FORGOTTEN LORE
VOLUME THREE

# AN ASSEMBLY OF MONSTERS

EDITED BY

## DANIELLE ACKLEY-MCPHAIL

NEOPARADOXA

Pennsville, NJ

PUBLISHED BY
NeoParadoxa,
a division of eSpec Books LLC
Danielle McPhail,
Publisher
PO Box 242,
Pennsville, New Jersey 08070
www.especbooks.com



ISBN: 978-1-956463-95-8
ISBN (ebook): 978-1-956463-94-1



Cover and Interior Design: Danielle McPhail, McP Digital Graphics

Illustrations: Art Credits - www.shutterstock.com
Cover:
Steampunk metallic frame with copper clockwork gears and blue banner isolated on black 3D digital © T Studio
Portrait of a medieval scientist working in his laboratory. Alchemist. Halloween. © Kiselev Andrey Valerevich
Interior:
Hand drawn line art human brain and heart halfs. Grunge sketch tattoo design isolated on white background vector illustration. Logic and emotion priority concept. © Croisy

# Our Literary Ghouls

Danielle Ackley-McPhail

Rachel A. Brune

James Chambers

Doc Coleman

Ef Deal

Keith R.A. DeCandido

Dana Fraedrich

John L. French

Teel James Glenn

Jessica Lucci

Christine Norris

Aaron Rosenberg

Hildy Silverman

Michelle D. Sonnier

Dacre Stoker

David Lee Summers

# Steampunk Titles by eSpec Books

### The Clockwork Chronicles
The Clockwork Witch
The Clockwork Solution
The Clockwork Discovery (Forthcoming)
(Michelle D. Sonnier)

Baba Ali and the Clockwork Djinn
(Danielle Ackley-McPhail and Day Al-Mohamed)

Echoes of the Divine
(Danielle Ackley-McPhail)

A Curse of Ash and Iron
A Curse of Time and Vengeance
(Christine Norris)

Spirit Seeker
(Jeff Young)

Sherman's Last Round-Up
(David Sherman)

Esprit De Corpse
Aeros & Heroes
The Order of Duval (Forthcoming)
(Ef Deal)

Crimson Whisper
(Ken Schrader)

# Steampunk Anthologies by eSpec Books

Forgotten Lore
A Cast of Crows
A Cry of Hounds

After Punk: Steampowered Tales of the Afterlife

Gaslight & Grimm
Grimm Machinations

Grease Monkeys: The Heart and Soul of Dieselpunk

The Weird Wild West

Other Aether: Tales of Global Steampunk

The Chaos Clock: Tales of Cosmic Aether

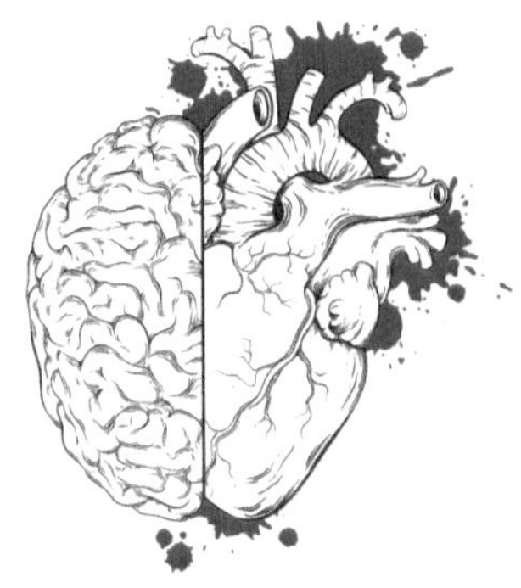

For all of those who stand against
the monsters.

# Jonathan Harker's Journal

*(Kept in shorthand.)*

## BRAM STOKER

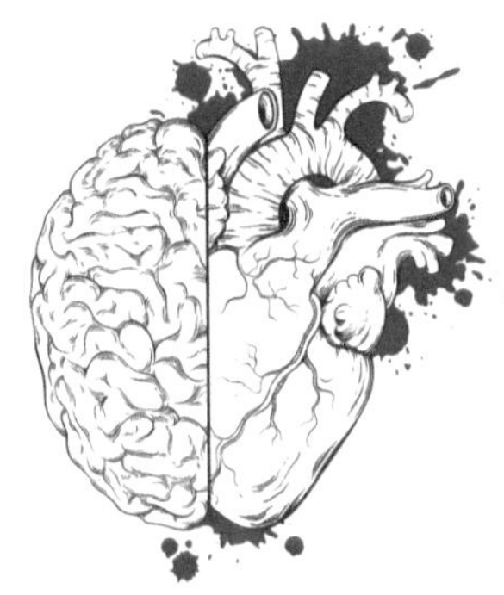

5 MAY. THE CASTLE. — THE GREY OF THE morning has passed, and the sun is high over the distant horizon, which seems jagged, whether with trees or hills I know not, for it is so far off that big things and little are mixed. I am not sleepy, and, as I am not to be called till I awake, naturally I write till sleep comes. There are many odd things to put down, and, lest who reads them may fancy that I dined too well before I left Bistritz, let me put down my dinner exactly. I dined on what they called "robber steak" — bits of bacon, onion, and beef, seasoned with red pepper, and strung on sticks and roasted over the fire, in the simple style of the London cat's meat! The wine was Golden Mediasch, which produces a queer sting on the tongue, which is, however, not disagreeable. I had only a couple of glasses of this, and nothing else.

When I got on the coach the driver had not taken his seat, and I saw him talking with the landlady. They were evidently talking of me, for every now and then they looked at me, and some of the people who were sitting on the bench outside the door — which they call by a name meaning "word-bearer" — came and listened, and then looked at me, most of them pityingly. I could hear a lot of words often repeated, queer words, for there were many nationalities in the crowd; so I quietly got my polyglot dictionary from my bag and looked them out. I must say they were not cheering to me, for amongst them were "Ordog"—Satan, "pokol"—hell, "stregoica"—witch, "vrolok" and "vlkoslak"—both of which mean the same thing, one being Slovak and the other Servian for something that is either were-wolf or vampire. (*Mem.*, I must ask the Count about these superstitions.)

When we started, the crowd round the inn door, which had by this time swelled to a considerable size, all made the sign of the cross and pointed two fingers towards me. With some difficulty I got a fellow-passenger to tell me what they meant; he would not answer at first, but on learning that I was English, he explained that it was a charm or guard against the evil eye. This was not very pleasant for me, just starting for an unknown place to meet an unknown man; but every one seemed so kind-hearted, and so sorrowful, and so sympathetic that I could not but be touched. I shall never forget the last glimpse which I had of the inn-yard and its crowd of picturesque figures, all crossing themselves, as they stood round the wide archway, with its background of rich foliage of oleander and orange trees in green tubs clustered in the centre of the yard. Then our driver, whose wide linen drawers covered the whole front of the box-seat—"gotza" they call them—cracked his big whip over his four small horses, which ran abreast, and we set off on our journey.

I soon lost sight and recollection of ghostly fears in the beauty of the scene as we drove along, although had I known the language, or rather languages, which my fellow-passengers were speaking, I might not have been able to throw them off so easily. Before us lay a green sloping land full of forests and woods, with here and there steep hills, crowned with clumps of trees or with farmhouses, the blank gable end to the road. There was everywhere a bewildering mass of fruit blossom—apple, plum, pear, cherry; and as we drove by I could see the green grass under the trees spangled with the fallen petals. In and out amongst these green hills of what they call here the "Mittel Land" ran the road, losing itself as it swept round the grassy curve, or was shut out by the straggling ends of pine woods, which here and there ran down the hillsides like tongues of flame. The road was rugged, but still we seemed to fly over it with a feverish haste. I could not understand then what the haste meant, but the driver was evidently bent on losing no time in reaching Borgo Prund. I was told that this road is in summer-time excellent, but that it had not yet been put in order after the winter snows. In this respect it is different from the general run of roads in the Carpathians, for it is an old tradition that they are not to be kept in too good order. Of old the Hospadars would not repair them, lest the Turk should think that they were preparing to bring in foreign troops, and so hasten the war which was always really at loading point.

Beyond the green swelling hills of the Mittel Land rose mighty slopes of forest up to the lofty steeps of the Carpathians themselves. Right and left of us they towered, with the after-noon sun falling full upon them and bringing out all the glorious colours of this beautiful range, deep blue and purple in the shadows of the peaks, green and brown where grass and rock mingled, and an endless perspective of jagged rock and pointed crags, till these were themselves lost in the distance, where the snowy peaks rose grandly. Here and there seemed mighty rifts in the mountains, through which, as the sun began to sink, we saw now and again the white gleam of falling water. One of my companions touched my arm as we swept round the base of a hill and opened up the lofty, snow-covered peak of a mountain, which seemed, as we wound on our serpentine way, to be right before us:—

"Look! Isten szek!"—"God's seat!"—and he crossed himself reverently.

As we wound on our endless way, and the sun sank lower and lower behind us, the shadows of the evening began to creep round us. This was emphasised by the fact that the snowy mountain-top still held the sunset, and seemed to glow out with a delicate cool pink. Here and there we passed Cszeks and Slovaks, all in picturesque attire, but I noticed that goitre was painfully prevalent. By the roadside were many crosses, and as we swept by, my companions all crossed themselves. Here and there was a peasant man or woman kneeling before a shrine, who did not even turn round as we approached, but seemed in the self-surrender of devotion to have neither eyes nor ears for

the outer world. There were many things new to me: for instance, hay-ricks in the trees, and here and there very beautiful
masses of weeping birch, their white stems shining like silver
through the delicate green of the leaves. Now and again we
passed a leiter-wagon — the ordinary peasant's cart — with its
long, snake-like vertebra, calculated to suit the inequalities of
the road. On this were sure to be seated quite a group of home-
coming peasants, the Cszeks with their white, and the Slovaks
with their coloured, sheepskins, the latter carrying lance-fashion
their long staves, with axe at end. As the evening fell it began to
get very cold, and the growing twilight seemed to merge into
one dark mistiness the gloom of the trees, oak, beech, and pine,
though in the valleys which ran deep between the spurs of the
hills, as we ascended through the Pass, the dark firs stood out
here and there against the background of late-lying snow.
Sometimes, as the road was cut through the pine woods that
seemed in the darkness to be closing down upon us, great
masses of greyness, which here and there bestrewed the trees,
produced a peculiarly weird and solemn effect, which carried
on the thoughts and grim fancies engendered earlier in the
evening, when the falling sunset threw into strange relief the
ghost-like clouds which amongst the Carpathians seem to wind
ceaselessly through the valleys. Sometimes the hills were so
steep that, despite our driver's haste, the horses could only go
slowly. I wished to get down and walk up them, as we do at
home, but the driver would not hear of it. "No, no," he said;
"you must not walk here; the dogs are too fierce"; and then he
added, with what he evidently meant for grim pleasantry — for
he looked round to catch the approving smile of the rest — "and
you may have enough of such matters before you go to sleep."
The only stop he would make was a moment's pause to light
his lamps.

When it grew dark there seemed to be some excitement
amongst the passengers, and they kept speaking to him, one
after the other, as though urging him to further speed. He lashed
the horses unmercifully with his long whip, and with wild
cries of encouragement urged them on to further exertions.
Then through the darkness I could see a sort of patch of grey
light ahead of us, as though there were a cleft in the hills.

The excitement of the passengers grew greater; the crazy coach rocked on its great leather springs, and swayed like a boat tossed on a stormy sea. I had to hold on. The road grew more level, and we appeared to fly along. Then the mountains seemed to come nearer to us on each side and to frown down upon us; we were entering on the Borgo Pass. One by one several of the passengers offered me gifts, which they pressed upon me with an earnestness which would take no denial; these were certainly of an odd and varied kind, but each was given in simple good faith, with a kindly word, and a blessing, and that strange mixture of fear-meaning movements which I had seen outside the hotel at Bistritz—the sign of the cross and the guard against the evil eye. Then, as we flew along, the driver leaned forward, and on each side the passengers, craning over the edge of the coach, peered eagerly into the darkness. It was evident that something very exciting was either happening or expected, but though I asked each passenger, no one would give me the slightest explanation. This state of excitement kept on for some little time; and at last we saw before us the Pass opening out on the eastern side. There were dark, rolling clouds overhead, and in the air the heavy, oppressive sense of thunder. It seemed as though the mountain range had separated two atmospheres, and that now we had got into the thunderous one. I was now myself looking out for the conveyance which was to take me to the Count. Each moment I expected to see the glare of lamps through the blackness; but all was dark. The only light was the flickering rays of our own lamps, in which the steam from our hard-driven horses rose in a white cloud. We could see now the sandy road lying white before us, but there was on it no sign of a vehicle. The passengers drew back with a sigh of gladness, which seemed to mock my own disappointment. I was already thinking what I had best do, when the driver, looking at his watch, said to the others something which I could hardly hear, it was spoken so quietly and in so low a tone; I thought it was "An hour less than the time." Then turning to me, he said in German worse than my own:—

"There is no carriage here. The Herr is not expected after all. He will now come on to Bukovina, and return to-morrow or the next day; better the next day." Whilst he was speaking the horses began to neigh and snort and plunge wildly, so that the driver had to hold them up. Then, amongst a chorus of screams from the peasants and a universal crossing of themselves, a calèche, with four horses, drove up behind us, overtook us, and drew up beside the coach. I could see from the flash of our lamps, as the rays fell on them, that the horses were coal-black and splendid animals. They were driven by a tall man, with a long brown beard and a great black hat, which seemed to hide his face from us. I could only see the gleam of a pair of very bright eyes, which seemed red in the lamplight, as he turned to us. He said to the driver:—

"You are early to-night, my friend." The man stammered in reply:—

"The English Herr was in a hurry," to which the stranger replied:—

"That is why, I suppose, you wished him to go on to Bukovina. You cannot deceive me, my friend; I know too much, and my horses are swift." As he spoke he smiled, and the lamplight fell on a hard-looking mouth, with very red lips and sharp-looking teeth, as white as ivory. One of my companions whispered to another the line from Burger's "Lenore":—

"Denn die Todten reiten schnell"—("For the dead travel fast.")

The strange driver evidently heard the words, for he looked up with a gleaming smile. The passenger turned his face away, at the same time putting out his two fingers and crossing himself. "Give me the Herr's luggage," said the driver; and with exceeding alacrity my bags were handed out and put in the calèche. Then I descended from the side of the coach, as the calèche was close alongside, the driver helping me with a hand which caught my arm in a grip of steel; his strength must have been prodigious. Without a word he shook his reins, the horses turned, and we swept into the darkness of the Pass. As I looked back I saw the steam from the horses of the coach by the light of the lamps, and projected against it the figures of my late companions crossing themselves. Then the driver cracked his whip and called to his horses, and off they swept on their way to Bukovina. As they sank into the darkness I felt a strange chill, and a lonely feeling came over me; but a cloak was thrown over my shoulders, and a rug across my knees, and the driver said in excellent German: —

"The night is chill, mein Herr, and my master the Count bade me take all care of you. There is a flask of slivovitz (the plum brandy of the country) underneath the seat, if you should require it." I did not take any, but it was a comfort to know it was there all the same. I felt a little strangely, and not a little frightened. I think had there been any alternative I should have taken it, instead of prosecuting that unknown night journey. The carriage went at a hard pace straight along, then we made a complete turn and went along another straight road. It seemed to me that we were simply going over and over the same ground again; and so I took note of some salient point, and found that this was so. I would have liked to have asked the driver what this all meant, but I really feared to do so, for I thought that, placed as I was, any protest would have had no effect in case there had been an intention to delay. By-and-by, however, as I was curious to know how time was passing, I struck a match, and by its flame looked at my watch; it was within a few minutes of midnight. This gave me a sort of shock, for I suppose the general superstition about midnight was increased by my recent experiences. I waited with a sick feeling of suspense.

Then a dog began to howl somewhere in a farmhouse far down the road—a long, agonised wailing, as if from fear. The sound was taken up by another dog, and then another and another, till, borne on the wind which now sighed softly through the Pass, a wild howling began, which seemed to come from all over the country, as far as the imagination could grasp it through the gloom of the night. At the first howl the horses began to strain and rear, but the driver spoke to them soothingly, and they quieted down, but shivered and sweated as though after a runaway from sudden fright. Then, far off in the distance, from the mountains on each side of us began a louder and a sharper howling—that of wolves—which affected both the horses and myself in the same way—for I was minded to jump from the calèche and run, whilst they reared again and plunged madly, so that the driver had to use all his great strength to keep them from bolting. In a few minutes, however, my own ears got accustomed to the sound, and the horses so far became quiet that the driver was able to descend and to stand before them. He petted and soothed them, and whispered something in their ears, as I have heard of horse-tamers doing, and with extraordinary effect, for under his caresses they became quite manageable again, though they still trembled. The driver again took his seat, and shaking his reins, started off at a great pace. This time, after going to the far side of the Pass, he suddenly turned down a narrow roadway which ran sharply to the right.

Soon we were hemmed in with trees, which in places arched right over the roadway till we passed as through a tunnel; and again great frowning rocks guarded us boldly on either side. Though we were in shelter, we could hear the rising wind, for it moaned and whistled through the rocks, and the branches of the trees crashed together as we swept along. It grew colder and colder still, and fine, powdery snow began to fall, so that soon we and all around us were covered with a white blanket. The keen wind still carried the howling of the dogs, though this grew fainter as we went on our way. The baying of the wolves sounded nearer and nearer, as though they were closing round on us from every side. I grew dreadfully afraid, and the horses shared my fear. The driver, however, was not in the least disturbed; he kept turning his head to left and right, but I could not see anything through the darkness.

Suddenly, away on our left, I saw a faint flickering blue flame. The driver saw it at the same moment; he at once checked the horses, and, jumping to the ground, disappeared into the darkness. I did not know what to do, the less as the howling of the wolves grew closer; but while I wondered the driver suddenly appeared again, and without a word took his seat, and we resumed our journey. I think I must have fallen asleep and kept dreaming of the incident, for it seemed to be repeated endlessly, and now looking back, it is like a sort of awful nightmare. Once the flame appeared so near the road, that even in the darkness around us I could watch the driver's motions. He went rapidly to where the blue flame arose — it must have been very faint, for it did not seem to illumine the place around it at all — and gathering a few stones, formed them into some device. Once there appeared a strange optical effect: when he stood between me and the flame he did not obstruct it, for I could see its ghostly flicker all the same. This startled me, but as the effect was only momentary, I took it that my eyes deceived me straining through the darkness. Then for a time there were no blue flames, and we sped onwards through the gloom, with the howling of the wolves around us, as though they were following in a moving circle.

At last there came a time when the driver went further afield than he had yet gone, and during his absence, the horses began to tremble worse than ever and to snort and scream with fright. I could not see any cause for it, for the howling of the wolves had ceased altogether; but just then the moon, sailing through the black clouds, appeared behind the jagged crest of a beetling, pine-clad rock, and by its light I saw around us a ring of wolves, with white teeth and lolling red tongues, with long, sinewy limbs and shaggy hair. They were a hundred times more terrible in the grim silence which held them than even when they howled. For myself, I felt a sort of paralysis of fear. It is only when a man feels himself face to face with such horrors that he can understand their true import.

All at once the wolves began to howl as though the moon-light had had some peculiar effect on them. The horses jumped about and reared, and looked helplessly round with eyes that rolled in a way painful to see; but the living ring of terror encompassed them on every side; and they had perforce to re-main within it. I called to the coachman to come, for it seemed to me that our only chance was to try to break out through the ring and to aid his approach. I shouted and beat the side of the calèche, hoping by the noise to scare the wolves from that side, so as to give him a chance of reaching the trap. How he came there, I know not, but I heard his voice raised in a tone of imperious command, and looking towards the sound, saw him stand in the roadway. As he swept his long arms, as though brushing aside some impalpable obstacle, the wolves fell back and back further still. Just then a heavy cloud passed across the face of the moon, so that we were again in darkness.

When I could see again the driver was climbing into the calèche, and the wolves had disappeared. This was all so strange and uncanny that a dreadful fear came upon me, and I was afraid to speak or move. The time seemed interminable as we swept on our way, now in almost complete darkness, for the rolling clouds obscured the moon. We kept on ascending, with occasional periods of quick descent, but in the main always ascending. Suddenly, I became conscious of the fact that the driver was in the act of pulling up the horses in the courtyard of a vast ruined castle, from whose tall black windows came no ray of light, and whose broken battlements showed a jagged line against the moonlit sky.

# LETTER 4

*To Mrs. Saville, England.*

## MARY SHELLEY

AUGUST 5TH, 17—.

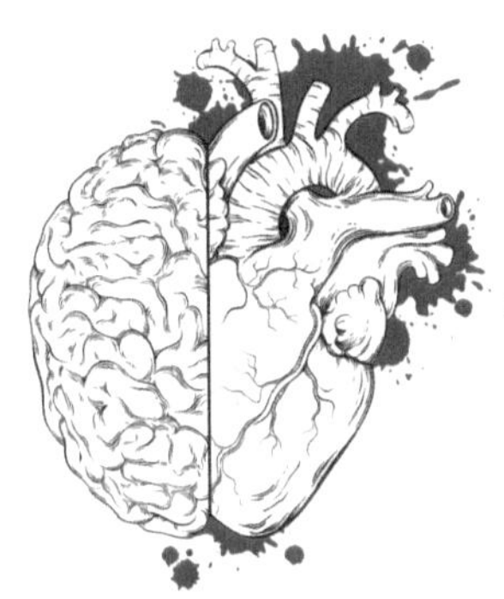

SO STRANGE AN ACCIDENT HAS HAPPENED TO us that I cannot forbear recording it, although it is very probable that you will see me before these papers can come into your possession.

Last Monday (July 31st) we were nearly surrounded by ice, which closed in the ship on all sides, scarcely leaving her the sea-room in which she floated. Our situation was somewhat dangerous, especially as we were compassed round by a very thick fog. We accordingly lay to, hoping that some change would take place in the atmosphere and weather.

About two o'clock the mist cleared away, and we beheld, stretched out in every direction, vast and irregular plains of ice, which seemed to have no end. Some of my comrades groaned, and my own mind began to grow watchful with anxious thoughts, when a strange sight suddenly attracted our attention and diverted our solicitude from our own situation. We perceived a low carriage, fixed on a sledge and drawn by dogs, pass on towards the north, at the distance of half a mile; a being which had the shape of a man, but apparently of gigantic stature, sat in the sledge and guided the dogs. We watched the rapid progress of the traveller with our telescopes until he was lost among the distant inequalities of the ice.

This appearance excited our unqualified wonder. We were, as we believed, many hundred miles from any land; but this apparition seemed to denote that it was not, in reality, so distant as we had supposed. Shut in, however, by ice, it was impossible to follow his track, which we had observed with the greatest attention.

About two hours after this occurrence we heard the ground sea, and before night the ice broke and freed our ship. We, however, lay to until the morning, fearing to encounter in the dark those large loose masses which float about after the breaking up of the ice. I profited of this time to rest for a few hours.

In the morning, however, as soon as it was light, I went upon deck and found all the sailors busy on one side of the vessel, apparently talking to someone in the sea. It was, in fact, a sledge, like that we had seen before, which had drifted towards us in the night on a large fragment of ice. Only one dog remained alive; but there was a human being within it whom the sailors were persuading to enter the vessel. He was not, as the other traveller seemed to be, a savage inhabitant of some undiscovered island, but a European. When I appeared on deck the master said, "Here is our captain, and he will not allow you to perish on the open sea."

On perceiving me, the stranger addressed me in English, although with a foreign accent. "Before I come on board your vessel," said he, "will you have the kindness to inform me whither you are bound?"

You may conceive my astonishment on hearing such a question addressed to me from a man on the brink of destruction and to whom I should have supposed that my vessel would have been a resource which he would not have exchanged for the most precious wealth the earth can afford. I replied, however, that we were on a voyage of discovery towards the northern pole.

Upon hearing this he appeared satisfied and consented to come on board. Good God! Margaret, if you had seen the man who thus capitulated for his safety, your surprise would have been boundless. His limbs were nearly frozen, and his body dreadfully emaciated by fatigue and suffering. I never saw a man in so wretched a condition. We attempted to carry him into the cabin, but as soon as he had quitted the fresh air he fainted. We accordingly brought him back to the deck and restored him to animation by rubbing him with brandy and forcing him to swallow a small quantity. As soon as he showed signs of life we wrapped him up in blankets and placed him near the chimney of the kitchen stove. By slow degrees he recovered and ate a little soup, which restored him wonderfully.

Two days passed in this manner before he was able to speak, and I often feared that his sufferings had deprived him of understanding. When he had in some measure recovered, I removed him to my own cabin and attended on him as much as my duty would permit. I never saw a more interesting creature: his eyes have generally an expression of wildness, and even madness, but there are moments when, if anyone performs an act of kindness towards him or does him any the most trifling service, his whole countenance is lighted up, as it were, with a beam of benevolence and sweetness that I never saw equalled. But he is generally melancholy and despairing, and sometimes he gnashes his teeth, as if impatient of the weight of woes that oppresses him.

When my guest was a little recovered I had great trouble to keep off the men, who wished to ask him a thousand questions; but I would not allow him to be tormented by their idle curiosity, in a state of body and mind whose restoration evidently depended upon entire repose. Once, however, the lieutenant asked why he had come so far upon the ice in so strange a vehicle.

His countenance instantly assumed an aspect of the deepest gloom, and he replied, "To seek one who fled from me."

"And did the man whom you pursued travel in the same fashion?"

"Yes."

"Then I fancy we have seen him, for the day before we picked you up we saw some dogs drawing a sledge, with a man in it, across the ice."

This aroused the stranger's attention, and he asked a multitude of questions concerning the route which the dæmon, as he called him, had pursued. Soon after, when he was alone with me, he said, "I have, doubtless, excited your curiosity, as well as that of these good people; but you are too considerate to make inquiries."

"Certainly; it would indeed be very impertinent and inhuman in me to trouble you with any inquisitiveness of mine."

"And yet you rescued me from a strange and perilous situation; you have benevolently restored me to life."

Soon after this he inquired if I thought that the breaking up of the ice had destroyed the other sledge. I replied that I could not answer with any degree of certainty, for the ice had not broken until near midnight, and the traveller might have arrived at a place of safety before that time; but of this I could not judge.

From this time a new spirit of life animated the decaying frame of the stranger. He manifested the greatest eagerness to be upon deck to watch for the sledge which had before appeared; but I have persuaded him to remain in the cabin, for he is far too weak to sustain the rawness of the atmosphere. I have promised that someone should watch for him and give him instant notice if any new object should appear in sight.

Such is my journal of what relates to this strange occurrence up to the present day. The stranger has gradually improved in health but is very silent and appears uneasy when anyone except myself enters his cabin. Yet his manners are so conciliating and gentle that the sailors are all interested in him, although they have had very little communication with him. For my own part, I begin to love him as a brother, and his constant and deep grief fills me with sympathy and compassion. He must have been a noble creature in his better days, being even now in wreck so attractive and amiable.

I said in one of my letters, my dear Margaret, that I should find no friend on the wide ocean; yet I have found a man who, before his spirit had been broken by misery, I should have been happy to have possessed as the brother of my heart.

I shall continue my journal concerning the stranger at intervals, should I have any fresh incidents to record.

AUGUST 13TH, 17—.

My affection for my guest increases every day. He excites at once my admiration and my pity to an astonishing degree. How can I see so noble a creature destroyed by misery without feeling the most poignant grief? He is so gentle, yet so wise; his mind is so cultivated, and when he speaks, although his words are culled with the choicest art, yet they flow with rapidity and unparalleled eloquence.

He is now much recovered from his illness and is continually on the deck, apparently watching for the sledge that preceded his own. Yet, although unhappy, he is not so utterly occupied by his own misery but that he interests himself deeply in the projects of others. He has frequently conversed with me on mine, which I have communicated to him without disguise. He entered attentively into all my arguments in favour of my eventual success and into every minute detail of the measures I had taken to secure it. I was easily led by the sympathy which he evinced to use the language of my heart, to give utterance to the burning ardour of my soul and to say, with all the fervour that warmed me, how gladly I would sacrifice my fortune, my existence, my every hope, to the furtherance of my enterprise. One man's life or death were but a small price to pay for the acquirement of the knowledge which I sought, for the dominion I should acquire and transmit over the elemental foes of our race. As I spoke, a dark gloom spread over my listener's countenance. At first I perceived that he tried to suppress his emotion; he placed his hands before his eyes, and my voice quivered and failed me as I beheld tears trickle fast from between his fingers; a groan burst from his heaving breast. I paused; at length he spoke, in broken accents: "Unhappy man! Do you share my madness? Have you drunk also of the intoxicating draught? Hear me; let me reveal my tale, and you will dash the cup from your lips!"

Such words, you may imagine, strongly excited my curiosity; but the paroxysm of grief that had seized the stranger overcame his weakened powers, and many hours of repose and tranquil conversation were necessary to restore his composure.

Having conquered the violence of his feelings, he appeared to despise himself for being the slave of passion; and quelling the dark tyranny of despair, he led me again to converse concerning myself personally. He asked me the history of my earlier years. The tale was quickly told, but it awakened various trains of reflection. I spoke of my desire of finding a friend, of my thirst for a more intimate sympathy with a fellow mind than had ever fallen to my lot, and expressed my conviction that a man could boast of little happiness who did not enjoy this blessing.

"I agree with you," replied the stranger; "we are unfashioned creatures, but half made up, if one wiser, better, dearer than ourselves—such a friend ought to be—do not lend his aid to perfectionate our weak and faulty natures. I once had a friend, the most noble of human creatures, and am entitled, therefore, to judge respecting friendship. You have hope, and the world before you, and have no cause for despair. But I—I have lost everything and cannot begin life anew."

As he said this his countenance became expressive of a calm, settled grief that touched me to the heart. But he was silent and presently retired to his cabin.

Even broken in spirit as he is, no one can feel more deeply than he does the beauties of nature. The starry sky, the sea, and every sight afforded by these wonderful regions seem still to have the power of elevating his soul from earth. Such a man has a double existence: he may suffer misery and be overwhelmed by disappointments, yet when he has retired into himself, he will be like a celestial spirit that has a halo around him, within whose circle no grief or folly ventures.

Will you smile at the enthusiasm I express concerning this divine wanderer? You would not if you saw him. You have been tutored and refined by books and retirement from the world, and you are therefore somewhat fastidious; but this only renders you the more fit to appreciate the extraordinary merits of this wonderful man. Sometimes I have endeavoured to discover what quality it is which he possesses that elevates him so immeasurably above any other person I ever knew. I believe it to be an intuitive discernment, a quick but never-failing power of judgment, a penetration into the causes of things, unequalled for clearness and precision; add to this a facility of expression and a voice whose varied intonations are soul-subduing music.

August 19th, 17—.

Yesterday the stranger said to me, "You may easily perceive, Captain Walton, that I have suffered great and unparalleled misfortunes. I had determined at one time that the memory of these evils should die with me, but you have won me to alter my determination. You seek for knowledge and wisdom, as I once did; and I ardently hope that the gratification of your wishes may not be a serpent to sting you, as mine has been. I do not know that the relation of my disasters will be useful to you; yet, when I reflect that you are pursuing the same course, exposing yourself to the same dangers which have rendered me what I am, I imagine that you may deduce an apt moral from my tale, one that may direct you if you succeed in your undertaking and console you in case of failure. Prepare to hear of occurrences which are usually deemed marvellous. Were we among the tamer scenes of nature I might fear to encounter your unbelief, perhaps your ridicule; but many things will appear possible in these wild and mysterious regions which would pro-voke the laughter of those unacquainted with the ever-varied powers of nature; nor can I doubt but that my tale conveys in its series internal evidence of the truth of the events of which it is composed."

You may easily imagine that I was much gratified by the offered communication, yet I could not endure that he should renew his grief by a recital of his misfortunes. I felt the greatest eagerness to hear the promised narrative, partly from curiosity and partly from a strong desire to ameliorate his fate if it were in my power. I expressed these feelings in my answer.

"I thank you," he replied, "for your sympathy, but it is useless; my fate is nearly fulfilled. I wait but for one event, and then I shall repose in peace. I understand your feeling," continued he, perceiving that I wished to interrupt him; "but you are mistaken, my friend, if thus you will allow me to name you; nothing can alter my destiny; listen to my history, and you will perceive how irrevocably it is determined."

He then told me that he would commence his narrative the next day when I should be at leisure. This promise drew from me the warmest thanks. I have resolved every night, when I am not imperatively occupied by my duties, to record, as nearly as possible in his own words, what he has related during the day. If I should be engaged, I will at least make notes. This manuscript will doubtless afford you the greatest pleasure; but to me, who know him, and who hear it from his own lips — with what interest and sympathy shall I read it in some future day! Even now, as I commence my task, his full-toned voice swells in my ears; his lustrous eyes dwell on me with all their melancholy sweetness; I see his thin hand raised in animation, while the lineaments of his face are irradiated by the soul within. Strange and harrowing must be his story, frightful the storm which embraced the gallant vessel on its course and wrecked it — thus!

# Contents

# The Progenitors of Gothic Horror

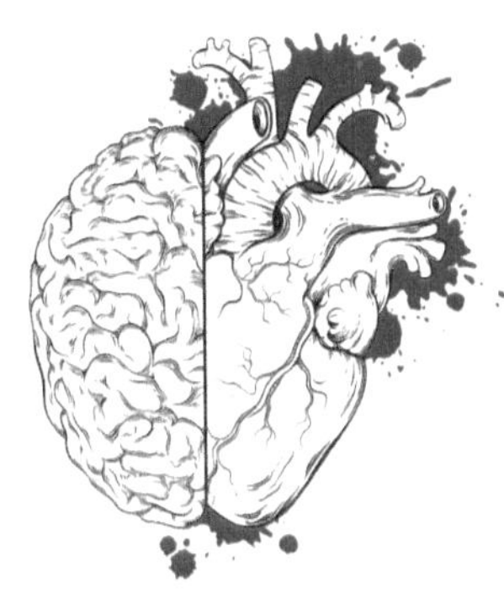

It is doubtful that any holiday spoiled by bad weather has proven quite so successful as the one undertaken in the summer of 1816 by Lord Byron, Dr. John Polidori, Percy Bysshe Shelley, and Shelley's soon-to-be wife, Mary Wollstonecraft Godwin. Known as "the year without a summer," 1816 witnessed severe climatic abnormalities which dropped the average global temperature by about one degree Fahrenheit. Evidence suggests that the anomaly was likely caused by the eruption of Mount Tambora in Indonesia in April of 1815, which clouded the atmosphere with enough volcanic ash and gases to block sunlight and induce a temporary "global cooling." Summer temperatures in Europe were the coldest of any on record, resulting in crop failures, major food shortages across the Northern Hemisphere, and, as fate would have it, the establishment of the Gothic literary tradition as we know it today.

Instead of enjoying the normally lovely summer weather in Lake Geneva, Switzerland, with outdoor recreation, the famous group of authors was forced by rain and cold to spend several days indoors. Boredom stoked creativity, a house party begat a storytelling contest, and the rest is history. It was here that Mary Shelley started writing *Frankenstein*, and here that Lord Byron penned a fragment of a tale which his traveling doctor, John Polidori, would take up and adapt into his 1819 short story "The Vampyre." These stories, of course, are commonly counted among the most important literary influences for Bram Stoker's *Dracula*.

Less widely known, perhaps, is the fact that Bram Stoker was also inspired by a holiday to write what would prove to be his most famous novel. It was not the weather that sparked Stoker's creativity in the summer of 1890, but the town of Whitby, an ancient coastal community in Yorkshire distinguished by its rich history, its stark beauty, and its stranger-than-fiction folklore. So inspired was Stoker that he set chapters six, seven, and eight of *Dracula* in the town and even lifted recent events into his plot, such as the 1885 wreck of the ship Dmitry outside of Whitby Harbor. Local flavor proved a fruitful strategy for Stoker, who worked meticulously to include real locations and accurate details whenever possible, elevating his reader's experience of horror with an air of realism.

Similarly, Mary Shelley's *Frankenstein* not only takes place in and around Lake Geneva, but also draws from Shelley's experiences traveling along the River Rhine in 1815. Of particular interest is her stop in Gernsheim, in Southern Germany's Odenwald mountain range, near Castle Frankenstein. Shelley must have been aware that Castle Frankenstein was also the birthplace of the notorious alchemist and occultist Johann Konrad Dippel, whose experimentation with cadavers was rumored to include attempts at soul-transference between dead bodies, just as both authors would have been aware of some of the highly publicized cases of suspected vampirism which circulated widely throughout the century. Shelley even wrote a line where Doctor Frankenstein referred to his monster as a vampire:

> *"I consider the being whom I had cast among mankind, and endowed with the will and power to effect purposes of horror, such as the deed which he had now done, nearly in the light of my own vampire, my own spirit let loose from the grave and forced to destroy all that was dear to me."*

Throughout the 19th century, advancements in science and medicine enabled scholars to reinterpret cultural mythology through new lenses, such as the germ theory of disease. Yet long-held "common knowledge" can prove difficult to dislodge outside of the ivory tower. The 19th century, therefore, bore witness to fascinating contests between—and, sometimes, confluences of—modern science and ancient myth. Bram Stoker's notes for Dracula, for example, contained an

1896 clipping from a New York newspaper describing a tuberculosis outbreak in rural New England which had been interpreted by panicked locals as a series of vampiric attacks.

Seven years ago, I had the pleasure of contributing to a four-month exhibition on these novels organized at the Rosenbach Museum in Philadelphia, PA. Running from October of 2017 to February of 2018, the exhibition celebrated the 120th and 200th anniversaries of *Dracula* and *Frankenstein*'s publications. Its title, *Frankenstein and Dracula: Gothic Monsters, Modern Science*, attests to the lasting relevance of these ahead-of-their-time tales.

Despite being published toward opposite ends of the long nineteenth century, these books have far more in common than what divides them. Bram Stoker's mother, Charlotte, seems to affirm this sentiment in a July 1897 letter to her son: "I have just read a review of *Dracula* in a London paper they have not said one word too much of it, no book since Mrs. Shelly's *Frankenstein* or indeed any other at all has come near yours in originality or terror" [sic]. The romance and mystery of long journeys and distant communications is a shared interest, for example, as both texts employ epistolary form to tell their stories through the limited perspectives of different characters. As the British Empire expanded, its growing population of readers was fascinated with the allure of far-off places—to say nothing of the Victorian fascination with demonology, occult science, and the esoteric arts. Indeed, probably the most important and enduring common theme between the two novels is that of contemporary medical science and technology (in other words, modernity) clashing with established societal norms and traditions, the old ways and meanings of the world.

Simultaneously with Shelley's writing, significant ethical debates raged in medical circles over the questions raised by Alessandro Volta's and Luigi Galvani's experiments with electrical currents and organic tissue—particularly the theoretical possibility of reanimating deceased bodies. Bram Stoker, likewise, used a variety of references to new and emerging sciences. Shorthand entries in Stoker's Lost Journal, such as "Story of man brought back to life in a dissecting room by the application of a new power unexpected," indicate his interest in the same possibilities that charged Shelley's imagination. A similar motif made its way into Stoker's notes and working drafts for *Dracula*; in what had been originally intended as the opening chapter of *Dracula*, which was later discarded, Jonathan Harker describes Count Dracula as an "old dead man made alive."

Stoker and Shelley's monsters not only challenge the finality of death by their creation, but also by their incomplete destruction. Consider the details of the method in which Count Dracula is defeated: a bowie knife, rather than a wooden stake, is thrust into his chest, after which the Count disappears in a cloud of dust. Shelley's ending is equally ambiguous, with Frankenstein's monster rafting off into the Arctic sea. Was this a conscious decision by each author to insinuate that their creations, along with everything that they represent, are quite possibly still alive? And that the many issues that their stories evoked will continue until they are resolved—if resolution is possible? At any rate, we must be grateful to them for leaving the door open for creative storytellers, like those gathered in this anthology, to breathe new life into these two enduring, familiar, yet horrifying creatures.

Ongoing fascination with the origins and inspirations for these iconic novels, as well as others, drives a global literary tourism industry of fans following in the footsteps of their favorite authors and characters, seeking to understand their thoughts and motivations. Certainly, any author's writing is affected by its social, political, and scientific context. The real question is about whether an author is "making a statement" or just writing organically with the aim of telling an entertaining story. In the cases of *Dracula* and *Frankenstein*, too little source material exists to satisfy our curiosity, and we no longer have the luxury of asking the authors.

Stoker only ever gave one interview about his writing of *Dracula*. In that 1897 interview with Jane Stoddard, published in the British Weekly Newspaper, my great-granduncle acknowledges the edifying potential of literature but emphasizes the importance of a reader's participation in discovering it:

*In a recent leader on* Dracula*… it is suggested that high moral lessons might be gathered from the book. I asked Mr. Stoker whether he had written with a purpose, but on this point he would give no definite answer. "I suppose that every book of the kind must contain some lesson," he remarked; "but I prefer that readers should find it out for themselves."*

In other words, we must do our part. Like the characters in these mysteries we so adore, we must work actively to plumb the depths, pursue the unknowable, and, in the process, perhaps, better ourselves through knowledge.

Dacre Stoker,
Bestselling Author and
great grandnephew of Bram Stoker

# THE WHITBY LIGHT

## JAMES CHAMBERS

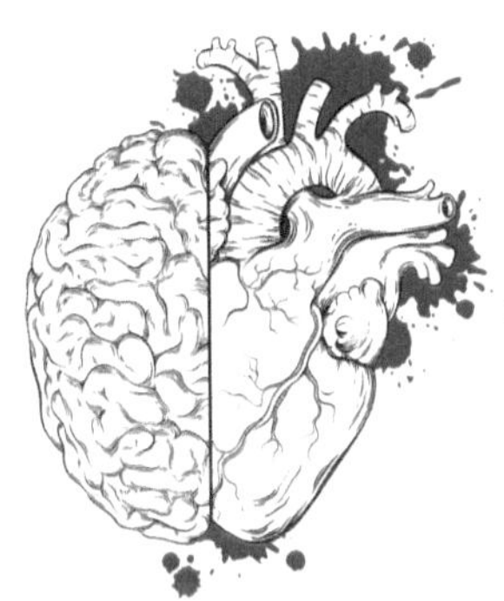

*"ON THE SUMMIT OF THE EAST CLIFF THE NEW searchlight was ready for experiment, but had not yet been tried. The officers in charge of it got it into working order, and in the pauses of the inrushing mist swept with it the surface of the sea. Once or twice its service was most effective, as when a fishing boat, with gunwale under water, rushed into the harbour, able, by the guidance of the sheltering light, to avoid the danger of dashing against the piers. As each boat achieved the safety of the port there was a shout of joy from the mass of people on shore, a shout which for a moment seemed to cleave the gale and was then swept away in its rush. Before long the searchlight discovered some distance away a schooner with all sails set…"*

*The Dailygraph, 8 August*

*October, the following year.*

"The *Demeter* ran aground here."

Archibald Barnes gestured with his walking stick at a mounded expanse of sand beside Tate Hill Pier. The chilling wind tugged at his gray-streaked hair and fluttered the hem of his topcoat. Gusts blasted the beach and peppered sand against the trio marking the location.

"*C'est dingue!* What a horrible night that must have been," Madame Marceline Rene said.

"Not nearly as horrible as the voyage for the poor crew," Morris Garvey said.

"Indeed, according to the ship's log they experienced the darkest of days before their tragic captain beached his vessel. Imagine the scene! A storm-tossed night, one of the worst Whitby has ever withstood—then a Russian schooner comes charging from amidst the clouds, waves, and lightning and thrusts herself onto the sand like a dying leviathan. Such excitement! People rushed to help, to witness, to scavenge, all for the lack of any means that might enable those ashore to bring home safely those at sea. Do you grasp what I'm pursuing, Morris?"

Morris rubbed his chin and gazed at the choppy sea against a cloudless and cold blue sky that seemed infinite. Ships of different kinds dotted the white-capped water like chess pieces moving of their own accord. "I can't say I do, Archie, but perhaps it's too much of a leap for me to make on such a beautiful autumn day."

"A shipwright in Marseille has been striving for years to build a machine to launch lines hundreds or thousands of meters from shore to imperiled ships and tug them into harbor. Is this what you have in mind?" asked Marceline.

"I'm aware of that gentleman's work, Madame Rene, but no, that's not what I'm after. That night we ran the new searchlight I built to guide ships in, it worked better than I expected. It lit the night with the brilliance of the sun itself, providing a view, clear as day, for all on shore to watch the ships fight to safety, and later to watch the *Demeter* crash to her doom. I saw that beam, that rod of luminosity reach out to the sea like the arm of phantom giant—" Archibald extended his arm toward the surf, spread his palm wide, and then curled his fingers as if cupping a bowl. "—and I asked myself what if that arm could be made solid and given a hand?"

"Sorry, Archie, despite the bright light you're talking about, I'm still in the dark," Morris said.

"Picture this. I throw the switch on the light. It flares to life, casts its beam far beyond the reach of any physical device, and blazes a troubled ship with perfect clarity. But this is not enough to save the vessel, no, only to ensure that we on shore may witness its life-or-death struggle while our feet remain safely planted on the ground. But, what if at the toss of a second switch that beam became a tangible, reassuring arc of force capable of containing the vessel it illuminated in a protective emanation then drawing it into port while shielding it from the sea's cruel violence? Ah, what then, Morris? What then, I ask you?"

Morris strode closer to the frothy surf, mulling over his answer, then turned and met Archibald's eager gaze. "I suppose, you'd have one hell of an invention on your hands."

Smiling broadly, Archibald nodded. "Imagine the possibilities. The potential to impel carts, lorries, and trains along roads and rails by application of such a powerful light. To pluck birds from the sky. Maybe even to draw down dear Selene herself, the moon." Archibald burst into an energetic laugh. "I exaggerate, forgive me, but I do very much pray you now understand the magnitude of my conception."

"It would change the world," Marceline said.

"I hope you don't consider me immodest if I agree with your assessment, Madame."

"That's all well and good, Archie, but between concept and practice yawns an abyss to shame the widest ocean. Have you got any notion at all of how to achieve such a thing?"

"Would I have invited the world-renowned genius of New Alexandria, inventor of the steam-powered chimney sweep, to a speck in the English Isles like Whitby if I hadn't?"

Morris gazed up at the East Cliff, where a churchyard encroached upon the bluff to the point that gravestones projected out over a cliff face gnawed and undermined by erosion. A dark shape paced back and forth among the marble slabs, a hound or mastiff of some kind. It stilled and, for a moment, seemed to gaze at Morris, before, with an abrupt leap backward, it vanished like a lingering night shadow before the encroaching dawn.

"No, I suppose not."

"Indeed, certainly not." Archibald walked up the beach, gesturing for Morris and Marceline to follow. "I wanted you to see the ground, the sea, the forces of nature arrayed against man's endeavors before I shared my work so you will comprehend the true scale of my undertaking. Now that we're thoroughly chilled to the bone by that ceaseless breeze, let's get ourselves to the warmth of hearth and home, and I'll show you what I've been designing."

Marceline shivered and wrapped her arms across her chest as the wind kicked up and stole her body heat. From a distance came the faint susurrus of Whitby as evening approached, disrupted only by the cry of an unseen animal from somewhere on the adjacent moors. A lonely howl. Morris doffed his coat and wrapped it across Marceline's shoulders.

"No, Morris, you'll catch your death," she said.

"I'll be fine. A little wind and sand won't harm me," Morris said.

"Do you think Archie can really build such a marvelous machine?"

Morris hesitated to answer. Archibald filled the moment by urging them to hurry to his waiting carriage. With a shrug, Morris guided Marceline ahead of him in clambering up and over a loose dune. Soon they sat sheltered from the nagging wind and jounced along the road into the hills outside Whitby where Archibald lived and worked. Not a long journey, but one filled with an awkward silence as Marceline's question, unarticulated but unavoidable, hung over them all. Archibald's quiet confidence and eager grin provided one possible answer; Morris's sullen patience offered another.

A great ruckus greeted them upon arrival at Archibald's classic, thatch-roofed, country home. A large barn, converted to laboratory and workshop, stood about thirty meters from the dwelling. Both structures leaked electric brightness into the dusk. The noise of a steam-powered generator contributed a steady din of mechanical clanks and huffs that blanketed the yard. Two men in lab coats prowled the grounds. One carried a shotgun. A man in a tweed suit escorted a young woman in a finely tailored cerulean dress toward the front door of the home, which hung wide open. Hardly waiting for the carriage to cease moving, Archibald popped open the door and leapt out, hitting the ground running.

"Eve!" he called. "My god, what's happened? Are you hurt?"

He reached the girl in only a few long strides. She threw her arms around him and pressed her face against his chest in greeting.

"Baker, what goes on here?" Archibald demanded of the man in tweed.

"Sir, it's that blasted beast been roaming the moors, came creeping around the grounds again. I saw it this morning and chased the damned thing off, but it returned and caught Miss Eve on her way between the house and the laboratory."

"Did it harm her?" Archibald gently broke the girl's embrace and held her at arm's length to examine her condition. "Are you hurt, dear Eve? Do you need a doctor?"

Eve smeared tears from her face with the back of her hand, calmed herself, then shook her head. "I'm uninjured, Father. The beast appeared out of a shadow, snarling and baring its awful teeth at me. It was as large as a mastiff but unlike any of the breed I've ever seen. It bore the stench of death about it and radiated a coldness from its withers that chilled me so deeply I couldn't as much as squeak out a call for help. I felt utterly frozen by its gaze. If Mr. Baker hadn't come by and chased it off with a plank of firewood, oh, heavens, I shudder to think…"

Pulling Eve to him again, Archibald offered her words of assurance and led her into the house. Mr. Baker joined the men in lab coats in their reconnaissance of the grounds. Morris and Marceline entered Archibald's home, grateful for its heat yet full of apprehension.

"Archie, could the beast have come inside while the door was open?" Morris said.

The words stiffened Archibald's back. "My god, we have to check. Madame Rene, please, would you kindly sit with Eve in my study. Second door on the left. Lock it after you and open it only for me or Morris. Eve, dear, now go and rest, collect yourself."

Without waiting for answers, Archibald directed Morris to investigate the second floor, while he cleared the first. The two men split up and heavy footfalls filled the house while fires crackled and spit behind the hearths in the parlor and the kitchen. Morris felt intrusive going from room to room at the top of the stairs, but he found them all bereft of any obvious danger or signs of the beast. Two guest rooms, the servant's quarters, Eve's room, even the master bedroom Archibald had once shared with his recently deceased wife all seemed placid and well-outfitted to offer comfort and peace. An open book lay face down on the nightstand beside Archibald's bed, a volume on spiritualism that struck Morris as an unusual reading selection for a mechanically minded man such as Archibald Barnes.

He returned to the first floor and joined Eve and Marceline in Archibald's study.

"All clear upstairs," he told them.

"Thank you, Mr. Garvey," Eve said. "I'm quite sorry to greet you with this trouble and hysteria after you've come such a long way to visit Father, but if only you had seen the beast as I did, felt its presence, the sheer horror it projected, but, no, of course, you must think me a weak and anxious child prone to spells of madness."

"Not at all, Eve," Morris said. "I've seen enough unexpected horrors in the world that I don't doubt your story or the beast's effect on you. Nor do I think you childish or weak. You're recovering your composure and your manners rather swiftly, aren't you? As for Marcy and I, we didn't travel all that far, just a diversion on our return to London from the annual conference of steam engineers in Edinburgh. Marceline presented a paper, and I sat on a panel of judges. Your father thought we might help him with a new device."

Eve nodded. "Sol's Hand, a machine to give substance to light."

The study door opened without warning. Archibald entered.

"Come now, Eve, don't give away my secrets so easily," he said.

"Sorry, Father. I assumed they knew."

"I was about to bring them into the shop and reveal all when we found you in distress. How do you feel? Do you need anything?" Archibald sat beside his daughter on a short couch and placed one arm around her. "The house is all clear now, but I'm sorry I wasn't here when you needed me."

"How could you have known? We haven't seen the creature for weeks. We all believed it had moved on or perished on the moors."

"You've seen this thing before? What is it, Archie?" Morris asked.

"A stray dog gone feral, I'm afraid. It doesn't seem rabid, but it's ferocious, and it has the most damnable fixation on my grounds and Eve, as if it's latched onto her scent like a bloody hound."

"How can we help you get rid of it?" Marceline asked.

"Tut-tut, let's not hear any talk like that," Archibald said. "My men will find and shoot it soon enough if it comes sniffing around again. I didn't invite you here to put down strays. You're here for more pleasant things, and now, if Eve feels up to it, I'd like to bring you over to the shop and let you have a gander."

"Yes, Father, of course, I'm perfectly fine now with all of you here," Eve said.

With that, Archibald escorted them from the house. Morris wished he could cling a little longer to the warmth they left behind, but the barn stood only a short walk away and possessed several wood-burning stoves that made it almost stuffy. Within its walls, a handful of men who hadn't joined the search for the intruding canine toiled at workbenches, using steam-powered drill presses, lathes, and pneumatic bolt guns, all dedicated to pieces and parts of a fabrication Morris could not puzzle from the fragments on display. A quarter of the barn stood in isolation, compartmented by floor-to-ceiling glass walls framed by iron beams. Archibald unlocked the door to this area and welcomed the group to his office.

Bookshelves lined the corner walls, stuffed with an overwhelming array of papers, journals, packets of letters, and volumes of every size and thickness. A broad drafting table filled one part of the office, a massive desk another, each piled with notebooks, blueprints, writing implements, rulers, calculating devices, and odd bits of glass and metal. Morris felt at home in the chaos, the outward dishevelment that testified to an active and engaged mind. It reminded him of the Machinations Sundry works and shop, which occupied a full block in New Alexandria. The glass walls muted the workshop noise, and Morris almost envied Archibald his sanctuary compared to his own relentlessly noisy workspace. Archibald allowed his guests to take in the sights of it while he beamed with pride.

"I think best in quiet," he said, "but I like to watch the fellows work. And it's important they see me with my nose to the grindstone, as they say, to set the proper example."

"My compliments, Archie. You've built yourself a lovely sanctum here," Morris said.

"Thank you, but what I most want to show you is this." Archibald stepped to the drafting table, unrolled several sheets of mechanical designs, and weighted them flat with random bits of glass and iron. "Sol's Hand will extend humanity's reach far beyond any current conceptions of distance, perhaps even to the infinite. Even now my staff labor to fashion everything we'll need to assemble the first prototype. Unfortunately, I've reached a few dead ends in bringing it to reality. I need your assistance with the lensing, the power source, the wavelength calculations, and a few other minor details. More critically, Sol's Hand, once perfected, will benefit immensely from your endorsement. At first, it will seem incredible, a hoax. People will scoff and turn their backs on it. They will require persuasion of the kind only the participation and affirmation of the world-renowned steam-technology inventor, Morris Garvey, can provide. I am certain they will ultimately welcome it, but we must put all doubts at ease, a task you can do better than any other. What do you say? Can you and Madame Rene help me bring this to the world?"

Morris joined Archibald at the drafting table and shuffled through the pages of designs. He waved for Marceline to join them. She too perused the equations and plans scribbled across the papers. Then she and

Morris exchanged glances, a silent communication that Morris knew well enough.

"All right, Archie, we'll play Prometheus with you," Morris said. "Let's see if we can't bring this new brand of fire to the world."

"And hope the gods don't exact too dear a price from us for doing so," Marceline said.

*October 14, letter from Madame Marceline Rene to her mother.*

*Ma Mére,*

*I am well and healthy and eating right, despite the questionable traditions of English cuisine, and I hope to return home to see you before the New Year. I am with Morris, of course, and you know that means unpredictable adventures, excursions to the fringes of science and technology, and diversions down some of the oddest paths you might imagine. We are presently engaged in such an endeavor with Mr. Archibald Barnes, a professional acquaintance of Morris's. He works us day and night. Such a taskmaster! I exaggerate, of course, because his work is fascinating and rewarding and we are eager to aid him in completing it. If successful, then Morris and I will have been part of the greatest technological leap the world has known since Morris first miniaturized steam power — or even since the invention of the wheel. I dare say nothing more until we obtain greater certainty of the outcome, but I promise to write to you before anyone else when we do.*

*Whitby, a port town, proves quaint in its dreariness. I find it tolerable but rather dull as a visitor. When the weather favors me, I walk the edge of the moors or through a nearby churchyard where the ruins of an abbey remain. Well-fitted for such constitutionals and quite conducive to the deep thought often required to unravel the answers to the mysteries we are exploring, the environs offer little for the imagination other than the prospect of an encounter with a stray mastiff supposed to roam the nearby wilds. The beast, perhaps, is a refugee from a Russian schooner, Demeter, which grounded here last year during a storm. Witnesses spied such a creature leap clear of the ship that night and flee into the tempest. Days later, a local man's mastiff was found dead, slaughtered, presumably by the beast. The mystery animal has become an object of local superstition, with some referring to it as a "witch dog" or "the Devil's own familiar." All quite entertaining! Now don't fret over my safety. I carry a pistol with me always on these walks, and you yourself have often complemented my marksmanship.*

*More interesting than Whitby is Mr. Barnes' daughter, Eve. Such a strong-headed and inquisitive young lady! We have quickly become close friends. I have taken her under my wing a bit. She aspires to accomplish much in this world that does not always offer women the easiest of paths. What little advice I can offer as to its navigation, I am happy to share. Eve, however, lives under some shadow I cannot reveal or define. I attributed it at first to the loss of her mother in the spring, but when she speaks of her it is with love and fond remembrance, the words of a child who copes admirably with her loss. No, I fear something else, a distraction of heart and mind which she hides from us all, especially her father.*

*Despite our labors and diligent efforts at engineering and science, a strange undercurrent runs though Mr. Barnes' life. Morris and I have noticed several volumes on spiritualism and occult subjects in his library and about the house — including the most astounding journal written by an Austrian physician whose experiments imparting life to dead flesh are fit to chill the soul and which I cannot credit as anything more than the fancies of a madman. Nor can I approve of Mr. Barnes correspondence with the Dutch doctor named Van Helsing, with whom he discusses matters of biology, physiognomy, theology, and folklore of the most awful nature — too awful even for me to put to words here! Suffice to say, I fear Mr. Barnes's darker predilections have influenced Eve though it might well be the other way round: Eve's odd and sullen secretiveness might have led Mr. Barnes to these unorthodox pursuits. Perhaps like so many of the misguided in mourning, one or the other harbors private hopes of reunion with their lost loved one.*

*I cannot say, Mother dear, I cannot say, nor shall I guess. I shall do only as you have raised me to do always: observe, reflect, cogitate, and confirm before acting. This little mystery in parallel to the great one we seek to solve with Mr. Barnes's makes my time in Whitby rather fascinating.*

"Are you ready, Archie?"

Morris called out from a platform erected atop the barn roof constructed to mount the first prototype of Sol's Hand. He strained to cast his voice through the November wind. It tugged and bit at him, exposed five meters above the ground, and he pulled the collar of the heavy coat he'd borrowed from Archibald closer around his neck. He adjusted the tinted glasses he wore to protect his eyes from the light. Somehow his words reached Archibald, on the ground, twenty meters away, where a hay cart waited for Morris to cast the beam upon it. The cart occupied a stretch of ground rendered perfectly level and smooth. Chalk marks denoted the exact positions of the wagon wheels, and lines of lime powder boxed in the conveyance to reveal the slightest touch of their wood. Lengths of twine stretched from all sides of the cart, connecting it to thin sticks poked into the earth, balanced to fall at the slightest movement. Everything stood ready to record even the minutest fraction of distance covered by the cart, and Archibald led several of his team surrounding the test ground to observe the experiment.

He waved to Morris, and shouted, "Beam one!"

Morris nodded and threw a switch on the lamp. Modeled after the one mounted above Whitby port, it turned night into day and painted the cart, its rigging, and the men around it in brilliant clarity. Several men cupped their hands above their eyes against its glare. It erased all shadows within its reach, deepening by contrast those beyond its sphere. The light hummed and radiated heat as the mechanism steadied and a specially built steam engine at the base of the barn settled into a powerful rhythm, pulsing out the power required for step two. As Morris watched Archibald for the signal, his eyes adjusted to the concentrated brilliance. A motion in the dark beyond the reach of light caught his eye. He tracked it along the moors, but when he looked directly, he saw nothing but deep black. Only when he looked away did he observe the shifting lines in the shadows. Then another motion grabbed his attention: Archibald waved for him to throw the second switch.

Morris waved back. He tossed the switch. The steam engine growled and chugged as it strained with whistling blasts and groaning iron pushed to its limits. The light flickered then blazed a thousand times brighter than before. Despite his tinted glasses, Morris raised a hand over his eyes. Sudden heat drew sweat to his brow, and the hum of the light rose in pitch and intensity until it rattled Morris's teeth.

Cries went up from Archibald's men. A great *whooshing* noise filled the air like the exhalation of a giant bellows. The light flared brighter still for several seconds before the filament exploded and produced a burst of glass and iron, a glowing shower that flickered in the dark.

Morris recoiled from the eruption, dropped to the platform, and covered his face as specks of superheated glass peppered him.

When he dared look again, when his eyes adjusted to the gloom, he saw the hay cart engulfed in flames. Archibald's team rushed to fetch buckets of water to douse it.

Beyond the conflagration, painted in the unsteady firelight—a light that spoke to Morris of ancient humans huddled around campfires, clinging to their fickle lifeline against the horrors of the dark—a figure moved. Morris tugged off his goggles. He saw her clearly now: Eve. She walked like a somnambulist, one foot deliberately stepping after the other, a pause between each footfall. Her eyes aimed straight ahead without focus. The hem of her dress dragged on the heather.

"Archie, it's Eve!" Morris shouted. "Eve! She's on the moors. Keep her away from the fire!"

Understanding dawned on Archibald. He raced to his daughter, then, leaving his men to extinguish the flame, hurried her back to the house. Morris clambered down from his perch, the shattered light forgotten, and rushed to inquire about Eve's condition. He found father and daughter in the study with Marceline.

Archibald paced back and forth in an uncharacteristic state of distress. Marceline held a white handkerchief spotted with blood to Eve's neck, which looked pale as ice. Even her face lacked any color, her cheeks nearly translucent, and her eyes glistened darkly. Her pupils gaped as wide and deep as abandoned wells.

"What is it? Shall we call for a doctor?" Morris asked.

"A doctor?" Archibald almost snarled the words. "What can a doctor do for her? She's suffering the same calamity as her mother, and, god help me, if I can't figure out how to help her, I'll lose her too."

"Dammit, Archie, speak plainly. The girl was only sleepwalking," Morris said.

"Not so, Morris. Show him," Archibald said. Marceline lifted the handkerchief from Eve's throat. "There is more to this than can be seen at a glance. I value your opinion above all others in matters of science and technology, my friend, but in this matter, you may perhaps lack the proper expertise."

Morris hunched to examine Eve's neck. Two pink and swollen puncture wounds an inch apart above her jugular vein wept beads of blood.

*November 4, letter from Madame Marceline Rene to her mother.*

*Ma Mére,*

*Morris and I have stayed with Mr. Barnes much longer than planned. Construction of Sol's Hand, which I told you in my last letter would be difficult, has proven even more challenging than he expected. I fear he pinned far too much of his hopes on Morris's intervention. Morris, of course, is brilliant and has led Mr. Barnes much farther than I suspect he would've gotten alone, but the first prototype set a hay cart ablaze then exploded, nearly blinding Morris and leaving several burns on his exposed cheeks. You can safely assume that was not the intended outcome.*

*Despite all our advances and cleverness, it remains true that some attainments simply lie beyond the reach of mere humans. Some secrets nature refuses to divulge; some forces she forbids us to harness. Yet still we dig for the knowledge and understanding to achieve Mr. Barnes's objective. Still, he pursues far more laudable goals than that Austrian doctor and the Dutch physician who seem to cast such long shadows over this home, whose works and ideas occupy every minute not devoted to his invention. Ah, but these are not the most depressing or worrisome thoughts that confront me here. Even more troublesome is Eve Barnes, whom her father believes is afflicted by a ghastly thing out of folklore and superstition, a vampire.*

*Can you imagine? Incredible, I know, that any person of science might heed such fantastic, outlandish ideas, but Barnes seems utterly under the spell of the Dutch physician, Dr. Abraham Van Helsing, a man of tremendous intellect and expertise, very true — which makes it all the more wildly irresponsible for such a man to advocate the existence of the so-called undead, corpses animated by supernatural evil, dead flesh hungering for nourishment from the blood of the living. Incrédulité! What madness! What can one do with such childish ideas, and yet…*

*Can I so readily dismiss the possibility? Morris and I have experienced our share of the chaos and darkness that magic and mysticism midwife into the world. It is an outrageous notion but one that somehow fits the known facts and follows on from the wreck of the Demeter, the very incident that precipitated Barnes's current work — and which, according to Van Helsing, ferried a tremendous, diabolical evil to England, which he played a key role in dispelling to its homeland. It seems somehow linked to the great dog that fled the wreck upon its beaching, to the mastiff it is assumed to have slaughtered. Barnes refuses to divulge all that Van Helsing has confided in him during their correspondence. He senses our skepticism and fears our reaction to the whole truth. We are surrounded by mysteries within mysteries.*

*In the meantime, Whitby grows drearier and less welcoming with the encroachment of winter, and we sleep little most days, preoccupied into the night with the toil of bringing Barnes's light into being and attending to the endlessly disturbed sleep of poor Eve. I yet hope to join you before the New Year. I shall write you again the moment I have news — hopefully of cheerier nature.*

"Damn this cold," Morris said.

He stamped his feet as he shut the front door behind him.

"Hush, Morris," Marceline said. "Some wish to sleep at this hour. Come to the study with me to warm yourself and talk."

Morris quietly closed the study door behind him. Marceline placed a fresh log on the fire then poured Morris a brandy while he stood at the hearth and opened his coat to the warmth. He sipped the spirit while gazing into the dancing flames.

"Fire has no substance," he said, low-voiced. "It jolts and hops like a phantom jester. What is our Sun if not a blazing sphere of flame?"

"What's that, Morris?"

"I believe, Marcy, that Archie has set himself an impossible task, to give substance to the eternally ephemeral, to control sheer untamable chaos, to organize entropy."

"In other words, Sol's Hand cannot be made to work."

"If it can, I'm damned if I see how. This isn't like building steam-powered gadgets to help the people of New Alexandria. This is…

trying to bind the natural forces of the cosmic order to our will. I'm afraid Archie's monomania for it allows him to avoid the reality of Eve's illness. It seems clear to me the girl shows signs of tuberculosis, and yet he does not treat her for it, does not permit any doctor to attend her, but relies on the advice of a man hundreds of miles away."

"He's treats her for something else," Marceline said.

Morris drained his brandy then scrunched his face before releasing a long breath.

"That's not treatment, that's superstition. Garlic wreaths at her window. A cross hung on her neck. To what? Scare off a mastiff that mesmerizes her to drink her blood? Dear god, Marcy, you and I know well what witches and sorcerers do. There are things beyond our physical world, demons and ghosts of a sort, but this — the corpse of a dog addicted to the blood of a young woman? It's horrible and ridiculous at the same time. How the world continues to hold Dr. Van Helsing in such high regard I cannot fathom, but then nor do I care much for tulips or windmills."

Marceline chuckled. "Now, Morris, you've never even met the man."

"I'm not sure I care to do so. I suspect I'd have trouble maintaining my manners."

Marceline carried the brandy bottle to Morris and refilled his glass.

"Well, what is there for us to do? Sol's Hand cannot be made to work. Do we dash Archie's dreams, leave his daughter to her sickly fate, and return to New Alexandria? I have promised *ma mére* I will visit before year's end."

"That would be the smart thing. Cut our losses. Perhaps the kind thing too if it spares Archie more time tilting at windmills. He's clever and resourceful and could accomplish much if he puts his mind in the right direction. If we stay what can either of us do for Eve? We aren't doctors, and Archie prohibits us from interfering in her case. To leave is the only sensible choice." Morris swirled the brandy in his glass, gazing at the fire through its amber veil. "Yet, I cannot bring myself to do so. I feel as if we are still needed here, at least to see Archie through testing the second prototype. A few more days, and it will be ready."

"Then let's stay through the week. If Sol's Hand should lend us its aid in that time, we can reconsider, but otherwise, we depart this bleak place. Agreed?"

Morris nodded and parted his lips to confirm his agreement, but a shriek from the night cut him off and raised every hair on his arms. Marceline dropped the brandy bottle, which shattered on the hearth.

"Eve!" she cried.

A second scream came from outside the house. Morris and Marceline raced to the front door and out onto the grounds. Morris grabbed a lantern from a hook by the front door. Others already scrambled in search for Eve. The white lab coats of Barnes's men shimmered in the wan moonlight. Baker and Barnes, himself, having emerged from the barn, called out Eve's name. Yet another scream sounded, but it seemed to come from a different direction than the other two, hampering the effort to locate the girl.

"Dammit, we'll never find her like this." Morris handed the lantern to Marceline. "Take this. I'm going to shed some more light on the situation."

Morris dashed into the barn and fired up the steam-engine that powered Sol's Hand. He worked dials and valves until the pressure reached its optimal measurement then clambered up the ladder to the rooftop platform. He emerged into the swirling night beside the second-stage prototype for Sol's Hand. Kneeling, he connected several wires and gauges he and Archibald had left for further inspection, then primed the power source to the light. When the pressure needle bobbed right below the red zone, he threw the first switch and directed the light onto the moors. They lit up like noon on a cloudless summer day, individual stones and branches of heather coming into crystal clarity. Morris swept the light slowly from one side to the other but exposed only empty ground. Then Eve screamed again. By instinct, he whirled the light in a new direction and captured two horrifying figures in its glow.

"Dear god, no," Morris uttered.

In the illuminated stretch of moors, Eve lay writhing on the earth, her nightgown spotted with mud and flecked with bits of heather. Her body convulsed with waves of a sensation Morris could not determine between anguish and ecstasy. Her face appeared paper white and flushed of all blood. Her arms, exposed where her sleeves fell back as she raised them, resembled bleached lengths of birchwood. Her weak hands clawed and beat at a dead black hulk that loomed over her, a mass of shadow given muscle, meat, and fur, and extending its long, ropy neck to Eve's throat. There, its snout pressed against her snowy flesh, jowls retracted to expose monstrously sharp teeth embedded into Eve's skin and sucking the blood that flowed from her wounds.

Following the light, Barnes, Baker, Marceline, and the others rushed in the direction of the screams. When they reached Eve and the demonic thing that assaulted her, the beast relented from feeding and leapt at the nearest man in a lab coat. It snarled, a cry from outside the bounds of nature. The sound rippled through Morris, a subsonic wave that curdled his soul. The mastiff spread wide its jaws revealing teeth more fitting for a shark than a dog, and then it snapped them shut around the technician's neck. They closed with an audible *clack*, and the man's head gouted blood onto the dog as it dropped to the ground.

Everyone screamed and shouted. Fear descended on them all. Morris saw the panic in their stances, their faces, their eyes limned in perfect sharpness by the light.

"The light," he whispered to himself.

He adjusted the focus until the beam tightened around the growling mastiff. Black hairs rose along the ridge of its back. It lowered its front, preparing to pounce again.

Morris threw the second switch.

The steam-engine jolted and gurgled. Power surged into the light. *It flared, brighter than the sun, brighter than a million suns,* Morris thought, as light poured through his closed eyelids, through the flesh and bone of his hands clamped over them. The twang of the filament sang like a chorus of cats on fire—then the light, once again, erupted, spewed forth a rain of hot iron and glass, and burned itself out. Morris shielded himself from the hot debris but found it necessary to pat out several embers burning into his coat. He gazed out over the moors, willing his eyes to adjust to the gloom, and when they did, he saw nought but darkness as clouds blew in to cover the moon.

Darkness… and a fiery form bolting out into the wild.

Howls drifted back to him against the wind. Horrible wails of pain and hunger, a voice like the call of something from beyond the grave. They came at longer and longer intervals, until finally the flaming mastiff fell still and burned, a fallen star way out on the moors. A column of smoke rose from its carcass, pale gray against black night.

Morris watched until it smoldered. After a time, Marceline appeared next to him, forced him to release his grip on the platform rail and guided him down the ladder.

*December 14, letter from Madame Marceline Rene to her mother.*

*Ma Mére,*

*We set sail today from London, bound for New Alexandria.*

*Quelle joie! I shall see you before the New Year as I promised!*

*Two days ago, we departed Whitby. Following the night the second prototype failed, Morris required time to recover from burns sustained when the device exploded. These have healed nicely, and he is as Morris ever is, fully himself again. Even Eve has taken a turn for the better. Since that awful incident, she has slept every night through without so much as a troubled dream. Her color has returned, as has her appetite, and Morris, who all but declared her terminal with tuberculosis, has happily recanted his amateur diagnosis. It seems even distant Van Helsing approved of the mastiff's fate. Burning, apparently, is a means of destroying the undead. Poor Archibald shared that much with us, at least, but he seems beyond all recovery at the loss of spirit the failure of his second prototype induced in him. Although he refused to discuss it directly, Morris and I have inferred from his ramblings and from the occult books and letters around him, that he believed that by trapping light into a solid form, he might somehow reclaim his dead wife from the world beyond.*

*Madness and tragedy. Death is not always the absolute end. But most often it is, and never have I known the methods of science to transcend what exists beyond death. Archibald hoped to change the world in more ways than he revealed to us at the outset. We three fancied ourselves a new Prometheus, and though Archie has suffered a grave and unique punishment for our hubris, we yet failed to bring new fire from the gods. Such a cost for nothing gained — except, I venture, a healthy future for Eve, and for that I am grateful.*

# The Last Priestess

## David Lee Summers

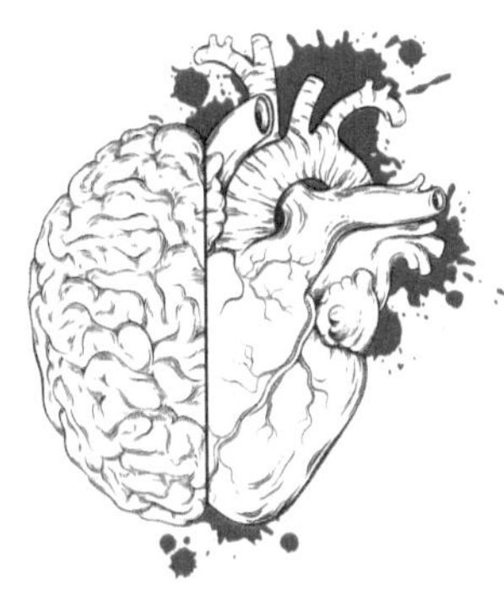

Dinella Stanton sat at a table on a terrace overlooking a lush, green garden under an azure sky dotted with bright clouds. Vibrant orange, yellow, and green buildings surrounded her. In the distance, church bells chimed. She sighed. She couldn't believe she had traveled by airship to Guanajuato, a city surrounded by mountains in central Mexico where the early autumn winds cooled the warm air. Back home in London, damp fog chilled the lengthening nights. And yet, despite the colorful buildings and pleasant weather, she couldn't shake a feeling of dread.

Dinella turned her attention to the sheet of paper in front of her.

*Dearest Mairi,*

*I hope this finds you well. I realize it's been far too long since I've written. However, a little over two weeks ago, Professor Harriman, whom we've discussed at some length, sent his manservant Talbot to my dwellings with an airship ticket and a most extraordinary request. As Talbot explained, the professor still wishes to resurrect a mummy even after our earlier misadventure with the Egyptian pharaoh. He would like to bring back a person from the past so they may relay their experiences first-hand. However, verifying that a particular mummy is an authentic pharaoh or other important personage consumes time and resources, and does not allow for the number of experiments the professor needs to perform to assure success.*

*Despite our harrowing adventures, he wrote a monograph for the Royal Society that was rather well received and it attracted the attention of the Mexican inventor and shipping magnate, Onofre Cisneros. The inventor has brought us to Guanajuato where there is a whole cache of mummies. They are not ancient nor are they people of renown, but they are plentiful and Mr. Cisneros has suggested that it is an excellent place for the professor to continue his experiments before trying to resurrect another Egyptian. We are currently staying at a home Cisneros maintains in Guanajuato.*

*I am along so that I may contact the spirits of any mummies he proposes to experiment on and then channel them into their mortal remains. I've insisted I secure their permission before attempting any experiments. But will the dead retain enough reason to agree? Or will they be lost in their own torment, lashing out as I disturb them? Alas, I cannot shake a certain foreboding about this errand.*

*Be sure to write with the latest news from the Scottish Highlands. You can post by return address, as I gather we may be in Mexico some months. At least the professor pays well. Give my regards to Alex and give Fiona love from her Auntie.*

*With warmest regards,*

*Dinella*

With that, she sealed the letter in an envelope then went inside, spending a restless night dreaming of vengeful mummies trapped in the professor's laboratory.

The next morning, Dinella awakened to the sound of distant spiritual voices. She didn't fully understand the language, but the tone sounded agitated and worried. She picked up the word "futuro" a few times. Odd. In her experience, spirits were usually trapped in the present or thought of the past, not the future. Unable to locate their source, she dressed and entered a cheerful room with high windows that helped to dispel her increasing sense of disquiet. The breakfast dishes had already been set on the table. Professor Augustus Harriman stood as she entered. With his long hair and bushy beard, she always found his name rather fitting. Instead of wearing his usual tweed jacket, waistcoat, and cravat, he wore a khaki jacket and jodhpurs, as though ready to embark on an expedition through the Sahara.

A moment later, Onofre Cisneros entered. He was a strong contrast to Professor Harriman. Neatly coiffed salt-and-pepper hair framed a craggy, but handsome face. He stepped over, lifted Dinella's hand, and kissed it, before pulling out her chair. Her cheeks warmed from the attention. She considered herself a modern woman without the need for a man in her life—let alone one many years her senior. Still, Cisneros's charming gestures made her smile.

Dinella took a few bites of breakfast, then turned to her host. "May I ask what attracted you to Professor Harriman's experiments? Bringing back the dead seems quite removed from building a transportation empire."

Cisneros laughed, then picked up a ribbon that had secured his napkin. He gave it a twist in the middle and held the ends together. "Are you familiar with Professor Möbius's loop?"

When Dinella shook her head, he brought it around to her and instructed her to run her finger around the outside. She did and was surprised to notice how her finger made a path to the inside of the loop and back outside.

Dinella's brow furrowed. "It's like there's only one side to the surface."

"No matter what path you take, you always return to the same point." Cisneros returned to his chair. "I believe history is like that. If we study the past, we can learn about the future."

Dinella felt as though the room's temperature had dropped as she remembered the spirit voices. "Like Ouroboros; the path to the serpent's tail also leads to its head." Although she understood the inventor's point, the image added to her foreboding.

"Indeed." Cisneros took a couple of bites, then wiped his mouth. "What's more, I find the professor's inventions fascinating. I think there may be many practical applications that can come from his work revitalizing tissues and building armatures that simulate human motion."

Dinella appreciated those reasons, but she had a more immediate concern. "I gather these mummies are at most a century old. If they died so recently, many must still have living relatives in the area. Will they object to us trying to contact their spirits?"

Cisneros flashed a reassuring smile. "I have already checked the cemetery's records concerning several of the mummies. I have that information should it be needed."

The three soon finished breakfast. As servants cleared the table, Harriman rose and retrieved a small, leather bag that resembled a doctor's satchel. Before she could ask about it, Cisneros led them outside to a nearby tram stop where several miners stood waiting. When the horse-drawn tram arrived, they climbed aboard and set off for the city's outskirts.

Dinella tensed as the inventor dove into an intense conversation with several of the miners in Spanish. This seemed no friendly banter. Rather the serious tone sent faint shudders traveling across her skin as the sense of something looming grew. She gave a little start as Cisneros turned his attention back to the professor and herself. "Please excuse my inattention. I started my career as a mining engineer. These men have… concerns that matter to me."

Stepping off the tram at the Santa Paula Municipal Cemetery, they faced a tall, arched edifice. Dinella shivered as she looked up at it, very nearly indulging a strong urge to turn away and find another tram. A sense of strong spiritual energy emanated from this place. She shored up her resolve and stepped forward with the others. Passing through the tall gates, Cisneros located a caretaker.

"Señor, might we pay our respects to the dead?"

The man held his hand out, and without hesitation, the inventor placed several silver centavos on his palm. With a faint smile and a nod, the man led them across the grounds, through a maze of tombs and statues, to a door. As he fumbled with a keyring to unlocked the entrance, Dinella labored to breathe, her chest tight in a way it never had been before when faced with the dead. The caretaker finally turned the knob and pushed open the door, revealing a set of steep stairs leading below ground.

She nearly turned and fled, but shook her shoulders loose and mentally took herself to task for her nonsensical agitation.

Glancing around the building's side, she noted several windows low on the wall. Would they be sufficient to admit some light to the underground space? Doubtful, she followed Harriman and Cisneros down the staircase. Although sunlight did filter into the catacombs, it still took a moment for Dinella's eyes to adjust to the dim corridor ahead.

When they did, she quaked.

More mummies than she had ever imagined existed in the whole world lined the corridor. Unlike the Egyptian mummies she'd seen, these were not wrapped in linen. Instead, they were either clothed or naked. The fashions of the clothed mummies resembled those of the city's living residents. This was not a comfort. Almost every mummy's mouth hung open in a silent scream. Scraggly hair covered their scalps. Eyebrows and mustaches still adorned faces. Some mummies wore boots. Others still had jewelry around their necks or on wrists. A few appeared to cover themselves as though out of modesty.

And then there were the spirits.

Panic rose within her once more and she kept her senses shielded. Dinella needed no séance to sense the souls swirling about her. She now realized they had been in her awareness since waking. Now up close, they jostled her like living people scurrying about looking for a way up into the light. Some with purpose, while others wandered lost. Earlier, their voices were almost indiscernible, but now they rose in volume. Behind her, an infant wailed. She whirled around and faced a mummified baby; mouth open wide, frozen in a shriek. Next to the baby stood a woman, head cocked at an unnatural angle, eye sockets empty, but clearly open—a mother who could never reach down and comfort her child.

The voices continued to roil around the space until they rose to a din. Dinella dropped to the ground in a crouch, covering her ears, her eyes squeezed shut. She gulped several deep breaths, then summoned her courage and looked up. Ahead of her, Professor Harriman had placed his bag on the ground. In one hand, he held a jar filled with ointment.

Tension coursed through Dinella once more. She shot to her feet, her eyes wide with outrage, but it was too late. As she watched, Harriman scooped ointment from the jar and rubbed it almost intimately on one arm of a mummified woman, then the other.

Her white hair intricately braided, the woman's eyes were closed and her mouth hung open like the others. She was clothed in the dusty, tattered remains of a dress. Dinella thought it must have been vibrant once, perhaps ceremonial even, but the color and patterns had faded with time. As the professor applied ointment to her face and neck, it seemed as though the mummy screamed a silent protest.

Despite the spiritual energy attempting to unbalance her, Dinella pushed forward. "What in blazes are you doing?"

The professor held up the jar. "This is the ointment I use to moisturize the tissues of ancient mummies. I wanted to see how it worked on these specimens."

"These are not *specimens*. These are the remains of *people*. No one has given us permission for this kind of…" Dinella sought the right word "…violation!"

Cisneros looked from Dinella to Harriman and then back. He smiled and suddenly Dinella wanted to smack the expression off his face, no matter how charming it might be. "I'm sorry," Cisneros said. "I'm afraid this is my fault. This mummy is known to me from my research. She came to Guanajuato from México City. According to the cemetery records, she had no family…"

"But you haven't asked *her* permission. You haven't allowed me to…"

A blood-curdling scream interrupted Dinella. It took her a moment to realize the mummy had drawn breath, wailing out loud at the top of her lungs. After a moment, she closed her mouth with a pop and a clack. Opening eyes untouched by decay, she glared at Dinella, Harriman, and then Cisneros. "¿Qué me estás haciendo?" the mummy rasped.

Eyes wide with awe, Cisneros recovered his voice first. "She asks what we're doing to her." He turned his attention to the mummy. "Mi amiga y mi amigo solo hablan ingles."

Professor Harriman tugged on his beard and leaned in close. "She shouldn't be able to speak. Her organs haven't been revitalized. My ointment merely revitalized her skin."

With that, the mummy took one stiff step forward, then another more swiftly. She thrust out her arm and grabbed Harriman around the throat.

"¿Por qué estás aquí?" After a moment, the mummy seemed to find the question in English. "Why are you here?"

Harriman struggled to free himself from her grip. "We wish to learn from you," he managed to croak out.

"We'd like to know about your life, your experience," Cisneros chimed in.

The mummy relaxed her grip and Harriman fell back to rub the red marks on his throat. She narrowed her gaze, then took an unsteady step toward Cisneros, who held his ground. "I know you. You've been here before." She then turned and pointed at Harriman. "It's not the past you should be concerned about. It's the future."

Harriman and Cisneros exchanged glances. "What do you mean, the future?" Harriman asked.

"You have awoken me, Tocasiuatl. My grandmother was the last priestess of the Spider Woman of the great city of Teotihuacan. She taught me her ways and placed my feet upon the great web of time. I have danced along its strands. I have seen the varied paths humanity has taken. There are dangers on every one, but the path you are on is especially perilous and *you*, Onofre Cisneros and Augustus Harriman, have made it so."

Dinella swallowed, then took a step toward Tocasiuatl. As she did, she noticed the mummy's dark brown eyes weren't cruel or cold, but they weren't kind either. They were the eyes of a person who mercilessly told the truth. "Has your spirit been here trapped in your body this whole time?"

Tocasiuatl shook her head. "I've been here, but not trapped. I can yet leave." She lifted her hand and pointed at Cisneros and then Harriman. "You wish to learn from me? So learn the evil of your choices!"

Cisneros gasped, recoiling as though slapped. "Evil? I have no intention of unleashing evil."

"Few people ever do, but you will cause great harm to this country's children. To *my* children!" The mummy turned. "Follow or I'll kill you now and cut away this tainted strand that way."

As they followed Tocasiuatl they passed the other mummies lining the catacomb's walls. The spirits in the corridor had quieted, as though in anticipation. The priestess climbed the stairs that led back out to the cemetery above. "We now travel along the web of time. With each step we move into the future." She opened the door and they stepped out into the daylight. The mummy led Dinella and the others through the cemetery gates. "As we walked, we moved forward some sixteen years." Outside, people strolled alongside the streets on errands. Dinella had a difficult time believing any time had passed.

Just then, she noticed an airship in the distance. Others on the street noticed as well and stopped to watch. It approached the large cathedral at the center of town, not far from Cisneros's house.

The inventor studied the large, silver vessel. "That's not one of mine. Is it American?"

Tocasiuatl cackled a dry, dusty laugh, lacking in humor. "Guanajuato is secluded, but not too far from the presidential palace in Mexico City. It's a good place for revolutionary activity."

"Revolutionary activity?" Harriman shook his head, confused. "Good God, man, what is she on about?"

Cisneros put his hand on Harriman's shoulder as though seeking support. "Porfirio Diaz has been president of Mexico for the last two decades. He is more like a despotic king than a president. I help people here who would end his long reign."

Again, Tocasiuatl cackled. "We have moved forward a decade and a half and he is still in power."

Cisneros and Harriman exchanged glances. "How exactly did we move through time?" Cisneros asked.

"Time is but a dimension." Tocasiuatl spoke in a pedantic tone, as though explaining the most basic idea. "Moving through time is no different than turning left or climbing stairs. You just need to know which direction to go so you're not swept along by the current."

Dinella continued to watch the airship as the others spoke. A hatch opened and several dark objects fell.

"What are those?" Dinella narrowed her gaze.

A moment later, several explosions rocked the town. The people around her shouted. Some ran toward the hills. Others ran downtown. Tocasiuatl held her place among the confusion. The airship thrummed its way toward them, dropping another payload of explosives. This time, the blast knocked Dinella off her feet. She cried in pain as her ankle twisted. Harriman, his beard covered in dust and cinders, helped her to her feet.

Body parts littered the path to downtown. Blood ran in rivulets to the gutters. Those few people who still lived, groaned in agony.

Cisneros ran toward them, already removing his jacket and tearing strips off of it to use as makeshift bandages.

"Stop!" Tocasiuatl called. "You cannot help these people, but know that Porfirio Diaz strikes from desperation." The mummy moved toward Cisneros. "You helped the miners and others build resources to strike out against the government, never considering the government would strike back."

Heedless of Tocasiuatl's words, Cisneros knelt beside a wounded woman, removed a shard of glass from her arm and applied a bandage. Harriman, coming to his senses, took some cloth strips from the inventor and tried to help another, but the blood came too fast.

The mummy grabbed the inventor's collar. "Come, we have more to see."

Cisneros stood and started to protest, but fell silent when the mummy glared at him.

The mummy led them down the street heedless of the wounded. As their journey continued, the air around them shimmered again. The bodies vanished and the buildings changed. Some vanished altogether. Others showed terrible cracks. Tocasiuatl pointed down the street. Six men wearing surgical masks held an unadorned wooden coffin on their shoulders. Behind them, marched another group. Dinella turned and faced the cemetery. A third group wielding a plain wooden coffin approached from another street.

"Are these the war wounded?" Dinella asked, and realized her ankle no longer hurt.

Tocasiuatl shook her head. "Worse. We've moved forward another three years. A terrible influenza epidemic marches through the world. It's even more fearsome than the humans who battled to unseat emperors and presidents who refused to yield power." She turned to a large house and put her hand on the door latch.

Cisneros placed his hand on hers before she pushed the door open. "Where's Mr. Harriman?"

Dinella looked around. Indeed, Augustus Harriman, who had been right beside her, was nowhere to be seen.

"One cannot be in two places at the same time." Tocasiuatl threw the door open.

"We can't enter without the owner's permission," Dinella protested. "We need to find the professor."

"And we will." Tocasiuatl's words came out cold and firm rather than reassuring. "You see, this is Augustus Harriman's house." She turned to Cisneros. "You helped him buy it, so he could be near the mummies. He has a laboratory here and has been working to resurrect them." The priestess led Dinella and Cisneros up a set of stairs, down the hall, and into a bedroom.

Dinella gasped. Harriman lay in bed, a wet towel on his forehead. His untied hair was a snarled mass on a damp pillow. His manservant, Talbot, started as the group entered. "My God," he said. "The professor said this might happen. I thought it was just the fever."

Dinella tried to understand Talbot's presence. He hadn't accompanied them to Mexico. Then again, if this was the future, it would make sense that he would eventually join his employer.

Harriman's crusty eyes fluttered open. He looked over at Dinella, Cisneros, and Tocasiuatl. "You're here. I don't know how I knew you'd be here, but you are. It's good to see you again. Both of you."

Cisneros stepped forward and took Harriman's hands. "It's good to see you, too, but what's happened?" Just then, Dinella realized that Onofre Cisneros's hair had turned white and more lines etched his face. She looked at her own hands and noticed a few dark spots along the back. She had aged as well.

"It's the flu, sir," Talbot said. "The Spanish flu. You do know about it, don't you?"

Dinella noticed that Harriman's manservant seemed nonplussed by the presence of a walking, talking mummy in the room.

"Yes, the Spanish flu," Tocasiuatl intoned. "There are strands of time where the professor turns his vast experience with the mechanics of life to the study of disease, preventing it where possible, and repairing those afflicted when it's not. On *this* thread, the professor remained in Mexico and continued his research into mummies."

On the bed, Harriman began to wheeze. His breath became a wet, crackling sound. He bucked as though trying to cough, but unable to clear phlegm. At last, he fell still, eyes staring into the distance.

"He is gone and we must move on as well," Tocasiuatl said.

"Wait!" Dinella stepped over and grabbed the mummy's arm. "You said you wouldn't kill him if he followed you!"

The mummy wrenched her arm from Dinella's grasp, then whirled and grabbed her by the throat. She didn't apply enough pressure to choke, but Dinella felt the terrible compression of her grip nonetheless. "*I* did not kill him," the mummy growled. "The Spanish flu is the monster here." With that Tocasiuatl released her grip and continued out the door.

The mummy had stepped outside by the time Dinella recovered herself and caught up with her. "We can't just leave Professor Harriman's body," she pleaded.

"It's too late for that by a year."

Dinella looked around. The pallbearers and their terrible burdens had vanished. She returned to the door and tried the handle. It was locked. "Where's Onofre?" She paused. "Mr. Cisneros?"

"We will find him soon enough." Tocasiuatl strode down the street. Dinella followed her. A gust of hot wind blew through Guanajuato's streets. The city had become eerily quiet. Dinella no longer heard the crying of mourners or the casual conversation of people going about their business.

They continued to walk toward downtown. As they did, Dinella noted more damage to buildings and streets. Soon, though, she discerned a lone voice. Tocasiuatl led Dinella to a plaza. In the center, a large man with a mustache shouted to the small, disheveled crowd. His face flushed bright red; Dinella worried a blood vessel on his forehead might burst. The man suggested that the disease came because people had gone against God's will. He said they didn't need masks. They needed to follow a righteous leader.

"He is called El Jefe," Tocasiuatl explained. Dinella understood the Spanish word to mean "the chief." "He appeals to people's emotions instead of their reason. He hopes to become México's next president. I have followed the thread of time. He will become a dictator far worse than President Diaz, joining with other dark forces only fifteen years hence. Many of time's threads point to a terrible war in the middle of the twentieth century. El Jefe controlling México could tip the balance of power toward the forces of darkness."

Dinella shook her head. "But this is the future." She added up the years on her fingers. "We're looking at events some twenty years hence? How are we responsible for this?"

Tocasiuatl didn't answer. Instead a familiar voice called out. "I fought to end tyranny in México these many years. I won't see another tyrant take Diaz's place."

"Onofre!" Dinella pushed her way through the crowd. As she reached the dapper and familiar form of Onofre Cisneros, two large men blocked her way. Two more grabbed Cisneros by the arms and hauled him toward the stage.

"Onofre Cisneros." El Jefe laughed. "The great inventor has deigned to come to one of my speeches. And what has the great inventor done? He acquired wealth for himself. He helped weak men take control of our country. México needs a strong leader, a leader who will use our strength, our airships, our navy, our great ports to bring peace and prosperity. We will no longer be slaves to the country across our northern border."

Cisneros shook his head. "You don't want peace and prosperity. You send the Indians to labor camps. You work the miners to death. You..."

El Jefe slapped Cisneros.

Dinella cried out and started forward. The two large men restrained her.

"You are a traitor to this country," El Jefe snarled as he pulled out a pistol and squeezed the trigger. Blood and brains exploded from the back of the inventor's skull. To Dinella's horror, the crowd cheered at the spectacle.

Dinella screamed.

One of El Jefe's guards moved to strike her, but was stopped when Tocasiuatl grabbed his arm. The mummy led Dinella back toward the cemetery. Everything was a blur as they walked. Tocasiuatl spoke, but Dinella barely registered the words. "Cisneros had always been torn about the right way to help the world. Build machines of war, or pursue science? They are not necessarily exclusive, but on this strand, he made choices that crippled México, along with much of the rest of the world. He could have made better choices. He could have funded medical research and education. He could have used his fleet of vessels to bring aid to those who needed it, instead of dropping bombs in retaliation for other attacks."

They entered the cemetery and walked toward the stairs leading to the catacombs. "You speak as though all this is a fait accompli." As they descended the stairs, Dinella noticed the air around her shimmering. "Is there no way to affect the future?"

"I am a dead woman who yet speaks the truth. Some would call me a monster. I am a woman of the past who has shown you the future. That makes me a paradox. The web of time has many paths. Changing the path you're on is as simple as taking a few steps in one direction or the other. It is as difficult as crossing to the other side of a Möbius loop."

For a moment, Dinella wondered how Tocasiuatl knew about such things, but realized that might not be so mysterious for a being who had just come back from the dead in physical form and could travel through time.

They walked through the corridor lined with mummies. Dinella still sensed the spirits around them. They seemed to be watchful and expectant. Two bodies lay on the floor ahead of them. Dinella rushed forward to find both Harriman and Cisneros on the ground. The inventor's hair was salt-and-pepper again. Harriman still wore his khaki suit, his hair dark. She held her hands under their noses. They breathed faintly.

She found Harriman's bag and emptied it onto the ground, shuffling through the contents until she found a bottle of smelling salts. She held them under each of the men's noses until they revived. Harriman sneezed. Cisneros held his head and moaned. "What happened?"

"I think we have a lot to talk about," Dinella said.

Harriman rose to his feet and approached the mummy, who once again leaned immobile against the wall, eyes closed. "Tocasiuatl? Can you hear me?"

Dinella stood and joined him. The spirits around her had gone back about their business. They milled about the room, but their presence no longer overwhelmed her. She tried to sense Tocasiuatl. "I think her spirit's gone."

"For good?" Harriman asked.

Dinella shrugged. She looked along the row of mummies. "In this crowd, who knows?" Then Dinella looked back at Tocasiuatl and realized her mouth no longer hung open in a silent scream. It was closed, as though she'd fallen into a serene slumber.

Dinella entered the observation lounge of the Airship *Larisa Carmesí*. A dozen or so people sat at clean, metal tables, some deep in conversation, some playing cards. She stepped up to the bar and ordered a glass of white wine. While the bartender poured her drink, a woman came up beside her. "I don't believe we've met, I'm Dame Eliza Waterhouse. My husband and I are just returning from Mexico City where we visited the pyramids at Teotihuacan."

Dinella smiled and thought of Tocasiuatl, the descendant of Teotihuacan's priestesses. Then she remembered her manners and introduced herself. "Perhaps we have similar interests. My employer and I are returning from Guanajuato where we viewed the mummies with Onofre Cisneros." She carefully omitted any additional details.

The bartender brought Dinella's wine and Dame Waterhouse flicked open a fan. "My, that's quite an honor. He owns this airship line. Not many people are granted an audience with the man himself."

"My employer is a scientist with… many interests. Mr. Cisneros funds his research."

Dame Waterhouse fanned herself. "Perhaps you'd care to join my husband and I in some conversation this afternoon?"

Dinella's gaze swept the lounge. She noticed Professor Harriman sitting at a small table near the gallery windows. "Most kind, but perhaps another time would be better." She inclined her head toward the professor.

"I understand," Dame Waterhouse said, though Dinella didn't think she did. "I look forward to chatting with you and your… employer later in the voyage."

Leaving the woman with her misconceptions, Dinella collected her wine and walked over to the small table. "May I sit down?"

Professor Harriman smiled up at her. "By all means."

She gazed out at the vista of sunlit clouds, which reminded her of the candy floss she'd enjoyed on a visit to Blackpool Pleasure Beach several years before. Occasionally the clouds parted, revealing the Atlantic Ocean's choppy waters below. Fortunately, it seemed the airship's crew had found a smooth airstream. She thought about Onofre Cisneros's home in Mexico, the veranda and the garden. She sighed as she felt a pang of regret about leaving Guanajuato.

"Are you sure going home is the right thing?" Dinella asked. "We won't necessarily avoid the coming war or the Spanish flu in England."

Harriman sighed. "I had begun to think I could control life and death itself." He faced Dinella. "I had begun to think you could help me understand what spirits were and how we could harness them." Harriman shook his head. "When Tocasiuatl revealed her vast control of time itself—when I *died,* for God's sake—I realized my understanding of the vastness of the cosmos has just started. I need to go back and rethink my priorities. Perhaps I can turn my skills to uses that are more productive to humanity. Maybe I can help restore dying organs or build prosthetic limbs."

Dinella nodded, agreeing that did sound like a better path for the professor's researches, but for a moment she returned to something else he said. "You remember dying?"

Harriman's brow furrowed. "Do I *remember* something that will happen in the future? It feels like a premonition." He scoffed. "I suppose that's exactly what it is. Though I hope it's a premonition that doesn't come true. At least not the way we experienced."

Dinella looked out at the bright, serene clouds. "Did you at least glimpse heaven?"

Harriman shook his head. "I just blacked out and a moment later I woke up on the catacomb floors." He paused and looked out at the clouds. "Sometimes I fear that's the truth of death. That there's just nothing. We merely cease to exist and it scares me to think there might be a day with no tomorrow." A tear ran down his cheek. Dinella reached over and took his hand. Harriman looked away, sniffing as he rubbed the tear away with his free hand.

"But we know there are spirits," Dinella said.

"Maybe they're just the ones who aren't ready for oblivion." Harriman sighed. "What about you? You could have stayed."

Dinella sipped her wine. "Revolution is coming to Mexico one way or another, but it's not my revolution."

"And yet, as you've told me, there are all those spirits in the catacombs. You could have helped them."

Dinella shrugged. "Could I? Tocasihuatl made it clear she controlled her own destiny. Those spirits knew where they were and what they were doing. Their human lives were cut short, but I believe they can find their way without the help of a stranger from England."

"So, what will you do now?"

"I suppose I'll just have to take a step to the left and cross to the other side of the Möbius loop."

# A Fearsome Tail

## Aaron Rosenberg

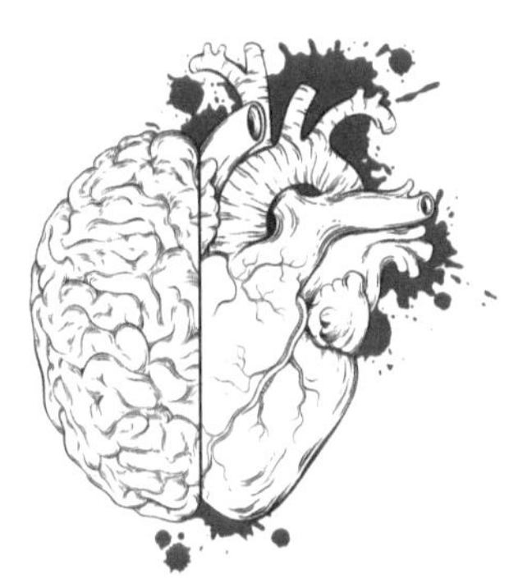

IT DID NOT TAKE PHILLIPE HURON LONG TO arrive on the scene, since he lived in the 7th arrondissement himself and thus Faubourg Saint-Germain was mere moments away, even without an autocar. Yet somehow a familiar blue-clad figure was already waiting for him at the front gate, collar turned up and hat brim pulled down against the rain.

"Inspector," Whitmer said, and he nodded back, Detective Dupin cawing a hello of his own from Phillipe's shoulder. The fact that the officer smiled fondly at the crow was not lost on Phillipe, though he pretended not to notice.

"What do we have?" he asked instead as they followed the front path up to a narrow, stately townhouse. "My wireless only provided the address and a sense of urgency."

As usual, Whitmer was nothing if not efficient. "This is the home of Madame Juliette Mailloux," she began, but he stopped her there.

"Mailloux? The same Mailloux who sits on the Board of Trustees at the Louvre? Renowned patroness of the arts?"

His officer shrugged. "Don't know, sir," she admitted readily. "Never heard of her, myself. But clearly she had money. And influence, since we were called out so fast."

"Had," Phillipe noted. "Has she died?"

"Not died," a new voice stated, as a man greeted them at the front door. "At least, I hope not."

Whitmer had fallen back a step, but Phillipe simply squared his shoulders and met the newcomer's gaze. "Préfet Lépine," he declared, dipping his head. Dupin let loose a subdued squawk, shuffling his feet. Even the crow was cowed by the head of the Préfecture de Police!

Louis Lépine nodded back. "Juliette is an old friend," he confided, stepping back to let them enter and then shutting the door firmly behind them. "I would appreciate your utmost concentration on this, inspector. All Le PP's resources are at your disposal."

"Understood, sir." Phillipe shut his umbrella and looked around, admiring the fine woodwork, the well-maintained antique furniture, the stand filled with a collection of handsome walking sticks, and the lovely artwork displayed on the walls. "What do we know?"

"We had a standing dinner date twice a month," the Préfet replied. "Myself, Juliette, and a handful of others. She did not attend the most recent one the night before last, nor had she sent word. I grew worried, so today I stopped by." He frowned. "I found nothing amiss, no signs of violence, burglary, or foul play. Yet Juliette is nowhere to be seen."

Phillipe had, with an apologetic shrug, slid past his superior and into the handsomely if stiffly appointed drawing room. From there he made a slow circuit of the first floor before proceeding toward the steep stairs. Whitmer shadowed him, as did the Préfet.

"No signs of forced entry on any of the doors or windows," Whitmer reported quietly as they ascended. "And plenty of what I'm guessing is expensive art, but nothing taken."

"Nothing except the owner herself, perhaps," Phillipe corrected. He made straight for the back of the upstairs hall, opening the door there to reveal a large bedroom. The bed was unmade and the wardrobe's front doors hung open. "Though it appears she may have departed of her own accord, as I cannot imagine a kidnapper would stop to gather spare clothes."

A set of glass-paned doors opened onto a small study, complete with its own wireless set and several pneumatic tubes, which most likely went to other portions of the house. Phillipe examined the items on the gilt-edged desk there, lifting an envelope to study it more closely. "Hm."

"What have you found?" Lepine asked, moving beside him. "Do you know what happened to her?"

Phillipe could only shake his head. "Not yet, no. But I believe I know where she went from here." He offered the envelope to his superior. "Arrived with the morning post two days ago, from the markings, addressed to her, and the letter is missing. No doubt she took it with her. But she no longer needed the address." He tapped the lines of neat script at the top. "La Galerie, Queues Poilues."

Whitmer was already tapping the name into her auto-locator. "Got it!" she announced triumphantly a moment later, when the device spat out a slip of paper. "It's in Bretagne, near Rennes, just off the Vilaine."

Lepine nodded. "Take a gyro and go at once," he instructed Phillipe. "This dismal weather isn't bad enough to prevent you. Bring backup if you like, and keep me updated."

"At once, sir." Phillipe turned to his officer, who had paled, but there was no time to wait for Parkins or even Beaumont. "Come along, Whitmer. We're about to go for a ride."

"Not a fan of flying, are you?" he asked once they were at the airfield and making their way through the gray drizzle toward the hangar reserved for le PP's collection of autogyros and balloons.

Whitmer shook her head. "Not really, sir, no. Sorry, sir."

He gave her a sympathetic smile. "Can't say I blame you, but don't worry. Shouldn't be in the air for too long." An airship would have provided a smoother ride, of course, but would take far too long. In any disappearance, time was of the essence.

His officer understood that, of course. She didn't offer any protests as Phillipe told the sergeant in charge what he needed, nor did she utter any complaints as they both climbed into the small craft. At least they were able to take one of the larger vehicles, and both of them sat on the back bench, with the pilot alone up front. Dupin fluttered about the small cabin a moment before alighting on the empty front seat's headrest, ruffling his feathers contentedly at the unrestricted view.

Whitmer did grip her armrest tightly as the rotors began to spin, and even harder when the little craft lurched and rose off the ground, the raindrops pelting it like stones. To distract her, Phillipe began discussing the case.

"What could have induced her to leave Paris in such a hurry, and without telling anyone?" He had to shout over the noise of rotor, motor, and wind.

His companion frowned, though he could see the relief on her face as she concentrated. "Blood or money," she replied just as loudly. "Only two things liable to get such a strong reaction."

He nodded. "She's a widow," he answered. "Husband died decades ago. No children, no siblings, if I recall. So blood seems unlikely. And she's rich—he was a judge, she was an heiress. So not money, either. What does that leave, though?"

"Art?" Dupin squawked, and Phillipe leaned over to ruffle the bird's head feathers.

"Yes, very good," he told his pet, companion, and friend. "Madame Mailloux is a veritable demon for the arts. News of some major find could have drawn her out easily." He had reclaimed the envelope before leaving, and pulled it out now to study it again. "Nothing to indicate who sent it, other than that it's from 'the Gallery.'"

Whitmer laughed. "Well, there probably won't be too many of those out where we're going!"

He nodded. Rennes was small enough, in and of itself. If this Queues Poilues used that as a landmark, the place must be tiny indeed.

The name itself was also odd. Why call a town "Furry Tails"? Perhaps it was a local legend, or an inside joke.

Either way, Phillipe would find out once they landed.

The pilot set down on a rocky outcropping at the top of a small cliff. "Closest I can get, inspector," he explained as the craft's wheels bounced along the rough terrain before finally coming to a stop. "Ground down there is too soft, 'specially with all this rain, we'd sink like a stone."

"Down there" was presumably the town of Queues Poilues, though Phillipe thought he'd rarely seen a sadder interpretation of the word. "Dump," Dupin declared, bursting from the cabin as soon as the door was opened and winging around the autogyro, water flying from his wings to spatter them all. "Dump!"

"That is unkind," Phillipe admonished his pet. Though, privately, he felt the crow spoke truth. A handful of buildings clustered along a winding road as if cowering from the forest pressing in around them, all of them grayed by exposure to wind and rain. Only the smattering of lights and the occasional wisp of smoke through the rain and fog convinced him the entire place had not been abandoned years before. The River Vilaine was just visible as a wide, dark ribbon winding through the trees to the south.

"You'd best head back," he told the pilot, straightening and stretching. Such small vehicles were not made for a man of his height! "Return tomorrow at dawn, and the same each day unless we call to arrange a different pickup." The pilot nodded, saluted, and a few minutes later had the rotors spinning again, while Phillipe and Whitmer picked their way down along the cliffside toward the dismal town below. He had brought his umbrella, of course, but the wind was too strong for him to use it, so he simply suffered the rain along with his subordinate.

"How did she even get here, if she did in fact come?" His officer asked as they made their careful descent. "Didn't you say she was quite old? This would be a difficult climb for her, especially in such foul weather."

Phillipe nodded. "Yes, although what little I know of her suggests a strong will. Perhaps enough to navigate this path, if she were motivated. And I had Beaumont check the travel logs—she hired an aircraft to bring her here two days ago. So we are on the right track, at least."

They made the rest of the trek in silence, broken only when they reached the first of the buildings below, which proved to be a small, sad little inn. "Le Bon Voyageur," Phillipe read from the sign out front. "Well, let us hope so."

Inside, the place had more vivacity, with a lively fire going in the large stone hearth, its flames casting a cheery glow about the room. Chairs and tables were spaced about the place, and a long bar took up the far wall, with a staircase to the side rising toward what presumably were bedrooms for rent. A handful of people sat drinking and eating, though any conversation ceased as Phillipe and Whitmer entered, shaking the water from their hats and coats.

"Welcome, sir and madam!" That was from an older gentleman behind the bar. "I am Matteo Épineux, the proprietor. Take any seat you like, there are some over by the fire if you care to dry off. Can I interest you in some hearty beef stew and fresh baguettes? And perhaps a glass of fine Bordeaux to accompany it?"

Phillipe nodded, claiming an empty table, and after a moment Whitmer awkwardly accepted the seat beside him. "I'm used to interviewing suspects and witnesses," she said softly. "Not dining with them." A chittering came from somewhere near the corner, and she grimaced. "Nor fending off vermin while I do."

He smiled at her. "Then this shall be another aspect of your education. And ignore the rats, as they will most likely do the same for us." When Épineux returned a moment or two later, bearing a bottle and two glasses as well as a basket of rolls, Phillipe turned toward him. "Merci, monsieur. We have come all the way from Paris, and your establishment is tres charming."

The man dipped his head. "Thank you, sir. Paris, eh? And you're with the gendarme, I see. Is there trouble?"

"We hope not." Phillipe accepted the wineglass, raised it in silent salute, and took a sip. Whatever else this place might lack, its wine cellar at least was up to snuff! "We are looking for someone. Perhaps you can help. Her name is Madame Mailloux. She is an older woman, slight of build, with silver hair. She walks with a cane."

Épineux frowned but nodded. "Oh, oui, I know her. Or at least, she was here a day or two ago. Dined here, then left. I know not where."

One of the other diners, a stout woman with the thick arms of someone who worked hard for a living, spoke up, though her companion tried to shush her. "I know where she went. To Benchurch. She said she was staying there, that it was all arranged."

That drew a collective gasp from the rest of the room. "What is this Benchurch?" Whitmer asked. She was tearing bits off a roll and offering them to Dupin, who accepted them with great grace and dignity.

"It's an old house, up on the hill at the far edge of town," their host explained after a moment, his voice more somber than before. "Grand old place, but no one's lived there in years. It's had a dark history, that place has. Even before the rats claimed it."

Phillipe nodded. "We will seek it out after dinner, and hope the rats will allow our visit. And what of a gallery?" His reply drew muttering from some of the residents, along with several hasty signs to ward off evil. He might have known such a small, isolated place would thrive on superstition!

But Épineux shook his head. "We have no such place here, sir. I'm sorry." Even after Phillipe handed him the envelope, the man still insisted the name was pure fiction. The questioning was clearly making him uncomfortable, and after a moment Phillipe allowed him to depart and fetch the rest of their supper. The skittering and scratching from the edges of the room seemed to increase as the rest of the room fell back into silence. Dupin was staring toward the corner with great interest, but Phillipe stroked his head and the bird subsided slightly.

"So she was lured here under false pretenses," he commented once the man had gone. "And whoever did it arranged for her stay at some old house away from everyone else."

Whitmer nodded. "It does sound suspicious, sir." She shook her head. "I hate to say it, but the lady may have met a bad end out there."

"Let us hope not," Phillipe replied. "But if she has, we shall at least find out who was responsible for it. After we eat," he added, for Épineux had returned carrying a covered tray, and the smell rising from it made his stomach grumble.

After all, there was little sense investigating on an empty stomach!

The stew proved to be excellent, and Phillipe was feeling quite contented as he strolled down the town's single road, Whitmer beside him and Dupin sailing along up ahead. The rain had subsided to a steady drip, leaving their surroundings hazy and damp and the ground squishy and treacherous, plus their trek was accompanied by the sounds of skittering on either side.

"I'm not a fan of rats," Whitmer confided as they walked, keeping her pocket torch out before her and her other hand close to her pistol. "And it seems we've piqued their interest."

"No doubt this place draws few visitors," Phillipe pointed out. "We are as much a novelty to them as they are to us — and just as little a threat, provided they stick to the shadows. And we stay to the light." That last was said to his crow, who had veered closer to the dark on his latest pass. Phillipe knew the bird wanted nothing more than to hunt some of those unseen rats, but there was no telling how many there were. He was not about to lose Dupin to a swarm of the filthy things!

"Grand" was certainly a good word for Benchurch, he thought as they came to the sturdy brick wall surrounding the place. The road had risen, and glancing back Philippe saw they were nearly at the same height as their landing spot. Behind the house, the forest soared upward, forming a formidable barricade. Against that backdrop, Benchurch was tall and solidly built, with heavy gables and thick mullioned windows. No lights gleamed from behind them.

He and Whitmer both aimed their pocket torches down on as he pushed open the wrought iron gate and led the way up the narrow, rain-slicked path. It had been fashioned as a series of steps and landings to accommodate the rising terrain, and Phillipe was breathing heavily by the time he reached the top and banged on the thick wooden door.

There was no answer from within, though he thought he saw a shadow shifting behind one of the curtains.

"Hello?" he called as he tried again. "Madame Mailloux? This is Inspector Phillipe Huron of the Préfecture de Police. Préfet Lepine sent us to make sure you were all right. May we come in?"

When she still did not reply, he tried the door. It was unlocked, and groaned softly as he pushed it open.

"Madame?" Stepping into the foyer, Phillipe shone his light about the place. The beam took in a marble floor, brocade wallpaper, and a dangling crystal chandelier. The long hall had tall pocket doors on either side and a winding staircase at the far end. At least it was dry, though he could hear water dripping somewhere farther in.

Turning to the doors on the left, he gestured for Whitmer to open them. She did so, eliciting a small puff of dust and revealing a large, dusty room beyond. The thick coating on the floor was undisturbed, save by scratch marks and what looked like tiny paw prints—and some a fair bit larger.

Next they tried the doors on the right. These opened more easily, and let onto an equally large room but one that had been at least somewhat swept clean. A bed had been placed along one wall, with a privacy screen around it and a small table beside it holding a pitcher and basin. Over in front of the tall windows sat a handsome desk covered in papers. There was a fireplace along the outer wall, and though it was dark now when Phillipe stirred the ashes with the poker he saw sparks of red amid the black and gray. That stirring upset the shadows, and an angry chittering rose from several places, the bits of light suddenly reflected in many small, beady eyes.

"She was here," he remarked, ignoring the vermin as best he could. "Not just now, but not terribly long ago, either. Within the past day, certainly."

Whitmer had gone to check the single door along the back wall. "Sir," she called now. "You should see this."

Joining her, Phillipe peered into a scene of utter turmoil.

It had been the kitchen, he saw at once, though it was too old to have any of the modern conveniences. Yet there was the washing sink and there the stove, with an old icebox alongside. A heavy, scarred wooden table had stood at the center, most likely used for both preparing food and feeding the staff. Pots and pans had hung from hooks along the wall, as had strings of onions, garlic, and other herbs and spices.

All of that was now scattered about the floor, along with the table itself, which had been overturned and shoved off to one side. Debris was caught against its top and legs, and more of that had been heaped in the room's far corner, where the wall bore signs of deep scratches.

As he watched, sections of that heap shifted, bits and pieces rising and falling as many small somethings moved beneath them. The noises were far louder here.

"Nest!" Dupin declared, taking a turn about the room before returning to roost upon Phillipe's shoulder. "Nest!" At least the crow heeded his earlier admonitions and did not attempt to disturb the clearly occupied pile!

"So it would seem," he agreed, petting the bird. "Yet could rats have been responsible for all this disarray? And what does that have to do with Madam Mailloux?" His eye caught on a gleam of black among the rubbish, and he strode forward, careful in case there were anything slippery beneath the trash, to retrieve an elegant ebon cane, its silver head intact but its sides scored and chipped. The pile heaved as he did, squeaks and shrieks erupting, but no rodents emerged to challenge him over the rescued item.

"She was here," he said, holding the walking aid up for his companion to see. "But it appears something awful has happened to her."

Whitmer nodded. She bent to capture something of her own, which at first Phillipe thought to be a large, pale needle or a single piece of oddly gray hay. Then he realized it was a whisker.

"Furry Tails," the officer whispered. "The name certainly makes sense now. And this, sir, belongs to a rat. But an enormous one. One big enough to carry off a small child—or an elderly woman."

"I am sorry, I should have told you." They had returned to Le Bon Voyageur, deciding to inspect Benchurch more closely in daylight, and Monsieur Épineux had brought them both steaming mugs of hot cocoa before taking a chair beside them. "It is a reputation we had all hoped to escape, you see." He grimaced at the constant sounds from the shadows. "Not that we can, really."

Phillipe shook his head, setting the mug to one side so Dupin could delicately dip his beak into the hot liquid. "So your town has a rat problem," he said. "Why not just hire an exterminator and be done with it?"

"'Cause they'll just get et, too," an old man by the fire declared. "It ain't the little ones ya got to worry about. It's the big uns, the ones in charge."

"What, you're saying people here get eaten by giant rats?" Phillipe asked.

The inn's other occupants all muttered at that. "Yes," their host agreed. "Exactly that. You've no doubt noticed we have more than our fair share of rats. But there are leaders among them, rats of enormous size, n'est-ce pas? Veritable monsters."

"And you are suggesting one of these carried off Madame Mailloux?" Phillipe frowned, rubbing at his jaw.

"It's true," the same old man insisted. "Seen it myself, a few years back. Beast big as a boar and black as coal snatched up a boy afore anyone could stop it. Disappeared into the forest with his prize, never saw the boy again."

The other residents all nodded agreement. "Saw one just the other night," a whip-thin woman with tired eyes said after a moment. "Gray rat, this one was, and it had an old lady clutched in its front paws." She shook her heard. "Poor thing didn't stand a chance."

Whitmer frowned. "Could that be Madame Mailloux?" she asked Phillipe quietly, laying the whisker on the table between them. "It would explain this."

Phillipe frowned. "No, it is quite impossible. There is some rational explanation for all this. And I will prove it."

Though, at the moment, he had no idea how he would go about accomplishing that.

The room Épineux showed him to was small and spare, but it was clean and dry and the bed proved long enough for Phillipe to stretch out on fully. Dupin perched on the footboard, head tucked down into his feathers, an inky guardian against bad dreams and intruders alike. Best of all, the rats evidently feared him or Dupin or both, because for the first time since entering town Phillipe heard no sounds of them. Relieved and exhausted, he quickly fell asleep.

Phillipe woke the next morning surprisingly refreshed. After his morning ablutions he made his way downstairs, finding Whitmer already there. She was speaking to several locals he recognized from the night before. The rats were evidently awake as well, judging by the noises from the corners, but he did his best to ignore those.

"The Turgots," the officer explained once she'd thanked them and moved away to join him at the same table they'd had previously. "Both have lived here their whole lives. Never saw Madame Mailloux before that one time, nor since. Never heard of her before, either. Said she appeared to be waiting for someone all through dinner, and left in a huff, alone."

Phillipe nodded. "Well done, Whitmer. We know someone sent her a letter from here, and that its contents were enticement enough to draw her here at once. But what did it say? And how did whoever sent it know that would work? For that matter, how did they even know who she was? And why bring her all the way out here, just to have her eaten by giant rats?" He muttered that last part with all the disdain he felt for such an idea, and Dupin flapped his wings as if to commiserate.

"Blood or money," Whitmer replied, smirking when he arched a brow in her direction. "That is what you said, n'est-ce pas? For her, but perhaps also for whoever lured her here. So either some sort of grudge, some attempt at control, or a play for money."

Phillipe nodded, both at her and then to Épineux, who had just brought out a tray covered with plates of steaming food and a jug of coffee. It was not one of the self-regulating type, just a simple earthenware pitcher, but the smell alone was enough to clear any remaining cobwebs from his sleep, and he gratefully poured a cup for himself and then one for his companion. Dupin cawed—the crow hated coffee, but happily accepted a waterglass instead.

"Yes, quite correct," Phillipe commented after his first sip. "So either someone here knew about her fortune or they knew her personally. But who?" He frowned, tapping his chin as he searched his memories for all he knew about the wealthy older woman. "Her husband was a judge, but she came from old money," he recalled aloud. "Her father was in textiles and manufacturing, owned several plants. Her mother... her family was in fisheries, I believe. And watermills. Along the Seine and also on the coast." He took another sip, letting the hot, caffeinated liquid do its work, and smiled as another scrap of information was jarred loose. "Carré. That was her mother's people."

"Carré, did you say?" Épineux had approached with a plate piled high with fresh croissants, butter, and jam. "Why, I know a Carré, Alain Carré. He was here last night, sitting with Elodie Dembour. He will most likely be in again this evening—many in town come here for supper."

Phillipe thanked their host, and he and Whitmer finished breaking their fast in companionable silence, punctuated by Dupin's occasional demand for treats. Afterward, the pair stood and, without needing a word, made their way outside into the rain and down the path toward the house looking down on the town.

It was time to see whether they could discern anything further about Madame Mailloux's stay at Benchurch.

"Here is her valise," Whitmer remarked. They had been making a slow, careful search of the room, the one that had clearly been occupied. "So whatever happened to her, she left her clothes behind." The bag had been pierced in many places by small, sharp teeth and claws, but the contents appeared to be undisturbed.

Phillipe nodded. He had crouched down by the desk, studying a dark spot Dupin had been pecking at. "Blood," he stated after smudging it with the tip of one finger. "Relatively fresh. Not a great deal, but enough if someone had, say, knocked her out from behind."

"No sign of drag marks, though," his officer said, joining him to examine the area. "And no furniture amiss. So perhaps not carried off by giant rats." She glanced apprehensively toward the shadows as she said this, as if afraid to anger them with such a statement.

Phillipe barely dignified that with a sniff, however. "Certainly not. This was the work of a person or persons, nothing more. All that nonsense about giant rats is exactly that. Aha!" He had crossed to the fireplace and now extracted a shred of paper from among the ashes. He'd missed that the night before, with only his pocket torch's light for a guide. "It's part of a letter. Listen:

> *. . . me Mailloux:*
>
> *. . . this abrupt and unexpected contact, but I have found*
> *. . . will wish to see. You are, of course, familiar with the works of*

*. . . oussin. Well, recently I discovered a handsome landscape*
*. . . believe to be one of his later works. I am no great expert,*
*. . . upon your greater knowledge and experience to confirm that.*
*. . . will meet you at Le Bon Voyageur, and will show you the piece.*
*. . . is a long journey, so accommodations will be prepared for you.*
*. . . meeting you, and hope this will be beneficial for us both.*
*. . . mbour*

"That could be 'Dembour,' could it not?" Whitmer asked. "And now we know Dupin was correct. It was art that drew her here with such haste." The crow preened at being validated.

"And not just any art," Phillipe agreed, rising and brushing off his trousers. "Unless I am mistaken, the author was claiming to have found a lost work by Nicolas Poussin himself." At his subordinate's blank look, he shook his head. "Truly, you must educate yourself in the arts more, Whitmer! A proper detective has at least passing familiarity in all such areas. Poussin is considered by many to be one of the first and finest painters of the classical Baroque style. Two of his paintings hang in the Louvre already, but it would be quite a coup for Madame Mailloux if she were able to secure a third."

Whitmer nodded. "But Dembour or whomever did not meet her at the inn, as planned. So she came back here, determined to wait for further contact or perhaps planning to ask around town. Only something happened to her first."

"Indeed." Phillipe sighed. "And someone. But one thing it was not, no matter what the villagers claim, was giant rats. We shall see if Madam Dembour can tell us more."

Elodie Dembour proved to be the sturdy woman who had directed them to Benchurch the night before. She worked as a washerwoman, and despite the continuing rain was busy wringing out bedsheets along the riverbank when Phillipe and Whitmer found her, having followed a narrow, slippery footpath away from the main road. "Never seen that before," she stated after he showed her the charred letter, carefully shielded by his umbrella. "And don't know nothing about no painting." Rats were now visible dashing along the water's edge, their little brown and gray bodies slick with rain, but they did not approach the human trio or the circling, eager corvid.

Phillipe studied her, but the woman appeared unconcerned, even when Dupin fluttered about her head. "Very well," he said at last. "It is entirely possible someone borrowed your name to disguise their own identity. But who? Have you seen anyone mailing a letter within the past week?"

She shook her head. "Not something I bother with, myself. But it weren't me."

There was little more to gain from questioning her, so instead Phillipe led the way back onto the street and stalked its length, hoping for any sort of clue. But nothing emerged, save more rats, who fled before him, disappearing back into their protective shadows and then glaring at him from that relative safe haven.

"Sir?" Whitmer asked, keeping pace alongside him.

"We know someone sent this from here," he told her. "And I believe Madam Dembour that she was not involved. So who was? And what has become of poor Madame Mailloux?" He shook his head. "Without more to go on, we may never know."

Dupin squawked. "Supper!" It was already growing dark, the shadows expanding to swallow up the buildings and the road, the constant rain aiding in masking the place from view.

"Yes, supper," he agreed, stroking his pet's beak. "We will hope this Alain Carré attends, and has some answers for us."

"That is him now," Epineux said, pointing to the man who'd just entered the inn. It was the same one who'd tried quieting Madam Dembour. "Alain!"

The man glanced up, startled. He looked on the verge of running, but after a second sighed instead and approached. He was small and slight, with wispy brown hair just starting to gray, and large eyes that made him look perpetually surprised. "Yes?"

"Do you know Madame Mailloux?" Phillipe demanded, straightening to tower over the man. "Are you related to her?"

Carré yelped, cowering before him. "What? No! I don't know what you mean!"

Phillipe remained there a moment before retreating a step. "You are certain?"

"Yes, quite certain!" Carré was all but falling over himself in an attempt to get away. "Leave me alone!" With that, the little man turned and fled.

"He has always been high-strung," Epineux admitted. "But it has grown worse of late. His wife passed a few months ago, and between that and his own ill health he has been unable to fish."

Phillipe exchanged a glance with Whitmer. "Where does he live, exactly?"

Carré's house proved to be one of the larger ones along the road, roughly halfway between the inn and the mansion. "A lot of house for one man alone," Whitmer remarked as they approached, walking carefully through the mud.

"Yes, but understandable for someone who came from money," Phillipe replied. He banged on the door, but heard no answering motion within. "Monsieur Carré! Open, please! We have a few more questions for you!"

They waited a moment, but still got no reply. Nor were there any lights on within, that they could see.

"Where else could he have gone?" Whitmer asked.

Phillipe started to reply, but was distracted by a large shape suddenly looming out of the shadows. "Who's there?" he called, shining his torch in that direction.

For an instant, the light caught on an enormous, jet-black shape with a long tail, a pointed nose, and beady red eyes.

Then it was gone.

"Did you see that?" he asked, and beside him Whitmer nodded.

"Yes, sir, though I'm not sure I believe it."

"Me either," he agreed, sweeping his light to and fro, scattering the shadows with each arc. "There!" A shadow shifted, moving quickly away from them. "After it!"

"I thought you said it couldn't be giant rats, that they didn't really exist!" his officer demanded as they chased the scurrying figure.

Phillipe didn't reply, saving his breath for running and his concentration for not falling.

The shadowy rat led them back to the river, but there Phillipe lost it amid the rain and fog. "Merde!" He stood catching his breath, and studied the area, hoping to spot his elusive quarry.

Dupin had circled overhead during the chase, and now returned to his shoulder "Boats!" The bird cawed.

Looking around, Phillipe saw that his feathered friend was correct. Several boats were visible along the Vilaine, most of them starting to return to shore now that night had fallen. One was already moored, a sturdy rope anchoring it to a wide old oak, and he noticed that it had settled into the mud around it.

"That one has not moved in some time," he commented, and Whitmer appraised the boat herself, nodding.

"Didn't Épineux say Carré'd had no luck fishing lately?" she asked.

Phillipe nodded. "Indeed he did, so perhaps he meant by boat rather than from shore. Let's go see if that belongs to him." He carefully picked his way along the soggy riverbank, Whitmer right behind him. Dupin, of course, soared on ahead, landing atop the boat's solitary cabin and waiting impatiently for the two humans to catch up.

The boat was a small steamer, and might have been handsome once. Now, it had clearly seen better days. Its paint was peeling and chipped, its brass steampipes dented, and its rear wheel missing several paddles. Yet through the small front porthole Phillipe thought he saw a flickering light.

"Hello, the boat!" he called as he approached. "Permission to come aboard?" Not hearing a reply, he grabbed the railing and hauled himself up and over, then reached down to give the shorter Whitmer a hand. Once they were both on the peeling, warped deck, Phillipe drew his pistol and his pocket torch.

"Monsieur Carré!" he shouted. "This is the police! Please do not give us any trouble!"

Still getting no reply, he crept over to the cabin and peered inside. He could see the wheel clearly, and a table behind it covered with charts and maps, but the small space was otherwise empty.

"Belowdecks," he mouthed at Whitmer, who nodded. She had armed herself similarly, and reached the door to the stairs first. Phillipe did not argue. If nothing else, she would have an easier time maneuvering in such a cramped space.

The door creaked when she opened it, but that couldn't be helped. They left it wide open as they descended the narrow steps into the boat's lower level. The front held a small galley and a tiny eating area. In back was a single door. Light glimmered beneath it, broken by the occasional shadow.

"Monsieur Carré!" Phillipe called again. "Please come out! We do not wish to harm you!"

When the door finally slid aside, it revealed not a man but a woman—an older one, silver-haired and fine-featured. She stood absolutely still, no doubt due to the arm around her neck and the knife at her throat.

"Put the guns down!" Carré demanded. Phillipe complied at once, as did Whitmer, and their pistols clattered to the floor.

"Back away!" Carré shouted next. "Back away now, or she dies!"

Phillipe nodded, slowly holding both hands out in front of him and taking a step back. "All right," he said in his most soothing voice. "No need for that."

The man shoved his elderly hostage forward, scuttling to stay with her. "You need to leave. Now."

"We cannot do that," Phillipe replied. "We have come all the way from Paris for Madame Mailloux, and cannot return without her."

"I'll kill her!" the panicked fisherman screamed. "I will!"

But Phillipe shook his head. "I don't think you will, actually. Otherwise, why haven't you already? That is why you brought her out here, is it not? So you could kill her and inherit her fortune? You are related, non?"

Madame Mailloux's mouth twisted. "We are, if only distantly," she answered, her voice cool and calm despite the apparent danger. "And if you had merely asked for my help, I might have given it. Instead, you lied to me, abducted me, and meant to kill me—but could not follow through with it. Pathetic."

Phillipe wanted to urge her not to antagonize the man, but then he noticed her smirk—and the way her captor's arm had begun to shake with rage. He had retreated further, and now found himself backed up against the galley, which gave him an idea. "Yes, it is, rather," he agreed, even as he groped behind him. He tried not to react as his hand closed around something slim, cool, and heavily weighted at one end. Perfect. "We see many reprobates in our work, but few so inept they cannot even follow through on their threats. Isn't that right, Whitmer?"

She stared at him, but she was clever and caught on after only an instant. "Oh, yes," she answered. "Trying and failing is one thing, but being unable to even try? That is just sad."

"Shut up!" What they could see of Carré's face was now bright red, and his arm was shaking so wildly it was a wonder he had not cut his cousin's throat already, if only by accident. "Or I'll—" And he pointed the knife at Whitmer.

That was what they had all been waiting for.

"Down!" Phillipe shouted, and Madame Mailloux obeyed by simply slumping to the ground. That left Alain Carré completely exposed. Phillipe leaped forward, wielding the heavy skillet he had found. The man stabbed at him but Phillipe parried with the heavy cookware, then punched the man full in the face. Alain staggered back, stunned, before collapsing on his rear, the knife dropping from his hand as he fell.

Dupin swooped in and stole the weapon in a flash, circling to waggle it triumphantly at Phillipe.

"Yes, yes, it's a lovely souvenir," he assured his pet, even as he reclaimed his fallen weapon, then stepped forward to help Madame Mailloux to her feet. "Are you all right, Madame?"

She nodded, leaning heavily on his arm. "Yes, thank you, inspector. I don't suppose you brought along my cane?"

"No, madam, but we will fetch it for you at once. And radio for our autogyro to pick us up as soon as possible." Glancing at the little room behind them, he saw a single cramped bed, some clothes—and what looked like an odd fur cloak. Slipping past to scoop that up, Phillipe found himself holding a gray rat costume. Which explained what the woman back at the inn had seen.

Whitmer had bound Carré's hands and dragged the man to his feet by the time he returned, so they made a strange little party emerging onto the outside deck, each gendarme guiding someone along. Phillipe brought the costume with him as well, giving Madame Mailloux his umbrella.

"There is just one thing I don't understand," Whitmer asked as they used the boat's retractable steps to reach the riverbank. "I can see why you would make it look like she had been killed by a giant rat, given the town's legends. But why have two costumes?"

Carré had mostly recovered by now, and shifted to glance over at her. "Two?" he asked. "I don't know what you mean."

"Your gray one, here," Phillipe said, holding up the costume he held. "And the black one we saw on the street."

But their prisoner shook his head. "I only made the one."

Phillipe exchanged a glance with Whitmer, knowing they were both wondering the same thing: If Carré had not been the giant black rat, who had?

Was that where the whisker had come from? It didn't match the fisherman's costume, either.

And how had her cane been so badly chipped and scratched? Surely no normal rat could have done such damage to it! Had Alain, to cement his story? Yet why go to that much trouble?

Perhaps, Phillipe thought as he led the way back to the main road, just perhaps, there was something to the town's stories, after all.

But if so, he would certainly never admit it.

# The Immoral Immortal

## Keith R.A. DeCandido

*Author's note: this story takes place eighty-two years after Mary Shelley's novella "The Mortal Immortal."*

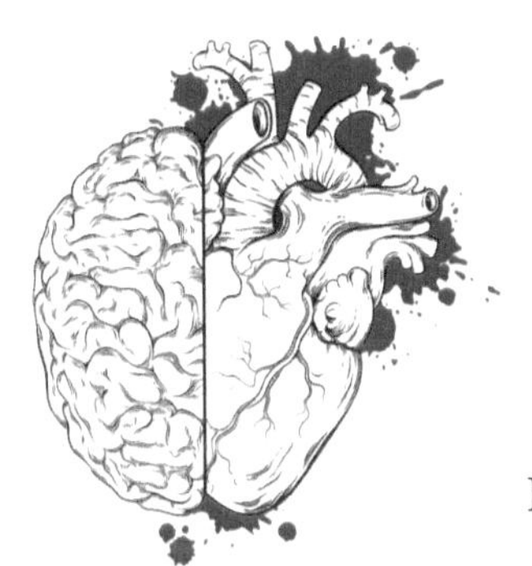

From the Desk of Field Marshal Douglas Haig, 1st Earl Haig, General Headquarters, British Armies in France

17 August 1915

My dearest Dorothy:

I had the most remarkable meeting this morning. We had an incident involving one of our dirigibles. I thought it best to inquire about the situation more informally at first. You know how much I despise paperwork, and courts-martial are time-consuming and distract from the war effort. We're here to defeat the Kaiser, not ass about with tiresome proceedings.

There were only three survivors of the incident, one of whom was the officer in command of the mission: Captain Windsor Agrippa, according to his file—though that was, it would seem, incomplete. More on that in a bit, my dear.

Captain Agrippa arrived in my office, escorted by my aide, Sergeant Dirk Plug.

After formalities were exchanged, and I had Agrippa take a seat, I said, "Captain, you were sent on a reconnaissance mission."

"Yes, sir."

"Standing orders for all balloon companies is surveillance. The route is picked, the dirigible is launched, you remain at an altitude of 12,000 feet, and you report back what you've seen."

"Yes, sir," Agrippa said again.

"Our airships have minimal offensive capabilities, and all balloon companies are under strict orders to *not* engage the enemy."

Once again, he said only, "Yes, sir."

"Captain, can you explain why, given the standing orders that I have just outlined, you took your dirigible to an altitude of 7000 feet and fired upon Jerry near Strasbourg?"

"The German forces were massing in far greater numbers than intelligence had believed. I thought it behooved us to prevent them from launching their inevitable attack. Our forces are weak in that area."

"Let me remind you once again, captain, that your orders were for surveillance and reporting back your findings. A proper battalion would have been mustered to deal with Jerry's forces in Strasbourg."

"That would have taken time, sir, and the German forces would have—"

"That was not your decision!" I snapped at the man for his effrontery. "Your balloon company consists of a dozen men, precisely none of whom are infantry. They are scientists and engineers and technicians, whose function is to operate the airship safely for its missions of surveillance and reconnaissance. They are *not* combat officers, and yet you took it upon yourself—again, acting against your standing orders—to bring them into battle. Ten of them are now dead."

To my horror, the man's response was to shrug! And then he misquoted *Macbeth*: "They would have died ere long."

"Hardly—as I said, captain, they are *not* infantry."

"That is not what I meant, sir. They will only live, what, a few more decades at best?"

"And who are you to decide that?"

"Their commanding officer. We are fighting a war against tyranny. I have lived under tyranny, sir, and it is not a pleasant thing. It is my duty as an officer in the Royal Army to do every-thing I must to prevent Germany's ascent."

"Including diving your airship into enemy territory, firing upon Jerry with a few rifles, having your dirigible hit with mortar and subsequently catching fire, and barely navigating back to base in an enflamed vessel, most of your crew having been killed by enemy fire or smoke inhalation?"

Agrippa nodded. "Including that, yes, sir. I did exactly what you do every day."

Drawing myself up, I clenched my fists. "I *beg* your pardon?"

"You routinely send your troops on missions from which they are unlikely to return alive."

"Yes—as I said, *infantry*. These are men who have volun-teered specifically for the task of fighting against the Hun. Your crew, however, did not volunteer for that."

"Death claims all of you, regardless of what you volunteer for, sir."

That turn of phrase caught my attention. "All of *you*?"

"Yes, sir."

I held out a hand, and Plug handed me a file. "You were given this particular assignment due to your experience with dirigibles, correct?"

"Yes, sir."

I read from the file. "You piloted an airship for the Mercier Company in France for ten years."

"Yes, sir."

I looked at my aide. "Sergeant?"

Pulling another file out, Plug said, "The Mercier Company went out of business in 1884."

"Yes, it did. What of it?"

"Your file claims that you were born in 1881," Plug replied. "Are we to believe that you piloted an airship before you turned three?"

Agrippa smiled. "You would be foolish to believe that, sergeant."

"In addition," Plug said, "I have been unable to locate a birth record for Windsor Agrippa in 1881, or in any of the five years on either side of that date."

At that, Agrippa shook his head and chuckled. Chuckled! The cheek of the man! "That is not surprising. I was not born within five years of 1881—nor was I born in England."

"Bloody hell," Plug said, then his face fell. "Excuse me, sir," he said hastily to me.

"Quite all right," I said with a dismissive wave. Plug's breach of protocol was as nothing compared to what I was hearing from Agrippa.

"I'm afraid," the captain continued, "that the misleading information in my personnel file extends to my family name. The last name 'Agrippa' is a tribute to the man who made me what I am today."

"A captain in the Royal Army?" Plug asked.

"No, someone who cannot die."

As you might imagine, Dorothy, it was at this point that I realized that the man had to be quite mad. But I let him continue speaking.

"I was indeed born on the fifteenth of July—but not in 1881. Rather, I was born in the Year of Our Lord 1510. I was apprenticed as a youth to Cornelius Agrippa."

The name meant nothing to me, but Plug surprised me by saying, "The alchemist?"

"Yes," the captain said with equal surprise to my own. "Since the rise of industry, I have met few who know the great alchemists of old. In any event, whilst apprenticed to Agrippa, I aided him in the creation of a formula, which he said would cure love. Too late, I realized he was speaking metaphorically. In truth, his potion severely retarded the aging process." He then smiled wryly. "I discovered that *after* I quaffed the brew, of course."

"And so you became immortal?" Plug asked snidely.

"Indeed I did, sergeant. I have lived for more than four hundred years. And I have seen much in that time. Two truths have come to light in those four centuries. One is that tyranny is something that is ever to be fought. The other: *you all will die.*"

My dear Dorothy, I don't mind telling you that I was almost physically taken aback by the intensity with which the captain spoke those last four words.

Again he quoted *Macbeth*: "You are all poor players that strut and fret your hour upon the stage and then are heard no more. Your lives are *so* shockingly brief. And yet, the population continues to increase with each passing year. There is no danger of the race dying out. No matter how many of you die—and that number is, of course, *all* of you—there will always be more. You say, field marshal, that there is a difference between you sending infantry to their deaths as opposed to my recent sending of technicians and engineers to theirs. To that, sir, I say nonsense. Everyone is sent to their deaths the moment they're born. The very least that I can do, as one who has been spared that particular fate, is to make sure that their inevitable deaths have meaning. Yes, ten of the people under my command died, but their deaths were for the greater good. If our side wins, then they died helping make that happen. And if our side loses, then they're better off dead than living under the Kaiser's rule."

A heavy silence descended upon my office following the captain's words. At this stage, I decided that I no longer cared about the veracity of his absurd claim to immortality.

"Your words are those of a madman, captain," I finally said. "You say you wish to improve the lot of the race, but you have no regard for the reality of our race. You promote the ghastly notion that we are interchangeable. There is a reason why I am a field marshal and the troops in No Man's Land are mere soldiers. Everyone has a place—and the place of the soldiers is to die for their country and for liberty. It is most assuredly *not* the place for random civilians or for engineers and technicians who are assigned to *surveillance* duty."

The captain merely sighed. "It is a pity that you believe that lie."

"It is no lie—it is the basis of our entire empire! The very empire you claim to be fighting for!"

Plug stood at attention. "Shall I prepare the paperwork for a court-martial, sir?"

"Not yet, sergeant," I said, and I could feel the disappointment radiating from Plug. "Captain Agrippa—or whatever your name might be—I prefer not to go through with the indignity of a court-martial. I also would just as soon keep your somewhat provocative words out of any official transcripts. Therefore I offer you this: you resign your commission, citing the trauma of the battle you were in. The official record will say that you were not prepared for battle—which, in fact, you were not—and you resigned due to the shock of losing so many under your command. The alternative is to be court-martialed, which I guarantee will result in your doing hard labor for the rest of your natural life. If you are as immortal as you say, that will be quite the wretched punishment, I would think."

For several seconds, the man just stared at me. His eyes, Dorothy, were pitiless.

But so was the gaze I returned. This man is a wretch, a fiend, completely unfit to serve, with no conception of the importance of life and the meaning of true sacrifice.

"Very well," he finally said. "May I be excused, field marshal, to write my letter of resignation?"

"You may."

He stood, clicked his heels, did an about-face, and departed.

"Good riddance to bad rubbish," Plug said.

The captain returned an hour later with his letter of resignation, which I accepted, and then instructed Plug to begin the paperwork to process the resignation. After which, my dear, I began this letter.

I wonder, having written this all out for your perusal, if perhaps the captain spoke the truth. If he has been alive for four centuries. Does immortality make a man into such a creature who loses all perspective on the value of life? And the value of death?

He said that Agrippa—the alchemist, that is—told him that the potion he supposedly drank would cure love. It would seem that he is indeed cured of love for the human race.

And yet, he claims to be trying to save us. His motives as he gave them were pure, even if his methods were despicable.

Enough. He is gone from the Royal Army and, as Sergeant Plug said, good riddance. We are well to be rid of him.

With loving regards,
D.H.

# A Sad and Bitter World

## Hildy Silverman

*"I leave a sad and bitter world; and if you remember me and think of me as of one unjustly condemned, I am resigned to the fate awaiting me." – Justine Moritz, Frankenstein, Mary Shelley*

15 August, 18 —

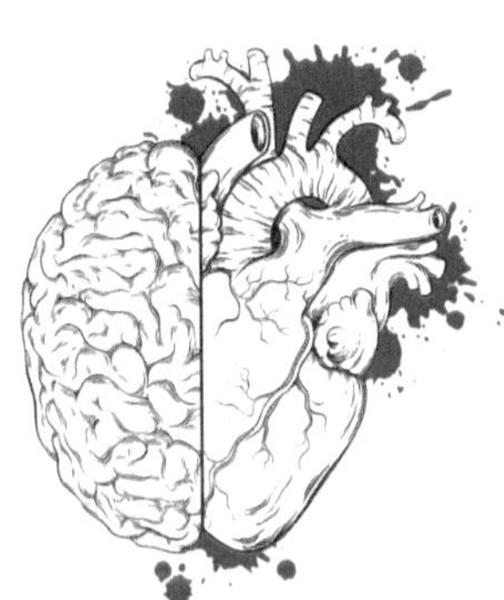

Dear Victor,

*I pray this missive reaches you aboard the Airship Prometheus, on which you have apparently secured continued passage to the northernmost reaches of the Earth, and that you remain in good health.*

*Does it delight you that I am utilizing your clever windup writing ball? It is so much faster and easier to correspond thanks to this machine, which has reaffirmed Geneva's reputation for producing the finest clockwork devices. It certainly produces letters kinder to the eyes of readers than those penned in my all-but-illegible handwriting. If only you had kept to developing such mechanical wonders and not ventured into —*

*Ah, well, no point dredging up what cannot be changed.*

*Thank you for the comprehensive list of the faults in my reasoning included in your previous letter. Despite them, I continue to assert that Death is indeed a parallel state of existence, rather than the terminus of linear life. In that spirit (forgive the pun), my project with the somewhat irascible Michael Faraday continues apace, albeit our progress has been slower than desired. Since I am the only member of the Frankenstein family still residing in our ancestral home, the responsibility for maintenance of our affairs has fallen to me. I do not intend this as condemnation, dear brother. Merely a statement of fact.*

*Faraday speculates that it is my longing for those we have lost that distracts from the goals he would prefer us to pursue. I confess that losing Father, darling Elizabeth, sweet William, and wrongfully condemned Justine does motivate my desire to prove that what humanity perceives as the ultimate end, Death, is in fact a miscomprehension. I am convinced that the dead continue to exist, albeit transfigured and transported to an alternate plane, upon which our living realm is superimposed. A palimpsest of existences if you will. Death denotes a separation, yes. Permanently so? That remains to be proven.*

*I imagine you scoffing as you read this, brother mine. Calling me fanciful, questioning my scientific reasoning – I know, like Father, you have always thought me ill-suited for such pursuits, expecting that I would enter into a career as a gentleman farmer. Perhaps you even question my sanity, which is ironic, given the accusations of madness levied against you. Yet despite them, your efforts to create life succeeded! You built an electrified bridge between the realms of Death and Life, dragged a soul (or was it multiple souls? Where does the soul reside exactly – within the whole of a body only or also its separated parts?) across into your creation. It is your very own work, Victor, which has inspired mine.*

*Others condemn your hubris for stealing God's fire, yet do not fully comprehend the nature of the flames. Even you deny it, which, given your perennial agnosticism when it comes to matters of faith, is unsurprising. Regardless, your journals, your copious research, continue to guide me. While I have no desire to snatch a flame, a soul, from the plane of Death and return it to Life without consent or trap it in a horrific assemblage of stolen corporeal remains, I do strive to invite a willing spirit to visit as its former self. In doing so, I intend to avoid the derangement that afflicted your Adam, which I suspect resulted from the incomprehensible spiritual agony of trapping a mosaic of disparate spirits within a single, monstrous form.*

*How I wish we could discuss and debate my pursuits across the dinner table! Alas, your quest to track down your creature continues with no end in sight, per your own admission. I fret that it might be some time before you return home – assuming you survive this ill-conceived pursuit. I ask you again: have you thought through what you will do should you succeed in running your rabbit to ground? Your creation is a murderer. He will not hesitate to destroy you as he did our beloveds, the losses of whom drove Father prematurely to his own grave. I understand wanting revenge, but you forget that your creature is Vengeance itself.*

*I continue to experience hours of despair, brought on by longing for human contact beyond professional engagement with Faraday and the staff, lawyers, and accountants who aid me in keeping our affairs in order. Socializing remains impossible given… well, I need not explain why our neighbors shun me, do I?*

*Know that I miss you, my brother, and despite the grievous, if un-intentional, misfortunes your activities visited upon our family, I hope and pray that you remain safe and return home before the year is out.*

*Affectionately yours,*

*Ernest*

Death was supposed to be a release from the torment of Justine Moritz's final weeks. The reward for a life of kindness, modesty, and devoted service; for surpassing any family's reasonable expectations of loyalty and forgiveness from someone who was, no matter how well-treated or liked, their servant. She had expected to enter Paradise to feast with the Lord and His retinue therein, basking in the eternal re-ward for a life, if all-too-brief, at least devotedly and righteously lived.

Then all the promises, all the lovely fantasies of the afterlife in which she'd been brought up turned out to be hideous lies.

Her suffering, her ultimate sacrifice, had been for naught. She was not welcomed by St. Peter, did not become an angel seated at the right hand of God. Instead, she *remained*, fated to wander the Frankenstein estate. It seemed even death offered no release from servitude. Al-though she no longer rose at dawn to bake cinnamon kanelbullar for the family's breakfast or tidy up after Little William spilled his cocoa or press the wrinkles from the family's clothes, neither could she wander the world to look in on those few friends she left behind… or even reunite with her predeceased parents.

Justine had felt insubstantial in life, now much more so in death. At least alive, she'd had the comfort of sensations, experiences, interactions with others. Now she wandered sightless and in silence; the pleasures of taste, of odors, of touching and being touched becoming increasingly distant memories.

*Ah, memories.* She retained those, along with their attendant emotions. Perhaps they were all she was now. Mostly, she remembered what she had lost while still in the full flower of youth. All the promise life had held, gone. Stolen by mistake… *No! By egregious oversight and rush to judgement, rather than an honest pursuit of actual justice, for poor little William's slaughter.* She had been tried and condemned with alacrity and not a single care for whether she was actually guilty. Which, of course, she was not.

Justine had loved William dearly, far beyond a fundamental concern for his welfare incumbent upon a nanny. She had considered him a little brother. How could she not, given she had known him since birth?

Brought into the Frankenstein family at the tender age of 12, she had been raised alongside Victor, Ernest, and their adopted cousin, her dearest friend Elizabeth. Although not their sibling — never that, unlike how Elizabeth was treated upon adoption by Alphonse and Caroline — Justine had felt a kinship to each. And they had made her believe she was loved equally in return.

But ultimately, the family failed her. Although they proclaimed disbelief that she might be capable of slaying little William and pled for her release from jail, protested at her sentencing, and stood aghast as she faced the hangman, they nevertheless allowed her to be executed. All their money, all their influence, and *none* of it enough to save her — or at least they had not been wielded with sufficient determination to do so.

She now also realized (with knowledge as certain as its source inexplicable) that Victor had known the truth all along. That he could have come forward and cleared her name. That she did not have to die and become trapped in this incorporeal, insubstantial, invisible… *nothingness.*

Her taciturn acceptance of her sentence, her grace in facing the gallows without railing against the unjustness of it all? Pointless. Worthless. Laughably naïve.

She enjoyed no heavenly reward, not even a peaceful oblivion. Meanwhile, neither Victor nor the true murderer, the monstrosity he'd created, had been punished. She knew these to be true also. That which had been Justine Moritz remained.

And grew enraged.

25 September, 18—

*Dear Victor,*

*I pray this reaches you via the local relay courier. Per your last, brief letter, the A.S. Prometheus was scheduled to dock for reinflation and service in Greenland, but you did not indicate how long you would remain docked there.*

*I am excited to share a leap forward in my project with Faraday (perhaps more accurately despite him)! The cage is nigh completion, and it is a marvel of modern ingenuity, if I do say so myself. In brief, we are using a small boiler conjoined with a miniaturized turbine to produce a magna-aetheric current. The resulting field suffuses and surrounds the cage, which in turn gives it the ability to contain the transubstantiated Self of one who has departed the Living plane for the adjacent realm of Death. Simply put (not to condescend, but we both know the aetheric sciences fall outside your purview), we have developed a ghost cage.*

*The next step is obvious: to test the effectiveness of that which we tentatively call the 'Frankenstein-Faraday Cage', we must part the veil between Life and Death.*

*Faraday has expressed… let us say uncertainty, over how unconcerned I am about locating a subject. "How, pray tell," he queried, "do you know where to find an inhabitant of your theorized otherworld? Do you propose we wander the graveyards, medium in tow? Given your brother's defilements, I don't think that a wise course of action lest we be caught and condemned for similar mischief."*

*"No need to take such risk." Gesturing to indicate my home, I explained, "Do you not sense them? This house is filled with potential subjects." For indeed, I have long felt them; the spirits of our lost family – God, so many! – wandering these halls. Sensed as if from a great distance despite our seemingly sharing the same spaces. That is how I bear my loneliness – by imagining how full our once-stately, now sadly bewebbed and dusty, manor truly is.*

*They are just beyond my ability to perceive them, Victor, their new existence layered beneath mine. What might it be like in that other realm? Are they all together again with Mother, enjoying an existence free of pain and suffering and the fear of being parted evermore? I certainly like to think so, for if I am right… if I can prove it, then humanity will also be released from its greatest collective dread: the inevitability of ceasing to exist.*

*Are you clucking your tongue, brother? Rolling your eyes?*

*Like you, Faraday would prefer we focus on uses for the cage that are considered more traditionally scientific. He only indulges me because the agreement we signed guaranteeing my continued financial support of this joint venture required pursuance of my goal first. Admittedly, my ambitions may well exceed our capabilities… nevertheless, while the idea of Man creating life held your fascination, dear Victor, so has Man deciphering death captured mine.*

*Please do respond when you are able. Despite our disagreements, I do value your opinions and eagerly await your thoughts on my progress. Also, to be frank, I grow increasingly concerned for your safety as you venture farther from home, heading into territories where much remains undiscovered and unknown. Despite your mistakes and the doubtless overwhelming guilt that drives you, I beg you again reconsider this risky pursuit.*

*I remain your devoted brother, despite everything, for you are all I have left.*

*With Affection,*

*Ernest*

Although the senses Justine enjoyed in life no longer functioned, others had replaced them. These allowed her to recognize and navigate her surroundings. She knew she was in the home where she'd spent most of her life. To a degree, she sensed the passage of time. She knew others, like her, wandered nearby, but could not interact with them. She even felt the presence of a living someone nearby, separated as if behind a wall. This nearly drove her to madness; the utter isolation despite not actually being alone.

Then, abruptly, it all changed.

Sensations flowed into her incorporate form. She saw — *blurred, dark figures moving about.* She heard — *faint voices, seemingly kilometers away.* She felt — *warmth defying the bitter chill of the void.* After existing so long without her living senses, only to have them even partially return, overwhelmed her so that she ceased her constant wanderings through the limbo in which she was trapped.

For the first time in an uncertain while, that which had been Justine stood still.

"More steam." A male voice. Vaguely familiar. "The vapor must be thick enough for a spirit to utilize it as a conduit."

"Ernest, we have been at this for three weeks." Another male voice, wholly unknown. Plainly irritated. "*Enough.* There are no spirits lurking here!"

An argument ensued. She could not follow it. However, she could more clearly make out the dark shapes of two men. After some time spent in an increasingly acrimonious dispute, one stormed away. A door slammed in the distance.

Justine propelled herself (what she did could not accurately be called *walking*, she just… moved) toward the remaining man. She sensed that she knew him, that he had been someone who mattered. She needed to see him more clearly.

More than that. She desperately longed to be seen.

31 OCTOBER, 18—

*Dear Victor,*

*I hope you do not mind receiving another letter from me so soon after my previous. I have not heard back from you yet but realize that could be due to distance rather than disinterest or misadventure. This I fervently choose to believe.*

*I could not wait to share something marvelously strange and wonderous that has occurred. Although you have doubted my beliefs and questioned my research, as a fellow man of science you cannot dispute facts, which I am about to share. I swear upon our bond as brothers and by our beloved, lost family, that the following is true:*

*I have enticed a spirit across the divide between our domain and Death's! It took weeks of attempts and pumping copious amounts of steam throughout the house (alas, this has quite worsened the mold issues in some rooms, but that is a concern for another time). Water amplifies spiritual energy, you see, enhancing the ability for ghostly* beings to materialize on our plane. Similar to electricity, water traverses the realms of Life and Death, forming a conduit through which spirits may travel between domains. Since bodies of water are known to attract spiritual activities and sightings, it stands to reason that if one wishes to aid a spirit on dry land in breaching Death's barrier, one must fill their parallel location in Life with sufficient moisture — the most obvious source of which is steam.

Alas, Faraday (who has disappointed me sorely, the foolish boor) has flounced off home to England determined to find a new patron for his project. I do not understand why he is so obsessed with electromagnetism when the potential of magna-aether is so much more exciting… but I digress.

The breakthrough occurred just the other night after Faraday's departure. I filled Elizabeth's old bedroom with such a volume of steam that I could scarcely breathe and waited. Within a half-hour, I beheld a displacement in the space between your late lamented bride's canopied bed and myself. Merely a flicker from the corner of my eye. But when I turned my attention upon it fully, a faint outline came into focus — a human form. It passed through the steam, wafting toward me as though gliding. Incorporeal, yes, but having crossed over far enough to recover some substance, though more gaseous than solid.

As you might imagine, my heart leapt into my throat! I regarded the figure, mouth agape. My thoughts were chaotic as I sought to identify who this apparition could be. Was it our beloved slain cousin, Elizabeth? Mother, perhaps. Too tall for William. Maybe an ancestor who long ago occupied our home? After all, it has been in the family for generations.

When she — for as the figure moved, I could see its outline was decidedly female — at last hovered before me, I recognized her with a start. Translucent though her visage remained, her ghostly features resolved to the degree that I knew…

Oh, Victor. It was Justine!

Yes, Justine, wrongly condemned and executed for your creature's heartless slaying of our baby brother. She who had been more sister than servant to us. Surely you recall her kindness, her pure and gentle nature. I recall how Father and Elizabeth wept bitterly after she was executed, relaying how Justine forgave all even as she resigned herself to her fate with dignity and grace. Such an injustice perpetrated upon her, especially knowing now that it was you, that it was your creation… ah, it is irrelevant, I know. Justine's tragic outcome cannot be changed.

Her shade spoke nary a word. Not surprising, given those rare few who manage to visit our plane seem unable to function within it. The very molecules of Life deny them substance, the ability to affect their surroundings or interact with the living beyond the faintest whispers or occasional physical outbursts achieved by poltergeists. No, Justine merely gazed upon me with colorless eyes, her glass features set in an unreadable expression through which I could see the portrait of our once-happy family on the far wall.

I confess I gave in to my shock. Seeing her again — I remembered her fondly from our times playing together as children. How she always giggled at my boyish antics, comforted me during my frequent illnesses. She taught me how to climb the sycamore in our yard when you couldn't be pulled away from your studies to do so. And remember those scrumptious cinnamon kanelbullar she baked? I can almost smell them as I write this, wafting from our long-neglected kitchen.

"Justine, dearest," I sobbed. "I have missed you so! Tell me, where have you been? What is your existence like beyond this Life? Have you seen little William, or Mother, or — "

Her expression, as faint as a distant reflection in a pond, transformed to one of such profound… sorrow? Disappointment? Misery? I cannot say for sure, but it broke my heart anew. In that instant, I knew — I cannot explain exactly how, I just did — that the realm of Death is a lonely one. Perhaps because I understand loneliness all-too-well, I could easily recognize the emotion in another. How it influences a soul, living or dead, in ways profound and disturbing.

How tragically unfair, I thought, that after all Justine endured, crossing over into Death's realm has not freed her, but rather her suffering continues apace! Only now, she could not even hope for the succor of release, as there is no death beyond Death. No hope of an end to her current phase of existence. Her pain, her loneliness, would be unending.

*I offered worthless apologies on your behalf, Victor, for your silence that cost her everything. For our entire family, which failed to adequately defend her. Perhaps it was not my place to make such apologies, given I was barely more than a boy at the time and could hardly be held responsible. Nonetheless, I felt it necessary to try. Even as I uttered regrets, however, I knew they were not enough. My penitence on behalf of House Frankenstein would not ease her eternal sorrows.*

*'Actions over words,' as Father used to say. I knew I had to make amends.*

*"Justine," I said, "if you can understand me, know that I have created a container for spirits, for your disembodied soul, which might alleviate your lonely state. It would allow you, for brief periods, to rejoin the living… insofar as the Living plane will allow. You could interact with me… with the living more fully. Only allow me to escort you to the parlour and – "*

*She reached out a translucent hand. I felt a brief chill against my cheek that soon suffused my entire head with an indescribable iciness, a cold that I imagine comes close to what you are currently experiencing, Victor. Darkness washed through me, overwhelmed my mind….*

*The next thing I can recall is returning to my senses lying upon the threadbare oriental carpet. Alas, the portable steam generator had run dry. Justine was gone; evaporated along with my manmade fog.*

*Do not fret, Victor. This is not the end of my tale. For I have realized that the divide between realms will be at its thinnest in a few days, on that occasion known as All Souls Day. That is when I shall fill the parlour with steam and immediately escort Justine's shade into the Frankenstein Cage (yes, I am calling it that now. Faraday lost the right to have his name attached to our invention when he buggered off in a snit).*

*Thus concludes my tale, if only for now. You may well remain incredulous, my brother, but please have some faith in me. Once I have brought Justine back to the land of the living, for however long a period as I am able, I will record such proof of my theories that even a skeptic like yourself will have no choice but to believe. I shall set up a kinetograph by the cage, to capture a succession of images of my achievement and share them with you – with the world – as irrefutable evidence of the Life/Death palimpsest.*

*My concern for your well-being has intensified to the point where it distracts me constantly, and I can ill-afford distraction at this critical juncture. Please, if you are capable, respond to this letter apace. Even if you are well out of range of relay courier service, a brief telegram stating you are safe would suffice.*

*Affectionately yours,*

*Ernest*

Justine experienced an emotion she had long forgotten: hope.

It suffused her as she once again passed from the void into the world of the living. The wall was easier to breach than before, as though it had been weakened somehow. On the other side, in the parlour where she had so often served the Frankenstein family their tea, she found Ernest—taller and older than she recalled, yet still slender and awkward as he had been as a youth. His hair, beneath a set of goggles with multiple ocular loupes perched atop his head, was unkempt. His waistcoat had stains and his trousers were in dire need of pressing. In life, his sorry aspect would have made her heart ache. Now though? She only felt contempt.

Ernest stood beside a large brass cage hooked up to some contraption she could not identify. "Come, darling Justine." His expression was one of eager delight as he beckoned. "There is naught to fear. This is my invention, the Frankenstein Cage. You have only to enter, and I will use it to bring you more fully into this realm of Life."

Justine wondered whether her phantom vocal cords could produce sound. Indeed, her attempt was faint and distant even to her own muffled hearing. "How… long?"

She could see Ernest straining to comprehend. Then his smile wavered. "Regretfully, it will only be temporary. At least for now, until I figure out a method for—well, if not to bring you back wholly, perhaps to make it possible for you to cross into the living realm at will and interact with those who reside here more easily."

She struggled to keep her rage in check. As she suspected, Ernest could not restore what had been stolen from her; merely tease her with temporarily restoration. Allow her to fully recall life only to freshly condemn her to death again. "Why? Pointless," she managed.

"I am sorry." More whining. "I wish I could offer more beyond brief respite from your current state. But... but surely, you would enjoy experiencing life's sensations again, if only on occasion." He lowered his head, plucked at the loose brass buttons on his waistcoat. "We can commune, like we used to, from time to time. Alleviate our mutual loneliness. Would... you *do* want that. Right?"

Justine drew closer. "What... you want." Her rising anger strengthened her seemingly disconnected voice. "Ease your conscience. Prove yourself. Companionship... however tenuous."

Ernest appeared taken aback. He turned away and began fussing with various knobs and levers on the mysterious device connected to his cage. "There is nothing to fear." His tone shifted to one of firm authority; all trace of the whinging manchild gone. "Once you have been restored to the degree possible, I've no doubt you will fully comprehend what I am doing for you—indeed, for the world—and become grateful."

She almost laughed but thought better of it. No, best to follow her plan, which she had devised after she had reached out for Ernest the other night. Her intent had been to silence his mewling, stop his worthless apologies by covering his mouth with her insubstantial hand. But in doing so, she had inadvertently discovered a more effective means of restoring herself, and exacting revenge, in one fell swoop.

"Afraid," she said, arranging her features into what she hoped was an appropriate expression of meekness. "Hold... me?"

Ernest hesitated. "Well, the magna-aetheric field is most likely harmless to living tissue," he mused aloud. "Although we never thought to test—"

"Please." She reached for him, caressed his cheek with her fingertips. Watched as his flesh prickled and he shuddered when they passed through. "I *need* you."

Ernest straightened his spine, expression resolute. Here was his opportunity to play the hero, the stalwart. As she had expected, he could not resist.

"Very well then." He pressed one more button. Gears spun. The hand of an embedded chronograph advanced a resolute tick forward. Then he entered the cage and smiled. "Come. I shall show you how it—"

She swept inside and wrapped him in her spectral arms.

Ernest gasped. She felt his body temperature plummet in response to her icy embrace. Death's realm was so very cold, as were those who resided within.

The chronometer marked the end of its countdown. The magna-aetheric current surged through the cage, surrounding it in a crackling deep gray field shot through with bolts of gold.

The barrier of Ernest's flesh, already demonstrably weaker than the wall between Death and Life, yielded entirely. Justine's spirit, or at least the warped, distilled essence of what had been Justine, passed into his spasmodically twitching body.

They threw back their head and screamed.

*3 November, 18—*

*Hello Victor,*

*I was so relieved to receive your telegraph confirming you were well. I also wish to congratulate you on successfully vanquishing the beast you unleashed upon so many innocents! How fortunate you chose to travel by airship to the frozen hellscape into which it had escaped, for if you had gone via steamship, I doubt your expedition would have ended in triumph. It would have been such a shame if you had perished before you fulfilled your duty to those slain, directly and indirectly, by your prodigal son.*

*As for me, or should I say us? We are pleased to announce that our own experiments have proven successful beyond our wildest ambitions. Yes, it is so — a denizen of Death has re-entered Life. We shall refrain from detailing all, as we prefer sharing our triumph with you once we are all, after so very long, reunited. Besides, it will be ever so much more effective to show you the kinetograph footage, which tells the tale better than we could ever hope to.*

*We eagerly await your return, dearest brother. We have such plans for your return. Do not keep us waiting long.*

*Until then, we remain,*

*Your brother,*

*Your humble servant.*

# The Man Who Was Not Me

## Doc Coleman

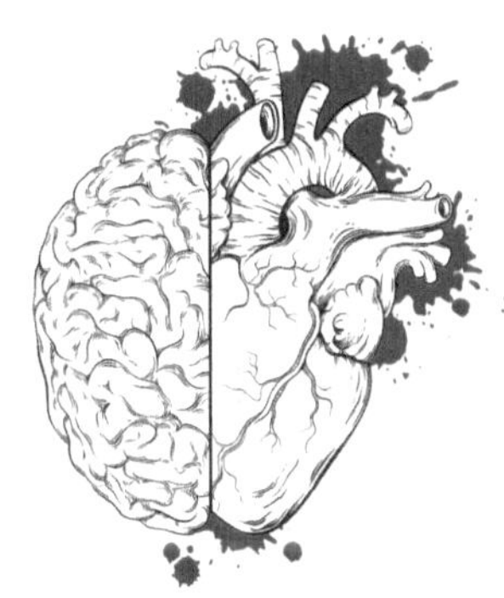

THE MAN WHO WAS NOT ME CAME BY MY DOOR again last night.

The day I first saw him, I took him for a reflection in a shop window. He was the very image of myself in better days. After a moment's confusion, I realized that he was wearing different clothing than myself, and while I stood still, he actively scanned the street.

I went about my business, thinking it just an odd coincidence until the next day when I was cornered by one of my customers.

"I'm so happy to hear your shop is re-opening!" he said.

"What?" I replied.

"You said yesterday that you expect to re-open soon. I'm so glad to hear it, Mr. Gladstone. Your work has always been exquisite and we are so looking forward to seeing your latest inventions."

I dug my right hand further under my stained coat and looked at him askance. "Mr. Shelley? You spoke to me, sir? You're quite sure of that?"

"Of course, Mr. Gladstone, you had a new coat on, and not the working coat you're wearing today. You gave me one of your new business cards!" He fished into his jacket and pulled out a small white card.

I snatched it from him with my left hand and looked at it. In neat, raised lettering the card read:

Gladstone and Co.
Mr. Horace Gladstone, Inventor and Proprietor
Repairs, Parts, and Custom Designs
Cheapside, London

I flipped it over, but the back was blank except for stains from my hands. "This isn't…" I began, but Mr. Shelley took the card back from me.

"I know, I know, you're not ready to advertise the new company name. So many details to work out! I understand. I do appreciate you trusting me with the advance notice," he said as he tucked the card back into his pocket. He put a gloved finger up against the side of his nose. "Rest assured, sir, I shall be the soul of discretion. I look forward to doing business with you again, Mr. Gladstone. I'll to be traveling to Spezia, in Italy, in a few months, and I'd love to be able to take some of your wonders along."

With that, he departed, and I wandered back to my shop, bewildered.

◉

I fumbled the key from my pocket and nearly dropped it in front of the door to the shop. Glancing at the door's dirty glass, I reassured myself that it still read "H. Gladstone Inventions and Repairs." I shoved the key into the lock, turning it first one way, then the other until it unlocked. Pushing the door open, I yanked the key out in the process, slipped inside, and closed and locked it, letting the darkness hide me from view.

The smell of old vomit assailed my nostrils, but I ignored it as my feet shuffled across the floor, sending empty bottles and bent and broken parts clattering ahead of me. The bottles tinkled as they rattled against each other and discarded cogs and bits of glass crunched under my feet. After a few steps, I noted a different sort of scuffing noise. A soft scrape as I moved my feet.

I looked down and saw a crisp, white envelope stuck to my shoe. I plucked it from the sole where a bit of dirt or muck held it. Someone must have shoved it under the door. I was about to crumple it up and throw it away when I looked at the writing on the envelope.

"Mr. Horace Gladstone" it said. In my own handwriting.

I shuffled through the discarded bottles and debris on the showroom floor, and pushed through a swinging door to the workshop beyond. Throwing the envelope down on the workbench, I lifted the glass of a lantern, pulled a long match from the pack, and struck it against the cast-iron stove. Lighting the wick, I flicked my wrist to snuff the match and dropped it into a kindling box by the stove. I winced as the flame sprung up when I lowered the glass back into place and the light intensified.

I flipped over the envelope, revealing a simple wax seal embossed with the initials HG. Opening a drawer, I pulled out the seal I use for my correspondence, one I made years ago, with a distinctive scratch along one edge. I held the seal next to the wax, and a ridge in the wax matched the groove in the metal. They were mirror images of each other, but I hadn't used the seal in months. Not since the accident.

I frowned. No one should have had access to my workshop. How was this possible?

I dropped the seal back in its drawer.

Pulling my right hand out from under my coat, I pulled it up, and set it on the corner of the envelope to hold it in place. The bandage on the hand was dirty, and soaked with blood in places. It throbbed as I put weight on the paper, and I could feel my bones grind against each other.

Grabbing a knife with my left hand, I sawed open the top of the envelope and fished out the page inside. There, written on clean white parchment, in my own hand, which I could no longer produce, it read:

*To Mr. Horace Gladstone,*

*My dear sir,*

*I am sure these tidings will seem strange to you. I wish you no ill will, sir, for indeed, your benefit is my own. I hope that I may be able to speak to you soon, about what may be done to rectify a situation affecting us both. I believe this can be done to our mutual benefit.*

*I remain your faithful servant,*

*Mr. Horace Gladstone*

I crumpled the letter into a ball, and threw it into the stove.

The following morning, I woke to find myself lying on the floor in a pool of my own sick.

I dragged myself up to sitting position, and sorted through the bottles scattered around me until I found one that still contained some of the cheap whiskey that was all I could afford. Raising the bottle to my lips, I replaced the foul taste of the sick with the bitter taste of rotgut.

Pulling myself off the workshop floor, I stumbled to the small apartment in the back of the shop. After stripping out of my soiled clothing, I flung the garments into a corner and foraged among the clothes on the floor for something to wear that wasn't quite as pungent. I piled my findings on a chair and dressed as best I could with one hand.

My right hand taunted me as I pulled on my clothing. The long, pale fingers poked out from the end of the bandage. Unconsciously, I tried to flex them, and they quivered in response as the weakened muscles did their best to respond. But that action sent a wave of searing pain up my arm. My fingers had escaped significant damage, but the palm of my hand had been dragged between two gears in the accident, crushing the bones within. The flesh beneath the bandage was now a combination of purple, red, and white scars that gave off a sickly-sweet scent.

I had seen a physician right after the accident. He wanted to take the hand right above the wrist, saying the damage was too great, and neither he nor anyone else would be able to rebuild the wreckage of my hand. Perhaps he was right. Perhaps. But my livelihood was in my hands, and what he asked was too much for me to contemplate. I refused the procedure and insisted he treat my hand as it was. He cleaned it and wrapped it in bandages, but cautioned me that it would have to be cleaned every day to prevent infection from setting in. He told me that infection would kill me much quicker than the loss of a hand.

For about a week after that, the doctor came by, changed my bandages, cleaned my hand, and tried to talk me into the amputation. He stopped when he found out I was unable to pay his bills.

By the time I was dressed, my stomach growled. The pantry was empty, so I had to venture out and see what I could scrounge. A crust of bread, or perhaps some light work that might be enough for another bottle of whiskey.

I made my way out to the shop, and spied a white envelope just inside the door. The memory of the previous letter clawed its way out of the whiskey-soaked fog of the night before. I spat my disgust. This one, as the other, was simply addressed to "Mr. Horace Gladstone."

I picked up the envelope and tore the end of it off with my teeth.

Fishing out the page inside, I flicked it open.

*To Mr. Horace Gladstone,*

*My dear sir,*

*I believe it is imperative for the two of us to talk. I regret I have no address to give you for your return message. If you would be good enough to respond, could you conceal a note beneath the planter in front of the shop. I will look for your reply there. If you are available to speak to me, I will come by the shop at the hour of ten this evening. I will gladly answer all your questions then.*

*I remain your faithful servant,*

*Mr. Horace Gladstone*

I crumpled the page into a ball and threw it across the shop. It bounced off one of the displays and rebounded among the smaller clockworks. I growled my irritation at this man. This man who wasn't me, this imposter who begged for my time. I resolved that I would not return until well after ten this evening, and I most certainly would not talk to this fraud.

I left the shop to scavenge for the day's sustenance.

For over a week, I continued to receive these letters shoved under my door. All written in my handwriting and signed with my own name. But this man was not *me*. A fact that I would think should make him grateful, and so he should leave me to my misery.

Each night, he left his letters insisting on his need to speak. Sometimes, during the days, he would appear on the street and call out to me, but I ran, evading him.

One night he chased me for several blocks before I managed to lose him. He nearly brought the constables down on me in the process. Each day I would escape him, but he kept up his pursuit. Each day he seemed to know the streets better, making it harder and harder for me to slip away.

Last night, I was scavenging in the alley behind the Wolf and Lamb when Peggy, the pub's cook, discovered me. Instead of chasing me off, as most others would, she took pity. She gave me a trencher of stew, with some meat in it, and slipped me couple bottles of ale to take home. I ducked around the corner and ravenously devoured the trencher. I returned to the shop early that evening, feeling warm and with a full belly.

I had popped open the first bottle of ale when I heard it: the front door of the shop rattling as someone tried it.

I took another pull from the beer and got up from my chair in the flat's small kitchen. Still holding my ale, I padded through the darkened workshop and made my way to the shop floor. While the store was in disarray, there were still a few items someone might try to steal. The really valuable items I'd sold long ago, but that wasn't widely known.

I slipped into the back of the storefront, and crept up a side aisle, trying to avoid the worst of the clutter on the floor. I wanted to surprise my would-be thief, not be spotted by him.

The shadow of a man in a top hat covered the door as it rattled again. I couldn't see him, but the streetlight behind him cast a stark silhouette. I moved to the front of the store to get a clearer look at him. I heard a scrape and a snick as he pulled a key from the door only to slide another one in. That key likewise turned and stopped, and he rattled the door again in frustration.

I leaned close to the front window, trying to get a better look at him as he fumbled with the next key on a ring of keys, when a woman's voice called out, "Mr. Gladstone?"

I jumped backward, thinking that I had been spotted, then realized that the intruder was likewise taken aback. He turned to the sound of her voice, and I saw him at last. It was the man who wasn't me! He had returned, but now he was trying to break into my shop! My grip on the bottle tightened, and I wanted to smash it into his face.

"Ah!" The imposter said, his tone light and cheerful, as if he hadn't just been caught trying to break into my shop. "Mrs. Clairmont. What a surprise to see you out so late! Although it is a pleasant evening, is it not?"

Mrs. Clairmont stepped into my field of view as she confronted the man, mistaking him for me. Her grey hair peeked out from beneath the dark shawl she wore over her black dress. The overall effect, and her own pale skin, gave her a spectral visage.

"Mr. Gladstone, this is not a social call. While you have been a good customer to my husband, and now myself, and I have been lenient given the difficulties that have beset you of late, there is a matter of several months back rent that I need you to address, or I will be forced to turn you out and let this space to another client. I have already received several inquiries. I cannot afford to put them off further."

I smiled as I looked at the imposter, wondering how he would deal with being hit up for the past due rent by my landlady.

He nodded, and reached up with his gloved right hand and doffed his hat. "I must apologize, Mrs. Clairmont, I have been remiss, and in putting my business affairs back in order, I have woefully neglected my account with you." He bowed to her, returning his hat to his head with a flourish as he straightened.

Mrs. Clairmont gave him a chilly frown. "I have no use for flattery, Mr. Gladstone. I *do* have need of payment."

He nodded and reached into his jacket. "Then, by all means, Mrs. Clairmont, allow me to make good on the account today and set your mind to rest."

He pulled forth a fat billfold and opened it with both hands. The wallet was packed with bills and I felt my jaw go slack at the sight of it. He began counting them out between gloved fingers. "How much, exactly, do I owe you, Mrs. Clairmont?"

The old woman swallowed at the sight of such a stack of bills. She certainly had not expected to be paid on the spot when she came out to confront him.

"Eighty pounds for four months," she said dryly.

"That much, is it?" he said, as he continued to count out bills.

She licked her lips, and said in a stronger voice, "Are you saying you don't have it, Mr. Gladstone?"

"What? Oh, nothing of the sort, my dear Mrs. Clairmont. I simply had not realized that I had fallen so deeply into your good graces. Now, I am expecting to re-open the shop soon. You see, I'll be taking on a few apprentices to help with the work, but it will still take some time to get them hired and ready…"

"If you cannot pay, I *shall* have to turn you out, Mr. Gladstone."

"No, my good lady." He pulled a thick sheaf of bills from his billfold and handed them to my landlady. "You misunderstand me. I simply thought it would be best for me to go ahead and pay the rent in advance. You'll find that is two hundred pounds, eighty for the rent already due, and one hundred and twenty for the next six months. By that time I am confident that we will be up and running again, and able to resume regular, on time payments."

Mrs. Clairmont gaped at the mass of bills she clutched in her hands, and I did as well. Where had this impostor gotten that much money? She held the bank notes up to her face and counted them.

"I trust this arrangement is to your satisfaction, Mrs. Clairmont?" the impostor asked smugly.

She cleared her throat before speaking. "It is, Mr. Gladstone. I pray your new venture goes well."

He nodded. "Thank you, Mrs. Clairmont," he said as he tucked his billfold back into his jacket. "Although, I would recommend that you put that out of sight. It would not do for some ruffian to spy it and decide to relieve you of it, Mrs. Clairmont."

She quickly stuffed the bills into a pocket of her dress.

"In fact, Mrs. Clairmont," the impostor continued. "Perhaps it would be best if I were to escort you home. Just to make sure you arrive without mishap."

My landlady nodded slowly. "That would be most kind of you, Mr. Gladstone."

From the shadowed showroom of my shop, I watched as the man who wasn't me escorted my landlady back to her apartments. What madness was this? The impostor was now paying my debts?

I stared after them for several minutes before returning to my small apartment and consuming the bottles of ale. My mind whirled, trying to come up with a plan of action to thwart this imposter. Sometime late that evening, I fell asleep in my chair.

The next morning, I awoke tucked into my bed.

Stretching out, I reveled in the feel of a good night's sleep on clean sheets.

*Clean sheets?*

The thought brought me abruptly awake, and I sat up in the bed. The curtains were drawn, but enough light spilled into the room around the edges that I could see that it was well into the morning. While there were still the familiar marks of dirt and smudges of grease on the walls and door, the room had otherwise been cleaned. The piles of dirty laundry were gone from the floor, and my boots had been set upright next to the dresser. The armoire no longer stood with its doors ajar and clothing draped over the doors and hung from the handles, but neatly closed.

The chair by the dresser now faced me. A pair of pants and a shirt were neatly folded on top of it, and a vest hung over the back of the chair.

I threw off the covers, and stood next to the bed, discovering that I had been dressed in a clean nightshirt. Not just a clean one, but a brand-new nightshirt.

My right hand had been re-bandaged with clean gauze.

When I stepped out of my room, I heard someone humming in the kitchen and the sound of something frying on the stove. The air was filled with the scent of cooking bacon.

I couldn't get into the workshop without passing through the kitchen, and there was nothing in the bedroom or the short hallway that I could use as a weapon. I did my best to slip into the room unnoticed.

"Ah, good morning! I hoped you'd be up soon," the man who wasn't me said. "I'm so glad we finally have the chance to talk for a bit."

He stood by the stove, a metal spatula gripped in a hand made out of brass and leather, gently stirring eggs in one pan while cooking bacon in another.

I moved sideways to the wood box, which had been restocked with firewood. Reaching in with my left hand, I grabbed a piece as a makeshift club.

He turned to me, and said, "Oh, come now. All I want to do is talk. If I had truly meant you any harm, would you have woken up this morning in your own bed?"

"How did you get in here?" I growled at him, scarcely recognizing my own voice.

"Dear Mrs. Clairemont was kind enough to let me borrow her spare key after I told her I seem to have misplaced mine. She was most accommodating after I paid the past due rent." He smiled, an eerie parody of my own smile. "Now, would you like to get dressed while I finish breakfast?" He motioned with the spatula back toward the hall and the bedroom.

I hefted the piece of wood, but he turned his back to me and re-sumed cooking. For a moment, I considered striking him on the back of the head, but I wasn't really sure what I'd do with him afterward. After staring at his back for a few seconds, I returned to the bedroom and dressed.

I stepped back into the kitchen wearing the clothes laid out for me but still carrying my makeshift club. The man who wasn't me was just placing the plates of food on the table. Equal portions of scrambled eggs, rashers of bacon, and bread. "Take a seat," he said, and waited for me to choose.

I sat in the chair closest to me. I didn't want to have to try to move past him. He dropped into the seat opposite me, and draped a napkin across his lap. He gestured with his metal hand. "Bon appétit."

I looked at the fork sitting on the left side of my plate and lifted the club again.

He pushed a mouthful of eggs onto his fork with his knife and looked up at me. "It's perfectly safe," he said, then lifted the fork and scooped the eggs into his mouth. He chewed briefly and swallowed. "See? I told you, I just want to talk." He continued eating.

I put the piece of wood on the floor next to my chair, then picked up the fork in my left hand. My bandaged right hand tucked into my lap. I gathered up a forkful of eggs, but again I hesitated.

"Who *are* you?" I asked.

He took a bite from a buttered slice of bread, replying as he chewed, "I am you. Or perhaps, it would be better to say that I *was* you. As near as I can determine, we lived the same life, were the same person, right up until a pivotal moment when you went one way, and I went another."

"The accident," I said, looking at his brass right hand.

He waggled the fingers of the hand. "Not really," he said, "but close. From what I've gathered from my visits to your world, it was most likely just after the accident. When the doctor offered to amputate the hand. In my world, I accepted his offer, and in yours, you did not."

I chewed on the eggs as I thought about what he had said. "But then, how are you here? If you're really me from another version of events, how can you be here?"

The man who wasn't me shook his head. "That I do not know. All I know is that I kept finding myself drawn here, into a world that wasn't quite like my own. I'd come home to find the shop closed and locked and all the changes I'd made undone. Then I'd turn around and I'd be home. I had begun to think I'd gone mad until I saw you in the street. Then I started to piece it all together." He paused, biting into a slice of bacon and chewing. "I don't think we were meant to go in two different directions. I think some power in the universe is trying to push us back together, make us one being again."

I shook my head. "That's not possible."

He leaned toward me. "But isn't it? In the span of the cosmos, a human life is just one tiny ripple, but the ripples all blend back into the wave. I can't go back to where you are, but I can help you build a life like mine."

He held his metal hand up in front of me, metal fingers of brass covered in patterns of black leather. "When I lost my hand, I remembered that I could still think. I could still design. I took on apprentices, and worked with others in the trade to make this hand, built to my design."

"You designed this?" I asked. I'd never seen anything quite like it. The movement seemed so… natural.

"Yes. My design. Now *our* design. The hand, the collar it mounts on, and the controls that use the movement of the muscles and activate the gears and pistons so it moves like a hand. It's not as dexterous as our hand was, but it makes life much easier."

I nodded, and looked closer at it. "Why the lines of leather along the inside of the fingers and palm?"

"Grip." He grimaced. "I went to Morton to see about getting the first prototype built. He wanted to do the fingers in smooth brass. I knew it wouldn't work. It would be just like those stupid pantos when they first came out."

"The mechanical horses? That's right. The saddles slid right off the first ones."

The man who wasn't me nodded. "And they glued leather to them to try and solve the problem, which is why they looked like a pantomime horse. Instead of glue, I built the leather pads into the design so they don't scrape off and they should last longer."

"Nice," I agreed. "But where did the money come from for this?" I gestured to his hand "And this," indicating the food on the plate this time, "or for the two hundred pounds you gave to Mrs. Clairemont?"

"You were listening?" He smiled that strange smile of his. "Well, my business is doing well. This," he gestured to the brass hand, "was an early prototype. Morton may not know anything about design, but he's a solid craftsman. We've entered into a partnership. I provide the designs and he does the manufacturing. The military is interested in it as a way of putting wounded soldiers back into action again. It looks like we're going to get Crown backing, so we've been able to get capital."

"Sounds like you're going to make a fortune," I said.

He nodded.

"Then why bother with me? Why not let me die my own miserable life and move on with yours?" I asked.

He tapped the table. "Because I keep getting pulled here. Day after day. I don't know why, but your life seems to be important somehow. I keep spending more and more time here. I don't know if my world can survive without yours. Without you. So I'm offering my help. For both our sakes."

"What kind of help?" I asked.

"I can provide some money to get you started. I can tell you how to approach Morton and what kind of deal he'll accept. And I can give you the plans for this." He gestured with his metal hand again.

This sounded too good to be true. "What's the catch?" I asked warily.

He pointed to my right hand under the table. "You're going to have to give it up. Part of the deal with Morton is that he has to think you're desperate to get your hand back. He won't even discuss it unless you've lost the hand. Besides, it's killing you. It's a miracle you haven't died from infection yet."

I nodded at his mechanical hand. "That will let me work again? That will give me my hand back?"

He grimaced. "It will let you work again. You'll be able to write, to draw. You'll be able to do some work, but this design isn't good enough to let you do master-level work. Maybe in the future we can come up with something better, but this is still a lot better than what you've got."

"So I need to go back to the doctor? Do you think he'll still see me? Are you able to pay off those bills, too?"

The man who wasn't me shrugged. "Maybe. I might have enough with me. But the bigger danger is if he takes too much of your arm. You need to retain enough of the muscle and bone to mount the collar and hook the muscles into the mechanism. If he takes too much, we'd have to start from scratch, and if he takes the arm at the elbow, it won't work at all."

I pushed back from the table. "What game are you playing? You bring me hope and then take it all away again? Don't you think I'm suffering enough?" I reached down and grabbed the club again.

He leaned away from the table but didn't stand. "No, wait! There is a way. I've been thinking about this. *I* can do the amputation." He pulled his right sleeve down, to expose the bottom of the brass hand, and a silver ring that ran around his arm where the metal ended and the flesh began. "I know how much of the flesh needs to be saved. And if he thinks you're desperate enough to have taken your own hand off by yourself, he'll treat you despite your debts. I'm sure of it."

"You want to take my hand?" I said, dropping the club. I grabbed my arm and held it close to my chest. I felt tears running in hot streaks down my face.

"I can do this. Please, let me help you," he said, begging for my permission.

I looked down at my shattered hand. *How long? How long until the infection turns to rot?* I thought.

"Do it."

He blinked at me in surprise.

"Do it before I change my mind!" I screamed.

He jumped into action, clearing the plates from the table and replacing them with a large cutting board. He produced a length of thin leather strap.

"I need to tie this around the arm to keep you from bleeding too much."

He moved me back to the table and rolled up my sleeve. Wrapping the strap around my arm, he looped it and pulled it tight, the pressure of it biting into my flesh and making me cry out. He paused as I gasped for breath.

"Keep going!" I told him.

He opened a drawer in my cupboard. Pulling out a large knife, he came around to the left side of my body.

"You're going to want to hold onto the table," he said. "This is going to hurt."

"Why are you doing this from there?" I asked him.

"When the doctor looks at your wound, we want him to think that you did it using your left hand. It's the only way to make this look believable.

I gripped the table with my left hand and braced myself for the blow. He gently grabbed my right hand in his left and raised the knife. I closed my eyes so I wouldn't see it coming.

The knife was sharp, and when the strike came, it slid almost painlessly between my ribs.

I opened my eyes, and tried to gasp for breath, but all that came was a gurgle in my throat. I looked down and saw the point of the knife slightly protruding through the fabric of my vest.

The man who wasn't me said, "Oh, that is going to be a mess."

He left the knife in my back and took his seat across from me. "It looks like I get to be a tinker for a little while. At least until I find someone better to become. Perhaps one of your customers? Mr. Shelley seemed interesting."

I reached for him, and the blood welled up in my throat and spilled down my chest. He pulled away from my weakened grasp.

"Hmm. I must have missed the heart. Well, it will just take a little longer."

He leaned forward and said in a conspiratorial tone, "Tell me, what do you think is more believable? The mechanical hand?" He held the back of his right hand in front of me. "Or a miraculous cure?" He turned the hand, and it transformed back into flesh and blood.

I tried to curse him, but only managed to vomit out more blood as I fell forward onto the table.

"You're right. The mechanical hand is more believable," he said, and then I heard no more.

# The Year Without a Summer

JESSICA LUCCI

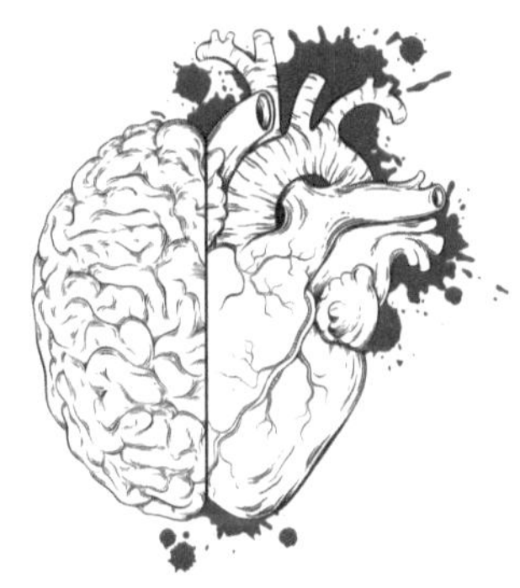

BLACK ASH SPAWNED LIKE A HEAVENLY PLAGUE circumventing the Northern Hemisphere. Across the globe from the glowing, flowing, spurting Mount Tambora, the skies grew dark with smoke. Though far distant, Cambridge, Massachusetts, home of Harvard University, was choked by brown skies and drowned by incessant rain. So began 1816, the year without a summer.

A small family sought a quiet summery sojourn one dry night. Bernard Prideaux, traveling bumbershoot salesman, and his wife Rose and daughter Isabella had been cloistered in a small inn together for weeks, avoiding rain and creditors. With a break in the weather came Bernard's proposal of a family excursion. Rose and Isabella dutifully and cautiously followed the patriarch away from the inn.

"Wait right here." Rose and Isabella obeyed. When he called their names, they followed his voice to the languid Charles River.

"Isn't this jolly? I've rented a rowboat for us."

The woman and young girl clutched their stoles tight around their shoulders as they shivered in the tentacles of wayward wind. This was not the evening either of them had hoped for. Yet they stepped carefully in to the watercraft.

As the mother and daughter watched the sky, a peephole opened through the dark clouds. The sight of a quietly smiling moon in a halo of stars enchanted them.

"Look, Mama! Libra!"

Rose looked where Isabella pointed.

"Yes, clever girl! The scales!"

"What about you, Papa? What do you see?"

Bernard assessed the sky slowly, then dully answered. "Clouds."

The family coasted along as the gears of the mechanical oars creaked with rusty effort. Once they reached a wide middle between two empty shores, the patriarch pulled the lever on the rod that controlled the oars, and pulled them into the small watercraft. He sat behind his stargazing family while the rowboat lost momentum.

Then, with a solid *thonk*, a moment that lingered between day and night, the lights in Isabella's eyes blinked out. Bernard raised the oar again, and swung the handle at Rose's head. Her face flung forward. Her hazel eyes popped out of their sockets. Her neck dislodged from its spinal cord.

The bodies, heavy with layers of evening dress, sank beneath the surface, disturbing the quiet calm of the murky Charles. Bernard paused to confirm that the bodies of his wife and daughter vanished out of sight. Then, without prayer, he lowered the lever and engaged the oars manually. His body buzzed with the feeling of power. The future was his, now that he would inherit his wife's family trust. *Which should have been mine all along*, he thought. But soon, he would be wealthy with the money that his wife's family had kept him from. Silent through the night, he returned to the dock.

Whiskey had never tasted so good to the jovial murderer. Celebrating a new life for himself, he bought the dwindling crowd at the publick house a round of drinks. Untethered from family responsibilities, the traveling bumbershoot salesperson could now build up his business without familial hindrance. They had always dragged him down and distracted him from his goals. *It had been good while it had been good, but sometimes a man's got to be free*, he reasoned. Or, with his new fortune, he could pause life for some well-deserved merriment. He raised another glass of whiskey to the bartender, full of hope and adrenaline.

*The Boston Gazette*, June 13, 1816, Cambridge, MA

Journalist: Frances Stein

The victims of a double drowning from Thursday evening have been identified. Twenty-nine-year-old Mrs. Rose Prideaux and her ten-year-old daughter Isabella Prideaux, both from Cambridge, drowned in the Charles River just after 7pm on Thursday. Their bodies were discovered Monday beneath the propellors of a steamboat.

It appears the two females were on a family rowboat excursion with the master of the family, Mr. Bernard Prideaux. The small boat was upset and the two victims were tipped from the vessel and inevitably drowned.

At this time it does not appear Bernard Prideaux activated a search of any kind. Witnesses indicate that Prideaux spent the greater of Thursday night at The Eagle Publick House.

Bernard Prideaux has been taken into police custody. An investigation into this matter is ongoing.

Cambridge Police and the Middlesex County Sheriff's Office are assisting the Massachusetts Bureau of Investigation, which has taken over as the lead agency in this case.

Massachusetts Bureau of Investigation agents are continuing to conduct witness interviews in hopes of illuminating the truth in this matter.

Updates will be released as further information develops.

Frances Stein had been sitting on the hard pine pew in the press corner of the courtroom for so long, she felt like the bones in her bottomside were going to bruise. She checked her silver pocket watch, a gift from her cousin Professor Avery Godwin upon her completion of her degree in journalism. It was eight minutes past, and the entire courtroom buzzed with anticipation. Today, a man would be declared guilty. *Today*, thought Frances, *justice will be served*.

She evaluated the press section of the courtroom that was cordoned off by black velvet ropes. Frances felt impeccable pride in her new profession. She had been first in line at the courthouse, so she could situate herself and get straight to work.

Frances fumbled with the unwieldy box on her lap. She could have relied on her ever-present notebook and pencil, but for this, she wanted to appear more official, more professional. She had written a series about this case, and knew everything there was to know about it—including Prideaux's guilt. This next article would be the masterpiece of her short career. She would be the first one to break the news about Prideaux, the murderer! And most importantly, for those two unfortunate souls, justice would be served.

Frances unlatched the handle of the copper box. She slid her fingers down the smooth metal to a small embedded button. She pushed this silver dot, and the top of the box sprung halfway open like a colossal book.

She balanced the apparatus with her knees, careful not to snag her new brown pants. She patted her notebook inside her vest pocket, just to make sure it was there.

Frances reached to the front of the box, and rotated a small silver knob, initiating a series of gears. With each twist of the knob, the gears spun smoothly, and from within rose her cousin's invention for her: a writing box. She carefully ripped a page from her notebook and clamped it to a flat metal rectangle bolted to the middle of the box.

Avery had built the writing contraption to her specifications, to provide unnecessary inspiration in her new endeavor as a journalist. Frances felt words forming in her head, trickling down her arms, to her fingers, to the springy panel of letters and numbers. She touched her right forefinger to the letter J. A corresponding stamp rose from a hidden well before the metal rectangle, and imprinted the letter onto the paper. She carefully pressed a series of additional letters, and looked down at her headline: "Justice."

Using the mechanical printer proved more challenging than writing in her ever-present notebooks, and it was also more cumbersome. Certainly too bulky and heavy to use on a daily basis. Heavy like the burden and duty Frances felt, sworn to expose the truth.

The writing box slid off her lap and she barely caught it by the handle before it could completely hit the marble floor. Too focused to be flustered, she twisted awkwardly and pulled the box back up and slid it across her lap. She was sure her peers in the press corner appreciated the pride she took in her work, and pretended not to notice them eyeing her fancy writing tool.

Soon, the courtroom grew hushed. The only sounds were the scratch of pencil on paper from the press corner, as well as a furious clacking sound. Frances had her byline ready.

Then there was the sound of heavy footsteps and the dragging of chains across the old oak floor. Bernard Prideaux was led to stand before the judge.

Frances heard the judgement, but was sure she had misunderstood beneath the blanket of sound created by her dedicated writing.

"Not guilty." How could it be so?

Frances shook with shock as she stared at Prideaux. She felt the uncharacteristic urge to swing the heavy writing contraption into his smug smile. But she didn't.

Instead she moaned. "How? How is this happening? What about justice?" A desperate glance at the jury was met with smirks.

Her vision faded to white and she felt like she could faint. She squeezed her eyes shut and grasped onto the contraption on her lap, the one steady thing she could count on at the moment.

She opened her eyes and could see clearly again. Chancing another glance at the jury, she grew suspicious. How much money had the bumbershoot salesperson bribed them with?

Her body went numb, her thoughts too frozen to write. All she could do was feel. Not shock, or anger, or resentment, but utter disappointment. Justice had not been served for Rose and Isabelle Prideaux. In a spiral of self-doubt and defeat, she decided to confer with her cousin, whose mind she trusted as well as her own.

Frances pressed one hand firmly to her forehead while with the other she grasped her cousin's.

"Not guilty! By a jury of his peers? More like paid-off strangers! And after all my investigation! Where is justice for those poor souls?"

Avery consoled her in the elitist yet loving tone they had adapted as a Harvard University professor in the growing field of Anatomy and Physiology.

"Frances, the court has sought answers, and we must trust the judicial system, or else we are doomed as a society."

Frances groaned and released her cousin's hand.

"But all my journalistic investigation- it was for naught! There is a murderer on the loose!"

Avery reached a long arm out and smoothed down Frances's unruly short hair.

"When is the last time you have eaten, or slept?" Frances rested her eyes for a moment. Avery gently released their soft grasp and crossed the concrete floor to a shelf lined with beakers.

"Tea?"

Frances mumbled a reply.

"I could make a bed for you on one of the gurneys." Frances suspiciously glanced at the beaker, and at the metal slab on wheels with something long and lumpy covered by a once-white sheet.

"I still do not understand how someone as civilized as you can perform this kind of experimentation."

"The body? Worry not about that. It will visit the university morgue and be incinerated, dust to dust."

"I find it rather macabre." Frances covered her nose with a kerchief from her suit pocket, unsuccessfully blocking the fragrance of death. Avery set the beaker on a tray next to a wide, lengthy table balancing rows of bubbling, smoking, glass tubes and bottles.

"Tea?" Avery repeated.

"No, thank you."

Avery gazed upon their beloved cousin. "You truly do look terrible."

"Better than whoever is under that sheet."

"You have your calling and I have mine," Avery answered lightly. Frances glanced at the table again.

"I cannot help but wonder—"

"It's my job to wonder, my dear, and your job to report."

"I also investigate."

"Of course, and in that way, I suppose we are the same. You seek the truth in society, and I seek the truth in science." Frances offered a brief wan smile.

"Whatever happened to right and wrong though? What about justice? Don't we reap what we sow?"

"No need to quote Galatians at me," Avery said. "I have read much of what I don't believe. I have also read unbelievable stories borne of myth, defined by science. The Christ figure himself rose from the dead one dark day. There is light in the darkness, just as death may begin new life."

"Your words trouble me, cousin. What you speak of implies unholy notions."

Avery laughed. "You of all people should understand. Your passion for justice is a human ideal, not shared by any other creature on this earth."

"My piety is based not on religion but in the reclamation of the right to live and be treated fairly. Laws must be enforced to protect this humanity. But what you are hinting at is—"

"—is a new breath into the old winds of science."

Frances blinked the blankness of exhaustion away. "I simply do not know what opinion I have to offer."

"When the day comes that the queries in your mind itch to be answered, of my visions of glorious new technology come to life, you are welcome to uncover the shroud of my secrecy." Avery squeezed Frances's shoulder affectionately. "Perhaps we should leave it at that."

"I wish I didn't know, much less suspect, what your motives are with the deceased."

"You are always about motives."

"Well, in this particular instance, it is not so much motives, as I have no explanation as to why you do these things you do in the dark. But I am aware of your plans. One does not wield a galvanizer for its medicinal value."

Avery strode over to the table of bubbling beakers. "But for now, tea?"

Frances rubbed her temples and closed her eyes. She reopened them and saw Avery looking hopefully into her face.

"I am not sure I want to see what goes on in this laboratory when the light fights dimly through the dark."

Avery held up two empty glass beakers and raised their eyebrows towards Frances.

"Yes, yes, I will take some tea." Frances supported her forehead with her hands, closed her eyes, and took a deep breath. She smelled the familiar: chemicals, smoke, and—of course—death.

"Prideaux," she moaned.

"Here you are, something to warm your bones." Avery handed her a glass beaker with clear green-tinged brown liquid. Frances eyed it warily. Moments passed, then she took a tentative sip. She let out a breath.

"I just wish that brute had confessed! No matter what the judge declared, all my evidence leads to him."

"Quite honestly, your attention to this case has become obsessive. Perhaps you can recuperate and rejuvenate."

"You may be right," said Frances, but both she and Avery knew she was devastated by the "not guilty" verdict of a man she was sure was a murderer.

"Since you have been placed on leave from the newspaper—"

"I was put on *probation*, not granted a vacation! Just because I asserted myself to the *Gazette*'s editor, and told him how if he did not allow my follow up piece, *A Murderer Among Us*, then that must mean he is in cahoots with Prideaux. It's not my fault he took offence to that. All I can do is communicate the truth."

"All I am saying is you deserve a respite. Take a sabbatical to the west where the air will clear your cloudy head."

Frances lifted her chin, her eyes rimmed with exhaustion.

"Just do not lose your mind."

Frances did not know if her cousin was being sincere or lovingly teasing. She decided she was too tired to care. Taking leave of Avery, she dragged herself outdoors to the waiting night.

No stars shone through the blackened sky. Frances pulled her flint switch from her jacket pocket. After a few futile flicks, the metal wick glowed an orangey hue, just bright enough so that she could see where her feet were taking her.

Cool air mixed with the solemn depths of the Charles River, forming trails of wispy whiteness. In the dim light of her flint switch, the fog seemed like floating white walls reflecting the flame. Frances crept along the narrow path through Harvard Yard, trusting her memory more than her sight.

A cold breeze rushed over her, and the light went out. Frances flicked the flint switch again, startling as a cloud of white vapor approached her. The light extinguished. Her thumb burned from activating the switch so many times. After a few more futile tries, the orange light shown again. The dim flicker now revealed two figures floating mere meters from where she stood.

Frances gasped, her breath threatening the light, but it maintained its low glow. She blinked hard, sure it was an illusion of the foggy night that had startled her. But the forms filled out and clarified as they wafted closer to where she stood, stunned. Anxious sweat trailed down the back of her pressed white shirt, but she was only aware of the chill in the unseasonably cold summer air. She took a few steps backward, but the white clouded figures still advanced toward her.

"Spirits, why do you haunt me so?" Frances asked, her voice clear but trembling.

The two figures hovered closer, until Frances could make out the facial features of a woman and a girl. The womanly apparition motioned for Frances to follow her. Without hesitation, she complied. There was a story here, a truth that needed to be uncovered. She followed the specters to the graveyard of the discarded: the childless widows, the indigent, the unclaimed. The figures hovered over two headstones engraved simply, "Mother," and "Daughter," with the year 1816 chiseled on each, the year of their demise.

Frances then realized whose ghosts she was seeing. It was Rose and Isabella Prideaux, the murdered mother and daughter! Their shapes were defined by the shadows cast from Frances's light. A woman and child in full evening dress, with matching stoles, just like the ones the pair had been wearing the night they were murdered. The mother whispered in the darkness, but Frances could not make out what was being said. She imagined that Rose was after the same thing she was.

Frances trembled like the flame in her hands. After all of her research, she felt like she knew Rose and Isabella. Felt the sorrow of their murder and casting away. She did not want to fail them again. Yet, as much as she was dedicated to this case, she was still frightened of the specters and their silent demand.

"You seek justice, as do I, and I imagine even more so. I promise to do my duty and deliver the justice you deserve." The white trailed ghosts glowed briefly in the shadows of monuments, then disappeared.

Most days, Frances walked. She delighted in the physicality of using all her senses to define the world around her. But today, she was in a rush. Her whole body was a whirlwind as she climbed aboard her velocipede. Her heart pounded even before she turned the key to activate the machinery. She wildly maneuvered through the slippery dirt road, barely avoiding horse dung and a wayward cow. Her curls swirled around her face, covering her bronze rimmed goggles. While despair over the not-guilty judgement had manifested as sluggish depression, her revived mission pushed hot blood through her veins in a rush of purpose.

She drove the mechanical vehicle half blind. From her small flat, across the landscape of flooded farms between shipyards, the entire route, her pulse thrummed in her ears. She needed to reach Avery at their laboratory. She just knew her cousin would be there, early in the morning.

With the frenzy of the enlightened, she relayed her unnatural experience and made an announcement.

"I have a plan to bring the murderer to justice. But it will only work with your assistance, your knowledge, your abilities. The time has come for you to share with me what really goes on here in the dead of night, your secret experiments, that till now I have kept a blind eye to. I need your help."

Avery soaked up this breathless inquiry. Self-preservation cautioned them to keep the secret that had remained hidden so well. But love and concern for their cousin's sanity won out.

"Together," begged Frances. "We can create an opportunity for justice to be served."

"You have me at your side." Avery assured her.

"Thank you!" She whipped her notebook out from the inside pocket of her vest, pulled her trusty pencil from behind her ear, and wrote.

> *Dear Mr. Bernard Prideaux,*
>
> *It is my delight to invite you to an Honorarium of Business, at our Independence Day Celebration at eight o'clock in the evening. You will be honored for your considerable sales of the latest design of bumbershoots, shielding Cambridge residents from excessive rainfall. You will be bestowed an honorary degree from the Harvard University School of Business.*
>
> *Harvard University Sciences Lecture Hall. Cambridge, MA.*
>
> *Sincerely,*
>
> *Professor Avery Godwin*

"Now," said Frances solemnly, gazing into her cousin's eyes, "lead me where you may."

Avery reached out and clutched their cousin's shivering shoulders. "You do not have to do this."

Frances's lower lip trembled. All she could think about were the figures of the mother and daughter, hovering over their graves.

"For justice, I will."

Frances and Avery waited for night to shield their desperate act. Then they rambled as quietly as they could with all their apparatus to the small burial ground where Frances had seen the spirits the previous night.

The cousins used small steam-powered diggers, each with broad shovels attached to a mechanical arm that dug the soft newly settled earth. They dug down, down. Then Avery lowered a short ladder they had brought in the self-propelled, wind-up wagon.

"You are suspiciously skilled and informed at this gruesome task." Frances scanned the dark graveyard. She didn't know what she feared more: coppers catching them in the act of grave-robbing, or the return of the dead mother and child.

"I cannot comment on that, Frances, but to say, if you follow my advice, we will complete this gruesome task before the lamplighters snuff out their flames and the pea-shooters rouse the wealthy with tiny pelts at their bedroom windows."

The bodies of the mother and daughter were still whole, but swollen from soaking in the Charles so long before they were discovered lodged between the propellors of a steam ferry. A sticky mess of ooze pulled at the corpses as Avery expertly pried the broken, propellor-slashed bodies from the caskets. Frances vomited and held her kerchief to her face. Avery handed Frances a shovel.

"Unfortunately, we are low on coal. If we want to be back before dawn, we must do this part the old-fashioned way."

Frances shivered in her cold sweat. She cried as she covered the empty coffins with dirt. She was disgusted with herself, horrified at her own actions, and so sorry that she had let the mother and daughter down by not being a better journalist. But mostly, she was afraid.

Bernard Prideaux strutted into the empty hall. New electric candles brightened the high ceiling. He was confused. Where were all the people to congratulate him on his honorarium?

"Hello?" he called out into the large room. At the trail of his voice's echo, a tall thin figure wearing a chemist's white coat entered the barren doorway.

"Why, Mr. Prideaux, how excellent to meet you! I am Professor Godwin. If you would follow me this way, we have another venue for your award." Avery led the murderer down the lift and across the hall. Bernard sniffed the cold, dead air. Soon he would finally be acknowledged as the brilliant person he was! Avery opened the massive doors wide. Bernard proudly stepped in, prepared for applause.

His practiced modest smile turned into a grimace. Sitting on a tall stool just ten feet from the door, was a woman with frizzy hair and lopsided eyeglasses. That pesky journalist! The one who had almost cost him his freedom! She held an iron rod in her hands and across one shoulder. He spun back to the egress, but Avery had already bolted a thick chain with a heavy lock through the door handles. Bernard turned again, and raised a fist into the air.

"What is the meaning of this?" His face flamed with outrage and embarrassment. He couldn't believe he had fallen for a loathsome ruse! "You dirty balderdash gossip! You'll get yours!" He stomped toward Frances, prepared to throw a punch.

"I wouldn't do that if I were you," said Avery. Bernard ignored them, ready for a fight.

Avery flashed a smile as Frances revved up the galvanizer, sparkling with electric brimstone.

"My new toy is ready to be experimented with. Frances, take aim!"

Bernard jumped back as Frances lifted the pole, using her shoulder for leverage. She kept one hand on the shaft, and with the other hand, activated the trigger. She aimed for his head, but gravity weighed on the heavy machine. The nozzle lowered as Frances readjusted the hard metal bearing down on her shoulder. The galvanizer aimed level with Bernard's crotch.

Bernard's hands darted down to shield his groin. Under Frances's threat, he watched as the professor circumvented him to two gurneys, with sheets covering what had to be human bodies. Frances had plugged her nose with melted wax, and Avery was used to the smell, but the decay of flesh attacked Bernard's olfactory nerves. He didn't know if it was better to breathe through his mouth or his nose. The smell of death was dominant in the chemical-filled laboratory.

Bernard stared as Avery lifted each sheet, bit by bit. He saw the professor attach clamps to bare ankles, then replace the sheet, and move upward, toward the arms, so each limb was connected to an octopus of wires leading to a hefty wooden box. The professor added a metal bowl to crown the scalps of the dead.

Bernard turned his gaze back to the journalist. "You little gnat! I demand you lower your silly weapon and release me!"

"The truth will set you free!" Frances felt brave, but the galvanizer was becoming too heavy for her to hold without wavering.

The professor continued their preparations, which they calculated had to be conducted in a certain order. They had planned on completing this last sequence of work before Bernard's arrival, but there had not been enough time. They fought the rushed feeling and willed their hands not to shake. They probed the bodies with a conductive rod, very careful not to remove the sheets.

The new electric lights flickered again. Bernard shivered, the air feeling colder every minute.

"You stupid wretches! Let me go! Do you know who I am?"

Frances maintained her aim between the man's legs.

"Yes, we know you are Bernard Prideaux, murderer." Frances stared into the man's eyes.

"You could never prove that, you spiteful flea!"

"I am not the one who needs to acknowledge the proof. You are."

"Mister Prideaux, if you would look toward me."

Avery stood between the two narrow metal gurneys. Bernard looked from one cousin to another, not sure where to set his sights. But gruesome curiosity corrupted his bravado and gave way to nagging fear. The sheets shifted, and two pairs of purplish grey feet confronted him. He gagged, the smell of rotting flesh overwhelming him.

Avery edged along to the back corner of the room, where there in the shadows, all the wires flowed. Bernard began to sweat.

"I do not know what you two imbeciles are playing at, but you've got to let me go!" Bernard took a heavy step toward Frances as he shouted.

"Not until justice is served." Frances was shaking but held her aim true.

"Keep your attention on the gurneys, Prideaux," said Avery. Then they called out to their cousin.

"Are you ready?"

Frances gritted her teeth and lowered her goggles. "I am ready for justice."

Avery pulled down their welding mask. Then they grasped an iron rod and twisted it to channel electricity. Bernard watched in horror as sparks fizzed like firecrackers in the professor's face.

The force of the electric current sent Avery flying backward into a bookcase. A cascade of medical volumes tumbled down on them, but Bernard's gaze remained fixed on the trail of sparks, traveling down the wires, to the clamps, to whatever was beneath those sheets.

When he saw the toes contort, he told himself it was a trick of candlelight. But when arms raised up from the sheets, with outstretched fingers, he roared with fright. Two figures sat up straight, sending the sheets to the floor. The faces contorted grotesquely.

Rose Prideaux's bugged-out eyes stared into her husband's. She hissed with a parched whisper.

Bernard scrambled back and fell, shielding his eyes from the sight of his guilt.

"Look upon them, you murderer! Look at your wife and child, and what you have done to them!" Frances felt feverish for this final judgement.

Isabella gazed at her papa with eyes that looked like boiled eggs. Bernard pulled himself to his knees, wet with urine and vomit.

"Admit what you did to them!"

The bodies stood with a wobble. The spirits within controlling their deteriorating shells. They reached their arms out to Bernard. He retched again, and as he spoke, bile dripped from his lips. Rose's bloated body took a squishy step toward him. Isabella followed suit.

"Confess!" shouted Frances. Through her veins burned a fiery rage she hadn't thought herself capable of.

Rose's saggy form lowered. She bent at the waist like a hinge and lowered her face to her husband's. Her loose eyes shook as she moved.

Bernard could feel coldness emanating from her. Cold like the Charles River. He squeezed his eyes shut, and when he dared open them, he saw that Isabella had stepped next to her mother, and was now also bent jaggedly down. He could not meet her eternal gaze.

"Confess!" shouted Frances again. The two bodies of the man's wife and daughter drew closer around him and his wet mess on the floor.

"Leave me be! That's all I ever wanted! To be alone!"

Rose stretched her disjointed arms toward her husband.

"Stop! Don't touch me!"

Rose did not retreat. Instead, she reached Bernard with a sticky embrace. Her skinless lips grazed his frothy ones.

"Okay, I did it! I murdered the both of you! Now let me go!" Isabella leaned over and placed her water-logged hand on her father's chest.

"My heart is beating so fast! I can barely breathe! Someone help me, please! Save me!" Frances and Avery looked on, frozen in a feeling different from fear, different from curiosity. This was something they could never have imagined, never in any of their research or calculations.

"What do we do now?" asked Avery, to no one. But their cousin was thinking the same thing.

"Send for the authorities. Then justice will finally be served!"

Rose's mouth opened wide and she screamed louder than a speeding locomotive's brakes. Her lolling eyes turned in her unstable head to face Frances. She spoke with a guttural growl. This time Frances deciphered the revenant's intention. Her foul mouth opened again to form the word.

"Revenge!" Mother and daughter both now embraced Bernard, and no matter how he screamed for them to cease, they persisted. Finally, after one last screech for help, bubbling froth foamed from his mouth. The revenants released him, and his dead body thudded to the floor.

Rose and Isabella helped each other up. Their spirits left their possessed bodies, which folded in a broken, mushy, heap. They floated above Frances and Avery, and curtsied.

The candles grew brighter. Then mother and daughter, hand in hand, dissipated into sparkles of snowflakes in the dim air.

"Avery, are you alright?" Frances watched her cousin approach the bodies.

"I am better than I could have imagined."

"What is that?" asked Frances, now noticing the wide syringe with a long needle in Avery's fist.

"Preservation serum."

Frances gasped. But a wild gleam shone in Avery's eyes.

"Your work here is done. But mine has just begun."

# Imagination Unbound

## Dana Fraedrich

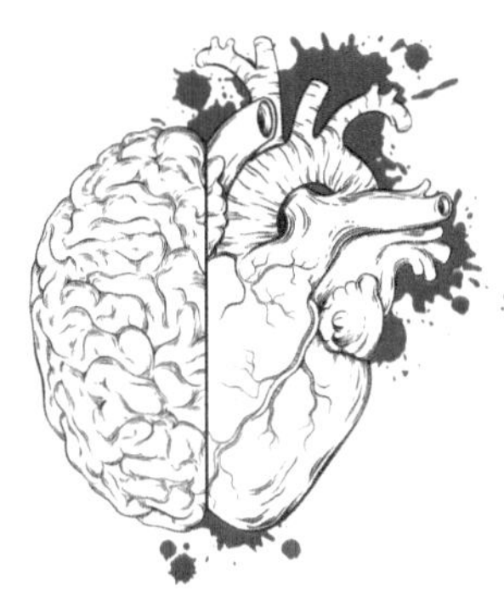

Night turned the city of Springhaven into an entirely different place, Robert observed. He'd been to the Agate district only a few times before, and though the area had fallen far from the shining arts and culture district it had been over a century ago—decimation by magical war will do that to a place—he found it was no different, at least in this case, from most of the rest of the city.

People, in his experience, were like bees. During the day, they buzzed about, swarming and filling all the available space. At night, they huddled in whatever hive they happened to favor at the moment. Whether it was a decadent gala in the glittering Ivory quarter, the dinnertime rush on a retired steamship-turned-restaurant in Cobalt, a chocolate house in Limestone, or an ordinary pub here in Agate, people sheltered together when the darkness took over.

That created a bit of an odd scenario for him now, given that, in his short tenure as a municipal surveyor, he'd never done a job at night. Of course, some assignments had gone long and stretched into evening, but it was proper nighttime at the moment, just past eleven, and they hadn't even reached their destination yet. Robert was used to the hum of people as he set out on an assignment, the clatter of horses and cabs on the cobbled streets. He heard muffled sounds of spirited—and spirit-fueled—joviality from a nearby tavern, but that was the loudest noise around. It faded away as they headed deeper in, toward the Char district. It had once been part of Agate, but now-extinct magic had scourged the area during the War of Light. Nothing grew there, so people said, and the walls, which had once bloomed with Agate's namesake shades of lilac and plum, had been irreversibly blackened. Robert found it all extremely silly. Clearly there just wasn't anywhere good for plants to grow, and people must not have found the right cleaning agent for such unique damage.

Even so, he had to admit this assignment was strange. Robert was beginning to see why the other gents at the office, all of whom were older and more established than him, had been so "generous" as to allow him to take it. But that, he mused, made for an opportunity to prove himself.

The group with whom he walked down the echoing, abandoned streets made for a motley bunch. He stuck near the builders. He already knew one or two of them, in a distantly professional way. And, as they were headed into an area that had been abandoned to time and the elements, the builders were the ones who'd be able to spot—and, more importantly, *avoid*—which bits of crumbling stone were in immediate peril of falling onto a person.

The accountants weren't much of a surprise, either. Accountants would at least attempt to keep keen developers within some semblance of a budget. The savviest businessmen seemed to always have one or two about.

The developer in question had come along as well, Mister Anthony Crackenthorpe. He led the charge, heavy mustaches at the front lines, and Robert knew he was only minutes from an enthusiastic explanation of all the magnificent things Mister Crackenthorpe had planned for the dilapidated area. Never mind that the builders, accountants, and Robert himself, as the team's surveyor, had yet to inspect the area and assess its state and the costs for these grand plans. And that they all had copies of the building applications, which already outlined said plans.

What was odd, however, were the handful of burly men he'd brought along, who looked like they made a living being large and intimidating. Of course, people said the Char district was haunted. Codswallop. But what had Mister Crackenthorpe been thinking in bringing these chaps? Were they meant to beat any preternatural forces to undeath?

As they walked, Robert leafed through the pages on his clipboard until he found the copy he'd brought of the last survey report done in the area. A small oil lamp attached to his clipboard lit the words before him. The accountants had similar apparatuses, while the builders wore miner's caps, so their heads smoked oddly as the oil in the attached lamps of the hats burned. Mister Crackenthorpe and his men all carried lightboxes, which were expensive and had small catadioptric lenses to increase the power of the small oil flame within.

A lot of what Robert had read back in the office about the Char quarter had contained superstitious nonsense, but he was nothing if not comprehensive. This most recent report had been the most objective, and thus, he pushed his spectacles further up his face and read over it again.

*DATE: Ninety Eighth Year of the Dawn Age,*
      *Eleventh Day of the Sun*
*SURVEYOR NAME: Dennis Gibson*
*AREA OF INTEREST: Prism Extravaganzaland Fun Fair*
*APPROX SIZE: 50 acres*

*REPORT:*
    *We arrived early in the morning to try and avoid the worst of the summer heat. Even so, I feel the oppressive air might have affected some of my fellows.*
    *The Prism Extravaganzaland Fun Fair covers a vast swath of land, but is tightly packed with buildings, which creates a complex network that is difficult to navigate. I believe the original intent of the design was to keep patrons inside and therefore part them from as much money as possible.*
    *We came first to a large loading and unloading station for an omnibus…*

Robert lifted his eyes from the report to gaze upon what had stopped the party in their tracks. A pair of bronze gates, now covered in a sickly green patina, stood before them. Above, in a curving arch, read the name of the place: *Prism Extravaganzaland Fun Fair*. Below that, straight across and in smaller letters was *Imagination Unbound*. Rusty chains and a heavy padlock held the gates closed, giving lie to the outdated proclamation. Every eye turned to Robert. He was the city of

Springhaven's official representative here, and thus had been given charge of the keys to unlock forbidden places.

He smiled in what he intended as congeniality, though the success of that intention could be debated.

"Not to worry, chaps," he said, striding forward.

As he extracted a ring of keys from his waistcoat pocket, the thin chain to which it was attached jangled loudly in that quiet space. "I'll have us inside in a jiffy." The key for the padlock fit, though a bit of cajoling seemed necessary to crack the rust that had conspired with time to try and fuse the lock into one, solid piece. It had been six years, after all, since the last survey of the fun fair had been performed. One of the large men came forward and reached for the stubborn lock, but Robert raised a defiant hand.

"Out of the question!" He enunciated each syllable hard, and even added one or two extra for emphasis. His tone suggested the large man had offered to commit a hefty blood sacrifice in order to break the lock. "This is city property, I'll have you know. Only an authorized representative is…" He faltered. Hauteur could not magic up synonyms for him. He finished weakly. "Authorized."

Mister Crackenthorpe approached, mustaches quivering with amusement as the developer laughed. "It's alright, old bean."

Robert had noticed he addressed everyone like an old school chum, and he wasn't certain he approved of such familiarity, no matter how much money he might give the city for this sad, derelict place.

"Mister Black here was only going to lend a hand," Mister Crackenthorpe went on.

"Unnecessary, but thank you," Robert replied crisply. "I really must insist on city protocol."

Crackenthorpe and his man did not argue and backed away to allow Robert to get on alone. Robert began to regret his insistence after another solid minute of struggle.

Movement inside the shadowy fun fair caught his eye. He gazed into the gloom, but nothing stirred. It had been naught but a flicker, and Robert decided it must have been a moth or some other nightly pest. At last, the lock's inner mechanisms loosened enough for Robert to grind the key around and pull the shackle free of the padlock body.

The gates themselves still moved with relative ease, but they shrieked like Old World banshees when they did. Every man gathered there clenched his teeth as the noise ripped through the night.

"If we might proceed with a little less fanfare going forward." Mister Crackenthorpe patted Robert on the shoulder as he passed. "For as long as possible, I'm rather hoping to keep the locals *in the dark*. You know how people can be about revitalizing an area."

He chuckled at his own joke while Robert bristled.

"I'd like to remind you that the sale of this unit, if an offer is made, will be a matter of public record, and anyone living within a five-mile radius will have the right to petition against the sale, according to Springhaven municipal bylaws."

Mister Crackenthorpe did not look back as he waved the words away, as he might a gnat. "Yes, yes. The city and I have an understanding." He was already heading toward the omnibus loading station.

"Topping that there's already a transport network in place," one of the accountants said. "We can offer an upgrade plan to residents to be able to use a hop-on, hop-off system to get around."

The idea, or at least what Mister Crackenthorpe had applied for, was to turn the entire former fun fair into a community of luxury flats and other high-end amenities. All, of course, would pay Mister Crackenthorpe well for the glorious opportunity to be a part of what the developer insisted would be the most sought-after accommodations for modern Springhavians. An "ideal community" was how the application described the scheme.

Robert took in what remained of the omnibus system. A few of the large vehicles moldered on the pavement. They were little more than gargantuan wooden boxes on wheels with a stairway attached to the back so that both the inside and top level could be populated with passengers. They would have been pulled by horses, as modern trams were, though these had no glass in the windows, just rounded openings all down the sides. The omnibus' once-jolly paint was cracked and peeling, many of the seats inside having been split open by some creature raiding the stuffing within… or perhaps in pursuit of other, smaller creatures that had made their home inside said stuffing.

That was an interesting point. Didn't all the rumors about Char say nothing could live here? But that was ridiculous when one thought about it. A cat wandering in did not vaporize upon placing a paw within its bounds, which were ambiguous at best. Things must live here; nature always took over what people left behind. To follow the thread, Robert walked over to the sagging omnibuses and squatted down next to one. The smell of rotting wood rolled off of it.

Aha! Dotted around the underside of the vehicle, clusters of small mushrooms peered back at him. Of course it was all just a bunch of superstitious nonsense.

A pair of large eyes gleamed through the darkness, caught by the faint moonlight trickling down from above. They moved, a quick jerk of whatever head they occupied. Robert cried out, letting fly a garbled swear, and leapt back. He lost track of his feet along the way and stumbled. He was rolling, fighting against his own body to regain balance as he shouted for the others to run.

People were there, Mister Black and his similarly behemothic associate first. Yes! Muscle would be helpful now. Robert pointed and gabbled about some *thing* on the other side of the omnibus. They went to investigate, and Robert waited for the inevitable sounds of a scuffle. None came. Mister Black returned, shaking his head. Robert was suddenly very aware of how this must look.

"I saw it!" he insisted. "It was right there!"

He squatted back down, now a safer distance from the omnibus and pointed. Nothing but shadows and mushrooms met his searching gaze.

One of the builders muttered something to one of his fellows. The other mimed drinking from a flask. Robert didn't understand what was happening. He had no explanation, or rather nothing that would improve his situation.

"I must have been mistaken," he heard himself say. "My apologies, gents."

A few more threw him or each other dubious looks, but no one replied. Mister Crackenthorpe resumed the tour. Robert allowed himself to fall to the back of the group and buried his face in his documents. He was a professional, blast it!

A low, small theater building squatted beyond the omnibus station. They headed inside that next—thank the stars the entrance was covered and therefore the lock here fared much better than the one on the gates.

The interior of the theater sent a chill down Robert's spine. It was a simple space. A faded poster told them this theater's only production had been *Getting to Know the Prism Extravaganzaland Fun Fair*. A bit of litter scattered across the floor, as seemed to be the case everywhere. It was the… lostness of the place that seemed to echo through Robert. The hundreds of seats bolted to the floor in tidy rows would have still been ready to accept patrons, if not for the mold growing over them. More grew down from a broken window near the ceiling. The thinning triangle of green extending down to the floor shone in the light of their various lamps, and Robert made a few notes about questionable air quality. Mister Crackenthorpe was blathering on about turning the space into a hospitality area for interested persons.

After the theater came the waxworks museum, which had once displayed models of notable figures from around Invarnis. Back then, of course, the continent had been unified under one royal banner, rather than the three large city-states it now sported. The report copy Robert had brought with him had things to say about this building too.

> *Most of the waxworks have softened over time and now lean against their fellows, their faces and shoulders grotesquely merged into one another. Those that have been exposed to direct sunlight have slowly melted into stunted, deformed versions of their former selves.*

Robert could not help but agree as the light of their lamps fell across the disfigured replicas of once-living people. The harsh, flickering shadows only added to the macabre display. Even the builders, usually such stout fellows, looked disturbed. Robert did not hear what grand vision Mister Crackenthorpe had for this building; he was too busy counting.

"Where has Mister Beddingfield gone?" he asked, interrupting whatever the developer had been banging on about.

All voices dropped as the party looked about them. Mister Beddingfield was one of the accountants. They lifted their lamps higher and looked from here to there like bobbing chickens. Someone jumped and let out a curse, having thrown his light across one of the deformed wax figures and mistaken it for one of their number. They called his name, but no one answered.

"I need everyone to sound off," Mister Crackenthorpe commanded. "Robert, old boy, go through the roll call, if you would."

Robert pressed his lips together in annoyance but read off the names. Only Mister Beddingfield was absent.

"When was the last time anyone saw him?" Mister Crackenthorpe asked.

Movement at the farthest edge of Robert's light caught his attention. He swung his clipboard in that direction, but only the horrible waxworks appeared under the glow. A scream ripped through the air. Outside somewhere. In the deep dark of the fun fair. It sounded *pained*. Terribly, terribly pained.

"We should get the Enforcers," someone said.

Thus was the strength of the Char district's reputation. The city's rather brutish peacekeepers did not even patrol here. The official line was that whatever lurked in Char, whether criminal or cursed spirits, they could fight and die amongst themselves out here.

Another noise sounded then. Something like a growl, deep and resonant, but it somehow also… rattled. Robert gulped as he slowly turned toward the noise. Every other man did too. Their lights barely limned a figure.

Robert could only just make out a massive bulk about it. A broad, arched back. Long, gangly limbs. Huge, curving, black claws. Spines down its head and disappearing into the gloom. And eyes. Such large eyes that reflected their lights like dull mirrors. Another shriek split the night outside. Chaos exploded.

Robert could not say when he began to run. Others did as well. The men cried out to one another, but words dissipated on the panicked air. Someone let out a yelp of terror behind Robert, who sped blindly in the direction he thought was the fun fair entrance.

Turning down an avenue, Robert scanned for the theatre, the would-be hospitality area. Where was it?! Behind him, a growl rumbled. Something swiped past his shoulder, something long, curved, and gleaming in the scant glow of Robert's clipboard light. He flinched and darted off to the side. He heard the shouts of his fellow party members here and there.

One sounded as if it wasn't far off: "Where is the exit?"

The sounds of pursuit behind Robert peeled off in the direction of the cried question.

Nothing else seemed to be following him. Robert ran on for a bit, as fast as he could, before pressing into the small space between two buildings. He tried to force his panicking brain to think rationally. Difficult, given the snarls, yowls, screams, and stars knew what other noises resounded from elsewhere in the fun fair. And he fought to stop his imagination from envisioning what those claws were doing to his fellow men's soft, meaty bodies. Robert gulped air, willing his pounding heart to slow. Even if he didn't find the exit, he could find a fence and climb out. He just had to pick a direction and keep going. *Away* from the noises. He'd eventually come across the boundary between the fun fair and the rest of Springhaven.

*Right,* he thought. *You're going to survive this. One direction. Now get going and keep going!*

Robert scanned the area outside of his hidey hole. Stillness greeted his eyes, if not his ears.

"The teeth!" someone was shouting. From where, Robert couldn't tell. Not nearby, but not far enough. He shut his ears before he could hear more about the teeth, and what they might be doing.

He hadn't been jogging long when he was forced to turn a corner. An enormous space opened before him. The words from the report copy he'd brought with him flooded his mind.

> *A large pool, full of fetid water, hosted the rusting carcass of a small boat, which bled orange and red into the brown swill — a man-made lake once used for aquatic shows. The jetty leading to it has deteriorated and sags in the middle, but was just passable if we walked single file along the unsunken portion…*

Robert's gaze fell onto the rusting vessel. Atop the cab lurked another of the monstrous, hulking creatures. It's dull-mirror eyes followed him as he spun to retreat, just before it threw back its head and released a high, shrieking, animalistic cry. Robert looked back only once to see its dark form leaping down into the shadows, undoubtedly chasing after him.

*Get out of their sight!* Robert's brain screeched at him.

Another tortured scream of pain echoed from elsewhere in the fun fair, and Robert ran so fast his legs burned like acid. He hardly knew where he ran, just so long as he lost the thing behind him. He heard its grunting breath with every stride.

Dash, turn, turn, dash. More turns. The wet, growl-like breathing faded with each one, and Robert escaped into a building with a door hanging open. It opened toward the inside, and Robert pushed it closed behind him. One of the hinges had detached somewhat, but Robert managed to shove the pieces back together through sheer brute force and desperation.

Then, he listened. An unpleasant choice given all that still resounded outside. Thank the stars the sound was muffled from here inside his escape, but that didn't stop more visions of disemboweled cohorts and feasting creatures from popping up in his mind.

At last, after several solid minutes of failing to hear the sound of pursuit, he peeked beyond the doorway. He found himself in a small vestibule. On the walls were posters of various sideshow features and fantastical creatures — sword and fire swallowers; a ghastly mermaid with long, needle-like teeth, contortionists, fetuses of various species preserved in jars. Robert did not look too closely at the images after seeing the illustration of the jar that purportedly had contained a juvenile frog-human hybrid.

In the large room beyond, only blackness met Robert's eyes. He debated staying put, but to what end? Could the things out there smell him? How well could they hear? He looked back at the uneven gaps of the door. They might even see his light through it, and it wouldn't take much to break open what he had managed to heave shut. Cautiously, he walked on. Perhaps there'd be something useful further in. Perhaps, if he was very lucky, this place would lead to the outside somehow. A man could hope, anyway.

Robert's light illuminated what the darkness hid, and more of the report floated back to his mind.

> *Menageries, cages, and stages for the oddities and oddballs show. The skeleton of a dog man — that is, a long-legged, quadrupedal canine creature with a human head — as well as a huge, moth-eaten dragon pelt from the Old World.*

> *Within this large building, there's a preponderance of broken glass, and the display enclosures are desolate. There are what appear to be the remains of large animals, though it's mostly ribcages and spines and leg bones. Very few skulls are present. Also, any of the skeletons of hoofed creatures appear to have been scattered, while many with long, pointed teeth remain perfectly intact. I am no zoologist and therefore cannot venture what may have occurred to cause this discrepancy between specimens.*

Robert spied the bones first. They were scattered now as they had been when his predecessor had come through here years before. Robert refused to speculate as to why they'd been cast asunder like this. The shelves that once displayed the jarred and preserved atrocities against nature sagged, and some had fallen from their braces. Robert did not look closer to see whether the odd lumps his clipboard-light just barely limned on the floor had once been the contents of the now-broken jars, nor did he see whether any remained unbroken. The stages, which rose so low they could barely be called such, punctuated the long, dark space. It seemed to go on forever. That gave Robert hope. His plan to keep going in one direction outside might have a chance of working in here.

His feet crunched over glass as he crept further and further through the building. Such a *lot* of glass. It was everywhere. Robert looked around and around and up. That was when he saw them, the tiny slits of night sky peeking through not just the ceiling, but the walls as well. What surrounded him had once been a great, glass greenhouse. Vines—dead or alive, it was impossible to tell—tangled all over the building, creating a nearly solid wall. Most of the glass panels must have broken beneath them or simply fallen out over the years. A few entire spots in the ceiling still remained uncovered. Through one of them, in the distance, Robert spied a great, circular metal frame…

> *We ventured to climb the Grand Wheel—a contraption of rusted gears and broken pulleys that once carried passengers inside of hanging capsules around and up, until they were over a hundred feet high in the air and could look over the entire fair and, indeed, even much of the Agate district itself.*

*The Grand Wheel,* Robert thought to himself.

Perhaps he could use it, climb just high enough to see which direction was the fastest way out. His decision made, he headed for the back of the exhibition hall. He found another door there, dashed out, and skittered from one hiding place to the next. He cursed his need for his light. It shone like a beacon. And he wasn't certain if the fact that many of the voices from before no longer cried out boded good or ill for him. He was so close to the Grand Wheel now. Robert felt hopeful that he'd soon be out. Faded but helpful signs painted onto the decrepit buildings told him he was going the right way. Then he turned the final corner.

Lying on the path like a huge, monstrous cat, one of the creatures gnawed on something hard, round, and bloody. Robert squeaked out a yelp of horror. He imagined he recognized the matted, blood-soaked hair covering part of the round thing. The thing's mouth, Robert now realized, was not jaws like those on a dog or bear, but rather a sort of short, wide trunk. The creature's head snapped up. The trunk slid off of the round thing with a wet schlooping noise. The beast's dull-mirror eyes locked onto Robert. It rose to its feet. He spun to run back the way he'd come. Behind him, emerging from the shadows, another of the creatures stalked him from behind.

Robert screamed and flailed as it knocked him to the ground. His shrieks of terror filled the night as a warm, wet something enveloped his head with a gurgle-sucking noise. He fought blindly. Something pierced his flesh. The world became slow and difficult until finally darkness overtook him.

Far within the deepest back alleys of Char, one of the smallest of the monsters beetled into a space between buildings. Not quite a square, but a largish, cluttered space created first by the organic growth of a once-prosperous section of city and then mussed by the later demolition of war. The small monster leapt onto the edge of a fountain, long dried up with a huge crack through the entire thing. Its head turned this way and that, as if seeking something. A moment later, another like it, but much larger, emerged from the darkness between an abandoned, building and a crumbling section of wall.

"There you are, Marlowe!" the smaller monster said, in a chirpy and not at all a very monstery voice. "I was worried some of those big'uns would get the better of you."

The larger one, Marlowe, replied, "One tried. He'll wake up later inside a tunnel."

"It'd be nice if they'd take the hint and sod off forever," said another voice. This one rang with more than a hint of annoyance.

A third monster entered the space, though he was more of a hybrid. Instead of the long claws, he had human-shaped hands, sheathed in smooth, black skin. And he wore regular, everyday black shoes. The smallest of them gripped itself by the spiny protrusions on its head and pulled, stretching its head and face and neck, until they came away as one piece. Beneath lay the head of a dark-skinned lad, who grinned brightly in the pale light of the crescent moon.

"Hey, Fulcrum! Didn't know you were joining us tonight."

Marlowe likewise removed his head to reveal that of a human, perhaps a few years older than the small one and sporting a stern expression.

"Catbird twisted an ankle," Marlowe said. "Had to bow out."

"Aw, that's a shame," the littlest monster said. "She'll have missed all the fun."

Fulcrum too removed his spiny cowl and glared at his small comrade. "Coal, you do know this is serious business, don't you?"

"Of course," Coal replied, still smiling, "but who says serious business can't also be fun? Everyone else had a good time. Right, Marlowe?"

Marlowe smiled in a wicked sort of way. "Yeah."

A small tendril of green poked its way up through the crack in the fountain, and Coal knelt to pluck it. "Bit of a shame we can't let anything grow."

"Strangleweed vines grow," Fulcrum said. "They're all over the Exhibition Hall."

Coal grinned again. "We stuffed the guy with the clipboard into those ones. Not gonna be fun extra-catting—"

"Extricating," Fulcrum corrected.

"—That one. Extricating himself when he comes to."

"Did you get all your props?" Fulcrum grumped. "I want to go."

Coal bounded over to his comrades. "Clover's got them."

The trio began to plod further into the Char district, chatting about the success of the night.

At one point, Coal asked, "Do you think we did it? Do you think they'll change their minds about building?"

Now Fulcrum grinned. It was not a nice grin. "If they're stubborn about it, I'm sure everyone will come together again for an even better spook shindie."

Coal's eyes grew wide. "Can you even imagine?"

# Notre Dame de Linceul

**Ef Deal**

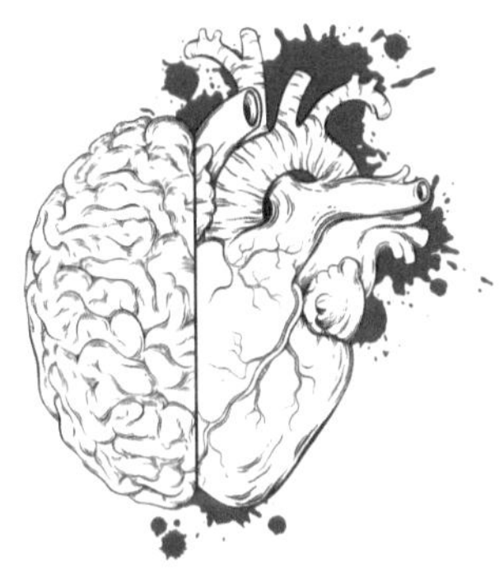

Windmills marked the crest of the Butte Montmartre, a silhouetted line of fat figures waving wild arms, their simple wooden engines whining and clacking in the night. Theirs had been the foundational power that had brought the city of Paris to its prominence in Europe and the world. Long before the industrialists had brought in their coal-fueled, steam-driven engines, the windmills established a line of farms and homesteads that gave the necessary sustenance to a growing city and a great civilization. The mists rising from the middens spoke of a simpler world even as they fueled a growing complex society of factories, industries, engines, and powers. A society with demands both ghoulish and germinal.

Inside a long-abandoned, dilapidated windmill hard up against the city wall, two companions prepared for their irregular nocturnal activity, a clandestine routine they had been assured would be sanctified —if not by the church, by the free thinkers of a future mankind especially in the world of medicine.

"You know this place is magic, don't you?"

Allard, one of those very large men, broad in the shoulders, heavily muscled, and light on brains, fidgeted with some of the gears that his mechanically-inclined companion had lying about on a workbench.

"Saint Denis. Patron saint of Paris. Got his head cut off. Picked it up and carried it all the way here. Saint Geneviève. All kinds of miracles.

She could make the dead come back to life. Do you think that's what the surgeon is trying to do?"

Hogg barely heard Allard's childish questions anymore, having no patience for the big oaf's dulled wits.

"Just so long as he pays us for these cadavers, he's helping this little piece of mankind. You and me."

"You do all the hard work," Allard said, pointing to the machine wherein Hogg sat.

"I couldn't do it without you, my friend."

"I know."

A chilling gust of wind blew through the slats of the tumble-down walls, raising dust and dirt. Allard hastened to wipe the gears clean and stack them neatly.

"Do you think they can see us?"

His deep voice, growing too loud for the hour and their task, brought Hogg up from the cockpit of his steel crab half buried in a tunnel, freshly dug the previous night, that led to the tiny church cemetery near the Porte de Clignancourt.

"Chut, you idiot. You want to tip off the flics? And put out that cigarette or someone *will* see us."

Hogg, barely a meter tall, slapped his large accomplice on the knees, then handed him a cable. "Keep alert and be ready to guide me out."

Allard crushed his cigarette. "I know the routine." He pointed vaguely to encompass the whole churchyard beyond the windmill. "Did you ever wonder if they see what we're doing to 'em?"

"Nope." Hogg checked and re-checked his helmet and goggles, pockets, and gloves to make certain all were secure. "They're dead. They're money. I'm going in."

"But you're the smartest guy I know. Why can't you get money for all your gadgets instead of stealing bodies?"

Hogg bit back a mean comment. Every time, Allard asked the same questions, made the same observations, forgot the answers Hogg gave. Why indeed did the military not see the wisdom in commanding a fleet of tunneling crabs? Why did they not appreciate advanced lenses for photography? Why did they turn down his mechanical soldier or subterranean gyroscope? Hogg didn't know, and he counted it all as prejudice against his diminutive stature. Surely no one that small could have big ideas, hein?

He climbed back inside the crab and initiated the clockwork engines, one to crawl and one to seize the coffin from underneath the fresh grave he'd targeted at the far end of the field. Assuming, that is, his compass and gyroscope had guided him accurately. Hogg trusted his calculations.

Hence his consternation when the crab was abruptly stopped less than halfway to its goal by an obstruction that had not been there when Hogg had crawled the tunnel the night before. With a snarl and a curse, he engaged the claws in an attempt to push the blockage aside and was surprised by a solid *clang* of the steel striking a large block of stone. He sat, momentarily confused, but then opened the claws tentatively, gauging their position around the block so he could close them around it. Once they seemed to accomplish that, he began maneuvering to pull it out of his tunnel in time to still get back in and retrieve the coffin from the grave before drawing attention to their endeavor.

Allard was slow to respond to the tug on the cable. Probably sneaking another cigarette. Hogg fidgeted inside the confines of the crab until he finally felt his accomplice's answering tug and engaged the reverse engines. Weighted down with stone instead of wood, the crab gained little traction, and the engines ground and whined until Allard pulled in earnest. By degrees the crab retreated and emerged with its find. Hogg popped out of the cockpit, his anger smoldering lest he let loose a stream of loud cursing, and he stomped forward to see what had thwarted his plans.

"That ain't a coffin," Allard observed with all the astuteness he possessed. "It's a sarcophagus."

It was indeed a sarcophagus of solid stone, Hogg didn't know what kind. He also didn't know the meaning of the message written along its side any more than the weird symbols that marked the lid.

"What does it say?"

"I don't know."

"I thought you could read."

Hogg glared. "I can read French. This isn't French."

Allard pondered the problem, then deduced, "Maybe the sarcophagus isn't French either."

Examining the thing, Hogg found the lid had been sealed shut, but the claws had left sizable gouges in the stone sides.

"We might be able to get whatever's in there out," he said, heading back into the crab to disengage the claws.

As steel retracted, the stone sarcophagus exhaled a noisome breath, and a lily-white arm slipped out of the hole. Allard yelped and stumbled back.

"Quiet, you moron!"

Hogg ran forward to see what had startled Allard. He grinned at the sight of a fresh body.

"Gold. Give me a hand."

Allard shook his head fiercely.

"Come on, you big baby. I can't do it myself." When the oaf folded his arms, Hogg sighed. Then he shrugged. "Hein. Twenty francs for me then, and you get nothing."

Frowning sadly, Allard surrendered. Together they worked at the hole in the stone until they wriggled the body from its entombment, then they sat back to behold their prize in wonder.

"She ain't dead," Allard said. "She don't look dead."

It was true. The woman was draped in her shroud, but the pale skin of her limbs was smooth and unblemished. No sign of decay, not even of the shroud.

"Maybe she's sleeping. Maybe she's one of them incorruptible saints. Or maybe…" Allard gulped. "A vampire."

Hogg scoffed. "All I know is, she's worth twenty. Let's go. I'll shove the crab and the thing back in the tunnel and cover it. You get the body."

He hopped into the crab to turn it around, secured the sarcophagus, and backed it all down the cleared tunnel. As he approached, he found Allard studying the markings on the lid. The body was gone.

"What did you do?" he called. "Where's the lady?"

Allard straightened and looked around like he'd just woken up. "Right—" He stopped, then scratched his head. "Oh, the devil. I told you she was a vampire!"

"Damn it, you clod! What did you do with her?"

"Nothing! I didn't touch her! I was looking at the letters and—" He wrung his hands, shifting weight from one foot to the other like he needed to pee. Tears welled up. "This is bad. This is very bad. They're not supposed to get up and walk away. Hogg, this is really bad."

Hogg kicked his shin. "Twenty francs bad. All you had to do was grab the body. Are you telling me she got up and walked away?"

Allard's eyes widened. He pointed ominously toward the distant graveyard, where a glowing figure moved along the rows of marker stones slowly, her arms spread as if conferring benediction upon the souls there. Hogg scratched his head as he watched her raise one hand toward the night sky. When a wisp of mist arose from a grave and ascended, Allard patted Hogg on the head.

"She's the Virgin Mary," he whispered in awe. "She's releasing that soul to heaven."

"Ouais, and chicken have teeth. Damn, wish I'd brought my camera." Hogg stalked off after the lady. "I'm going to see what's going on.."

Allard followed reluctantly. While Hogg flitted from gravestone to gravestone, hiding himself, Allard simply strolled, knowing he'd never be able to hide his bulk.

The lady glided, occasionally pausing to "release a soul," as Allard would say. When she reached the edge of the cemetery, she paused and turned to look back at her pursuers. She acknowledged them with a slight bow, then continued on in the direction of Montmartre.

"What do we do?"

"Follow her."

"Ho, the devil. That's the Virgin Mary, and you want to hunt her?"

She moved with grace, turning her head from left to right as though seeking something familiar. Hogg and Allard kept their distance but never let her out of sight as she climbed the Rue Damrémont. At this hour, Montmartre would likely still have some revelers. For his part, Hogg was curious to see what she would do among the guinguettes and taverns.

Couples trickling out of the taverns or stumbling down the street passed her by without notice. She stopped at a darkened cafe where a lone man sat outside, smoking. Hogg held Allard back and watched as the woman opened her arms. The man stood and went to her. To Hogg's shock, she kissed the man, intimately, like an old lover. When she stepped back from him, he crumpled to the pavement, wisps rising from his body.

As the woman turned, Hogg and Allard scuttled back into an alley, pressing to the wall to escape her view. The seconds pounded in Hogg's ear until finally she appeared, but instead of passing them, she halted in the alleyway, silhouetted by gaslight. Hogg held his breath, but Allard, the buffoon, couldn't help gushing.

"She's so beautiful."

She half-turned to them, again with that slight bow, then continued on her way to the cemetery.

"What's she doing?"

"I don't know."

"Should we follow her?"

Hogg smacked his leg. "There's a fresh dead body. Still warm. Twenty-five francs. Let's go."

They came out of the alley, but they found no sign of the lady in the shroud.

"Notre Dame du Linceul," Allard murmured. "Our Lady of the Shroud. She blessed us."

"She blessed us with a body. Come on."

Adopting one of their means of avoiding the flics, Allard hoisted the body of the dead man over his shoulder like a drunk buddy.

"He's not bleeding."

"Better still."

Allard chuckled. "He's still, all right."

They left Montmartre and headed to the back door of the surgeon who would reward them handsomely for their haul.

Not surprisingly, it didn't take long for Allard and Hogg to burn through their francs. Meanwhile, no rumor of any murder came to their ears, nor any word of the unusual sarcophagus, so they counted themselves safe. When another funeral was scheduled, Hogg went that night to scope out the cemetery and ready the crab to tunnel. To his surprise, the pale, graceful figure of the shrouded woman again drifted among the graves.

She turned his way, nodded, then moved out to the boulevard. Hogg followed cautiously, more curious than afraid. Though she strolled casually as a woman might stroll the Champs-Élysées window-shopping or taking in the air, Hogg suspected her goal was a bit more sinister—and perhaps more profitable for him. His stature might prevent him from making off with the body, but he still had enough francs in his pocket to buy an accomplice to haul for him.

She eschewed the tavern district this time in favor of the warehouses. When she reached the second one, a man posted outside the gates accosted her.

"You're out late, chérie. Shouldn't be out by yourself. Come here."

To Hogg's delight, he grabbed her wrist and yanked her into his embrace, kissing her brutally. She didn't fight him, nor did she hold him as she had held the other. Nevertheless, the man's grip eased just before he too sagged to the ground. She glanced at Hogg, nodded, then began her walk back to the cemetery.

Hogg scratched his head as he stood over the corpse. No wounds, no blood. Poison kiss? Suck out their life? What was her secret? He shrugged, considering his options. He doubted he could conscript another warehouse guard to help, but now he wasn't sure he had time to get to the taverns where he could hire someone.

A tap on his shoulder startled him. He yiped to see the lady had returned. She again nodded to the body.

"I'm not… " He indicated his own stumpy form. "I can't lift him," he explained.

She took a moment, then bowed and moved off.

Frustrated, Hogg snatched his hat off his head and threw it to the ground. With much effort he pushed the body into the doorway and curled it over, then tucked his cap over the face so it looked like a vagrant sleeping. He went back to the boulevard to wait until a suitable candidate appeared. The man agreed to three francs and happily carried the body to the surgeon's back door without pursuing gainful employment on a regular basis. By then it was too late to complete his task at the cemetery, which meant Hogg would have to forgo the funeral the next day, and Allard would be out of luck and out of his share of the warm-body bounty. He was sure the lady would make it up to them.

He wasn't wrong. The following night, while Allard expected the routine of Hogg retrieving the fresh coffin via the tunnel, they instead followed the ethereal shrouded woman, "Notre Dame de Linceul," as Allard insisted on calling her. That, or "the Lady."

"I think the Lady blesses us because we released her from the sarcophagus," he said.

Hogg had entertained the same thought, which made him uneasy. What was she? A demon. A ghoul, a real ghoul. Had she been alive while entombed in stone? Would those markings tell anyone the answers? The surgeon was educated; maybe he'd know somebody who knew somebody who'd know. Hogg made a mental note to bring his photography equipment to get a record of the sarcophagus.

The Lady blessed them with a drunk old woman this time. Allard carried her like a child in his arms.

"So I think she knows what we do with them," he concluded. "Notre Dame de Linceul."

Hogg wagged his head. His obtuse accomplice never questioned the provenance of their benefactress. He made up his mind to come to the cemetery in daylight to get tintypes of the writing and symbols.

For the next few weeks, each night they visited the cemetery, the Lady received them and led them forth as she hunted down prey, providing them with fresh corpses. Meanwhile, Hogg got his tintypes and took them to the professor at the School of Antiquities recommended by the surgeon. He also found himself a safe place to cache his sudden riches lest their nocturnal endeavors were discovered, or worse yet, someone robbed his room. Though he had advised Allard to be as wary, the big oaf claimed he was big enough to beat down anyone trying to rob him.

"You're going to get rolled," Hogg warned. "They'll come at you with a knife, maybe a gun. You have to hide that money."

"I did hide it. It's under a floorboard under my bed."

"Chut! Don't let anyone hear you say that." Hogg slapped him on the knee with his cap.

Allard grinned and pointed to the distant graves. "They're dead."

Hogg sighed. "At least you got that part into your head."

As the surgeon handed over the bounty that night, he also handed over a note from the School of Antiquities. "You boys are being careful? It's quite the epidemic. Handling all these bodies, don't want you to succumb too." He winked.

Hogg chuckled. "I think we're on the right side of it."

"Just be careful. Cholera comes on quickly."

*Cholera?*

"These all died of cholera?" He gulped with a guilty look toward Allard, who had toted so many bodies over the past few weeks.

"Be careful," the surgeon said again.

Paris stank. From the rancid charnel of the surgeon's lab to the sour stench of the brick factories, from the manure piles of the farms to the sewage trenches along the roads, Paris was a noxious nightmare. Hogg huddled over a pint of ale in a Pigalle guinguette, where Nini-la-Folle sang on Thursday nights to a badly-tuned-piano accompaniment, and unfolded the letter from the Antiquities professor. He expected to find a translation of the runish language and an explanation of the symbols. Instead, he read:

*My dear sir:*

*I implore you with all earnestness not to touch or attempt to open the container upon which these images captured in tintype were found. The baleful markings give every indication of a prehistoric evil that early Germanic tribes called "Peacemaker." A variety of myths from the Scandinavians down to the Parisii tell of a great evil that fell from the outer darkness into this world giving birth to disease and pestilence in order to feast upon the dead. The tintypes you provided indicate Peacemaker was captured and bound by "blood magic" into the container. Regardless of whether we can believe tales of monsters from the expanse of the universe or of the power of mere mortals to bind such creatures, I can assure you that whoever sealed this container believed it to possess the power to decimate populations, and it therefore most likely harbors a danger to all who attempt to open it. I can only suggest you notify the University Museum who will reward you handsomely for such a significant archaeological find.*

*Sincerely yours,*

*Professeur M —*

Hogg fingered the letter idly as he pondered its content. He could not accept that the Lady was evil, much less a creature from outward space. Allard's belief that she was the Virgin Mary made more sense, and Hogg didn't believe that either. He liked to think of himself as a man of science, even if his life's works had amounted to nothing. He'd always hoped he'd be accepted into the Academy one day, but not this way — through the back door of a surgeon's laboratory, snatching bodies, peddling flesh. Someone like Hogg, 100 centimeters of brilliance, could never be accepted as an equal to someone like Faraday, Brunel, or Jacqueline Duval. He should have known he'd be outcast by an unenlightened society.

Having his name attached to a major archaeological find wouldn't be a bad way to thumb his nose at the world. Enough money to invest, maybe go somewhere, lie on a beach in the West Indies.

That would leave Allard out of a source of income. Maybe a few tintypes of the Lady herself could garner him a bit of a nest egg. And honestly, Allard didn't need Hogg just to follow the Lady around and pick up her droppings. So long as there were bodies and surgeons to pay for them, Allard would be okay financially.

Except he was so obtuse he probably couldn't remember the way to the surgeon's back door without Hogg.

No, he would assure Allard's income before leaving, but leaving with a lot of money and some scientific credit was the right decision.

He headed back to the windmill to begin work on a new system for his photography, a system that might make the development of the tintype simultaneous with the ejection of the slide. He tinkered and hammered and wired through the rest of the morning, pausing around noon for some coffee.

Sunlight streamed through tattered slats, setting the gold symbols on the sarcophagus aglow. Hogg perused them again, trying to find indications that some great evil threatened Paris. A rectangular spiral, a box with an arrow pointing northwest, three concentric circles, something that looked like a fish standing on two legs, a single inverted triangle. How could anyone make a clear interpretation of it, much less construe a creature from beyond?

A shift in the air made him shiver and glance about. Diaphanous and aetherial, the Lady watched him from the foot of the sarcophagus. The cerement that draped her entire body but the willowy arms that had escaped its folds gave no indication of its cultural source—no cross, no ankh, no symbols like the ones on the sarcophagus. Still, Hogg couldn't deny that in her presence, he felt safe, he felt a beneficence, he felt forgiven.

He rubbed his nose, acknowledging his sins before her as he cleared his throat and addressed her.

"They say you're not from here. You're not human. I know that's true enough after seeing what you do."

The drafts billowed her shroud, but she remained unmoved. She made no indication she understood or was even listening.

"See you over the graves pulling something out of them. Then I see you with these people, something comes out of them. Then the surgeon says they all got cholera. Don't know what to make of it all."

The Lady lifted her head slightly, raising her left arm in that way that seemed like a prayer.

"Ouais, that's what I thought. You ain't talking. That's all right. You keep your secrets. But you keep Allard safe, hein? You're not gonna hurt him?"

He bent back to his photography project, creating a chamber he would attach to the camera so the plate would slide automatically into a developing bath, ignoring the Lady's silent vigil for the next two hours until he felt the first pangs of hunger. He set aside his screwdriver and wiped his brow.

"Got to eat," he said. "I don't suppose you eat."

To his surprise, the Lady bowed slightly. Was it a nod? Yes, she did eat, or yes, Hogg was right? He shrugged.

"Shall I bring something back for you?"

For answer, she turned and left the windmill, pausing at the door to make sure Hogg followed her. She descended the hillside into the village where she began to bend her head this way and that toward each doorway, slowing, and finally stopped and faced the door of a narrow farmhouse where, amid the barking of a dog and the flustered clucking of chickens, a baby wailed and screamed in pain. She waited patiently for several long minutes, her arms spread in their beneficent call, and after a few minutes, the door opened.

"No, no, no, no." Hogg held his breath. "Don't do it," he pleaded silently.

But the farmer's wife gazed adoringly up at the shrouded Lady and passed the child into her arms before closing the door again. Hogg watched the Lady snuggle the child, leaning in to nuzzle its tiny face. The crying stopped. It gave a short giggle, then was silent.

"Oh, no. Oh, no."

She turned back and glided toward him. He stood frozen as she drew so close he could smell fresh dirt as she laid the dead baby in his arms. Hogg could barely breathe, barely speak.

"Wh-what did you do?"

But the Lady was already climbing the path up to the windmill.

*She thinks we're eating the bodies. She thinks she's feeding us.*

Hogg wept silently as he followed, having no idea what to do with the tiny corpse in his arms. He doubted the surgeon would want it, but he couldn't be sure. On the other hand, how could he explain a baby? Obviously not a drunk off the street, not a murder victim, not a vagrant found in a doorway. Also not wrapped in burial clothes, therefore, clearly not snatched from a grave.

Miserable, Hogg took the infant into the windmill and set its little body on the sarcophagus. The Lady was nowhere to be seen. Hogg sat on his workbench, smoking steadily, his stomach churning. Evening came on, and with it Allard carrying frites wrapped in newspaper.

"I got these for you," he said, then he stared at the baby. "What's this?"

Hogg scowled. "Our Lady of Peace."

Allard snorted and laughed. "Our Lady of Farts?" When Hogg didn't laugh, he repeated, "*Paix*? *Pets*? Get it?"

Hogg sighed. "She thinks it's my supper."

Allard pondered that in his slow way, then said, "That makes sense, I suppose. She sends the souls straight to heaven, and we take the bodies away, so..."

"No. It does not make sense." Hogg slammed his fist on the sarcophagus side near the dead baby. "Why would the Virgin Mary think we're eating people? Why would she give me this to snack on? What do you think she really is? Because it's monstrous!"

Ducking, Allard shrank back, frightened by his companion's anger. "Monster?" He shook his head vehemently. "She brought us hundreds of francs. Hundreds, maybe a million. She's not a monster. We're the monsters. People die, they get buried, waiting for Judgment Day. We steal them and the surgeon chops them up, the ones we bring him. So they never get resurrected when the Christ comes back. So, no, we're the monsters."

"All these bodies she brings us, they have cholera!" Hogg shouted. "We could die!"

"Everybody dies, Hogg."

"Well, I don't want to die of cholera."

"We haven't gotten sick," Allard argued. "She's keeping us safe. She blesses us. Don't you?" he said, turning to the Lady who had reappeared among them.

He drew closer to her, gazing in wonder and love into her veiled face. "We set you free, and you set us free by giving us money. Ain't that right?"

Hogg bowed his head, frustrated. "Allard..."

"She loves us. She's no monster."

The Lady raised her hand to Allard. Hogg's chest tightened as she reached for the big man. He hurried to come between them and shoved Allard back from her.

"Don't let her touch you!" He whirled on the Lady looming another half meter over him, and wagged his finger at her. "Show him your face," he said. "Go on, take off that shroud and show us your face."

He grabbed his modified camera and loaded it with a freshly prepared tintype slide. He turned the lens on the Lady and said, "Come on. Show him. Show the world what you are!"

He threw the focusing cape over his head and framed her shrouded face. When he snapped a photo, the slide popped into the developing chamber. He slapped another slide in and and came out from under. He stared into the beautiful face of the Lady of the Shroud.

More than glorious, her serene smile and the depths of sorrow in her dark brown eyes spoke of wisdom, compassion, and a deeper love than Hogg had ever known. The love he was told God had for all mankind. A caring, caressing love. A love that knew what Hogg did, understood why he did it, and desired to reassure him he was known and forgiven. Her eyes, wide and glistening with tears, met his, inviting him in, begging him to accept her with as much loving generosity.

"She is *so beautiful,*" Allard said in a hushed voice.

Hogg went back under the cape to be certain he could capture such exquisite pulchritude. He pressed his eye to the lens, then screamed with a terror that burst from the depth of his heart. Reflexively he snapped the photo as he fell backward, striking his head on the sarcophagus and dropping into darkness.

Allard hurried to Hogg and lifted him into his arms.

"Hogg! Hogg!" He looked up at the Lady. "He's dead. He's dead! How come he's dead?"

The Lady smiled her loving smile. Covering her face again, she glided from the windmill.

Torn, Allard watched her go. He should follow her. He should continue the routine he knew. But Hogg…

Allard burst into tears, hugging his dead companion. "I don't know what to do next," he blubbed. "She wants me to go with her. She wants me to carry on. Hogg, Hogg. I will miss you so much."

Blinded with tears, he set his friend down on top of the sarcophagus next to the dead baby and wiped his nose in his sleeve as he combed back Hogg's hair, caressing him as one would a child, but as he turned to follow the Lady, he accidentally kicked the tripod leg. The camera crashed to the dust and the newly built developer fell apart, revealing the final two tintypes in stunning detail.

Her shrouded face, her open arms, the graceful bend of her neck. *Notre Dame de Linceul.*

Then…

Ophidian eyes. Gaping saurian maw ringed with a hundred tiny, sharp teeth. Hooked tongue whipping toward the photographer's screaming mouth.

Allard studied the two portraits for a moment. Shoving the first in his pocket, he laid the other on Hogg's chest and kissed his brow. He followed the Lady out into the night.

# A Legacy of Fangs

*A Van Helsing Tale*

## Teel James Glenn

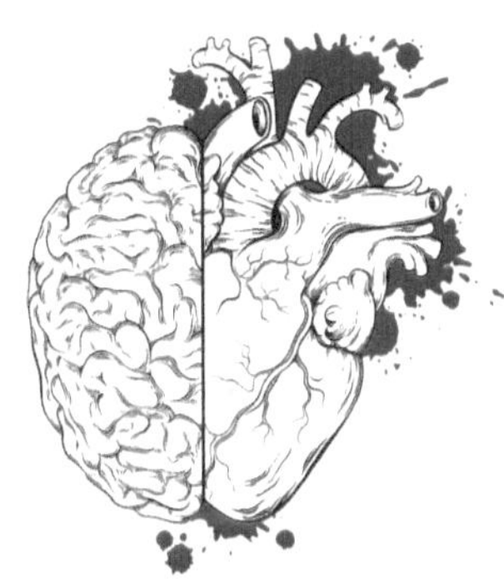

I write this account for you, grandson, as I am long in the tooth now. I have lived my life in accordance with the ancient edicts of our family and hope to have made you proud. I thought to tell you of a stranger that came to our land and the mark he made.

Aye, it were a simpler time then, not so many of these clinkers on the road and the sky were not yet filled with the great behemoths of the air steaming from the continent to dip on our shores then skip across the big waters to far-off America.

Oh, we had an occasional dirigible stop by with mail before it went across the ocean, and some of our local farmers had themselves steambots to replace their old, worn-out mares, but here in Killkracke it were a simple life, much like it had been for our ancestors.

Good Queen Victoria were on the throne in England and a body could walk a few miles down the road without ever looking behind for fear of some gashing steam carriage running them down.

I were fit young and strong, and it were up to me to watch over our people in the family tradition. And as constable it fell on my shoulders when the murders happened, for me to find the killer.

Aye, they were bloody things, all four young girls taken in the fullness of their youth by some creature of the night in four successive months. Each on the second night of the full moon.

We searched day and night, using the dogs to track, but try as we might we found no trace of any killer, man or beast, as the hounds balked at tracking, the scent of whatever creature it was seeming to confound them. We followed the physical tracks that were clear at the sites of the deaths, animal tracks that seemed to be of a large beast, but always they went to rocky ground or into a stream as if the beast knew we would try to track it. Cunning it were, not normal cunning. Monstrous cunning.

After the second death the word reached the county seat in Cork City and they took a dim view, thinking us country folks had not the brains to find our own behinds. When the third happened and I had not found the culprit they thought they should send an expert, a foreign fellah by the name of Van Helsing.

Now it was the day before the fifth full moon and I was in the town center to meet the expert fella, a Dutchman. It was a fine spring day and the steam coach from the capital came clanking and huffing into the village square.

He came down the ramp from the coach with two-wheeled steam-bots carrying his bags. The Dutchman was a bit older than me, of medium height, strongly built, with his shoulders set back over a broad, deep chest. His poise seemed to tell of a thoughtful and powerful man.

"Professor?" I says, extending my hand as I took the measure of him. His face was clean-shaven with a hard, square chin, a large resolute, mobile mouth, a good-sized nose, rather straight, but with quick, sensitive nostrils. He had big, dark blue eyes beneath busy eyebrows and a broad forehead.

"I'm Conri Mac Tir, constable of this here county and of this lovely town, at your service. They telefaxed that you were coming." He fixed his eyes on me as I stepped up to greet him.

"Yawh," he said in a clear voice. His handshake was firm, and I liked that he looked me directly in the eye. It didn't hurt my opinion of him that his hair was as red as mine. He touched his chest over his heart and gave a small nod. "Is good," he said. "We take my bags to hotel, then we investigate, time is short is it not?"

"As soon as you wish," I said. We walked down the cobbled main street, with me waving to the curious townsfolk. Back then we didn't get many strangers in the village.

"I wish to see where the last girl died," the Dutchman said, all business.

He were city folk and so city impatient, not that I could blame him. The pressure to find the killer before there were more deaths weighed on my shoulders. And Bridget Rose McConnell, the last of the slaughtered colleens, was a sweet thing and cursed be the one that took her from us.

I welcomed any solution to the horror and was not so arrogant to think I had all the answers, and in fact, at that moment I had none.

"It's just a bit out of town," I told him when we dropped his bags at the inn.

He was all for heading out directly and we did so afoot, as the path the poor dead girl had taken was not accessible by one of the steam carriages. He seemed to revel in the physical activity, which made me respect him as most city folk seemed soft to me, always 'why walk when you could ride.'

The spot where the body of the last poor girl were found was off the main road, up a little used path to the old settlement. A fire two decades before had taken most of the buildings and no one had bothered to rebuild, so only decaying skeletons of the dwellings were left. It were eerie even in the afternoon light, the ground still blackened, with only the stone church and a few of the peat houses looking much like dwellings anymore. It was just off a path between the old church and the girl's home.

"You say that the tracks of the killer all went to rocks or water at each site?" The Dutchman studied the ground around where we found Bridget Rose's mortal remains.

"Her father had said she went to the old churchyard once a week to place flowers on the old graves that had no family members left." I said, "A sweet angel."

"I have read the reports of the other deaths," Van Helsing said. "The nature of the wounds—"

"They were the same with Bridget Rose," I said. "Raw wounds, great tears in the flesh. Horrid."

"This is no surprise," the Dutchman said. He walked the whole area with his eyes on the ground and then asked that we walk toward the abandoned church and the graveyard beside it.

"I can see she had done her work," Van Helsing said as we surveyed the fresh flowers on half a dozen old graves. "Indeed, an angel and she seems to have met a devil."

I stood by while the old gentleman looked around the graveyard as if he would find the answer on that once-hallowed ground. He stooped to take one of the flowers from a grave and sniffed it.

"Yawh," he said after a long moment where I thought he might tear up as he replaced the flower. "A devil for certain."

"Well, what do you want to do after this, professor?" I asked. "We've done again all that I had—and I have to say I am at a complete dead end. I've lost the scent altogether."

The Dutchman looked at me with an odd expression, his mouth in a ghost of a smile.

"You are certain the young women were killed where you found them, not somewhere else and then brought there?"

"A sad truth," I said. "It was clear each girl was surprised and killed with almost no chance to run; the tracks made that clear. And the blood loss in the area around each made it clear the beast killed them on the spot."

"And it did not feed?"

"No, there was no evidence of that," I said with disgust. "It killed, it would seem, for the sheer joy of the slaughter. They died in absolute agony."

"And did you use dogs?"

"Yes, but they seemed to shy at the spoor of the beast," I said. "They would follow for a short distance then suddenly stop, became skittish, and would not go any further."

He pondered this, his right hand tapping over his heart, apparently a nervous gesture. After a time he said, "You have a map of the area?"

I did.

I took a map of the countryside and spread it on top of a wide gravestone. On it, I had marked where the other bodies were found, including the latest abomination where Bridget Rose died.

"Here we are," I said, pointing out the graveyard on the paper.

"And so," The Dutchman said pointing to the map. "Here is the place of each death. Do you notice that they all are spaced evenly from each other, though the center of their circle is not the town?"

"Yes, I noticed that," I said. "But it did not suggest any pattern."

"Ah, perhaps, if you were to look at them in isolation, but this is where we will look for our monster." He pointed at a space at the center of the marks.

"What do you mean?"

"Notice how each of them are in a different location outside the town—this is a beast trying to throw us off, but not being very bright, yawh? Each death is the distance from this central place, a distance that one could reasonably travel in night and safely return to a den again by dawn."

He indicated an area that I had not thought any beast would den in the area.

"That is the Snowdon Manor House," I said. "And the small village of Shane's Folly—only a dozen huts, really, that had housed the workers that served the old English landlord in times past. There are so many people in these areas, why would a hunting animal avoid all those people and go so far afield?"

"An animal would not," Van Helsing said. "A natural animal. This creature we hunt is a thing of the devil, a supernatural beast."

"You believe in such things?"

"I believe the English playwright Shakespeare spoke of 'things not dreamt of'—I have seen and dealt with such things, most recently in the Carpathians. It is the reason I did not come earlier here—would that I could have prevented the fourth death."

"But what sort of beast could be so savage? So cunning?"

"In the Carpathians, they speak of men who can transform into beasts—wolves. And in the nights of the full moon in France, the Loup Garo is accepted as existing."

"Really?" I did my best to sound shocked.

"So it is that an animal of an unnatural reality—guided by a human intelligence—might be careful to hunt far from its den." The Dutchman raised his eyeline to look off in the direction of Snowdon Manor. "The light it goes, yawh? Soon darkness will make investigation impossible, constable," he said. "Also, I am tired. Let us return to the inn that we may dine. And early tomorrow—"

"Yes," I agreed, trying to hide my anxiousness about the coming full moon. "It's always better to face monsters in daylight with a full belly, eh?"

"Yawh," he agreed with a jovial smile. "As Shakespeare also said, "Man does not live by bread alone—it is good to have beer and beef as well.""

The walk back to town was uneventful but I suspect we both stepped more briskly than with our outward journey.

That night in the pub, the Dutchman proved to be an amiable drinking companion, speaking freely of home, his family — now deceased — and of his various adventures. He was quite a learned man, but that did not stop him being a fascinating storyteller, and I could not help but think he had a bit of the Irish in him.

Most curious were tales he told of his battle with a Transylvanian nobleman who had made a pact with dark forces for eternal life.

"It's a wild tale, for sure," I said when he concluded his story on a hair-raising battle in the mountains of Europe among a tribe of Eastern Travelers. "I'd say it's hard to believe, were you not looking me directly in the eye and that you had lived it."

The Dutchman laughed. "Yet I did live it, but you must admit it is no more so than the old tales of the Wolves of Ossory in your own country."

"How so?" I said, not quite liking him suddenly bringing up old tales.

"The legendary figure of this land, *Laignech Fáelad*, who served the people, was said to be able to transform into a wolf at will," Van Helsing said.

I laughed at that myself. "Every schoolchild knows that old tale, it is said his descendants gave rise to the Kings of Ossory. But — wolves have been extinct for centuries in Ireland."

"I know," he said. "Why your ancestors bred your wolfhounds. For once wolves were very plentiful here."

"Are you saying someone might have brought one here or trained a dog to do these killings?"

"Anything is possible," the Dutchman said. "And with that I should leave you for the night, constable, I am not a young man and must have my rest."

"Goodnight, professor, I have to coordinate the townsfolk and some deputies to set up watch posts for tomorrow — we have warned all the people to stay indoors, but there are always some who do not listen. I'll see you bright and early, and we can take a steamcart to Shane's Folly."

"I shall be ready," he said with an attempt at a formal bow, though he wobbled slightly. "Fear not, we will defeat this evil. Sleep well."

The next day we got a later start than I wanted for my need to coordinate with the men from town to get watchers set about. I were determined that this full moon, no one would die.

So it were late morning before we rolled into Shane's Folly. That hamlet is no longer there, grandson, but it were northwest of Killkracke, a cluster of peat houses in the old style that was home to some farmers and a stone blacksmith's shop. All the way there in the steamcart the next morning the Dutch fellah unnerved me a bit, seeming to know more than he was telling me, but I could not press him too close.

"I don't see why an animal would den in so populated an area and travel so far to hunt," I said, hoping he would confide in me what he knew.

"One who expects to be hunted might," he said, "one controlled by a devious and evil mind."

"Where can we begin to look for such a mind?"

"Perhaps here, in this little hamlet," he said. "I would assume not just anyone would have the skill or wit to make such a pact with the forces of evil, for it is said that—in the Balkans, at least—only a pact with the devil and the forces of evil gives one the ability to transform to bestial shape."

"But anyone can be evil," I observed. "A heart can turn to evil for many reasons, desperation, cruelty…"

"Such pacts require study, the learning of ancient spells," Van Helsing said. "Devils, it seems are picky, eh?"

The steambot clanking into Shane's Folly brought out the inhabitants, who seldom had visitors, and almost never ones driving a'bot.

"Mac Tir," Maryanne Chappell called as I climbed down. She was the unofficial 'headman' of the little hamlet since her father, a blacksmith who served that function had passed away two years before. She was a tall, darkhaired lass with a ready smile but a temper that kept all the lads around in line. "What brings you out this way? Not another girl after the McConnell child…?"

"No, thank the Lord," I said. "No one since Bridget Rose, but the moon is coming full, so I wanted to make sure you warned your folk to take care."

"You don't have to tell us," she said. "We lock our doors these days like we never did. Have you any idea the beast responsible?"

"We're working on it, Maryanne," I told her. I turned to introduce Van Helsing, but the Dutchman had wandered off and was walking the perimeter of the hamlet, his eyes fixed on the ground, his hand tapping over his heart as if he were impatient.

"Professor," I called. He looked up at me, and for a moment, his eyes seemed hooded, even angry. Then his face lit in a gentle smile.

"Yawh," he said. "I was just looking."

"For what?"

"Ah," he said. "I was not sure, but there was nothing. I think we must continue to look."

We had Maryanne show us around the hamlet, and I talked with all of the folks we met. The Dutchman followed behind, his hand still nervously tapping his heart but he said nothing. We kept at this for some time, and when we had spoken to everyone we had made a wide circle of the hamlet.

It was only then, when I felt we had exhausted all places a den could be, that I blurted out, "Excuse me, professor, but time is wasting. You were supposed to know more about this than me, fellah, but I ain't seen it," before I could stop myself.

This made the Dutchman laugh. "I did not mean to be so obtuse, constable. I just wanted to be absolutely certain with my postulations before I said anything. I think we would be better served if we go to this manor house you spoke of. It is near?"

"Yes, it's up the road a piece. But night is coming, time grows short."

"Yawh, but still, let us walk? Good for the circulation."

As startled as I was, I could do nothing but agree. We set off walking toward the Snowdon Manor House. I can tell you, grandson, I was impatient, for this expert seemed as lost as I and the first night of the full moon would be upon us before we knew it. We *had* to find the killer!

"Why not ride," I asked when we were out of the hamlet. I'd been the one to decry the soft ways of the city folk, but it seemed we were wasting time to walk the kilometer to the manor. As we left the main track to head up the long dirt road he saw my apprehension.

"I have a reason to progress slowly, constable." He stopped by an outcropping of rock that cast a shadow across the path.

"I feel I have progressed too slowly already; that I've failed so far," I said. "I admit I am stumped, if I were not I might have resented the government sending in an outside expert, but I feel you're holding something back from me."

The Dutchman shook his head, his expression becoming somber. "I understand your concerns, Constable Mac Tir, as my methods are my own—I can only ask that you trust me a little while longer, I believe we are very close to your killer. I think by nightfall we may have an answer."

There was something in the sincerity of the fellah that made me want to trust him—that, and I had no clew myself to pursue. He did seem to have experience with such goings on, and there had been little more than a local rowdy for me to deal with for an age. Certainly, no crime like the murders of colleens.

"As you say, professor, I will trust you, but it is not an easy thing for me to be passive." This brought a chuckle from him.

"I would think not, Mister Mac Tir. I would think you are used to being at the head of the pack, not bringing up the rear, eh?"

Once more, grandson, he seemed to know more than he should, but I felt at road's end for what to do, for to confront him directly for his insinuations could spell disaster—he represented the government, and as you know, outsiders really don't know how things are here. So, I simply nodded when he indicated we should move on toward Snowdon Hall.

We came upon the once magnificent manor house as a layer of clouds darkened the sky prematurely.

"Looks like a storm brewing," I commented as we walked up the wide circular carriage way to the manor.

"Yawh," the Dutchman said. "Who lives here?"

"English fellah," I said. "Doctor Chaney, who is some sorta distant relative of the late Snowdon family. He don't come into town much."

"A doctor you say?"

"That is what I've heard, but what sort, I have no knowledge."

"How long has he been here?"

"Two years," I said. "The place was empty for a long time after the old Earl passed."

"He has not done much to maintain the grounds," the Dutchman said as he looked at the disreputable shape of much of the building. Some windows showed cracks, the flower beds in front were overgrown, and there looked to be some damage to part of the roof.

"Funny that, he's had enough loads of materials shipped in for it. A number of the merchants were happy for his business."

Van Helsing strode directly up to the front door of the building, raised the brass knocker, and struck it. The sound echoed hollowly.

"We are losing time, professor," I protested. The sky was darkening almost to twilight though it was only mid-afternoon. "If there are any clews out here for where the monster's den is, the rain will erase them."

"Perhaps," he said as he tapped his hand over his heart again. "So, it is good we get in out of the weather, yawh?"

Before I could respond, the door swung open, and a steambot butler painted in livery colors appeared. The machine had a single central eye on its dome top and spoke from his grill. "Good day, gentles. How may I serve you?"

"We are here to see Doctor Chaney," the Dutchman said.

The 'bot clicked and buzzed, then said. "Who may I say is calling?"

"Constable Conri Mac Tir," I interposed myself. "And this is—"

"Just a visitor assisting the constable," Van Helsing quickly cut me off. I said nothing but shot him a look of surprise. He gave me a calm, reassuring smile.

"Please enter and wait," the 'bot said then spun and clanked away.

We stepped into the foyer, closing the door behind us just as the sky opened and a downpour started. When I looked at him with a questioning expression he said, "It is better sometimes to keep cards close to the vest, as the Americans say, yawh?"

We waited in silence while the sound of the storm roared into a full banshee scream and the rain began to pelt against the building like pagan drums.

"The good doctor does not seem to be much on social graces," the Dutchman said. He studied the space before us, all the while his hand tapping on his heart in his now usual manner.

I had to agree with him, however, for the smell of the interior of the manor house was musty as if the building had not been lived in for some time. As I looked closer at the hall, the space beyond also seemed not to have had much attention.

"Makes a fella wonder what all those supplies were destined for," I said. A moment later the 'bot butler rolled back and stood before us.

"Please follow me, gentles," the machine intoned. "The master will see you in his workroom."

The 'bot whirled about and led us along a marble-floored hallway to the right. I took the lead while the Dutchman followed, his eyes scanning left and right, his hand now pressed firmly over his heart. It made me worry if he had a condition that should warrant my attention.

As if I needed more to worry about.

I could only hope that a storm might keep both the townsfolk and the killer in. And give me another month to hunt them down, since the Dutchman seemed to be as lost for suspects as I.

The corridor. which I suspect had been grand in its day, was as dingy as the foyer had been; the floor-to-ceiling windows had obviously not been cleaned lately and would benefit from the downpour.

The gaslamps lit automatically along the corridor as we rounded a turn to what must have been a wing of the main building. Here, there were more signs of it being lived in, the floor worn, with a number of crates and building supplies lining the walls.

The 'bot stopped before a closed double door. It was a massive portal of dark wood with a crystal lock on it. While the 'bot hummed the tone to unlock the door I whispered to the Dutchman.

"This is a waste of time, professor," I said. "There is a killer out—"

"I ask only that you have patience and stay alert," he said. "I think we shall soon have answers. We could not do much out there now in any case."

His last statement, at least, was true, for the storm had reached a peak fury, hammering at the windows, and the sky was as black at night outside. It felt like an ill omen…

The massive doors opened wide, spilling bright yellow light out from the room ahead of us.

"Come in," a reedy voice called. "It is not often I get visitors."

The room before us appeared to have once been a ballroom, now converted into a workroom, with large metal structures along most walls. There were strange lenses in an array as well, with the whole thing butted up against a floor-to-ceiling window, much like a telescope might have been, though not like any telescope I had ever seen or heard of.

There were also stone panels aligned on an interior wall, such as I had seen in museums. They were covered with hieroglyphs and images of Egyptian gods.

"Ah, yes," the lord of the manor said with a chuckle, "It is an impressive collection, isn't it? Took me decades to amass and decipher."

The man who stood in the center of the room was the most extraordinary figure I had ever seen.

He wore a purple velvet, old-style coat and waistcoat, was tall with narrow shoulders and long arms, and had a long, thin neck on which was perched an oversized head. He had a shock of black hair worn long that formed a wild halo around his skull, emphasizing a wide, high forehead.

It was the eyes of this unusual figure that was most arresting, however. They were wide with watery blue pupils that one of a more literary bent might call 'poet's eyes.' They were hypnotic and powerful when he focused them on me.

"Doctor Chaney," I managed to say. "I am Conri Mac Tir."

"Yes," he said, exaggeratedly bobbing his head, "So my 'bot Jarvis said." He held up a pince-nez to peer at we two visitors. "But who is this distinguished gentleman with you, constable? He seems somehow familiar."

He took a step toward us, then, dropping the glasses to dangle on the lanyard around his neck, he clapped his hands and did a little jig.

"Ah yes, I know now!" He laughed. "Oh ho! Distinguished indeed."

I looked to my companion whose expression remained dour.

"Do I have the pleasure of addressing Professor Abraham Van Helsing, MD, D Ph, D litt?" Doctor Chaney said.

The Dutchman clicked his heels and gave a slight bow. "I am he. Have we met?"

"Not at all," our host said, "but I attended your lecture series in Geneva three years ago, on the value of ancient documents on the sciences — lost arts and such. It was most instructive." The tall man giggled and bowed. "Most instructive indeed!"

The man waved at the array of lenses that pointed out the window. "You see before you the fruits of my labors, which followed understanding that came to me after your so informative lectures."

"To what end?" the Dutchman said. "These seem —"

"Extreme?" Chaney said. "Ha, just so. Extreme to the outer edges of knowledge."

I could feel a tension between the two, suddenly and Van Helsing gave me no indication why.

"Knowledge without moral compass is evil," the Dutchman said.

Our host's aspect abruptly darkened. His eyes narrowed, and his jaw clenched. "So, you know?"

"I merely suspected until I saw this apparatus," Van Helsing said.

"I should have known they would send you," Chaney said. "For are you not also a metaphysician and student of alchemy?"

"Professor?" I asked. "Are you saying this man has something to do with the deaths?"

"Yawh, constable," he said. "He has stumbled on the secrets of the ancients—the transmutation of matter."

"You mean like the Philosopher's Stone? Lead to gold?"

"And human to more," Chaney said. He stepped to the center of an elaborate diagram on the floor which I had not noticed before. "The jackal-headed god, the cat-headed goddess, and the other deities of Egypt were not metaphors. They were *fact!*" He touched a lever just at arms' reach and the machinery of the 'telescope' whirred.

Abruptly the tall man was enveloped in a silvery glow. I felt a strange electric charge in the air, a tingling all over my body. He looked directly at us and grinned in the maddest way.

"Using crystals, I have harnessed the power of moonlight." The machines hummed louder and the glow around Chaney intensified. "I have enough power stored from the last months and I will replenish it with tonight's—after you are dealt with."

That was when Professor Van Helsing reached under his jacket to a pocket by his heart, pulled out a crystal cross, and held it up. "I rebuke you and your evil, doctor," he called. "And in the name of holy justice call on you to surrender!"

At that moment the figure of our host proceeded to vibrate wildly, his head whipping back and forth, his long hair flying, his limbs flailing, and he began to change.

The man's face pushed out and his hair transformed into shaggy fur. Chaney emitted a high-pitched yell that became a snarl as his teeth grew into fangs. His head now elongated 'til it was more beast than human.

Suddenly there stood a two-meter tall, two-legged monster, covered in fur, with savage-looking claws and madness in his eyes.

Professor Van Helsing stood his ground, holding the now glowing crystal cross before him, his expression fixed in grim lines, showing no fear. When he spoke, it was in a calm, even tone.

"Now would be a good time to change, constable. This will hold him back but will not stop him."

To say that I was stunned, grandson, was to understate by a Cork mile! But I had no chance to stay so for long as the snarling beast came toward us in a slow, confident stalk.

What could I do? No time for secrecy anymore, now was time for self-preservation. So it was that I said the family prayer to the Morrigan, great red she-wolf of our ancestors and I changed.

In ten heartbeats, I was in my full wolf form, and I met the approaching beast in a battle of teeth and claws. The monster came at me crouched, almost like an ape in its posture, but with fangs gleaming and oversized, clawed, hairy hands.

I do not lie that I was sore tested by the claws of this false wolf who slashed me many times as we fought, rolling locked together. He tried to get his hands around my throat, but I kept my muzzle at him, so he had to fend me off. He had the size of me and fought with the fury of the damned, but I fought with the heart of the clan within me and held my own.

While we battled, the Dutchman went to the lens array and disassembled the crystal discs. My opponent saw this and, with a renewed surge of savagery, tried to force me off him to get to the professor.

In desperation, the false wolf drew a hand back to strike, but I lunged forward and latched my jaws on the fur of his throat. I worried and tore at him until, at last, the monster gave a great, gurgling roar and, with a final howl of defiance, sagged lifeless at my feet.

I returned to my human form at once, kneeling by the corpse, the wounds of my battle fading, though I was still covered in the blood of the mad doctor. I looked over at the Dutchman who had disassembled the array. He seemed to be saying a prayer as he touched the crystal cross to his lips, then turned to face me.

I got shakily to my feet, and for a long moment, the Dutchman and myself faced each other in silence.

"How did you know?" I finally asked him. "And when?"

"I knew you were werewolf from the beginning, Constable Mac Tir," Van Helsing said. "You sniffed me when we met."

I was stunned. "How…?"

"That Transylvanian prince was not the only creature that I have faced down who aligned themselves with darkness," Van Helsing said. "Including shapeshifters."

"Yet you trusted me?"

He smiled, a genial expression that seemed out of place with the bloody carnage around us. "My dear wife—who was driven mad after one of my earlier battles with evil—gave me this blessed cross when we married. It is an old relic that vibrates in the presence of evil. I always wear it by my heart, and it revealed your truth."

"What now?" I asked. Our secret had been guarded for ten generations since we served the Kings of Ossory, and here, this stranger knew. Revealing our truth could mean disaster. "What will you tell the world?"

"Nothing," he said. "It has long been known that the wolf beings of Ireland are guardians of the people, so I knew the killer must be an aberration. You may continue to protect your pack."

There was a sudden lash of lightning outside the window as the storm continued unabated.

"Then, professor, since we are stuck in here until this storm clears, let's see if this poor excuse for a dog has a decent stock of whiskey in this place. He's left a bad taste in me mouth."

And so it was, grandson, that for the first and last time in our history, an outsider came to know the secret of Clan Mac Tir.

# A Clockwork Heart

## Christine Norris

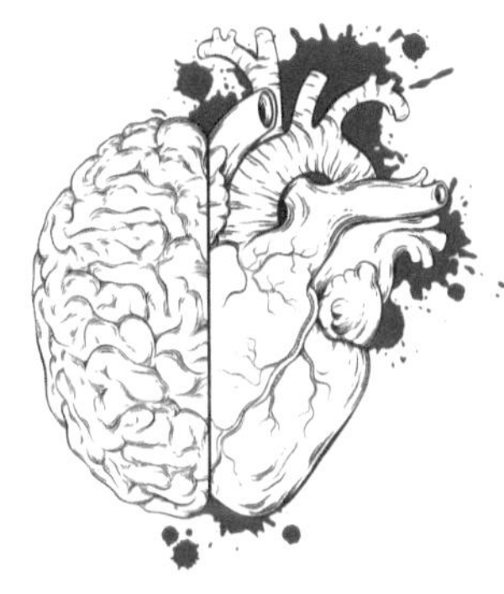

MARIE GASPED FOR BREATH AS SOMEONE SHOOK her awake.

"Time to wake up, princess." Her kidnapper hovered over her wearing a smile that made her skin crawl.

Marie pushed herself upright. They rode in a private train car. It was moving, but the rain-lashed windows showed nothing but night. She put a hand to her aching head. "Where are we going?"

"You'll see." The man handed her a cut-crystal glass of water. As he reached toward her, his sleeve slid above the wrist, revealing a metal arm. When he flexed his gloved fingers, brass rods glided inside the cage of the lower arm. Marie pulled her curious gaze away before he noticed.

"Drink that. It'll help with the headache."

She stared at him, reluctant to take anything from a man who had abducted her literally from her doorstep. He chuckled and set the glass on the table beside the chair. "Sorry about the chloroform."

Marie shifted in the unfamiliar upholstered chair. "Why?"

"You'll have to ask Mr. Fuguet." The train slowed, and the squeal of brakes punctured the quiet.

"Who?"

"My employer." The man lifted one eyebrow. "He has commanded your presence."

The train slowed, then, with a hiss of steam, stopped. Marie's abductor handed her a warm cloak while he donned the Petersham and bowler hat he had been wearing when he knocked on the door of the apartment she shared with her father above their toy shop.

Marie was escorted down the steps and onto the deserted platform. The rain had stopped, leaving everything shiny and dripping. A sign above the ticket window said *Bryn Mawr*. They were well outside Philadelphia, on the Main Line. Where the wealthiest Philadelphians kept their summer homes to get respite from the heat and odor of the city.

"No time for sightseeing." The man pushed her into a waiting carriage. A short but smooth ride later, they stopped in front of an elegant manor. Marie was unceremoniously shepherded inside. They met no one as they marched through the foyer, down the hall, and into the library. A trim man in his early thirties waited in a wingback chair beside the fire. He sipped an amber-colored liquid from a tumbler. A book sat open on his lap.

"Mr. Fuguet?" Marie knew she recognized the name when her captor had said it on the train. One of the wealthiest industrialists in Philadelphia. In fact, he had visited the shop just the previous day, to her father's great delight.

Mr. Fuguet looked up from his book. "Ah, Miss Ryan. I trust you had a pleasant trip? My valet treated you well?"

Marie stood dumbfounded. "Outside of kidnapping me, yes. Is there some... toy emergency that requires my help at this hour?"

Mr. Fuguet laughed. "How delightful. Yes, an emergency of sorts." He set his glass on the small table beside him and closed the book. "I've been looking for you for quite a while."

He stepped over to the shelves and pulled down a handful of books. "I have spent years studying the writings of the most advanced thinkers of the modern age. Franklin and his kite." He pulled a book from the top of the pile and tossed it on the floor. "Faraday and Tesla." Another two books hit the floor with a loud *thump*. "Dr. Victor Frankenstein. More recently Alexei Faber, experimenting with hypothermia to extend life indefinitely." He shook his head sadly as he tossed a leather-bound journal on top of the others. "That poor child. Unfortunate. Of course, there's Van Helsing and Jekyll, who had the most *absurd* theories." Mr. Fuguet lobbed the last two volumes to the floor. His hands empty, he put his back to the shelves.

"Their work has been incredibly useful. I have achieved so much, but ultimate success has been illusive. That is why you are here."

Marie stared open-mouthed, barely able to process the lecture. Mr. Fuguet pinned her with his gaze, until she realized he expected a response. "I'm sorry, I don't understand."

"Your gift, of course." Mr. Fuguet picked up the small book he had been reading when Marie had entered. "Let me show you where you'll be working for now."

Marie, still perplexed, followed the gentleman through the house to a small room at the far end. It may previously have been a pantry but had been transformed into a workshop.

Mr. Fuguet ushered Marie inside. "Everything you need is here. You have until dawn. More than enough time, if your father has not exaggerated your skills."

"Sir, I still don't understand."

"I expect results." He handed the book to Marie. "My notes. In case you would like to peruse them before you begin."

As he closed the door, he gave Marie a look that made her shiver. "I don't think I need to tell you the penalty for failure."

Marie could barely get the words out. "P-p-penalty?"

Mr. Fuguet nodded. "I couldn't have you telling anyone what is going on here if I were to let you go. If it comes to that, your father will be compensated for his loss. Good night." He shut the door behind him.

Marie pulled at the door. Locked. There was no keyhole on this side, so she couldn't even pick the lock. She pounded on the wood, shouting for help. Tears poured down her face as she screamed between great, gasping breaths. She received silence in reply.

Realizing it was a useless endeavor, she faced the tiny, windowless room. The workspace consisted of two tables and a chair. One table was covered with a variety of tools. On the other sat a mechanical toy bird. Marie wound it and watched its wings flap as its metal beak opened and closed. A music box inside played a sweet tune as the bird went through the prescribed motions.

*What am I supposed to do with this?* As the daughter of a toy maker, she was well acquainted with this type of novelty, having tinkered in her father's shop and built a few clockworks for her own amusement. Her specialty, however, was dolls. Handmade, beautifully painted dolls. Metal and gears held no attraction for her.

What "special talent" had her father claimed Marie possessed to impress an important customer? She couldn't imagine it was something worth abducting her in the middle of the night over.

Marie opened Mr. Fuguet's journal, hoping for some hint. She skimmed the pages. Many were full of mathematical equations that made no sense to her. One was labeled "alchemical formula transformation – Ferrous to Aurum."

A page about halfway back held a short paragraph that caught her eye, sending another shiver rippling through her.

> *Experiments combining clockwork and organic material are promising, however, the tissue decomposes too quickly. There is not enough time to complete the work before the flesh degrades. I have likewise attempted animation through both chemistry and electricity, with fleeting success.*

> *Faber's work with Aether has compelled me to search ancient texts and to travel to the far reaches of the globe. The Vatican. Greece. The sands of Egypt. Deep in the German forests and mountains of Romania. There I found the answer. Technomancy. A gift I do not possess. Success depends on finding a person so blessed. The search begins!*

She gasped. What was Technomancy? Whatever it was, obviously Mr. Fuguet was convinced Marie could do it. She slumped into the single chair and wept. *Oh, Papa.*

The door creaked open. Marie looked up, hopeful, as a figure in a dark cloak stepped inside.

"Why are you crying?"

Marie wiped her eyes with the sleeve of her dress. "Because this is likely my last night on earth." She stated it matter-of-factly. Things could hardly get worse.

"Are you ill?"

Marie let out a cheerless laugh. "I almost wish I were. Who are you?"

The figure kept their hood raised, shielding their face from view. "Unimportant. If you are not ill, why would this be your last night on earth?"

Marie sniffed. "I have been given a task. I'm not even certain what it is, but if I fail I am to be murdered." She paused. "Have you ever heard of Technomancy?"

The stranger leaned against one of the tables. "Are you in need of a Technomancer?"

"It seems so." Marie indicated the journal. "I have no idea what it has to do with that little clockwork bird, but the two seem to go together. Technomancer you call it? I am not one, whatever that is. I can't complete the task, which seems to require a Technomancer, so I will be murdered in the morning."

Her visitor's hood bobbed again. "That sounds perfectly horrible." They paused. "What would you give me if I saved your life?"

"What do you mean?"

"I believe I was perfectly clear. A straightforward exchange."

The girl stared at the stranger in disbelief. "You're going to help me escape?"

"No. But I will help you not be murdered. If you don't want my help, I'll be on my way." The visitor turned toward the door as if to leave.

"Stop!" Marie shouted, then covered her mouth with her hands and waited to see if her outburst had been overheard. The visitor stood with their back to her, their hand on the doorknob. After a minute of silence, Marie lowered her hand slowly.

"Yes. Please. Help me."

"You still haven't answered the question."

"Oh." Marie looked down at herself. "I can give you this, if it's acceptable." She pulled the ring from her finger, a plain silver band, and held it out to the stranger.

The visitor took the ring, and it disappeared into the folds of the cloak. "It will suffice." The stranger pushed back the hood of the cloak, revealing a boy of nineteen or twenty with a shock of reddish hair. He bent over the clockwork bird and stroked it with one gloved finger. With his other hand, he reached into his mantle and pulled out a peculiar, long-handled tool. Gears had been attached to the side of the handle, which widened and flattened at the end. On the opposite side, a series of rings had been attached, set one inside the other.

"You may want to take a step back."

Marie obeyed, her eyes wide. The visitor pulled off one glove and held the tool in his bare hand. White-blue sparks crackled around his arm, like bits of lightning. The hair on Marie's arms stood up, and she continued backward until she met the door. The bolts traveled down the stranger's arm to his wrist and hand, then gathered around the handle of the odd tool. The gears spun, and the rings extended like a telescope.

The boy moved the tool over the clockwork bird's tiny body. Lightning and smoke arced between the objects. Both raced along the toy finding the seams and disappearing inside.

The rings retracted and the boy stood straight. "That should do it."

Marie exhaled — she had been holding her breath without realizing it. "Do *what*? I'm sorry, I still don't understand."

The stranger put the tool in his pocket and shook his hands, flinging off excess bits of lightning like drops of water. "Wait."

Marie stared at the bird. *Chirp.* She leaned closer. The clockwork songbird's tiny beak opened and closed. It flapped its wings and walked across the table. When it cocked its head and looked right at Marie with living eyes, she shrieked.

"Where is the music?"

The strange boy held out his hands. "Gone. The toy bird is now more... bird. Alive, so to speak. It won't last forever, it's too simple a mechanism. But it should be enough to satisfy the... man who put you here." He pulled up his hood and stepped to the door. "Now, I must go. Good luck."

"Wait!" Marie ran after him. "How did you do that?" Despite still being a prisoner, what she had just witnessed was far too strange to let go without explanation.

"Technomancy, obviously." The boy reached for the doorknob.

"Please take me with you," Marie cried.

He hesitated. "I cannot. You should be safe enough for now."

Marie grabbed the edge of his cloak and clutched it for dear life. "What if I'm not? If Mr. Fuguet thinks I did this and wants me to do it again?"

"Then maybe I'll see you once more." The boy opened the door and slipped through. Marie reached for it, but the knob pulled from her fingers. She tried to follow but it was already locked. Marie slammed her fist against the door. The rest of the night she spent cursing the boy's face, her father, and Mr. Fuguet.

In the morning, her captor opened the door. Extremely happy with her supposed achievement, he held the former clockwork toy, delighted.

"Amazing. As I have studied the great scientists, I have also read every scrap I could unearth on Technomancy. I've spent a fortune.

And now look! Your father was right when he said there was magic in your fingers." His gleeful, almost unhinged laugh made Marie uncomfortable.

"I'm glad you're pleased." Marie balled her hands into fists and pressed them to her sides to stop them from shaking. "Can I please go home now?"

Fuguet's gaze turned cold as he looked at her over the bird's head. "Certainly not." He set the bird on the table, where it continued to *chirp* and flap its wings in an attempt to get its metal body into the air.

Marie's voice trembled. "Why?" She could not imagine what machinations rolled through Mr. Fuguet's mind.

"I have another test, of course. This evening. I need to know your limits, if you have any." He tapped the table with one finger. "Meanwhile, my valet will see to your needs." He marched out of the room, past the man with the mechanical arm.

The valet made a mocking bow and smirked. "My lady." Two staff members entered behind him, one with a cot and a chamber pot, and one with a tray of food. They deposited their burdens and left without a word.

"Until this evening." The valet shut and locked the door. Marie kicked it when he had left, furious. She was in the exact same predicament the red-haired boy had found her. Anger wouldn't fill her belly, however. She attacked the tray of eggs and sausage.

After her meal, she yawned. Exhaustion pulled at her. Begrudgingly, she crawled into the cot and fell asleep almost immediately.

In her dreams, a flock of living clockwork birds chased her down a never-ending corridor full of locked doors. She woke a few minutes before the valet delivered her dinner. The roast beef and new potatoes were delectable but sat like a stone in her belly. A terrifying feeling of trepidation crept over her.

When she finished, the valet returned to collect her. Marie, her stomach churning like a stormy sea, snatched up the journal and followed him to another workshop, twice the size of the last. Something larger than a bird had been placed on the workspace at the far end of the room.

Mr. Fuguet tilted his head in what might have been an endearing manner if not for his intent, almost crazed stare. "We are clear about the terms, yes?"

Marie was afraid that if she opened her mouth, she might vomit. So she only nodded.

"Have a pleasant and productive evening."

The door closed and locked. Morbid curiosity dragged Marie past the tables of tools to the item on the workbench. She stopped short, with her hand across her stomach to stop from disgorging her dinner. It was a rabbit. The creature's gray fur lay smooth, its black eyes open and staring. Marie touched it with a shaking hand and recoiled. It was cold and hard. The lamplight glinted off of the animal's paws. With a ragged breath, Marie looked closer. The claws were made of metal.

"Oh, thank goodness." She inspected the animal more closely. The fur was real, but the eyes were glass, like a taxidermy. Carefully, she opened the rabbit's mouth. Metal teeth, and far back inside the throat, springs and gears. It was, again, a clockwork. The most realistic clockwork she had ever seen, but a clockwork, nonetheless. That didn't change the dire nature of her situation, but it made the task less terrible somehow. Though she found that a Technomancer could make metal creatures come to *life* somewhat disturbing.

She flipped open the journal, found a technical drawing of the rabbit, and read Fuguet's notes.

> *The rabbit's skin has been treated, like a lady's coat, so that it won't decompose. This is one step I would like to reproduce with the Final Project. Flesh is much more difficult to work with, however, and does not retain its elasticity. More questions! And still, a Technomancer is essential to success. I have searched every watch and clock shop in the city. Not even the Rittenhouse family seems to possess the gift. I will find her. I must find her.*

Marie threw the book across the room.

"Hey, watch it!"

Marie's mouth fell open in surprise. The boy stood there, the journal in his hands.

"No need to throw things at me." He set the book on the nearest workbench. "I see you're still here."

"I told you it was likely." Marie did not bother to hide her irritation. "I'll ask again for your assistance, please."

The stranger glanced at the rabbit. "A bit trickier. I'll need to use Aether. But I can do it. Payment?"

Marie was prepared for his request. She slipped a fine silver chain with a thimble threaded onto it from around her neck.

"This was my mother's." She held it out to the boy and blinked back tears at letting it go.

He took it gently and tucked it into his cloak. Again the odd-looking tool appeared in his hands. When the lightning and smoke gathered around his arm, Marie watched closely, in case Mr. Fuguet had any questions about the procedure. If he asked to see the tool, she didn't know what she would say. Maybe she'd leave that bit out.

A pungent, metallic smell permeated the air, like after a thunderstorm. The energy crackled down his arm to his hand and then the tool. The gears spun; the rings extended. Smoke and lightning enveloped the creature's body and disappeared inside. The boy exhaled deeply.

"Took a bit more than expected. This one will last quite a bit longer, I should think."

Marie inspected the rabbit. Its nose twitched. An ear moved. When it hopped across the table she jumped away, startled.

"That is both amazing and horrible." She turned to the boy. "Mr. Fuguet is mad. I am terrified what he will ask of me next. Can you please just take me with you?"

The boy pulled up his hood and turned away. "I'll see you tomorrow. I promise." He slipped out of the door and was gone. Marie, after half an hour of cursing and stomping the confines of the workshop, throwing tools and making a general mess, lay on the worktable and slept. The rabbit curled up beside her.

Mr. Fuguet was ecstatic when he saw what had happened overnight. He twirled around the workshop, the living clockwork rabbit in his hands.

"Unbelievable. When I think how long I've looked for you…" He put the rabbit down and his hands behind his back. "One last test this evening, and then I will know for sure."

When Marie was again locked inside the workshop with food and a cot, she didn't bother with hysterics. She ate her breakfast, then cleaned up the workshop. With nothing else to do, she paged through Mr. Fuguet's journal, hoping to figure out what the last test might be. Pages of boring notes about his experiments, both successful and failed. A diagram of the valet's mechanical arm was opposite one of a drawing of a similar leg. Marie wondered if the valet also used that device.

Near the very back was a detailed diagram spread across two pages. She turned it one way and then another, confused. When she figured out what it was, Marie dropped the book to the floor.

*He's insane. He has to be for him to think that it would work, even with the help of a Technomancer.* There was no doubt in her mind that animating this — unspeakable creation — would be her next task.

With a shaking hand, she picked up the book and paged past the profane image. Notes about the experiment were scrawled across another five pages. She skimmed them, her horror only growing as she came to the last words.

*Once I master this final barrier, nothing will be out of reach. Immortality will be in hand.*

The valet entered with her supper. Marie glanced at his mechanical arm, covered by his shirt, and shivered. She managed a few bites, and then pushed the rest around to make it look as if she had eaten. When Mr. Fuguet arrived to collect her, his smile and encouraging words did nothing to assuage her feeling of dread. Instead of a third room on the ground level, she was taken to the library.

"Close your eyes, please. No peeking." Mr. Fuguet kept his voice light, but the command was clear.

Marie complied. She heard footsteps, muffled by the carpet. There was a sound, like something sliding.

"You may look."

When Marie opened her eyes, her surprise was overwhelmed by fear. One of the bookshelves had disappeared, revealing a twisting stone stair. The valet pushed her toward the opening, and she fought to keep her breath steady, though her body trembled. All three of them followed it down, far below ground. The stair ended at a plain oak door.

"My personal workshop." When Mr. Fuguet smiled, Marie saw all of his teeth and was reminded of a wolf. He made a great show of unlocking the door's three complicated locks, then opened it with a flourish into a cavernous chamber. Stone walls around, thick wooden beams above. Dozens of gas lamps burned brightly.

Tables were scattered about, covered by a variety of tools and projects in different stages of completion. Shelves lined one wall and held jars of strange specimens suspended in liquid.

Marie dragged her feet across the room, panic building like a bubble in her chest. Beside the table at the far side of the room sat a strange machine, covered in dials and gauges. It was taller than she, with an enormous coil sprouting from the top. Something large lay on the table, covered by a sheet, steam spurting from underneath. Somewhere nearby, something ticked loudly.

"Your final test, Miss Ryan." Fuguet folded his hands in front of him and rocked on his heels. "Succeed, and you become my muse. A life of luxury in exchange for sole command of your gift. Any other result…" He shrugged in an apologetic way, then left, the valet following in his footsteps. Marie shuddered as the door shut behind them with an ominous *bang*. The locks were secured, their bolts driven home with a definitive sound that echoed through the chamber.

She looked over the apparatus beside the table. The gauges were all labeled: *respiration, cardiac function, musculature.* Buttons and levers surrounded each indicator. Pipes ran between the front of the machine and the table, ending beneath the sheet. Whatever was on the table was also the source of the ticking.

Marie approached the cloth-covered table as if it would bite her. With a fleeting hope that she was wrong, she pulled off the sheet.

It lay before her, a waking nightmare. Limbs, fingers, toes. The chest was bare, but the lower half was covered by trousers. Marie didn't dare touch the skin for fear she might scream and never stop. If she didn't know better, she might think it was a life-sized doll. The torso had been fitted with a door that revealed inner workings of springs and gears. Inside, the mechanisms were active and moved with precision. All of it connected to a brass clockwork heart, set in the center of the chest.

The automaton took up the length of the table, at least six feet. Its eyes were closed, and Marie had no desire to see if they were glass, like the rabbit's, or something more. As horrifying as the creature was, she was unable to look away. The drawing in Fuguet's journal had been disturbing, to see that he had followed through with his unholy experiment was revolting.

Marie's gaze traveled to the creature's face. The features were soft, almost angelic. Full lips, a well-formed nose. In any other instance she would consider him handsome. The top of the head was covered in thick, dark hair. A button stuck out from behind one ear. Knowing it was imprudent, she pressed it. The top of the automaton's head split down the center and opened with a *hiss*. Inside was a mass of gray, wrinkled jelly.

Fascinated and repulsed, Marie stared at it, disbelieving.

If the boy appeared, he could absolutely *not* bring that – *thing* – to life. Marie ran to a nearby table and grabbed the longest screwdriver she could find. Her breathing came in gasps as she considered what she planned to do with the tool. One quick jab into the soft jelly of the brain, and this monster would never wake, not even with Technomancy. Or at least she hoped not.

"What are you doing?"

Marie jumped and dropped the screwdriver. The red-haired boy ran toward her, his face a mask of shock. She hadn't even heard the door open. "How did you get in here?"

The boy shrugged. "Fuguet likes security, but hasn't figured out how to use anything but a mechanical lock. Easy to pick for someone like me. I'll ask again, what are you doing?"

"Stopping a madman." Marie bent over to pick up the tool. "I may not be able to bring it to life, but I can make sure no one else does either." She pulled her hand back, ready to thrust it into the exposed brain.

"Hold on!" The boy caught her hand before she could strike. "Do you think this will stop him? He will just start again."

Marie relaxed her arm. Of course he was right. "What choice do we have?"

The boy gently pried the screwdriver from her hand and examined the automaton. "It's as we feared."

"We?" Marie squeaked. "Who is *we?*"

"My employer. And others. We've had reports he was searching for a powerful Technomancer. A very specific one. He was fed some... misinformation... that unfortunately led him to you."

Something suddenly became very clear to Marie. "Is this why you refused to help me escape?"

He shrugged sheepishly. "I had to get him to bring you down here. I've been looking for the entrance to his laboratory for months."

Marie balled her hands into fists, apoplectic. "You left me here so you could find *this*? Wait, how did you find me?"

"I said I was sorry. And I found you by following the psychic energy from the ring and the thimble." He reached into his pocket and handed both back to her. She snatched them from his hand with an indignant look.

"Hey, it's not like I asked you for your first-born child." He leaned over the infernal clockwork man. "Damn. Didn't think he was anywhere near this close." The boy tossed his cloak to the floor, the Technomancy tool already in his hand.

Marie grabbed his wrist. "You're not actually going to *do* it, are you?"

The boy huffed. "I can't let him keep it. We can't destroy it. Are you going to carry it?"

She jerked her hands back. "You can't. It's unnatural. It's not even a person, just a shell that you're going to... I don't even know what. Reanimate? Is that the word?"

"I don't know what it might be yet, and neither do you. It deserves a chance." The boy stood beside the automaton, holding the tool over its head. "Please be quiet so I can concentrate."

He closed his eyes and started again. Lightning and smoke gathered around not only his arm but also his torso, circling him like a serpent. The bitter, pungent scent of a storm hung heavy over the room. The gears on the tool spun so fast they blurred. The rings extended. Marie scuttled back, trying to put as much distance between herself and the thing on the table as possible.

The lightning and smoke poured from the boy to the tool, then leapt into to the creature's open chest and disappeared inside. The doors on his chest and head closed, leaving behind only smooth skin and hair.

"I hope that was enough." The red-haired boy waved the tool, which had returned to its original state, over his head. He leaned both arms on the edge of the table. "I don't have energy to try again."

Marie didn't have the courage to speak. She prayed the boy's efforts had failed.

He reached beneath the table and disconnected the pipes. "If it didn't work, we'll have to think of something else." He looked up at Marie. "Hey, are you listening?"

Marie didn't hear a word. Distracted by the creature, she pointed.

A finger twitched. The hand moved. With a groan, the automaton sat up.

"Hello," the boy said. The creature swung his legs around and stood, then swayed against the table. "Whoa, easy. I'll give you a minute to get your bearings, then we'll need to go." He glanced at Marie, who hadn't budged. "All of us."

Marie's insides performed acrobatic feats as the automaton took his first steps. The creature's movements were jerky and uncertain, and he towered over both of them.

"All right?"

The creature nodded roughly. When he turned his head and looked at Marie, she shrunk back against the life-support machine.

"He won't hurt you," the Technomnacer said.

Marie scoffed. "How do you know?"

He paused before he spoke. "The brain. When I brought him back, I felt what was going on in his brain as it, um, started up."

"You what?" Marie's stomach soured. "Have you felt a lot of brains?"

"No, actually. Technomancy usually deals with things that have never been alive, like the toy bird and the rabbit, giving them a boost. Making them more alive, though their core being remains all metal. This was a first. I felt kindness. And confusion, and fear. This is Fuguet's fault, not his." He used his head to indicate the creature. "You can stay behind if you want, but you know what will happen if you do."

Marie kept her eyes on the creature as he shuffled toward them. She pushed her terror down but could not stop the shiver that ran up her spine like the lightning used to bring the automaton to life. The ticking of his clockwork heart grew louder until it seemed like it was all Marie could hear.

"Wait!" The creature stopped just feet from the other two.

"We can't wait," the boy replied. "What are you doing?"

Marie thrust the journal into his hand, then grabbed a hammer from the nearest workbench. "You're right. Fuguet will start over. We should make that difficult, don't you think?" She ran to the shelves and smashed every jar. A thick liquid with a strong odor poured out all over the books and notes on the worktable.

"Excellent idea." The Technomancer grabbed a wrench and ran to the equipment that had been attached to the automaton. He made quick work of it; gears and springs flew into the air, and every gauge was shattered. When he finished he dropped the wrench. "That was extremely satisfying."

Despite their situation, Marie laughed. "Well done..." her words trailed off, having no name to hail him by.

The red-headed boy grinned back. "I suppose I shouldn't make you guess, should I? Reggie."

They both startled as the automaton took the opportunity to pick up the nearest mechanical experiment and rip it apart with his bare hands, scattering bits across the room.

Their work complete, the three of them gathered at the door.

The saboteurs crept up the winding stair. Reggie and Marie's steps were light and quick. But the automaton struggled with both his joints and his balance, and the clockwork heart's ticks reverberated.

"So much for a sneak escape," Marie grumbled.

Reggie opened the library door and peered out. "All clear." They stole across the darkened room and into the hall.

"This way," he whispered, beckoning them toward the back of the house, across soft, footstep-dampening carpets. In the lounge, a set of French doors opened onto a terrace and the safe camouflage of night.

Reggie peered between the curtains. "I have a carriage waiting down the road. We'll cut through the gardens and be there in a flash." He carefully turned the knob and pushed the door open. The next instant, an alarm sounded.

"Oh, there you are. I've been looking for you."

The voice cut through Marie like a knife. She didn't need to turn to know who it was.

"Did you think there were no detection devices in this house? How stupid do you think Mr. Fuguet is?" The valet moved into Marie's field of view. "So who are you, chap?" He pointed a pistol at Reggie. "Her beau, perhaps?"

Reggie chuckled. "Nope. She's kind of a pain in the ass, if you haven't noticed."

"That's the truth." The valet held the pistol higher and leveled it at Marie. "Good work, by the way." He looked the automaton up and down. "Mr. Fuguet will be *very* pleased."

"I hate to tell you, but I'm not the Technomancer. My father lied." Marie glanced at Reggie.

The valet clucked. "Oh, I see. One of Agatha's, I imagine?"

Reggie did not reply.

"In that case, I suppose we no longer need you, do we, little girl?" The valet clicked back the hammer on the weapon. "I'll be sure to leave you where your father can find you."

Marie shrunk back and closed her eyes. The shot was deafening. She braced herself, but there was no pain. Her eyes flew open.

The automaton stood between her and the valet. Reggie pulled a weapon from his cloak and fired. A bolt of energy hit the valet in the chest. The henchman sailed backward and crumpled to the floor, motionless.

Reggie grabbed Marie's hand and pulled her onto the terrace.

"Stop!" Marie turned back. The automaton hadn't followed. He faced them; a hole punctured the center of his chest.

Reggie ran to his side. "Can you run?"

The automaton nodded. He was halfway across the terrace before he fell to his knees.

"No!" Marie pulled on him to stand. The ticks of his clockwork heart slowed. He turned and looked into Marie's eyes.

Blue. His eyes were blue. A single tear ran down his cheek as he collapsed.

Marie threw herself across his body. "Get up. Please." The automaton's eyes stared, unseeing, up at the night sky. She pressed her ear to his chest, but there was nothing.

"We have to go," Reggie said quietly.

Marie choked back sobs. "He saved me. We can't leave him."

"I hate to do it, but he's too heavy. We'd never make it."

The thunder of footsteps coming from the house pulled Marie's attention from her sorrow. She ran beside Reggie through the garden and toward the woods. Once they were safely beneath the trees she looked back. Three people stood on the terrace, the light from their lanterns falling on the body of the automaton. He lay there, still and silent.

"Find her!" Fuguet ordered as he emerged from the house.

"I'm so sorry," Reggie whispered. "There was nothing we could do."

Marie and Reggie disappeared into the woods. Half a mile of rugged terrain, tripping over rocks and tree roots, with Fuguet's men close behind. At last they stumbled onto the road and the waiting carriage. A teenaged girl sat in the driver's box. There were no horses.

"There you are," the driver shouted as she hopped down. "I was beginning to worry."

Reggie held the door open, and Marie jumped inside. "Sorry, Penny. We ran into some complications, and they're right behind us."

Penny slammed the door shut and jumped back into the driver's box. Marie noticed that the coach vibrated, like a train car.

"Hang on," Reggie warned. "It's a bumpy takeoff."

The carriage jolted forward, then raced off down the road and into the night.

"We should be safe for now." Reggie breathed a sigh of relief and fell back against the seat. "I'll get you home before the sun is up."

Marie stared out of the window. The vision of the automaton dying, wouldn't leave her mind. The look on his face. "Your employer. Agatha, is that her name?"

"Yes."

"She wants to stop Fuguet?"

Reggie nodded. "Among others. I can't really talk about it."

Marie locked her gaze with Reggie's. "Take me to her."

# To Those Who Are Ancient

## Danielle Ackley-McPhail

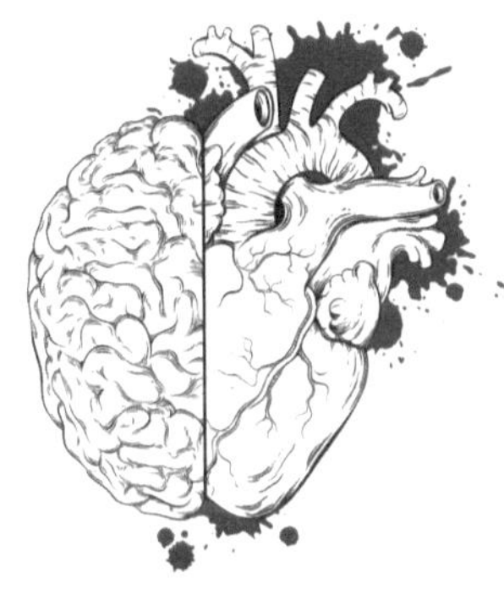



*I have not written down my thoughts since my peculiar journey began, an Angel in pursuit of death's shadow, but I find I need the comfort of these trusted pages, now more than ever before. They haunt me, you see. In every manner of the word, they haunt me. Those souls that I have not been able to guide on their way. Their aether selves tattered and torn as I have never seen before. Their gazes tripping on madness and melancholy. They want saving, yet every grace that has been granted me toward that task has failed. They linger still despite my every effort.*

*A.A.F.*

Aleta Angelina Fabricio set down her fountain pen and stared out her workroom window, taking solace in the restored courtyard once more burgeoning with rosebuds and marigolds and flowers she still had no names for. Where the shattered fountain once stood she had built an arbor on which she grew grapevines and placed a bench beneath its shade. When she was not lost in her tinkering or drawn off to herd spirits, she sat there to enjoy the evening breeze, quietly reminiscing about her family. She had found peace despite her isolation. Or perhaps because of it. No spirits lingered here, only memories.

As comforting as her sanctuary was, however, this time it held no answers, nor solutions. For three seasons she had served as Santa Muerte's Angel, a shepherd of wayward souls. But in the last few months she had come upon teyolia she feared were truly damned. Damaged and unhinged, with aethereal strips ripped away, lost in the torment of their fragmented selves. Incomplete echoes of all they had once been. Angel felt their pain with every breath drawn in their presence, reminiscent of the jolts from the steam-turbine resuscitation device that had summoned her back from her ill-advised journey to the land of the dead. She did not know how to help them, and Santa Muerte remained silent, so for now, Angel avoided such spirits when she felt the precursor of that pain, though it was to her shame that she did so.

She flinched, startled out of her musings by the careful grip of talons alighting on her shoulder, catching in her shawl. A harsh, chuckling caw sounded by her ear as her corvid companion Ujer tucked his sleek-feathered head beneath the fall of her hair, all but blending in with her raven locks. Gently, he tugged her earlobe with his beak, chuckling and clicking in comforting tones.

With a chuckle of her own, Angel reached up both to ruffle the crow's crest and hold him steady as she stood. Closing her journal, she placed it back on the shelf with her father's many tomes. As she did so, her belly grumbled, causing Ujer to chuckle once more, bobbing on her shoulder in his mimicry of the way her father used to belly laugh.

"Ay, pequeño! You are so fresh!" As she left the workroom, she raised a hand to shield her face as Ujer briefly fluttered his wings for balance before folding them along his back.

Despite the bird's antics, Angel's thoughts continued to dwell on those tormented souls that haunted her. She had not realized it before, but, just as her belly grumbled, so too did those spirits hunger. Not for food, but for those missing fragments of themselves. With a sigh, she raised a hand to her temple and rubbed at the building tension. Understanding the problem did not provide a solution.

She could, however, settle the matter of her belly.

Entering the kitchen, Angel went to the coal-fired stove and the pot of beans and rice she kept simmering there. Scooping some into a tortilla, she wrapped it neatly and took it out into the courtyard, settling on her bench, wreathed in the heady scent of grapes and roses.

The harsh whisper of Abuela's voice drifted through Angel's thoughts, *"Aleta Angelina Fabricio!"*

Were she still alive, her grandmother would not have approved of Angel's meal, or the lackadaisical manner with which she ate it, but anything more elaborate seemed too much effort for just herself, and she kept no pigs to feed on scraps. She found comfort in the memory of Abuela's scoldings, though. Strangely, those were the moments her grandmother most showed her love. But Abuela's was not the voice of reason Angel needed to hear today.

"Mami," she whispered, in the place she felt closest to her mother. "What should I do? How do I help them?"

All that came to Angel's ear was Ujer's happy little murmurs as he dipped down from her shoulder to filch bits from her dinner. Angel finished the last few bites before he could snatch them and settled back against the bench. Ujer squawked his protest and fluttered from her shoulder. Perching on the arbor overhead, he plucked her grapes in defiance.

In truth, she had not expected a response. Angel had guided both her mother and brother on their way. Had herself gone to the underworld at great risk and without summons to ensure Mami and Maximo safely crossed over Apanohuaya, the river that all souls forded on their journey to the afterlife. But there were many paths through the underworld of her Aztec ancestors, and many places a person's teyolia might go once released from their mortal form. By the tales Angel learned at Abuela's knee, her mother, Angelina—having died trying to birth Angel's brother, Maximo—was destined for Cihuatlampa, the place of women. There, in the western heavens, those who died fighting the gods for their child's soul became Cihuateteo, divine women, as honored as any other warrior who died in battle.

Many grew up fearing the divine women and blaming them for ills, leaving offerings to placate them as they would demons instead of celebrating the bravery of those fallen mothers, but Angel knew the true stories and revered the spirits.

She shuddered again, only just realizing the chilling bite the evening breeze had taken as the sun dipped down below the hills—guided by the Cihuateteo and other fallen warriors—leaving her in darkness. Again... no answers, no solutions. Drawing her shawl around her shoulders, she went inside and to her bed.

Angel woke surrounded by obsidian darkness. Though her soft feather mattress had cushioned her body what seemed like only moments before, now she stood, cold seeping up through the soles of her feet. Turning a slow circle, she searched for the golden glow of the path she'd so often encountered when Santa Muerte summoned her to the realm of the dead.

There was none.

Barely a glint of luminosity distinguished the cold, rocky hills from the arch of the underworld. In the distance, the harsh clatter of bone knocking bone mocked her, so unlike Santa Muerte's melodious clacking.

*This is not your time. This is not your place.* Xolotl's words echoed in her too-fresh memories of when she'd taken it upon herself to breach the underworld.

Angel remained where she stood, lest she lose her way, her spirit doomed to wander without the goddess's guidance or the god of death's intercession. All around her, subtle movements disturbed the mist that blended ground with sky. Elusive whispers tormented her ears, screaming, wailing, taunting. She jumped as a sudden battle cry rent the silence, echoing with rage and tortured notes of longing. Something aethereal swooped down upon her, clawed, pallid hands grasping while bare teeth and bone gleamed from beneath a loose stream of luxurious ebony hair.

Scattering feathers and loosing raucous caws, Ujer startled from his perch as Angel bolted upright in her cot. She would like to think she yelled an answering battle cry, but pure terror plucked at her nerves, tightening her chest until she could scarce breath. Echoes of her scream mocked her as she drew gulping breaths and unfisted her reluctant hands from the bed clothes.

Angel's legs trembled as she swung her feet to the floor and faint shudders rippled down her back. Below the hem of her nightgown her flesh appeared chalky in the moonlight, casting her for an instant back into her night terror. Setting her jaw, she stilled her body and drew deep, slow breaths. Such foolishness. It was but a dream. One she had no desire to revisit this night.

Pushing to her feet, Angel took her robe from the peg beside the door and slipped it on, wrapping it tightly around her chilled body. In the darkness she moved through the hacienda to the kitchen where she lit one of the lamps before stirring the embers in the stove and adding fresh coal. She then took Abuela's cherished tin of chocolate down from the shelf and made herself a cup, sweet and rich and creamy and warm with spices. On her way back to her workroom, she grabbed the lamp and a small bunch of grapes from a bowl on the counter, a peace offering for Ujer.

Placing both beside his perch, she sipped her chocolate and considered her father's books. Mostly his journals—and hers—but among them stood a few books of bound fiction. Fanciful musings by the likes of Shelley, Verne, and Wells. She could not read them... could not read English. But Papa had been a learned man and used to read them aloud to her. While she'd marveled at the science such luminaries envisioned, her heart ached for Shelley's creature. So many fragments torn from other bodies, slaved together but ever separate, always reviled. To form such a misbegotten offspring. Sheer madness. And to what end? To play at creation? Such a premise led only to damnation.

Something in the thought vied for her attention only to dance away before she could grasp it.

She drew her hand back from the tome in question once she realized she'd reached to draw it out. Even if she were able to read it, now was not the prudent hour. Instead, she took up the lamp and stepped back. Turning, she slowly left the room. As if swept along in an unrelenting current, Angel came to stand before her mother's door. She had not been inside since she and her father had prepared Mami's body for burial.

Fingers trembling, she turned the knob.

Nothing. Moonlight streamed across the neatly made bed revealing only dust. And yet, she could hear the echo of Abuela's voice rife with reverence murmuring tale after tale of their Aztec ancestors to Angel and her mother, all while the three of them mended clothing and knitted shawls and any number of other domestic chores in the chairs by the window while Papa toiled outside. Too many echoes to glean from. Too much pain in the remembering. Of the four of them, only she remained.

Angel closed the door and returned to the workroom.

Almost without thought she stood before her father's books once more. Rather than reach for one of Papa's journals, she found herself giving in to her earlier impulse and grasping Senora Shelley's chilling and audacious book. As Angel opened the cover with care, she at last understood her father's fascination with the tale. Before his death, he had been obsessed with reconnecting with her mother's spirit. Angel had not realized until now that he had contemplated anything further. Across the endpapers, in his fine, precise hand, her father's thoughts lay bare to her:

> *Could this be the answer? Is the premise sound? The science? I have seen as such with frogs at the University, but muscle stimulation only, never to reanimation. Yet my mind, my heart clutches at any potential. I have tried most everything else to reunite us save the unforgivable sin. But if so, where to begin?*

> *Such machinations. The calculations alone. Were I even to fathom a path forward, I cannot say I dare such extremes lest I succeed and my darling Angelina hate me even as the creature hated his maker.*

> *Oh, but if there were a chance. If my love and I could be rejoined this side of the underworld. I am sorely tempted. I dare say I would even consider a journey to Mitla to petition Mother Aleta's 'cloud people.' Perhaps they might share their wisdom, might tell me if my love would look favorably upon such efforts.*

Fingers trembling once more, Angel closed the book and returned it to the shelf.

Papa had succeeded another way, if not as intended. But something he wrote stayed with her... the cloud people. Ancient and noble souls, buried at Mitla... the earthly gateway to the underworld. They were said to intercede on behalf of those below. Perhaps she would find answers there. Guidance to help the fragmented souls that haunted her. She would make arrangements in the morning.

The sun was high in the sky by the time Angel began her journey.

First, she banked the coals in the stove and prepared the house for her absence, then she gathered the unending pouch of marigold petals and her aether glass, a small, palm-sized contraption refined from the original, much larger spirit window she had devised to send Abuela's spirit on her final journey, to much the same effect. About the size of a lady's handheld mirror, two polished lenses of concave glass with aether trapped between them, secured in a rubber gasket sealed with wax, allowed Angel to guide lost souls on their final journey with much less fuss. Usually. Grimacing, she slid the items into a satchel along with her tool kit, her current journal, and a fountain pen, before filling a second satchel with provisions and her shawl.

She then arranged for her neighbor to care for her livestock and hitched her mule to the wagon for the drive to Oaxaca, where she exchanged them temporarily for the use of the blacksmith's mare, a much more efficient means of traveling the thirty miles to Mitla.

Curse efficiency. She missed the seat of her wagon.

Groaning, she shifted, grateful for the support of the bedroll and provisions at her back. She shielded against the sun's glare as she searched ahead for Ujer, telling herself she need go just that much further. Only, the contrary bird kept moving, always in sight, but never closer.

Angel took a drink from her canteen and urged the mare forward… And forward… And forward again. Until at last something other than cacti and scrub brush lined the widening path. Ahead, Ujer perched on the thatch roof of a simple shrine, a cihuateocalli—a goddess house— from the looks of the statues on the altar visible inside. *Cihuateteo*. Divine women, in traditional pose, legs tucked beneath them, and clawed hands raised. Bare breasts full and rounded, but their faces only bone. Amatetéuitl—paper banners—festooned the shrine, along with fresh offerings of tamales, toasted corn, and bread formed like butterflies. Each statue bore its own character, shaped in tribute to one fallen, in the old way. The honored way. These offerings were not left by ignorant ones placating demons, but by someone honoring the Cihuateteo.

Why had they never done so for Mami?

Only, Angel knew. Papa had never let her mother go, and these were not the ways he was raised on. But Abuela… Perhaps her mother's mother had likewise clung to Papa's desperate hopes, if only in her secret heart. When Mami and Maximo had lost their battle for life, Abuela had served as midwife, had administered the sacred prayer:

> *My little one, my daughter, my noble woman, you have wearied yourself, you have fought bravely. By your labors you have achieved a noble death, you have come to the place of the Divine. Go, beloved child, little by little toward the Cihuateteo and become one of them; go, daughter, and they will receive you, and you will be one of them forever, rejoicing with your happy voices in praise of our Mother and Father, the Sun, and you will always accompany them wherever they go in their rejoicing.*

But perhaps in her heart of hearts, Abuela likewise had not let them go.

Angel drew her mount to stop before the shrine, off to the side of a well-worn crossroads. Dismounting, she entered with reverence, noting the adornments of the five figures. Each bore a warrior's headdress: feathers, a crown of skulls, or the semblance of a fierce beast. All wore knotted belts of vipers and simple skirts. Bits of fragrant copal held the banners in place, filling the shrine with a sweet, citrusy scent, and some worshippers had left little folded notes before one of the statues. Petitions? Or messages for the fallen?

She had too much respect to look.

Overhead, from his perch on the roof, Ujer cawed an alert. Angel ducked outside in time to see a man scurry past, the lead rope of a donkey clutched in his left hand while the right rapidly made the sign of the cross over and over as he muttered prayers of protection. Or so Angel presumed, for she could not make out the man's words, except, perhaps, "vampiro." But surely not…

Of course, those who demonized the Cihuateteo did liken them to vampires, claiming such fed off the souls of unwary men and small children on those days they descended from the heavens, causing palsy and eventually death.

Such nonsense went against everything Angel had been raised to believe of the divine women. Those honored as warriors would not behave as monsters. Surely…

But a kernel of doubt found purchase as the echo of a warrior's battle cry rose in Angel's thoughts, and she nearly flinched away from the memory of pallid hands clawing for her.

By the time the man moved past, the sun had nearly sunk behind the hills, and it was too dark to go on. Angel took care of the mare and herself before the light was completely gone, then laid out her bedroll in the shelter of an overhang across from the shrine. It was a warm night, and she forwent a fire, using her satchel for a pillow and her shawl as a blanket.

For a long time, she stared up into the heavens toward the western sky, where Cihuatlampa lay — the place of women. Though she tried not to dwell on her underworld encounter, she could not get the

Cihuateteo from her thoughts. Two faces to one tale. Which bore truth? Or was it both?

Angel drifted off to her wondering, only to be torn from sleep by a jolt of pain, fresh and hot and so much worse than any that had come from a teyolia before. She jerked upright only to fall back with a groan and twice the number of stars in her vision than could be accounted for by the sky. Dizzy, with a pounding in her head rivaling that of a drum, Angel crawled clear of the overhang and pushed herself to her feet. A cool glow lit the crossroads and the shrine. At first, she thought it the moon, but clouds shrouded the heavens. She turned her gaze to the shrine and the ache in her chest tightened.

Five glowing forms stood within the goddess house, facing outward as if in defense. Majestic and fierce. Pale blue light radiated from their corporeal bodies. Sorrow limned their features as they looked out into the center of the crossroad. A sixth figure stood there facing off against them, glowing like the others, but in a yellow hue so pale as to be almost white. She was as like the others in all ways, save bare of adornment, as if her teyolia had not completed its journey. Chalk-white limbs snatched at the sky as the sixth spirit threw back her head and raged, loose tresses thrashing around her skull.

A gasp slipped through Angel's lips, and the Cihuateteo turned her way sending her scrambling for the satchel containing her aether glass. As she worked the flap open, something leapt upon her, slamming her to the ground. Rolling, Angel drew out the glass and held it up before her, praying the spirit would pass through.

She would always wonder how a skull screamed without flesh.

The sixth figure reared back. It screamed once more in defiance before darting away, a mournful voice crying out in the night, searching, always searching for her child's soul.

*Two faces to one tale, indeed,* Angel thought. Before she could consider that any further, a deep groan brought silence to the night as the birds and the insects fell still.

Turning toward the sound, Angel realized that the remaining Cihuateteo had withdrawn. Moving closer, her steps shifting on churned-up dirt where the roadway was disturbed, she peered into the shrine. In the shadows where the divine women had stood lay a dark mound. With another groan, it shifted and slowly sat up. Angel stared into the eyes of the man who had passed by earlier. He appeared dazed, his features tight with pain and fear. The left side of his face hung oddly slack.

With her other vision — the one perceptive of spirits — Angel noticed the stranger's teyolia had been rent, a piece very nearly torn away at the site of the palsy. Shuddering, she recalled the maddened Cihuateteo's clawing hands. Was that what had happened here? The traveler, caught unaware by the raging figure, had scrambled back to the shrine in search of protection? It appeared he'd found it from the very souls he'd feared, but the damage had clearly been done. Wisps of aether clung to the spiritual wound as if trying to mend the tear. Angel glanced down at her glass. It was the only one she had. The first. But she could remake it.

Returning to her satchel, Angel took out her tool kit and hurried back to the man's side. She grabbed a razor blade from her tools and carefully cut through the gasket holding the two lenses of the glass together. Aether seeped from the gap at an alarming rate. Angel shoved it toward the man's face so rapidly he recoiled, only to come up hard against the wall of the shrine, halting his retreat.

When he tried to cry out, the palsy garbled the sound.

"Shhh… It's okay. It will be okay," Angel murmured, gently blowing the aether toward the wound. Like attracted like until the rent drew closed, slowly, awkwardly, like a big bandage wrapped over a small cut. The man visibly calmed as his lax muscles began to twitch, and then firmed up. To Angel's vision the aether drew in tighter and tighter until a dense, thin line formed like a scar. Relief flooded the man's gaze, tinged with confusion. And then, as with those bearing physical wounds needing much healing, slumber drew him down.

Angel arranged him more comfortably before retrieving her things and bringing them back to the shelter of the shrine.

In the morning, the man was gone, having left a tamale in token of thanks beside Angel's makeshift pillow. Sitting up, she broke her fast. Magically, Ujer appeared, side-hopping closer and cocking his head. She held the last piece out to him before he decided to snatch it on his own.

Angel frowned.

Such hunger. Such mind-numbing hunger.

Not Ujer. The teyolia. The Cihuateteo that did not realize she was Cihuateteo. Angel still felt the pain radiating from that tortured soul.

She had not understood. But now she did. A woman's heart… a *mother's* heart always searching, never finding. Left with no other purpose. But how?

Driven by impulse, Angel tethered the mare within easy reach of both grass and water, then settled down in the shrine to meditate, letting her mind work over the pieces of this mystery within her own grasp.

It was early evening before all the threads fell into place.

"She's still fighting," Angel mused aloud. "Still trying to snatch her child's soul from the gods. She does not know she lost."

It felt right. And also, very wrong.

"Is this what happens when a soul isn't properly sent on?" Angel murmured aloud.

Though she struggled to stay awake, to reason out if her theory was correct, Angel slumped, then nodded, then slept as the air grew chill and a cold glow lit the crossroads.

A jolt of pain hit Angel like an electric shock to her soul. Gasping, her back arched and her eyes flew open just as a chalky hand clawed at her. Her own hand shot out and locked around the Cihuateteo's wrist. Somehow, she held. Looking up into that death's-head grin, Angel only felt the pain. The ache of longing. The heart-rending agony of loss. This mother had been battling for a very, very long time.

Compassion welled within her until Angel finally realized what this weary soul needed.

"My little one, my daughter, my noble woman, you have wearied yourself, you have fought bravely." Angel whispered, fervently and heartfelt, hearing the echo of Abuela's voice in every word. "By your labors you have achieved a noble death, you have come to the place of the Divine. …*Go*, beloved child, little by little toward the Cihuateteo at long last and become one of them…"

The universe raised no objection at Angel's embellishment. Quite the opposite, as a sense of peace settled over her being as she finished. The Cihuateteo's hand relaxed in Angel's grip as she closed out the long-overdue prayer. As Angel finished, the spirit faded, rising like the last of the embers spiraling to the heavens.

Angel released a shuddering breath.

"Well done, my angel."

Angel yipped, clunking her head yet again, this time on the structure of the shrine.

Looking up she spied Santa Muerte standing before the goddess house. Beside her swayed the Cihuateteo's 'child'… a man-shaped collection of anger, fear, and pain; a composite of mindless swatches not quite complete, scraps of teyolia snatched from those ensnared souls that had vexed Angel so. They rippled and swayed, pulling taut then billowing, unable to free themselves. A sickly green glow bled through the gaps.

Angel sobbed, her hand trembling violently as she reached out, hundreds upon hundreds of jags of pain piercing her soul. Pain she shared with the collective before her. Pain she needed to heal.

With the memory of the restored traveler fresh in her mind, Angel bent her will to exacting those results in reverse, slowly drawing off the aether bindings stitching those fragments together like Shelley's creature. As each scrap slid free, it swirled in a joyous ribbon dance until Santa Muerte pursed her semblance of lips together and absorbed their aether into the underworld, leaving not one strand remaining.

"Why now?" Angel demanded once the goddess was done, too weary to be reverant, or even polite. "Why not when I called?"

Santa Muerte cocked her head, her aether layer dipping in a reproving look. "Cihuatlampa is not my realm, child."

Rather than vent her frustration, Angel considered the goddess's words, slowly nodding as realization dawned. "I had to deal with the mother first… to send her on her proper way."

"Well done, my angel," Santa Muerte repeated. "Now, you must complete the task."

Angel groaned in realization. All of those souls… so many souls. They were still out there, waiting to be reunited with those ribbons of themselves that Santa Muerte had just sent on.

Her chest ached already with anticipated jolts.

"But why the grown, who are already formed? Why not…"

Angel paused as a shudder shook her. All the damaged teyolia had been adult; the creature formed from their parts had been in the semblance of a man.

"Why not infants? So much closer to the child lost?"

"To those who are ancient, all are as children," Santa Muerte murmured as she turned and glided away, her fingers bones clacking gently, melodiously in farewell as her form faded in a swirl of pale marigold petals drifting on the wind.

The divine had their own way, and Angel doubted she would ever fully understand them.

As the glow of the petals slowly faded in kind, she flinched, startled out of her musings by the careful grip of talons alighting on her shoulder, catching in her shawl. A harsh, sleepy caw sounded by her ear as Ujer tucked his sleek-feathered head beneath the fall of her hair, all but blending in with her raven locks. Gently, he tugged her earlobe with his beak, chuckling and clicking in comforting tones.

Reaching up to ruffle his crest, Angel sighed and held him steady as she gathered her things. Dreading the thought of mounting once more, she led the mare by her halter and turned the three of them back toward home.

# Evil Obscura

## Rachel A. Brune

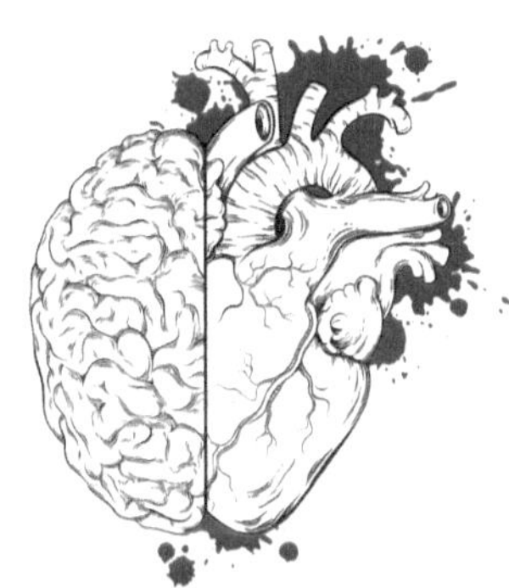

*Compilers' Note: The following narrative derives from the papers of the estate of Colonel Lady Marta XX and Lady Lydia XX. Their great-granddaughter, who discovered them in an old trunk while preparing the estate for sale, donated them to His Majesty's Museum of Early Air Warfare. Together, they provide an unvarnished and fascinating account of one of the little-known perspectives of the Crimean War — that of a tactical combat officer commanding a Troop of Light Airships. While the papers unfortunately refer several times to the presence or action of the supernatural, this historian believes that the recorder used those terms as shorthand for the technology or unexplained science used by their opponent. Further research is needed in this area.*

*These papers have been edited and annotated for clarity and to protect the privacy of the XX estate throughout. Any further inquiries should be directed to the Archives Department of the Museum of Early Air Warfare.*

ORDERS (PART ILLEGIBLE)
DATE: (OBSCURED.)
CLASSIFICATION: HIGHEST DISCRETION
FROM: HEADQUARTERS, HER MAJESTY'S 11TH AIR TROOP CAVALRY
TO: CAPTAIN LADY MARTA XX, BRAVO TROOP (LIGHT), 2ND BATTALION (COMBINED)

With General Lord Shelly's compliments, you are to proceed to the objective named "Farrier" Lat./Long. (*coordinates obscured*) to reconnoiter and rescue if it may be possible the Duchess Ygritte de Trefurant and retrieve any information regarding the rumors of the Imperial Chief Machinist Tarkov and reports of the progress on the mechanism known as the "Evil Eye."

Acknowledge upon receipt, yours, etc., etc.

Major Kelly Parker, Adjutant

*(Compiler's Note: The Duchess Ygritte de Trefurant was stationed with the 11th Air Troop overseeing the field deployment of her most recent innovation, the interval stabilizer that enabled the H17 Troop Transport to navigate altitudes three times higher than its previous maximum safe height. It is believed that her abduction was a crime of opportunity and not, as has been speculated, related to the rumored connection between the de Trefurant family and their industrial relations with the House of the Imperial Machinist Tarkov.)*

JOURNAL OF CAPTAIN MARTA XX
(DATE OBSCURED.)

Dearest Lydia, this was meant to be a letter, but as you reported my last appeared almost a single block of ink from the censor's unfriendly ministrations, I have purchased this small volume and will fill it with what I mean to say. Perhaps if I fall, some enemy may glean a bit of knowledge, but our unfriendly surroundings have the locals reporting on our comings and goings with some regularity, and you may read of our unvarnished exploits in the *Times* without my poor additions to the text.

The orders that sent me arrived from Bttn HQ, presented by a young private with great haste before I'd even had time to change my wool socks or repair the pulled stitching in my weapons belt. Indeed, I had not time to wipe the bloody dirt from my hands before the grime smudged half the ink.

We have been fighting these weeks against the hard line of the forests that cover the sharp hills in this area. The dense cover stymies our air formations and at night any sleep comes uneasy. There are whispers of men and women beset by unknown means by fiends who use the forest to attack and retreat at whim. Indeed, only this morning we woke before dawn and flew to extract a troop of infantry soldiers that had sent a rushed wireless call for rescue.

Our four mini-dirigibles made haste, escorting one of the large troop-transport airships. We flew our drones ahead as doctrine and *Sir Alexander's Manual of Air Warfare* demands, but the limitations of their ocular transmission did not prepare us for what was left on the ground. Of the fifty-nine berths in the transport, we filled barely half a baker's dozen with the remains. I do not wish to trouble you with the description; suffice it to say that Mr. Wilham's shop in the market could not ~~have prepared even that butcher for the~~ I am sorry, my dearest. These visions are fresh on me. If you are still reading, your artist's eye would be working overly.

And still, that symbol, I see it before me still, worked in blood, that of an eye… staring…

I may strike through this last, my Lydia. Perhaps I shall still keep this from you. But the strange nights and shadowy days lie heavy on my mind, and I must unburden myself or the dreams…

In any case, our orders await, and I hear my sergeant calling for last inspections. He will be here in a moment, and I must be ready. Our minis are faster than any dreams, and once in the air, I know this shadow will be stript away by the sun above the trees. We pursue an adventurer and woman of science, the Duchess Ygritte, who I am sure should have known better than to venture past the protection of our front lines, but I hold a similar woman dear in my heart and know more than most the futility of arguing with her. As for the "Evil Eye," I am sure that once we come upon it, we will see that it is no murderous boggart that cannot be explained by the sun of science.

Ah! The mail call. I will send my letter of platitudes and a small token — a ticket stub from the Grand Railroad Station here in XX. Perhaps you will receive it, if the censors do not seize it for their own use. Perhaps they can use the stains upon it to spin their own tale of dashing wartime heroics. You will not hear such from me.

Until next time.

*Compiler's Note: The Marquesa, grandmother to Lady Marta, was a refugee noble from the Eastern European states who provided valuable service to Her Majesty's intelligence department during the course of*

*the war due to her close familiarity with the region, language, and culture. It is unclear the meaning of "charm" referred to by the signatory and alluded to later in Lady Marta's journal; this item was unfortunately not included with the artifacts retrieved from the estate.*

LETTER FROM MARQUESA ANNA PIETROVNA SMITH TO CAPTAIN MARTA XX (C/O BRAVO TROOP, HER MAJESTY'S LIGHT AIR CORPS)

*(Date Obscured)*

*Dearest Marta,*

*I read with excitement and consternation the latest reports from the front. Excitement as I know firsthand the daily progress and setbacks of our struggle, consternation at the thought of my granddaughter at the mercy of the winds that slice through the mountains of my youth. If I have timed this correctly, you will not have left on your mission just yet. The wonderful machines you command may not lose the sky, but I beg of you to pin the enclosed charm to your sleeve, as I taught your mother. I pray you will humor what may seem the superstitions of an old woman from the same mountains through which you ride the winds. But you yourself may see — may have already felt — the darkness more than night that follows you under the cover of the forest.*

*Your loving grandmother, etc., etc.*

*Anna Pietrovna*

* * *

LADY MARTA'S JOURNAL EXCERPT, UNDATED.

Dearest Lydia,

I wrote earlier of my desire to launch my mission as early as humanly possible. And thanks to the efforts of Sergeant Wilcox, we lifted before dawn, our four minis rising in perfect formation, the drones darting out like hummingbirds to chart our course. We are traveling due west now, the dawn at our backs, the untraversable peaks to our north.

I cannot shake the sense of dread that refuses to lift. My hopes that the sun would wash away uneasy dreams are not to be realized; the day broke under a thick, unyielding layer of cloud and fog that reaches down and drizzles its lanky fingers under our flying leathers.

The forests have begun to turn with the season, and even the brilliant scarlets among the dark, thick pines fail to lift my spirits. I had hoped the letter from my grandmother would offer some small note of comfort, but now I cannot escape the horror of the charm she sent. I do not know why I followed her instructions and pinned it inside my sleeve. I feel it rustling there now. That charm—that eye—that same symbol written in the blood of fallen soldiers—

Official Report of Engagement of the Enemy (OREE)
0214
Date: (Deliberately Obscured)
Location: 5 km ESE Objective FARRIER


At approximately a half hour after dusk, our drones detected small flames burning through the canopy below. Shortly thereafter, an unknown number of crude arrows, dipped in some form of oil and set aflame, were launched at our position in the air. Three arrows struck our first mini-dirigible, which rendered its flight hydraulics inoperable and forced a landing short of our rendezvous site. The rest of the troop, aided by our drones, pursued the unknown attackers, whose position was only identified by the torches they held aloft to light their arrows.

We landed in a clearing ESW of the attackers, who turned to face us, their retreat foiled by the rocky terrain and a sharp cliff rising up behind them. We engaged them with our dirigible weapons, then alighted to pursue the final stragglers, as they took cover within the trees where our weapons were ineffective.

We interrogated the last surviving member of the band and learned that they had indeed kidnapped Duchess Ygritte, but they had been attacked by a swarm of ten men wearing the livery colors of the Imperial House, who had decimated their numbers and taken the Duchess from them.

Although we attempted to glean any further information on the Imperial device known as the "Evil Eye," we were unsuccessful and the man succumbed to his injuries shortly after. We are sending this report with the crew of our downed mini-dirigible, and will proceed to our final objective in pursuit of Duchess Ygritte.

Signed,
Captain XX

*Compiler's Note: This section, along with a select few others, was carefully cut from the journal and placed in a thick envelope addressed to Lord Dino von Hicks, sibling to Colonel Lady Marta XX. Our reasonable conjecture leads us to understand that the colonel wished to preserve these documents, but intended them for her sibling's receipt, rather than the more delicate sensibilities of Lady Lydia. We discovered no clue that indicated why the package was never mailed.*

*Technical Addendum: Throughout, then-Captain Lady Marta refers to her "weapon" and her "blade." Like most of her commissioned comrades, the "blade" refers to the heavy officer's blade presented upon the purchase of her commission; far from decorative, these swords were highly functional. A receipt found in the estate's ledger indicates it was purchased in 1846; although some families chose to present a family legacy to newly-commissioned officers, the XX estate indicates that no such legacy blade existed. Indeed, the whereabouts of this blade are currently unknown.*

*As for the "weapon", we can only assume that Lady Marta was issued the standard SW-127 40 .cal steam-propelled, air-cooled, dual-ammunition sidearm typically carried by all members of the Light Air Corps.*

* * *

JOURNAL EXCERPT OCTOBER 13, 18XX

~~Dearest Lydia~~

I have found the turmoil in my heart and mind too great to set these words down with ease, even knowing that you will not see them until a very great time has passed. And still, my own confusion and shadow weighs upon me… I do not know why I should have left those details from the official reports; I attempt to write them down as even with only a week's time between our encounter and now, they begin to fade and I question if I even… I shall write what I remember in the order it happened as simply and quickly as I can and hope that what I set down may be enough to keep these memories and the nightmares they bring at bay.

You know the basic narrative from the official reports. But they cannot capture the soul-drenching fear of the soft *shrrk shrrk* of the arrows as they grew larger, the light from their fires reflecting in the copper struts of the drones and fins of our mini-dirigibles. One unlucky hit could spell the sudden end to any of our troops. Yet, the haste with which our enemy fired or the crude nature of his weapons, either sufficed to disable the flight controls from one of our minis, and leave it merely stranded instead of destroyed.

We landed farther towards the destination and alighted, pursuing the men who had attacked us almost before the dirigible had settled. Any hesitation our troops might have had at launching an attack through the forest as dusk drew shadows was lost in the desperation with which our foes struck at us and the ferocity with which we met them. Our troop's weapons whined and burst, the rounds raining a death of metal shrapnel upon them which their crude arrows could not turn. My blade grew bloody as it slipped and pierced my opponent, and I lost myself somewhere in the gruesome dance. My breath grew quick and my arm wearied until, as I could not raise my blade for fatigue, I realized that all had gone quiet around me.

We had driven our attackers against the floor of a ravine, a stark cliff rising behind them. It was surrounded on three sides by the forest, and only this slight clearing provided relief from the gathering gloom. They had made this their camp. The feeble flames of a cook fire threw monstrous shadows against the night. It was only as the fury of the battle faded that I realized two things.

First, the men and women who attacked us had seen more than one fight that day; bodies lay strewn around the clearing. What had killed them—they showed no wounds I could say with clarity. Some lay in pieces, guts and brain matter slashed to ribbons and strewn in paths across their corpses. Others, intact except for a single, roughly circular hole ripped through their torso, had died in the throes of a desperate fear still written on their tortured face.

A few of the bodies bore signs of having been ministered to, with their arms crossed and feet bootless, prepared for burial. The blood around all these bodies had gone brown and cold, contrasting with the fresh splashes on those we had slaughtered and on my own blade.

The second realization—a sight that chilled my own blood and put a lie to our report. For there, on the bodies of each of the slain men and women, and repeated in a grisly mural painted on the cliff, was the sign of the mysterious Evil Eye.

◉

*Compiler's Note: The final documents consisted of the debrief upon return from the mission, which was so disintegrated as to be illegible and unusable. The following journal pages, containing Lady Marta's depiction of the scene detailed in the brief and addressed to her brother, was post-dated several months after the incident, as she recovered from wounds sustained in the battle. We caution the reader to view judiciously the description of the marvels contained therein, as time and memory have foiled the most diligent of archivists, let alone the emotion-fueled sensational report of events months previous by a soldier who had spent much of that time recovering from the fog of soldier's heart.*

I do not know if anyone should read this, even you, brother Dino. I have spent the past months recovering, they tell me, from the fatigue of soldier's heart, and that has affected my memory, my ability to communicate, and even think coherently. I myself feel as if I have been swimming underwater in a dark lake, unsure if I am heading to the light of the surface or descending farther into the dark. And all the time, ~~I feel as~~

How do I describe the haunted feeling, as if he still pursues, of the demon Tarkov who wielded the Evil Eye with such vicious malice. If I were to glance behind me, in the shadows, I would not be surprised to see the orange gleam of the monster Eye. Does my mind tell me the true details, or is this another fever that has fallen

~~I cannot My dearest~~

~~It gleamed~~

~~I cannot I can't I am drowning and all the water is flames that I cannot find my way out for the love God I CAN STILL SEE THE DEMON EYE~~

*(Compiler's Note: There are several pages missing from the journal before the narrative begins again on a fresh page.)*

To return to where we were at the end of the first night, we left the butchery of the camp behind us. I sent the crew of our downed dirigible to return on foot with the hasty account of our engagement and proceeded ahead with our remaining three crews. We flew our drones ahead, but approached on foot to limit our chances of detection.

Our objective, named Farrier by our orders, was on a slight crest, nestled between two sharp, impassable peaks. There was only one narrow path that led from the main road to the castle above, barely wide enough for two loaded carts to pass. It was the sort of remote stronghold that the advent of air cargo transportation had allowed.

We left the road, approaching the grounds through the forest. The cover of night quickly dissipated, and although we felt the extremity of our mission, I decided that it would be courting failure to approach as the dawn arose and betrayed our position, so we made camp and slept fitfully under the trees.

~~As night fell, we~~

These details are unimportant. We made it to the castle, entering unawares. It was not as difficult as one might imagine, or perhaps I don't remember clearly given what was to follow. It could have been one night. It could have been many. But we crept through the halls. They were dark. Or perhaps they were lit by sputtering candles in the black, iron sconces. I seem to recall the light splashing our shadows against the stone walls like a jerky pantomime show for Hell's imps to attend.

My hand never wavered, tired and fatigued as we were, the weight of my blade the one solid thing in my grip.

At last we came to a vast room. Perhaps at one time it was a ballroom, but now the tapestry-draped walls enclosed something rather more sinister. I led my troop into the chamber, Sergeant Wilson on my left, his weapon at the ready. Before us stood a maze of tubes and gears and shadows. To our right, a cabinet of organic curiosities held the remains of animals I am sure never roamed any natural landscape, their eyes and hides and nails twisted and deformed.

Sergeant Wilson grunted and pointed to the left. A large desk sat, covered with paper upon which had been scrawled arcane notes. Models of weird forces, engraved with unknown runes, sat dormant, as if awaiting the right spark of hellish energy to demonstrate their power. A woman sat in a chair before the broad surface, her bright red hair vibrant even in this murky space.

Motioning to Sergeant Wilson to stay behind, I approached. It quickly grew apparent that the woman was dead, the unnatural paleness of her limbs the result of the slashes that rent her face and torso, spilling blood and viscera down her skirts and staining the floor under her desk. Despite the violence visited upon her, she sat, rigid, staring ahead with lifeless eyes, her right hand still grasping the pen with which she had been writing.

And on the page, row after row, in a cramped and shaky hand, the words, "The eye the eye the eye the eye…"

A scream from behind us tore my attention away from the corpse of Duchess Ygritte. I turned to see my rear-most team disappear in the shadows, their shrieks cut off so abruptly the silence left behind rang in our ears.

Skittering… like the long claws of a dog with far too many limbs… a shadow on the wall dancing from the lights of too many candles. Sergeant Wilson whimpered. A tear rolled down his face, though he held his weapon steady.

It came into view. As one, we fired, the deafening sound of our weapons in that space echoing until it became one long tortured cacophony. And as if in some nightmare of the Devil's making, the rounds that we fired made no difference. It shambled toward us and ripped the first soldier in half from head to toe, each side sloughing apart before the man had time to blink or realize he was dead.

The only part of the creature still human was the black and gold livery he wore, with the gold embroidered sash of the Imperial Chief Machinist Tarkov. His ~~arms, legs~~ – LIMBS. His limbs, with too many joints, too many of them to be real… Did I see them, moving, jointed, the nails on the ends grown far too long and curved wickedly like a dagger, blood dripping and other, darker things. ~~He~~ It ~~moved~~ scuttered like a crab, forward, sideways, too fast to catch it and two more soldiers fell under our own bullets. Tarkov barely slowed to rake the next two, disemboweling them, spilling their bright red and dark brown viscera across the ground.

I stood, frozen, out of ammunition. Sergeant Wilson fired twice more, then reached for another magazine to find none left. Stepping forward I raised my blade.

Tarkov stopped. And then he…

Smiled.

He smiled.

Oh God, Dino, as I think of it now, I wonder if it is a dream or if the image burned into my sight could have been true. His mouth full of too many teeth, like a ravening wolf. And things, embedded within. But the horror even worse than Tarkov's teeth, worse than the bodies of my men and women lying in their own offal, worse than the final sob as Tarkov whipped his claws around and ripped out Sergeant Wilson's throat…

Was the Eye.

It gleamed and shuddered, rotating and palpitating, a sickly orange flecked with bits of bilish green and pale pink. Centered in his chest, it rolled independently of Tarkov's gaze, a nauseating independence that brought the taste of vomit to my mouth. A black pupil in the center sucked the light from the room. My gaze couldn't bear to stay more than a moment on the Eye, but I recognized its symbol. I'd seen it written in blood more than once on this mission.

The monster that had been Tarkov raised one of its hands, claws vibrating, and I lifted my blade, expecting to join the rest of my soldiers in the afterlife. And then, inexplicably, Tarkov smiled.

"I know you."

My shock at the words must have showed on my face.

"Your grandmother… the traitor… I thought they might send you after…" Too many teeth gave its words a slobbery slur. "You see, I needed just the last equation—" Saliva dripped down its chin.

I stepped back, hoping desperately to find a way out, knowing the only choice would be to somehow make it around the monstrous Eye and then run slipping through the congealing remains of my soldiers.

"You kill those who work for you?" My voice cracked, dry and strained.

"They demanded more… money." The monster shrugged. My mind almost didn't comprehend the gesture, it seemed so uncanny—the Eye followed the motion. "She gave me the last key."

The last key to the Eye. Then, my mind did not comprehend past the screams I choked back, but now it has become clear. The Eye was an eldritch marriage of steam and science, with something darker and more arcane beneath its pulsating surface. Tarkov had sought mastery of the Eye, and in doing so, had become something miscreated, inhuman.

Tarkov laughed, a deep giggle that set my teeth against each other, and attacked.

I raised my blade, dodging the claws, slashing three fingers from one hand. They landed wetly on the floor as Tarkov lunged at me with his other limbs. The rest of the room faded. All I saw before me was the rolling, protuberant Eye.

The charm on my arm clicked and in the space of half a breath had torn through the sleeve of my uniform to create a thin copper shield. Tarkov's limbs hit the shield with enough length to graze deep furrows down the side of my head and neck even as I lunged forward aiming with the point of my blade.

The steadfast steel stuck on the Eye for one heart-stopping moment, and I lost control of my bowels before pushing farther forward.

Tarkov shrieked and tried to rear back. I screamed as his claws broke my skin, pierced my torso and legs. Our grandmother's present held firm, but his reach was too much to defend against all together. One limb, and then another, and yet another gripped me in tight embrace.

The Eye tried to roll, but I pushed my blade until the hilt sank into the darkness of the pupil. As I touched the wet, pulpy mass, I shielded my gaze, waiting for the claws to slash, unmaking me like so many others before. I welcomed the darkness, the infinite beyond, grateful that I would not have to face my failure or the wasted lives that lay spread around, still gleaming wetly in the dull light of the laboratory.

I waited for a death that did not come.

*Compiler's Final Note: Here ends the extracted journal pages. The next entry, some several weeks later, does not reference any of the previous events. Captain Marta returned to service after a year's convalescence. She rose to the rank of Colonel and commanded a brigade of His Majesty's Air Troops in the Anglo-Afghan War. Shortly after, she retired to civilian life. Further information about her life and her family faded into obscurity until the discovery of the correspondence at her estate.*

*This paper has been published under the auspices of the Department of History, Cambridge with generous thanks to the Archives Department of the Museum of Early Air Warfare for their gracious assistance.*

# The Lambton Wyrm
### *A Story in the Clockwork Chronicles Universe*

## MICHELLE D. SONNIER

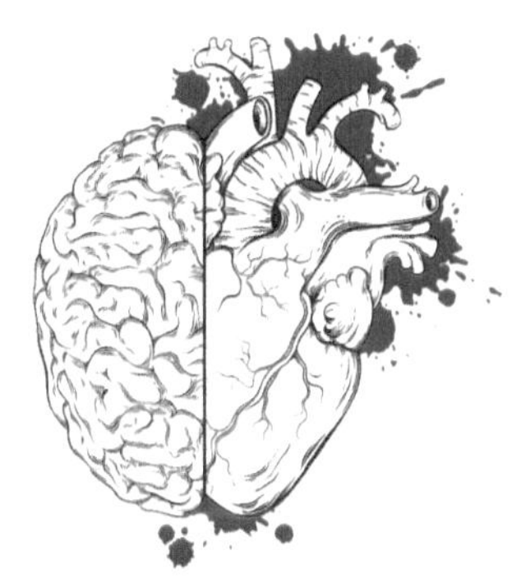

A STACCATO RAPPING ON HER BEDROOM window startled Arabella out of her reverie. At first she saw nothing framed in the window, but then spotted a large raven wheeling against the glowering gray sky, picking up speed.

She hurried to wrench up the sash, diving out of the way just in time. Feathers skimmed the top of her head. She heard a few wing beats, then the scritch of talons gripping wood.

Arabella raised her head to eye the messenger raven, now perched on the back of her chaise lounge. He hopped from foot to foot, bobbing his head and clacking his beak. Hauling herself to her feet, she dusted off her skirts, muttering, "There's no call to laugh at me."

"Quork!" the bird exclaimed and bobbed his head emphatically one last time.

Her mechanical messenger birds would never be so cheeky.

Arabella examined the warrant medallion that lay against his chest. "Prankster, thy name is… Bran. Don't you have something for me?"

Bran drew himself up into a regal pose, extending one leg toward Arabella. A small leather quiver, closed on both ends, opened easily to Arabella's fingers. She pulled out a tightly furled letter and flattened it on the seat next to her.

"I'm sure you can find your way to the kitchen," Arabella murmured distractedly. "The ladies will happily coo over your handsome feathers and feed you tidbits." With a farewell croak, Bran launched himself off the chairback and flew through the doorway to the rest of the house.

Arabella turned the letter over. The wax seal was cracked from being rolled in the message case, but it still held. The address was a bit blurred from a long trip through the gloomy autumn weather, but the hand was unmistakable. She'd known it all her life. But why was Amelia writing to her? Of course, they were sisters and family fealty ran strong in all witch households, but they had never been especially close. Amelia preferred the company of her older sisters, not the youngest of the brood. She mentally shrugged and snapped the wax seal.

*Arabella,*

> *You must come to Lambton immediately. I hardly know what to call the monstrous thing that is harassing us, but you are the only person I can think of who might be able to bring us some peace.*

> *Make sure to bring…*

> *Make haste,*

> *Amelia*

A small blob of red wax covered the word telling her what to bring. Arabella frowned. It was not like Amelia to be so careless with her correspondence. Carefully, she worried her fingernail against the wax until she got enough purchase to try prying it up. She hoped that she could ease it away gently enough not to tear the paper, and discover what Amelia needed so desperately for her to bring. The wax snapped.

Magic flooded through Arabella's body; magic so strong that even the most muddle-headed mundane would have felt it. Dread swirled in her belly. Unwinding like a living creature to crawl up her throat and seize her breath, as a compulsion seeped into her bones. A geas. The burning need to go immediately to Lambton overwhelmed Arabella. Nothing would douse the fire but to travel north, almost to the border of Scotland, and present herself to her sister.

Even as she feverishly stuffed necessities into a valise, under the all-consuming desire to go and go *now*, a different flame flickered in Arabella's breast. She growled through clenched teeth as she finished her packing. How dare Amelia? How dare she force what Arabella would have willingly given?

The geas tormented Arabella as the train screamed north up the track. She paced her private compartment, three steps up, three steps back, like an exotic cat in a cage. Her skin crawled and itched with the compulsive need to be in Lambton, making it impossible to sit, sleep, or in any way enjoy her two-day journey on this marvelous steam-powered creation.

Even so, she caught glimpses of what a pleasure the trip could have been for a technomantic witch like herself, from the mechanical hole punch the conductor used to mark tickets that glimmered like a tiny fairy; to the unending streamers of golden light that painted the floor in regular patterns as the machinery of the undercarriage responded to the pull of the locomotive. But every time her mind wandered from the singular purpose of getting to Lambton, the geas spell viciously pulled her back.

Arabella alighted from her train carriage disheveled and strained. She scanned the platform around her, but the cursed weather confounded her. Light drizzle kept everything uncomfortably damp while streamers of fog wound through the crowd obscuring faces. Arabella felt her spirit rise as Amelia hurried out of looming fog bank, waving to get her attention.

She held herself stiff as Amelia embraced her, kissing her cheek. At her sister's touch, the burning compulsion at last lifted, like a damp chill burning off beside the heat of a fire. All of Arabella's frustration, anger, and betrayal bubbled up. But before she could say word Amelia whispered into her ear. "Ari, I need to explain, please don't be angry…"

Before Amelia could continue, a haughty voice emerged from the fog. "Amelia, I realize you have not seen your sister in some time but really, there are rules of decorum in public."

Amelia flushed and stepped away from her sister, dropping her eyes as she murmured, "Yes, Mother Hamilton."

The woman who accompanied the strident voice cutting through the fog stopped in front of Arabella, looking her up and down. Amelia's fiancé hovered behind his mother, his expression strained. The woman reminded Arabella of her own mother, composed and severe, but older and thinner.

Arabella lowered her eyes and sank into the most graceful curtsy Mother taught her. "Miss Arabella Leyden of Blackstone House, at your service. It's a pleasure to meet you…" She trailed off and anxiety knotted her stomach. She couldn't remember the name of Amelia's future mother-in-law, nor even her title.

Amelia blanched. "Sister, dear, may I present you to Beatrix Frances Hamilton of Aberdean House, Lady Dunham and Viscountess Lambton." The viscountess extended her hand to Arabella with a raised eyebrow aimed at Amelia.

"It is an honor, my Lady." Arabella took the woman's fingertips and curtseyed over her hand, a tingle of magic shivering over her skin. Lady Lambton was a strong enough witch for Arabella to feel, even without an affinity for the earth-based magics. She also possessed titles of mundane peerage, a formidable woman indeed. And one who owed fealty to a House that had *not* backed Arabella during the Trials.

Lady Lambton withdrew her hand with a sniff. "At least your manners are better than your sister's." Arabella caught Amelia's flinch out of the corner of her eye. "I dare hope you are competent enough to take care of our little problem."

"Now, Mother…" Nathaniel began.

"Now nothing," his mother cut him off. "I have already deemed your bride-to-be acceptable. Her bloodline is impressive, after all. But her manners have clearly been spoiled being raised in the cosmopolitan south." She flicked a glare at Amelia. "*We* abide by the old ways."

Arabella ground her teeth, struggling to maintain her composure. The witches of Blackstone House certainly did *not* give the old ways short shrift. But before Arabella could draw breath to defend her House, a desperate voice rang out through the fog.

"My Lady! My Lady!" The sound of hurried footsteps preceded a middle-aged gentleman emerging from the fog. By his dress he was one of the house servants of Lambton Castle. He stumbled to a stop in front of Lady Lambton, panting, bent over with his hands on his knees.

"For Brigantia's sake, Godwin! Pull yourself together."

"Apologies… My Lady…" he gasped out. He swallowed hard and drew himself upright, wobbling as he did so. "The Wyrm has returned. It's already taken a cow from the Cooper's pasture. Now it's in the Chesterton's lower fields going after their sheep."

"Time to get to work, girl." The viscountess nodded to Arabella, then turned on her heel and marched off into the fog. "Godwin," she called over her shoulder. "See to Miss Leyden's luggage."

Arabella crossed her arms as she turned to Amelia. "I think you had better explain a few things."

Amelia blushed and twisted her hands together. "Well… you see…"

"Perhaps you lovely ladies can have this discussion on our way to the Chesterton's fields?" Nathaniel took Amelia and Arabella's elbows and guided them off the train platform. "We can take my pony trap."

It was disconcerting how quickly the train station disappeared behind them in the fog. All around, banks of swirling mist obscured the landscape. A shiver tickled Arabella's spine. The fog reminded her a bit too much of the unsettling dreams that had plagued her of late. The thick air muffled sounds. She couldn't see, she couldn't hear, the entire world reduced to the cramped pony trap and a few yards of packed dirt. Beyond the miasma around them might very well be absolutely nothing, a void waiting to swallow them. Turning away from the unsettling view, Arabella leveled a hard gaze on her sister

"Sister dear? Pray tell me why did you feel the need to *compel* me to come? And why does your future mother-in-law seem to believe I am hired help of some sort?"

Amelia, squashed in between Nathaniel and Arabella, reddened. She kept her eyes straight ahead, refusing to look at her sister.

"I didn't think she would come to the station at all," Amelia said. "And I didn't think the Wyrm would appear precisely when you arrived. I thought I'd have the ride back to the castle to apprise you of the situation."

"You're avoiding my questions," Arabella huffed. "Perhaps we should start with just the one. Why the geas?"

Amelia dropped her gaze down to her hands in her lap and spoke in barely a whisper, "I wasn't sure you would come if I told the truth."

Arabella's eyes blazed. Had she not always served her sisters as they trained and cast their spells in service of the family and Blackstone House? Had she ever shirked her sororal duties?

Amelia lifted her eyes to her sister. "I know I have not always been kind to you, Arabella. There is no excuse for how we… *I* took you for granted. After the way we all treated you…" Amelia bit her lip, blinking away tears. "I wouldn't have blamed you if you hadn't come."

Arabella swallowed back the hot retort balanced on her tongue. A witch must always keep her temper. Without control, a witch's magic had been known to blight fields or kill bystanders. She closed her eyes for a moment to calm herself. "I can't say that I am at peace with everything that happened in our girlhood. However, you are my sister by both blood and House. Even if I could find a way to morally abandon my duty to you, I would not. We shall deal with the... impertinence... of your geas another time."

A sob escaped Amelia. She dabbed her eyes with a lacy handkerchief.

Nathaniel cleared his throat. "Perhaps I should tell you the story of the creature while my dear bride composes herself." Nathaniel favored Amelia with a small smile.

"Well, now... Let's see... A few hundred years ago, one of the witches in our family line made a dire mistake in her spell experimentation and created a ravenous creature known as the Lambton Wyrm. The details of how it all came to be are really quite boring. I prefer to focus on the positive part of the story, that the family took responsibility and our foremothers managed to tame the beast enough so that it only needed a sacrifice once a week! Why, most of the time we feed the Wyrm from our own flocks and herds. We only ask the villagers and cotters to contribute every few months..."

"Nathaniel, you need to tell her the truth," Amelia murmured.

Nathaniel pulled a face. "Do you really think so?" His voice dropped to a whisper that Arabella had no trouble hearing in the close confines of the pony trap. "She's not family."

"She's my family!" Amelia hissed through gritted teeth.

Nathaniel paled a little. "Yes, yes. I certainly see your point, my dear." He leaned across Amelia to give Arabella a conspiratorial wink. "We have the utmost trust in you, but you really mustn't share this with anyone else."

"I feel honored," Arabella said acerbically.

Nathaniel grimaced. "The part about my family creating the creature in the first place is true enough. Great-great-however many greats-grandmother Alyse really was more than a bit mad. Brilliant, but not quite all there. The part we, the family, tend to leave out is that we've known how to destroy it for quite some time."

Arabella narrowed her eyes. "How long is quite some time?"

Nathaniel cleared his throat. "Just a few generations, really. Can't be more than a hundred years..."

Arabella caught her squawk of astonishment before it left her throat. She sat with the idea for a moment, the idea of a noble family allowing some sort of monster to terrify their people and eat their precious livestock on a regular schedule, even though they knew perfectly well how to stop it. "But why?" she finally asked.

"Mother says that it's the only way to keep the mundane people from turning on us as they did to the Irish witches. She says you city witches are too insulated from the changes in country folk attitudes. They don't remember the Dark Ages so much when they can't read." Nathaniel gave Arabella a pleading look. "We've never allowed it to hurt people, not once we knew how to control it! And most of the livestock it eats comes from our lands!"

Arabella held up her hand to forestall any further justifications.

"Whether or not your foremothers were right and moral, and whether or not your mother is correct about the differences between city folk and country folk is beside the point. Something has changed and now you expect *me* to fix it. What changed?" Arabella asked.

Nathaniel nodded. "The Wyrm seems to have some other master now. People swear they've seen a rider on its back, but no one can get close enough to be certain. Mother's control spells have become ineffective; she can no longer touch its mind. We have no idea when or where it will show up, nor what or how much it will eat." He paused, flicking a glance over at Arabella. "And it seems to have armor on parts of it now."

"It's a hotchpotch of metals," Amelia put in. "Copper, brass, steel, tin—almost like a tortoiseshell cat. Quite the patchwork of color. The local earth witches thought they could control it through the metals, but they say they can't grab hold. It just keeps slipping through the fingers of their magic like sand…"

"That was when Mother finally started hearing the gossip from London about your peculiar power," Nathaniel said. "She demanded Amelia prevail upon you to solve our little predicament."

"So." Amelia asked, her voice subdued. "Will you help us?"

Arabella let out a frustrated sigh. "I don't see that I really have a choice, even without a geas." She glared at her sister. Amelia looked away, blushing.

"Let me think," Arabella murmured as she settled back and worried her bottom lip with her teeth. After a moment she said, "Nathaniel, you said your foremothers knew how to destroy the beast? How?"

He swallowed hard. "You need running water, and a lot of it. The Wyrm can regenerate as long as its blood is close to its body. The water would wash it all away before that could happen."

"Does it still have blood? Or has its new master changed it so much it's no longer a creature of flesh?"

Nathaniel paled but didn't answer. He brought the pony trap to a gentle stop. "And here we are!"

Arabella peered about her into the unchanging banks of mist. "How can you tell?" she said, dubiously.

"I've lived on these lands all my life. I have an excellent sense of direction." He shrugged with a sheepish grin. "I just seem to always know where I am."

As Nathaniel handed the ladies down from the trap another voice called out of the mist.

"Is that you, milord?"

"Yes, Chesterton," Nathaniel called out. "We came as quickly as we could."

A middle-aged man with a bristling beard and a limp materialized from the fog. "You've not missed the bugger. It's already savaged my best ram because the daft thing tried to protect his ewes. And now my best shepherdess, down from me cousins in the Highlands, is out there trying to protect the herd because she hasn't got the good sense…" He noticed Arabella and Amelia with a start. He tipped his cap. "Pardon my language, ladies, I didn't see you there."

Nathaniel handed Mr. Chesterton the pony's reins. "No time to waste. That thing moves quickly. We don't want to miss it." He hopped two steps up the tall verge, stopping at the top to hold his hand out to the ladies.

As they stepped up, the hazy air closed in behind them. It was just the three of them standing in long grass surrounded by banks of white fog. So much like her nightmares… Arabella shivered and surreptitiously pinched the inside of her wrist. When she didn't bolt awake in her own bed, she reached out and clutched Amelia's hand. Nathaniel took Amelia's other hand and they trooped off together across the mist-shrouded grass. It didn't take long for Arabella's soft little boots and the hem of her dress to get soaked.

They hadn't been walking long when the round and weathered stones marking the boundary of the field appeared first as a gray smear across the horizon. The demarcation sharpened as they drew closer. Nathaniel confidently turned right and followed the line of the wall.

"I hope we will not have to go into the field proper, but if we do the stile is over here," he said.

Arabella trailed her fingers across the bumpy top of the wall, reveling in the sensation of something solid and decidedly un-dreamlike. That was when the sounds caught her attention.

First, chugging.

Then, clacking.

Then a hiss, sibilant over the distant mechanical chorus.

Arabella closed her eyes and let her magical senses rove. There was something out there. Something beautiful. It sang to her. The pistons of an engine formed the pounding base of the song. They drove the gears that meshed in hissing, rhythmic harmonies. Small bits of metal—legs?—clicked together in a tinkling glissando, up and down, swirling around the melody of the machine.

Then a fleshy squelch interrupted the music. Another wet sound, like a stone plopping into a deep mud puddle ruined the steady baseline. Out in the fog an unearthly screech tore across mundane hearing. Arabella flinched.

In front of her, Amelia stopped. Arabella let go of her sister's hand and surged forward on her own, eyes closed. She tried to block out the off-tempo organic sounds interrupting her mechanical chorus. Her hand still trailed down the brick wall. She met the wooden upright of the stile, tracing her hand upward languidly. Arabella mounted the weathered steps of the wooden stile as if the act were the most familiar thing in the world to her. She kept her eyes closed, almost holding her breath.

At the top, she finally opened her eyes. Her gaze lighted on the source of her music. The Lambton Wyrm moved sinuously across the wet grass through the lightening mist. And most of it was indeed beautiful, to Arabella. The magic swirled and danced endlessly through, around, and below the gleaming metal carapace, covering most of the sickly white flesh beneath. The lights twinkled across the softening fog like nothing Arabella had seen before. She saw what Amelia had meant about the riot of color along the shell. It should not have been so lovely. But the colors mixed and surged through the movement of the machine to create a stunning piece of art. Arabella gasped in wonder.

"It's beautiful."

"Beautiful? Sister, do you need spectacles?" Amelia asked.

Amelia's tone pulled Arabella's spirit a bit closer to earth. She looked at the machine with more discerning eyes. It looked almost exactly like a millipede writ large. Not as tall as a steam locomotive, but nearly as long. It did not need a track to run on because it ran on dozens and dozens of tiny feet that distributed its weight well enough that the whole contraption did not sink into the damp turf. The head of the beast showed more of the Wyrm than any other part. A huge brass piece with uneven spikes covering the lower jaw. An iron mask gripped so tight it seemed to be painted across the creature's eyes and led up to a bronze box covered with levers. Behind the levers sat an ordinary leather saddle, and upon that saddle sat an ordinary man hauling on those levers and cursing the beast he rode.

The sound of frantic *baa*-ing broke out of the mist. Mr. Chesterton's sheep ran franticly toward the stone fence, herded from behind by Mr. Chesterton's brave cousin. The Wyrm increased speed and chugged after them. The whole spectacle rushed right for the stile in the fence. Arabella focused on the oncoming machine, putting the cries behind her out of her mind. She needed to understand. She pushed her senses out further and…

The rider's head whipped up and fixed a gaze on Arabella. He jammed levers down, and the creature shrieked in agony, shaking its head back and forth. The rider clung tight and knocked a fist into another lever. Screeching, the creature leapt forward.

Nathaniel's arm clasped around Arabella's waist from behind just as the wooden stile exploded from the Wyrm's impact. As she and Nathaniel hit the ground with splinters raining down above them, Arabella heard metal scrape across stone. Then the noise and magic disappeared into the distance, leaving her bereft. She whimpered.

"Are you alright?" Nathaniel demanded as he lifted her gently from the grass. "Speak to me, Arabella! Are you alright?"

"Why did you do that!" Amelia fell to the ground on her knees at Arabella's side. "You could have been killed!"

Arabella shook their hands away. "I'm fine, I'm fine." To prove it she hauled herself to her feet without help, only to wobble, much to her dismay.

A dark head popped up over the remains of the stile. "Hallooo! Are ye all in one piece o'er there?"

"No thanks to you!" shouted Nathaniel. "Why did you lead that damn thing toward her?"

"Keep the heid!" the shepherdess shouted back. "I was protectin' me flock. I did nae even see her standin' there like a gormless loon."

"I said, I'm fine!" Arabella pushed away Nathaniel's hands even as she swayed harder. She shouted up to the shepherdess, "Was that the first time you've seen the creature? What can you tell us about it?" Nathaniel grabbed her elbow as she almost toppled over.

"If'n ye don mind me sayin', ye don look so fine to me, lassie." The woman said, her brow furrowed in concern. "T'isn't the first time I seen the damned beast, but t'is the first time I seen it so close. Hope it's the last time, aye..."

Arabella tried to nod, but a sharp pain stabbed behind her eyes. She gasped.

"The name's Dannie Mac. Ai need to get me flock home afore that blighter returns. Ye caen find me at my cousin's, the Chesterton farm. Take care o' yerself, lassie." Her head started to disappear below the ruined stile again.

Arabella wanted to leave the melancholy bleats of sheep behind her. Just go to Lambton Castle and lay her aching head on a soft pillow, putting the world out of her mind for just a little while. But the Wyrm was still out there, doing Goddess knew what.

"Wait!" she called out to Dannie Mac.

"Eh?" she called as she popped back up.

"We must find this beast before it does any more damage. Did you see which way it went after it hit the stile?" Arabella asked.

Dannie frowned as she looked off into the fog. "It seemed to be headed for the gate at tha lower end o' the field."

"Then that's where we have to go." Arabella pushed away from Nathaniel and marched toward the mangled stile with purpose.

"There's no way we can chase that thing foot," Nathaniel called to her back. "We're not fast enough."

Arabella turned to Amelia. "Does your telepathy reach as far as the castle?"

"I can reach there without a problem," she said.

"Good. Call for horses to meet us wherever we are," Arabella said. She looked up at the deep gray sky above the fog that was finally breaking up. "Have them bring rain gear too. I think we may need it." She clambered over what was left of the stile leaving Amelia and Nathaniel with no other choice than to follow her.

Dannie Mac's suspicions proved true. As Arabella, Nathaniel, and Amelia found the lower field gate shattered, rain began to fall.

"Sometimes I don't like being right," Arabella muttered.

Nathaniel sank down to his heels to get a closer look at the grass outside the gate. He pointed to his left, north, and said, "I think it went that way. There's not much in the way of tracks but the grass is freshly torn."

They turned north, trudging uphill in the steadily increasing rain.

Four shattered gates and three fields later, the Lambton Castle Head Groom delivered them horses, rain gear, and stoneware flasks of hot tea. Fortified, they continued their hunt. Although the rain made the search miserable, it also made it easier since mud showed the creature's tracks better than dry grass.

Arabella's heart fell to the pit of her stomach when she spied the first patch of earth with crisscrossing tracks. Looking across field, she noted other patches of crossed tracks all over the field.

"The master must have better control of the beast now. He's laying down false tracks." Arabella groaned.

"That way!" Nathaniel called, pointing west. "I know my lands. That's the most sensible place for him to go if he wants to hide."

"Wait!" cried Arabella. "We can't just chase it. We'll always be one step behind. We need to find a way anticipate where it will be."

Nathaniel frowned. "How?"

Arabella shushed him. "Give me a moment." She centered herself, pulling her focus from the world around her. She listened for the music of the Wyrm. At first she found only silence, but then, off at the very edges of her senses, the click of gears and hiss of pistons sang to her. The music was more aggressive now, almost martial in tone.

"Out the gate and to the east," she called as she kicked her horse into motion.

"But the tracks turn west out of the gate," Nathaniel said.

Arabella called back over her shoulder. "Feel free to chase the old tracks, I'd rather go straight to the beast."

Pushing her horse as fast as she dared in the slick mud, Arabella headed for the source of the song. Nathaniel and Amelia were hot on her heels with only a moment's pause.

It wasn't long before Arabella completely lost her sense of direction. The heavy rain made one low stone wall look much like another, and grass was grass. Occasionally they crossed a path of churned-up mud.

The Wyrm was certainly leading them on a wild, winding chase over the wet countryside. Arabella kept driving them forward toward the increasing music.

They finally came upon the creature. Arabella's heart stuttered. The Wyrm was not alone; it was chasing a young boy wrapped in a voluminous wool cloak. The boy scampered up a hill toward a huge oak rising at the edge of yet another field. He dashed about in a serpentine manner. The Wyrm could not make such rapid shifts at speed. *Good boy*, Arabella thought as she urged her horse closer.

"Nathaniel," Arabella said. "Get up that hill and be ready to grab the boy. I'm going to slow the Wyrm down."

Nathaniel slid off his horse and made his way up the back side of the hill.

Arabella's world narrowed to herself and the Wyrm. She reached out and twined her magic within its inner workings, jamming the gears that drove the many legs of the beast. A screech jangled through the music of the machine. Arabella put her hands over her ears in agony, but dare not stop her assault. The driver applied more power and pulled against Arabella, gaining inches up the slope. Up above it, the tearful boy sobbed as he tried and failed to pull himself up the wet trunk.

Digging deep, Arabella pushed more power out and halted the Wyrm for a moment. It slid back an inch, then clawed that inch back. Amelia put her hand on Arabella's shoulder, offering her support and raw power. Arabella shook her head.

"Water," she gritted out through her teeth. "Put more water into the ground beneath it so it can't climb."

Without a word, Amelia gathered her own power and pulled more water to the sodden earth around the Wyrm. The ground beneath it turned to a huge slick of mud. The great machine slid back down the hill while its legs worked frantically.

"A river runs through a gully a few yards away," Amelia murmured to her sister as she continued to draw water under the beast.

"Let's get it there." Arabella grunted. "The moving water can strip the oil and grease from the gears, and they will seize up."

The screeching and howling of the machinery continued to claw at her ears and soul as she and Amelia joined forces to push the Wyrm across the field to the swollen river in the gully. Everything from her bones, to her flesh, to her spirit ached and burned. But she kept pouring more power in her working. If the Wyrm made a move away from the gully she held it fast. If the Wyrm made a move toward the gully she allowed it, even encouraged it. Arabella's breath came in gasps.

The Wyrm, the horses, and the witches made their way down the field, yard by stolen yard, until they reached the lip of earth that held out over the gully. Water surged below.

"Just a little more," Arabella cried out. She and Amelia redoubled their efforts, screaming to the sky. The Lambton Wyrm went still and the earth crumbled away beneath it. It tumbled into the water, great metallic crashes echoing out even over the drumming rain as billows of steam hissed toward the sky. Amelia sobbed and sagged over her saddle.

Arabella grasped her sister's reins with a trembling hand and nudged her horse toward the edge. She peered down into the tangled wreck below them. The saddle behind the Wyrm's head was empty. The driver might have been thrown clear, cast into the river itself. Or he might have managed to get to the other side and run away, abandoning his beastly steed.

Whichever proved true, that was a problem for another day.

"That machine will never run again," Arabella breathed.

Amelia's eyes lost focus as she cast her own magic out. She cried out in pain, curling over in the saddle. "It's alive!" she cried.

"What's alive?"

"The Wyrm! Under all the metal, the Old One is still alive. It hurts. He's in pain! We must save him, Ari! He's going mad from the pain." Amelia turned to her sister and sobbed.

"Or was it already mad? It's been marauding on this moor for hundreds of years." Arabella tried to put a comforting hand on her sister's shoulder.

Amelia flinched. "It hurts!" she wailed, wrapping her arms tight around herself. Arabella maneuvered her horse so she could whisper in Amelia's ear.

"We must put it out of its misery. You're in contact." She paused. "You could stop his heart."

Amelia shuddered. "I can't. I can't."

Arabella forced herself to draw on her near-exhausted power again, for her sister.

The metal in the rushing water held fast, no oil, no grease smoothed the way for motion. There was nothing she could do there. But the mysterious brass box on the top of the beast's head gave her the answer. The controls the rider used connected to rudimentary batteries, that then connected to thin wires stabbed deep into the creature's brain.

"I'm so sorry," she whispered, and send the energy left in the batteries coursing into the suffering creature's skull. Amelia and the creature screamed together.

The Wyrm fell forever silent as Amelia's sobs filled the air.

"Are you both alright?" Nathaniel rode up to them. The boy sat on the saddle in front of him, Nathaniel's rain gear wrapped around them both.

"I do not think your people will be troubled by the Lambton Wyrm any longer," Arabella said. "But Amelia and I have exhausted ourselves and would like nothing more than a hot bath and a good meal."

"You have certainly earned it," Nathaniel said. Arabella handed the reins for Amelia's horse to him. They all turned away from the gully, letting the tired horses walk home. Amelia slumped over, clinging to her saddle, silent sobs shaking her shoulders. Arabella rode next to her sister, so close their knees touched. She would never mention the geas again. Amelia had certainly suffered enough.

# To Feel the Sun Again

## John L. French

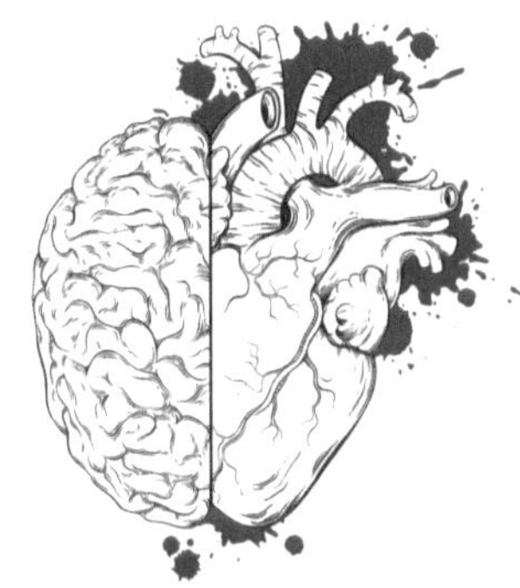



*The journals of my great-granduncle Victor Frankenstein have finally arrived. My agent in Geneva, a Mr. Sigerson, located them among the effects of an Inspector Vernet. Vernet had investigated the strange occurrences surrounding the death of Victor's wife, Elizabeth, whose maiden name I have taken for my own, the name Frankenstein being now both a joke and a curse. Obtaining Victor's journals was not inexpensive but fortunately money was not a problem. There is the income from the Frankenstein estate, which I receive as the sole heir, as well as quarterly payments from that book which that woman Shelley wrote.*

*Now, with the journals of Victor Frankenstein in my possession, I can continue the work my great-granduncle began, to conquer death so that no one must die unless they wish to do so.*

The storm arrived. Thunder crashed. Lightning was captured by the Franklin rod attached to the roof and traveled downward into the copper mesh surrounding the dead body.

"Live, damn you, live!" Caroline Lavenza shouted at the corpse. "You've been injected with the Elixir of Life. You've been exposed to the storm. Why won't you live?"

The storm passed; the smell of ozone came in through the open window. Still the body, that of a young woman who had been condemned as a slit-purse, just lay there. If the metal net had not still been hot, Caroline would have beaten the body with her fists. (She had done that once and still had the burn scars on her hands.)

*I'll have to wait until this damned thing cools before I call the Resurrection Men to remove it,* she thought, then smiled ruefully at the irony of what the graverobbers were called and what she was trying to accomplish. She hated dealing with them but "needs must" she told herself. At least Thomas, tall and thin, and William, shorter and rounder, were both very polite, even deferential. Still, Caroline could not get past how they made their coin even as she acknowledged that by using their services, she was no better than they.

While waiting, Caroline again went over her great-granduncle's journal. *That woman got it wrong,* she thought, not for the first time. *Imagine thinking that Victor succeeded on his first attempt. No, he tried and tried with animals, failing time and again before he brought that dog to life. Poor beast, to awaken scared and confused on his table. So frightened was it that it growled at Victor, then leapt from the window, only to break three of its legs in the fall. Victor had to put it down — again.*

*Or maybe Shelly deliberately omitted certain facts, like lightning as a catalyst, so as to prevent others from attempting to recreate Victor's work. If I ever see her, I'll ask her.*

*What am I doing wrong,* she asked herself even as her reading told her she was doing everything right. Maybe there were impurities in the elixir, either then or now. *The water here is filthy, but I boiled it. But there's nothing that indicates Victor did. Maybe I'll have Mr. Sigerson obtain water from Ingolstadt.*

Caroline looked at the body. The mesh had cooled. It was safe to remove it. When she did, she looked at the naked woman on the table. *So lovely,* she thought. Not that she had inclinations that way. As far as she knew, she had no such inclination for either sex. But she could appreciate beauty when she saw it. Yes, she had been a lovely woman. A bad thief but a lovely woman.

Tired, no, exhausted, Caroline decided to retire. *I'll remove and dissect the brain tomorrow. I'll send the Resurrection Men a message to get the body overmorrow. Maybe by then, I'll have thought of a new approach.*

Two days after her latest failure, Thomas and William came for the body.

"This'll be our last visit, missus," William said. "There's something that lurks in the boneyard. Willy here thinks it's a spook of some kind. And it may be that we was followed here. We didn't see nothing but in our line of work you gets a feeling, ya know. And I think someone might be watching your place as well. But we'll take this one and that'll be the end of it."

*And now what am I to do?* Caroline asked herself. *Abandon my efforts? Do like other ladies of my station and host parties and work at charities?*

As she thought this, she missed what Thomas was saying, something about,

"...and get yourself one of those automaton things. They're steam-powered, you know. I hear tell that you can set them to any task—moving, hauling, cleaning, even protecting against intruders. That's what some shops down in the Hollow use them for. Course, they don't think much, clockwork instead of brains, ya know. Ha, be something if they could think, wouldn't it? So, is the body in its usual place? Willy, you fetch it. I'll bring the cart around."

*Automatons? Of course! I could replace the clockwork with a human brain. But where would I get...?*

"Thomas," Caroline said quietly, "I understand why you can no longer supply me with bodies, but what about... just the brains? That's where my research was tending anyway, the study of the human brain."

Seeing that Thomas was hesitant, Caroline quickly added, "Your payment would remain the same."

"Willy, get in here."

The men huddled closely, talking in whispers. A few times Willy looked at Caroline.

"Missus," Thomas finally said, "I think we can do it for ya. Willy here has a gal what works in the charity ward at the hospital and me, well, I got friends in the morgue. And since you're paying regular price, we'll even put them in that preservative juice to keep them nice and fresh for you. I'll send you a message in the usual way when we've got some. For now, we'll be off. Mind you, keep an eye out for lurkers. A pretty woman like you, if I may be so bold, can't be too careful. And think about getting one of those automatons. From what I hear, Rossum makes the best ones. Almost human they are, or so I've heard."

"Thank you, Thomas. I believe I will look into them. You and William take care when you leave," Caroline said as she handed them their fee and a little more for their advice.

"We will, missus. Thank you, missus."

FROM THE DIARY OF CAROLINE LAVENZA

*My idea of placing human brains inside mechanical bodies was as big a failure as were my experiments with corpses. None of the brains I placed in the automatons brought them to life, as it were.*

*I must confess that after my most recent failure I became a bit unhinged, beating the chest of the automation and reinjuring one of the hands I had previously burnt. This caused me to let out a stream of very unladylike invectives.*

*I do not know what I am doing wrong. The clockwork that guides the machines should work more efficiently when replaced by a human brain. Instead, it works not at all. I tried installing the brain in conjunction with the clockwork but with no success. I tried replacing the steam that powers it with a Franklin battery, reasoning that if electricity brought Victor's creature to life, it should do the same for mine. Again, failure.*

*Perhaps, the methylene dioxide solution in which the brains were preserved was the problem. (Imagine, a solution being the problem. An impossibility outside of science.) I asked Thomas to transport the brains in alcohol — ethanol and wood alcohol, two brains each. Another four failures.*

*There are, of course, other procedures I can try. Thomas and William will be bringing me more brains from the hospital and morgue, this time preserved in the elixir of life itself. I will try one directly, then if (or probably when) that fails, I will run current through the next elixir-soaked brain. If a storm arises, I will expose one of the automatons directly to the lightning and observe the results, which I expect to be a ruined machine.*

*Unless I succeed, when I am left with only the brain I was born with I will cease my efforts of trying to bring Victor Frankenstein's work back to life. To the probable relief of my neighbors, many of whom already stare at me and whisper behind my back, I will move from here. I might marry. A husband might make a nice companion. Perhaps once I try it, I might develop the inclination. Or I could go to France and work on coal tar derivatives. We shall see, dear Diary, we shall see.*

"Here are the brains, you requested, Missus, in that special juice of yours. How goes the research?"

"Not as well as I hoped, Thomas. In fact, I think these are the last brains I will need from you."

Thomas breathed out a sigh of relief. "That's good to hear, Missus. Not only have questions been asked at the morgue and the hospital, but I had Willy shadow me and he thinks we're still being followed. And tonight I think I saw someone lurking about your place. You're taking precautions, aren't ya?"

"Yes, knowing you were coming I deactivated the guardian automaton but will turn him back on once you leave." She handed him an envelope. "Your fee, plus extra for all you've done."

"Thank ya, Missus. And good luck to ya."

Eight more tries, eight more failures, plus one ruined automaton.

"You're useless," Caroline said to the large, inert piece of metal on her examination table. "I might as well put the clockwork back into you. Maybe I can sell you back to Rossum. Or just sell him my idea of using a Franklin battery. I might try to improve on that idea by attaching solar-energy gatherers on the outside to help recharge the Franklin. At the least, I might be able to recoup something from this ill-fated venture."

Caroline paused, listened for and heard the clanking noise of the guardian automaton. Satisfied it was still patrolling the grounds, she looked at the heap of metal that had been its mechanical companion and finally looked at the inactive machine on the table.

"I still don't why it didn't work."

A voice came from the shadows. "Because the brains you used were dead."

A tall, well-dressed man stepped into the light of the Davy Electric Arc Lamps that illuminated Caroline's workroom.

"Who are you? How did you get in here? What do you want?" As Caroline asked this last question she wondered what in her workroom would make a suitable weapon. If he was there to steal, he could take whatever he wanted. If, however, his intentions were to… interfere with her, she would fight him to the death—hers or his.

"I apologize for frightening you, Countess Frankenstein…"

"I'll have you know, sir, that my name is Caroline Lavenza."

"That is what you call yourself, but you are a Frankenstein." As the man spoke, Caroline detected a slight accent, Eastern European perhaps. "But let that go, one should be able to call oneself whatever one wishes. Please let me assure you that… Madam Lavenza, please, put down that spanner. You'll be more likely to harm yourself than me."

Caroline lowered the spanner but did let go of it.

"Again, let me assure you that I have no ill designs on your property, your money, or your fair self. I come as a supplicant, in need of your help and your skill."

"Do you usually seek help from women, or even men, in the dark hours?"

"I must, for the dark hours are the only ones available to me."

"How did you get in here? Why did my automaton not stop you?"

"It is but a fallible machine that employs sound and light sensors. As for me, I move quieter than a thought and am invisible to things with mirrors that detect light."

Caroline had read and studied not only history and science but also myth and legend. In addition, she had not only read Mary Shelley's novel but also John William Polidori's novella. So she knew with what she was dealing.

"So tell me your name, vampyre, and what you want from me."

"I want to feel the Sun again."

Caroline looked at him, as if judging his sincerity. Coming to a decision, she said, "Very well, come into the house."

Soon the vampyre was seated on the couch in her drawing room. "Can you drink… wine?" she asked, playing the hostesses for the very first time.

"I can drink wine and enjoy it, though it provides no nourishment. So thank you."

Wine was served. As was the custom in certain houses, Caroline allowed her visitor to choose a glass, then drank from the other one.

"Very good, Madam. My compliments. Earlier you asked me who I was. "Please, call me 'Vlad.'"

"No last name? No honorific?"

The vampyre shook his head. "Just Vlad."

"Very well. Vlad it is." If Vlad was expecting Caroline to allow him to call her by her first name he was disappointed. "Are you the one who has been lurking outside my door?"

"If there was someone there when I approached, I did not notice them."

"Then it was you who was following the Resurrection Men. Why?"

"They intruded upon my cemetery, exhuming and carrying off the deceased. This is an excellent wine, by the way." Vlad poured himself another glass.

"*Your* cemetery?"

Vlad shrugged. "They were digging too close to my crypt."

"Your… crypt? Oh, yes, of course. I also dislike having my rest disturbed. So why follow them?"

"Why else? To see where they were taking the stolen bodies. They led me to this house and when I found out who owned it, I knew you were the answer to my prayers."

"Forgive me, Vlad, but I did not think your kind prayed."

"Every morning before I rest, I pray for the end of my curse and my torment. When I found you, when I learned who and what you are, I dared hope that my faith had been rewarded. Can you help me?"

Caroline did not know whether to believe this… creature or not. She reminded herself that even "The devil can cite scripture for his purpose." But his request intrigued her. Even if, as she suspected she might, she failed, at the least she would add to her knowledge.

"What would you have me do? Prepare the elixir of life and inject it into your undead body?"

Smiling, the vampyre replied, "It would be interesting to see what the result of that would be. Would the elixir fully restore me to life? Would it shock me into a coma from which maybe the lightning would revive me? Or would I die the true death?"

"If the latter, both your curse and torment would end."

"Yes, they would. But I do not want to chance it. As I said, I wish to feel the Sun again. So I propose that you place my living brain into a mechanical body to which you've added solar receptors."

"You've thought this out."

"Ever since the first Rossum made his first automaton. But obviously I cannot operate on myself."

"Obviously." Something made Caroline lean forward and take the vampyre by the hand. It was cold to the touch and when her finger sought and did not find a pulse, she suddenly broke away.

"Do not use your glamour on me again, Vlad. Or you will never see the Sun."

"Again, my apologies. It is my nature, which I will endeavor to control." Vlad stood, then knelt before her. "Madam Lavenza," he entreated, "you are my only hope. May I count on your help?"

"Get up," Caroline said, a bit harshly. "Sit there." She indicated a chair across from her. "What's this about needing brains that are alive?"

"As familiar with death as I am, I assure you that once something is truly dead, it remains so, and no elixir or lightning will bring it back. Perhaps the brain that Victor used was only mostly dead, with still a spark of life left in it. Who can say? If his creature were still alive I doubt even it could tell us. But a living brain, that might work."

Caroline thought for a moment. A living brain instead of a dead one. It was the one variable she had not considered. She began to plan the operation. Apparently, her ancestor had gotten lucky. Maybe twice lucky, the dog may not have been fully dead itself.

*I could do this,* she decided, *but I would have to be as lucky as Victor was. Unless…*

"Very well, Vlad. If you're willing I am. But first…"

"Yes, Madam?"

"I will need some living brains to practice on."

Vlad smiled again. "That, Madam, will not be a problem."

A few days later, when the night was halfway over, there was a knock on the tradesmen's door. Caroline had been expecting it and when she answered, Vlad entered bearing a bulky object.

"Is that…"

Vlad did not answer. Instead, he carried it through to the workroom and dumped the body on the table.

"Your first living brain, Madam."

Under the glare of the Davy Lamps, Caroline examined the body. It was that of a young man not much past his twentieth year. His shirt was torn and there was a savage wound on his neck. Looking at Vlad, she saw that his lips were red with blood, the young man's blood.

*I had not expected this*, she thought. *No, I had expected it but not to be confronted with it. This is more than receiving a dead body. This is being complicit in another's death. No, he's not dead but soon will be. How can I…*

"He won't last much longer, Madam," Vlad prompted. Then, as if reading her thoughts, he said, "He would have been dead already but for your needs. Our needs, really."

*He's right. This man, or one just like him, was fated to die. Creatures like Vlad must feed and so this body is no different than the ones Thomas and William brought me.*

"Let's get to work."

With Vlad's assistance, Caroline cut open the skull and removed the brain, quickly immersing it in a vat full of the elixir. Electrodes were attached to monitor the brain's activities.

"How does that work?" Vlad asked.

"It's similar to the telegraph, only instead of clicking, a pen records the impulses. So now we wait."

A few impulses, a few lines, then nothing.

"It's a start. There would be no reaction from a dead brain."

"Then, Madam, it appears as if we need more brains."

"Vlad, how do you…"

He knew what she was asking. "The streets of London are dark. Even on those streets lit by gas lamps, there are shadows. I wait in those shadows until someone walking alone passes by. Then I feed."

"And what of the body?"

"I usually leave it to be found. Except for tonight and the nights to come. And too bad for anyone who sees me."

"And what about…" Caroline looked at the now dead body.

"I will take it and leave it for the scavengers to find."

"Scavengers?"

"Best you don't know, Madam."

With the third brain, Caroline began circulating the elixir. With the fourth, she added a mild electric current. Each time the lines came then stopped. But each time the lines were longer.

In between her experiments with the brains, Caroline worked on designing Vlad's new body. A system to circulate the elixir, a reservoir to contain it. An improved sensory system to allow him to see and hear. Most importantly, the solar collectors placed on the outside of his mechanical body would not only help power it but also to feel the Sun.

"The collectors will feed the battery. But even then, the battery will not last forever. It will need to be replaced regularly. As will the elixir."

"So I should hope nothing happens to you."

"Exactly."

The seventh brain. Seven people nearly drained. Seven bodies left for the scavengers. And in the excitement of their increased successes, all thoughts of a possible watcher were forgotten.

"It's working," Caroline said, observing the results of their seventh attempt. "The brain is for some reason pulsing, and the electrical activity is not ceasing. We may have done it."

Caroline walked over and looked at the brain in its glass home. "I wonder what she's thinking. All alone in her mind with no sensory input. Is she slowly going insane or is she dreaming of a better life? We'll never know.

"We'll let this go on for another day. Then, to be sure, we'll try to replicate the results with another brain."

"I don't think that's wise, Madam. I've noticed an increasing number of constables on patrol and even a few detectives from Scotland Yard. Word of the disappearances must have gotten around and some of the bodies may have been found."

"You're right, Vlad. So if she's still 'alive' tomorrow night, you will start your new life the next morning."

Vlad knew he would not be able to speak once the operation was a success. After carefully considering his final words, he said to Caroline, "Thank you."

Two tables were placed side by side, the vampyre on one, a newly purchased automaton on the other. Vlad felt the bone saw cut into his head then imagined Caroline reaching into his skull to remove his brain. His last thought was, *Have I done the right thing?* Then he knew no more.

He awoke in a standing position. How? he asked himself, then remembered that the table on which he lay tilted. At first, there was nothing but his own thoughts, then his sensory array started.

Sight first. Vlad thought that something had gone wrong, but soon realized that his vision was monotone — black, white, and shades of grey. As a creature of the night, he decided he could live with that then realized he would have to. The first thing his new body saw were the remains of his old one.

He had expected that "he" would have crumbled into ash. Instead, "his" body was mostly intact. He thought it a strange thing for one to see himself dead.

Hearing—every noise was crisper, sharper, louder. He would have to ask Caroline if there was a way to control the volume.

Caroline. Where was she?

"Turn your head to the left."

He did, and there she was.

"Walk around the table to me."

He was clumsy at first, almost falling twice. But then he gained full control over his legs and walked to Caroline as smoothly as his mechanical body would allow.

"Forgive me but I have to say this. It's alive. Or rather, you're alive." He would have smiled if he had lips to move. Instead, he pointed to the living brain that was still in its glass jar.

"Her? I think I'll put her in another automaton as a companion for you. But that's for later. It's morning. Are you ready to feel the Sun again?"

Vlad nodded but as he did so, there came multiple crashes. He heard them first, then Caroline reacted to the sounds.

Loud voices called out, "Police, no one move."

"Quickly, Vlad, go stand with the others. Make no move. They may have me but don't let them have you."

He obeyed and was standing with the other automatons when the police barged into the workroom.

A large, gruff-looking man with greying hair and a brush mustache approached her. "Caroline Frankenstein, also known as Caroline Lavenza?" She nodded that she was. "I am Inspector Abraham of Scotland Yard. Madam, you are under arrest."

"What for, Inspector? I have done nothing wrong."

"That body on the table and the brain in the jar would argue otherwise. Plus we wish to question you about a series of disappearances that seem to center around this house. A few brainless bodies as well. I should warn you that anything you say will be taken down and used against you in your trial. Be advised we have your accomplices in custody and that they are cooperating."

"Which accomplices are these?"

"The pair you hired to burke the bodies. They've already given statements. Now go along with the matron there."

As the matron took her arm, Caroline could not help but look at Vlad. He had obeyed her and remained unmoving but a small part of her was disappointed that he had not sprung to her rescue.

"Don't worry about those machines, Madam. We'll take good care of them and after your trial, they will enter the service of Her Majesty."

From the journal of Adam Frankenstein

*From my place of concealment, I watched my "cousin" Caroline being taken away. I hated to do it. The bodies taken from the earth I could forgive. They were too long dead and Caroline did not have my creator's gift. But once I heard about the disappearances and observed that man bringing bodies into her home, I knew I had to act. I could not have her repeating my creator's evil. A word in the right ear brought the Yard. I hope they treat her well. I hope she does not hang.*

Vlad waited until Caroline's workroom was empty. Most of the police had departed, taking with them the living brain and his old body. Two constables remained to guard the scene. It was easy to escape them. He was just another mechanical man, they paid him no attention. When they were elsewhere in the house, he simply walked through one of the doors they had broken down.

And walked, and walked, and walked. He had nothing else to do. He knew the solar receptors on his metal skin would not be enough to keep the battery charged. That one day the battery would die. Then so would he.

*I will be dead, but it will have been worth it. For thanks to those receptors, I can feel the Sun again.*

# About the Authors

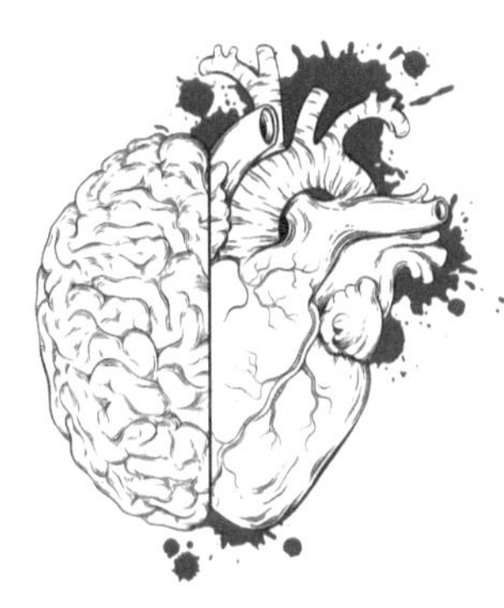

Award-winning author, editor, and publisher **Danielle Ackley-McPhail** has worked both sides of the publishing industry for longer than she cares to admit. In 2014 she joined forces with Mike McPhail and Greg Schauer to form eSpec Books.

Her published eight novels include *Yesterday's Dreams, Tomorrow's Memories, Today's Promise, The Halfling's Court, The Redcaps' Queen, Daire's Devils, The Play of Light*, and *Baba Ali and the Clockwork Djinn*, written with Day Al-Mohamed. She is also the author of the solo collections *Eternal Wanderings, A Legacy of Stars, Consigned to the Sea, Flash in the Can, Transcendence, The Kindly Ones, Dawns a New Day, The Fox's Fire, Between Darkness and Light, Echoes of the Divine*, and the non-fiction writers' guides *The Literary Handyman, More Tips from the Handyman, LH: Build-A-Book Workshop*, and *The Literary Handyman Library* omnibus edition. She is the senior editor of the *Bad-Ass Faeries* anthology series, *No Longer Dreams, Heroes of the Realm, Clockwork Chaos, Gaslight & Grimm, Grimm Machinations, A Cast of Crows, A Cry of Hounds, Other Aether, The Chaos Clock, Grease Monkeys, Side of Good/Side of Evil, After Punk*, and *Footprints in the Stars*. Her short stories are included in numerous other anthologies and collections. She is a full member of the Science Fiction and Fantasy Writers Association.

Danielle lives in New Jersey with husband and fellow writer, Mike McPhail and four extremely spoiled cats.

**Rachel A. Brune** is an Army veteran, former military journalist, novelist, and editor of the creepy and macabre. She is the founder and chief editor at Crone Girls Press, an indie horror micro-press specializing in anthologies. In 2022, she became Senior Editor of Falstaff Books' new horror imprint, Falstaff Dread. She lives with her spouse, two daughters, one reticent cat, and two flatulent rescue dogs. The first book in her werewolf secret agent series, Cold Run, was published in 2022 by Falstaff Books.

**James Chambers** received the Bram Stoker Award® for the graphic novel, *Kolchak the Night Stalker: The Forgotten Lore of Edgar Allan Poe* and is a four-time Bram Stoker Award nominee. He is the author of the short story collections *On the Night Border* and *On the Hierophant Road*, which received a starred review from *Booklist*, which called it "…satisfyingly unsettling"; and the novella collection, *The Engines of Sacrifice*, described as "…chillingly evocative…" in a *Publisher's Weekly* starred review. He has written the novellas, *Three Chords of Chaos, Kolchak and the Night Stalkers: The Faceless God*, and many others, including the Corpse Fauna cycle: *The Dead Bear Witness, Tears of Blood, The Dead in Their Masses*, and *The Eyes of the Dead*. He also writes the Machinations Sundry series of steampunk stories. He edited the Bram Stoker Award-nominated anthology, *Under Twin Suns: Alternate Histories of the Yellow Sign, Where the Silent Ones Watch*, and co-edited *A New York State of Fright* and *Even in the Grave*, an anthology of ghost stories. His website is: www.jameschambersonline.com.

**Doc Coleman** never dreamed of being a writer. He dreamed of being an actor, of making movies, and telling stories. He dreamed of going to space. He just didn't work hard enough at it. So he ended up going into IT.

But he always had a way with words. He still wanted to tell stories.

One day a friend told Doc that it takes 10,000 hours to master a new skill. He didn't know how true that was, but he did see something in that that was true: You don't get better at things you don't do.

So, he set about getting better at writing.

He started a blog, writing about something he did know about: technology. About six months later, he started writing short stories. And submitting them.

Doc's stories have appeared in The Ministry of Peculiar Occurrences' Tales from the Archives, the Way of the Gun Bushido Western

Anthology, the Steampunk Special Edition of Flagship magazine, and in the charity anthology Paradise Found: Tales From the Library. In 2017 he published his first novel, *The Perils of Prague,* the first book in the Steampunk Comedy/Adventure series The Adventures of Crackle and Bang. In 2018 he published *The Shining Cog and Other Steampunk Tales,* a collection of Steampunk short stories. In 2025, he plans on publishing the second Crackle and Bang Adventure, *The Kindred of Kali.*

Doc has been a perennial guest at Balticon, RavenCon, Capclave, and Continual. He is also known as a narrator and a voice actor.

When he isn't juggling projects, making a living, or mainlining podcasts, Doc is a gamer, an avid reader, a motorcyclist, a home brewer and beer lover, a fan of renaissance festivals, and frequently a smart-ass. He lives with his lovely wife and two cats in Germantown, MD.

**Ef Deal** is a musician, a poet, an editor, a video editor, and an author of science fiction, fantasy, and horror. She's been writing and composing since she was nine years old. Her short fiction has been published in numerous online zines and print anthologies including *The Magazine of Fantasy and Science Fiction, A Cast of Crows* from eSpec Books, *Dangerous Waters* from Brigid's Gate, Chris Ryan's *Soul Scream Antholozine,* two anthologies from Speculation Publications, and most recently in eSpec Books' *A Cry of Hounds* and *Other Aether.* She is currently public relation coordinator for *eSpec Books,* assistant fiction editor at *Abyss&Apex* magazine, and video editor for *Strong Women ~ Strange Worlds.* Her novel *Esprit de Corpse* from *eSpec Books* is the first in a steampunk paranormal romance series set in France, featuring the gifted Twins of Bellefées, who tend to show up in other eSpec Books anthologies as well. When she's not writing, she plays bugle in the Blessed Sacrament Golden Knights drum and bugle corps, and is a member of the Buglers Hall of Fame and the New Jersey Drum Corps Hall of Fame, honored for her contribution to playing, teaching, directing, and arranging. She lives in Haddonfield, NJ, with her husband Jack and her chow chows Corbin and Rory. She is a member of SFWA and HWA. Her website is www.efdeal.net. Follow her blog *Talespinner* at efdeal.blogspot.com.

**Keith R.A. DeCandido** has been an avid fan of Mary Shelley since he was a college student studying 19th-century literature, and still lists *Frankenstein, or The Modern Prometheus* as his favorite novel. He's the author of more than 60 novels, more than 100 short stories (one of which is "What You Can Become Tomorrow" in *Three Time Travelers Walk Into…*, which featured Mary Shelley), more than 50 comic books, and more nonfiction than he's entirely comfortable counting. Recent and upcoming work includes the debut of his new urban fantasy series *Supernatural Crimes Unit* in 2025; the fantasy novels *Phoenix Precinct* and *Feat of Clay*, both the latest in series of his also published by eSpec; the *Resident Evil* graphic novel *Infinite Darkness: The Beginning*; the urban fantasy short-story collection *Ragnarok and a Hard Place: More Tales of Cassie Zukav, Weirdness Magnet*; a comic-book adaptation of his 2021 serial-killer novel *Animal*; several stories in *Star Trek Explorer* magazine; short fiction in the anthology series *Sherlock Holmes: Cases by Candlelight*, *Phenomenons*, and *Thrilling Adventure Yarns*; and stories in the anthologies *Weird Tales: 100 Years of Weird*, *Multiverse of Mystery*, *Eliminate the Impossible*, *A Cry of Hounds*, *Joe Ledger: Unbreakable*, and *The Good, the Bad, and the Uncanny: Tales of a Very Weird West*, as well as two anthologies he co-edited, *Double Trouble: An Anthology of Two-Fisted Team-Ups* (with Jonathan Maberry) and *The Four ???? of the Apocalypse* (with Wrenn Simms). Keith writes about pop culture for a variety of essay collections and anthologies, most prolifically for the award-winning web site Reactor Magazine (formerly Tor.com). He's also a musician (currently percussionist for the parody band Boogie Knights), a martial artist (a fourth-degree black belt in karate), and an editor of 35 years' standing (though he usually does it sitting down). Find out less at his mediocre web site at DeCandido.net.

**Dana Fraedrich** is a dog lover, self-professed geek, and author of the steampunk fantasy series Broken Gears, which includes the Amazon bestseller, Out of the Shadows. Dana's books are full of secrets and colorful characters that examine the many shades of grey that paint the world. She can often be found attending book festivals and fandom conventions and co-hosting the Steam-Powered Movies podcast.

Even from a young age, Dana enjoyed writing down the stories that she imagined in her mind. Born and raised in Virginia, she earned her BFA from Roanoke College and is now carving out her own happily ever after in Nashville, TN with her husband. Dana is always writing; more books are on the way!

**John L. French** is a retired crime scene supervisor with forty years' experience. He has seen more than his share of murders, shootings, and serious assaults. As a break from the realities of his job, he started writing science fiction, pulp, horror, fantasy, and, of course, crime fiction.

John's first story "Past Sins" was published in Hardboiled Magazine and was cited as one of the best Hardboiled stories of 1993. More crime fiction followed, appearing in Alfred Hitchcock's Mystery Magazine, the Fading Shadows magazines and in collections by Barnes and Noble. Association with writers like James Chambers and the late, great C.J. Henderson led him to try horror fiction and to a still growing fascination with zombies and other undead things. His first horror story "The Right Solution" appeared in Marietta Publishing's *Lin Carter's Anton Zarnak*. Other horror stories followed in anthologies such as *The Dead Walk* and *Dark Furies*, both published by Die Monster Die books. It was in *Dark Furies* that his character Bianca Jones made her literary debut in "21 Doors," a story based on an old Baltimore legend and a creepy game his daughter used to play with her friends.

John's first book was *The Devil of Harbor City*, a novel done in the old pulp style. *Past Sins* and *Here There Be Monsters* followed. John was also consulting editor for Chelsea House's *Criminal Investigation* series. His other books include *The Assassins' Ball* (written with Patrick Thomas), *Souls on Fire, The Nightmare Strikes, Monsters Among Us, The Last Redhead, the Magic of Simon Tombs*, and *The Santa Heist* (written with Patrick Thomas). John is the editor of *To Hell in a Fast Car, Mermaids 13*, C. J. Henderson's *Challenge of the Unknown, Camelot 13* (with Patrick Thomas), and (with Greg Schauer) *With Great Power …*

You can find John on Facebook or you can email him at him at jfrenchfam@aol.com.


**Teel James Glenn** has killed hundreds and been killed more times — on stage and screen, as he has traveled the world for forty-plus years as a stuntman, swordmaster, storyteller, book illustrator, bodyguard, actor, and haunted house barker. His writing has been published in dozens of novels and his poetry and stories have been printed in over three hundred magazines including Weird Tales, Mystery, Black Cat Weekly, Tough, Pulp Adventures, Mad, Cirsova, Silverblade, Heroic Fantasy, Blazing Adventures and Sherlock Holmes Mystery.

His novel *A Cowboy in Carpathia: A Bob Howard Adventure* won best novel 2021 in the Pulp Factory Award. He is also the winner of the 2012 Pulp Ark Award for Best Author. And he was a finalist for the Derringer short mystery award in 2022.

His short story "The Clockwork Nutcracker" won P& E's best steampunk story and has been expanded into a novel. Epic ebook award finalist. P&E winner "Best Steampunk Short", a P & E finalist for "Best Fantasy short, Collection" and his novel "Callback for a Corpse" was a second-place winner in the CWR Poll as best mystery.

**Jessica Lucci** is a poet and steampunk fantasy author who writes about modern issues while maintaining historic integrity. She makes her home in Waltham, MA, USA.

Her poetry has appeared in *The Edible Anthology of Poetry Greatest Hits*, edited by Peter Payack, and also in *Lucidity Poetry Journal*. Her poem, "Australopithecus," from her poetry book, "How Can I Steal a Purse," was recently nominated for a Rhysling award. Her steampunk novel *Subton Switch* was a finalist in the 2019 Lesfic Bard Book Awards for science fiction. Her short story "Annabel Lee" was featured in the anthology "A Cast of Crows." Other works include *Waltham Watch*, *Gustover Glitch*, *Salem Switch*, *Steampunk Leap Year*, *Steampunk New Year*, and *Steampunk Pride*.

Once Upon a Time, **Christine Norris** thought she wanted to be an archaeologist but hates sand and bugs, so instead, she became a writer. She is the author of several speculative fiction works for children and adults, including *The Library of Athena* series, *A Curse of Ash and Iron*, and contributions to *Gaslight and Grimm* and *Grimm Machinations*. She is kept busy on a daily basis by her day job as a school librarian in New Jersey. She may or may not have a secret library in her basement, and she absolutely believes in fairies.

**Aaron Rosenberg** is the best-selling, award-winning author of over fifty novels, including the Twin Cities Cryptids urban fantasy/ cozy series, the DuckBob SF comedy series, the Relicant Chronicles epic fantasy series, the Areyat Islands fantasy pirate mystery series, the upcoming BEO Files urban fantasy series, and, with David Niall Wilson, the *O.C.L.T.* occult thriller series. His tie-in work contains novels for *Star Trek*, *Warhammer*, *World of WarCraft*, *Stargate: Atlantis*, *Shadowrun*, *Mutants & Masterminds*, and *Eureka* and short stories for *The X-Files*, *World of Darkness*, *Crusader Kings II*, *Deadlands*, *Master of Orion*, and *Europa Universalis IV*. He has written children's books (including the original series STEM Squad and Pete and Penny's Pizza Puzzles, the award-winning *Bandslam: The Junior Novel* and the #1 best-selling *42: The Jackie Robinson Story*), educational books, and roleplaying games (including the original games *Asylum*, *Spookshow*, and *Chosen*; work for White Wolf, Wizards of the Coast, Fantasy Flight, Pinnacle, and many others; the Origins Award-winning *Gamemastering Secrets;* and the Gold ENnie-winning *Lure of the Lich Lord*). He is a founding member of Crazy 8 Press. Aaron lives in New York with his family. You can follow him online at gryphonrose.com, on Facebook at facebook.com/gryphonrose, and on X (formerly known as Twitter) @gryphonrose.

**Hildy Silverman** writes in multiple genres, including science fiction, fantasy, horror, and blends thereof. In 2020, she joined the Crazy 8 Press authors collective (https://www.crazy8press.com/), which publishes novels and anthologies by its membership. In 2013, her short story, The Six Million Dollar Mermaid, which appeared in the anthology *Mermaids 13: Tales from the Sea* (French, ed.), was a finalist for the WSFA Small Press Award. In 2005, she became the publisher and editor-in-chief of Space and Time Magazine (www.spaceandtimemagazine.com), one of the oldest small press genre magazines still in production, and ran it until 2018. She is a past president of the Garden State Speculative Fiction Writers and a frequent panelist on the science fiction convention circuit. For more information about Hildy, including a complete list of her published work, please visit www.hildysilverman.com.

**Michelle D. Sonnier** writes dark urban fantasy, steampunk, and anything else that lets her combine the weird and the fantastic in unexpected ways. She even writes horror, although it took her a long time to admit that since she prefers the existential scare over blood and gore. She is the author of *The Clockwork Witch, The Clockwork Solution*, and *Death's Embrace* and has published short stories in a variety of print and online venues. You can find her on Facebook (Michelle D. Sonnier, The Author). She lives in Maryland with her husband, son, and a variable number of cats.

**Dacre Stoker** is the great grandnephew of Bram Stoker and the international best-selling co-author of *Dracula the Un-Dead* (2009), and *Dracul* (2018). Dacre is also the co-editor of *The Lost Journal of Bram Stoker: The Dublin Years* (2012). He has published *Stoker on Stoker Dracula Revealed (2022)* a companion book to his informative audio-visual presentations. In 2022 Dacre and Robert Eighteen Bisang published *Dracula Annotated for the 125th Anniversary*, a culmination of years of research, this version includes many of the passages edited out of the final *Dracula* typescript, including the first three chapters and the original ending.

Dacre is a native of Montreal, Canada, he taught Physical Education and Sciences for twenty-two years, in both Canada and the U.S. He has participated in the sport of Modern Pentathlon as an athlete and a coach at the international and Olympic levels for Canada for 12 years.

Dacre has consulted and appeared in recent film documentaries about vampires in literature and popular culture. *The Real Vampire Files* (2010 History Channel), *The Tillinghast Nightmare*, (2014 Historical Haunts), *Secrets of the Dead* (2015 PBS), *Mysteries at the Museum*, (2017 Travel Channel) *Legend Hunter* (2019 Travel Channel) *American Vampires* (2022 Fox Nation).

Dacre currently hosts tours to Dublin Ireland, Whitby England, and Cruden Bay Scotland, to visit places where Bram Stoker lived, was educated, worked, researched, and wrote *Dracula*. He also leads groups to Transylvania to explore both the life and times of the historic Vlad Dracula III and also the locations where Bram Stoker set his famous novel.

**David Lee Summers** became a steampunk in 1987 when he used a nineteenth century telescope on Nantucket to examine the evolution of distant pulsating stars. Since that time, he has published thirteen novels and numerous short stories and poems spanning a wide range of the imagination. *Owl Dance, Lightning Wolves, The Brazen Shark,* and *Owl Riders* comprise the Clockwork Legion steampunk series. His other novels include *The Astronomer's Crypt, Vampires of the Scarlet Order* and *Firebrandt's Legacy*. His latest novella is a World War II-era cryptid tale called *Breaking the Code*.

David's short stories have appeared in such magazines and anthologies as *Realms of Fantasy, Cemetery Dance, Straight Outta Tombstone, Gaslight and Grimm,* and *After Punk*. He's been twice nominated for the Science Fiction Poetry Association's Rhysling Award.

In addition to writing, David has edited the science fiction anthologies: *A Kepler's Dozen, Kepler's Cowboys,* and *Maximum Velocity: The Best of the Full-Throttle Space Tales*. When not working with the written word, David operates telescopes at Kitt Peak National Observatory. Learn more about David at www.davidleesummers.com.

# Our Children of the Night

Algie Lane
Alicia M Rabb
Allyn Gibson
Andrew Kaplan
Angelique
Anonymous
Anthony R. Cardno
Arne Radtke
Barrott
Beth Kee
Beth Lobdell
Bill Dowling
Bobby Zamarron
Brad Jurn
Brenda Huettner
Brendan Lonehawk
Bridget Wilde
Buddy Deal
C.A. Rowland
Carl Ball
Carol Gyzander
Carol Jones
Cat Treadwell
Cerise Cauthron
Christine Norris

Christopher D. Abbott
Christopher J. Burke
Chuck Michalik
coleman
Colleen Feeney
Connor Bradley
Crohnicgamer
CthulhuChris
Dagmar Baumann
Dale A Russell
Danielle Ackley-McPhail
Danny Chamberlin
David Myers
David Salmansohn
Devil Tree Media, LLC
Dino Hicks
Dirk Plug
Doc Coleman
Donna Hogg
Doug Hancock
Douglas G. Yeager
Dr. Rasa and Jaq Greenspon
Duane Warnecke
Ef Deal
Elaine Tindill-Rohr

Eric Schumacher
"Filkertom" Tom Smith
Gary Phillips
Gav I.
geoffrey thorne
George W Minor
Gillian Christopher
Gina DeSimone
Glassfane
GMarkC
Greg Levick
Hadrosaur Productions
Jacen Leonard
Jack Deal
jacob farber
Jakub Narębski
Jamie René Peddicord
Jason 'XenoPhage' Frisvold
Jennifer L. Pierce
Jennifer Whitworth
Jeremy Bottroff
Jocelynne Weathers
John Keegan
John L. French
John Schoffstall
Josh Ward
Juanita Nesbitt
Judy McClain
Julie Brannon
Karen Krah
Karen Palmer
Kathy Brady
Kelly Pierce
Kendall Varnell
Kevin Meares
Kierin Fox
Krinsky
Krystal England
Kurt Beyerl

Larien
Laura Anne Gilman
Laura Inglis
Laura Walker
Laurent Weber
Lee Mary Hawkridge
Lexi Taylor
Lisa Kruse
Lorraine Anderson
Lynn P.
Madeleine Holly-Rosing
maileguy
MAllder
Mari Hersh-Tudor
Marie Devey
Maryanne Chappell
Matthew
Melanie Ball
Mia Emerson
Michael A. Burstein
Michael Barbour
Michael Rosenberg
Miriam Seidel
Morgan Hazelwood
No Acknowledgements
Paul Drollinger
Paul Ryan
Raven
Richard Novak
Richard O'Shea
Richard Parker
Richard Stone
RJHopkinson
Robby
Robert H Hudson Jr
Ronald Miller
Samantha Bryant
Scott Pearson
Scott Roche

Scott Schaper
Shaun
Shawnee M
Shervyn
Sheryl R. Hayes
Sonia Koval
Stephanie Franklin
Stephanie Lucas
Stephen Ballentine
Stephen Buchanan
Stephen Chappell
Steve Pattee
Susan Carlson
Susan E. Wilson
Thomas P. Tiernan
Thomas Wikman
Tibbi
Tom B.
Tom Most
Tony
Tracy 'Rayhne" Fretwell
Trainor Houghton Whyte
Ty Drago
white beard geek
Wingnut
Yosen Lin

# What con story will you tell?

Interested in exploring the world of Steampunk? Look no further than the annual Telltale Steampunk Festival. Offering a captivating journey into an alternative version of the Victorian era, this event celebrates creativity with a range of activities suitable for the whole family. Dive into author presentations, participate in engaging workshops, and join thought-provoking panel discussions. Test your skills in Tea Dueling, showcase your attire in the Costume/Regalia competitions, and get in on the excitement of the silent auction. As night falls, immerse yourself in enchanting musical performances. Peruse a bustling room of vendors offering exquisite artisanal goods and handcrafted treasures from some of the finest talents in the mid-Atlantic region.

Find us online:

TellTaleSteampunk.com and facebook.com/telltalesteampunk

## Special Thanks to our Sponsors:

Airship Oddities • Captured Curls • Corsets & Cogs • Doctor Gus
Dana Fraedrich, Steampunk Fantasy Author • Dodson Designs• Gear Grinder
eSpec Books & The Hornie Lady • Gadgetometers • Heiress Gaming
Scarves of Holding • Silverwolf Leather • W Designs by Dianne

## Special Thanks to our Best Friends of Edgar:

Anita Adshead • Regina Barry • Matt Black • Stephanie Cansian • Barbara Craig
Ef Deal • Tina Good • Haley Farson •Chad Forsyth • Stacey Haberberger
Jeremiah Kornspan • Peter Koumparoulis • Melissa Lachetti • Michael Lake
Sean Lake • Justin Minor • Jacqueline O'Hare • Angela Pishko • Heather
Rachiele • Amanda Reith • Jazz Reith • Rachel Sanchez • Cathy Simmons
Sandy Slinger • Terry Smith • Cindy Terranova • Barbara Walker • Royal White

www.ingramcontent.com/pod-product-compliance
Lightning Source LLC
Chambersburg PA
CBHW060707190726
48289CB00002B/571